JODI TAYLOR is the internationally bestselling author of the Chronicles of St Mary's series, the story of a bunch of disaster-prone individuals who investigate major historical events in contemporary time. Do NOT call it time travel! She is also the author of the Time Police series – a St Mary's spin-off and gateway into the world of an all-powerful, international organisation who are NOTHING like St Mary's. Except, when they are.

Alongside these, Jodi is known for her gripping supernatural thrillers featuring Elizabeth Cage, together with the enchanting Frogmorton Farm series – a fairy story for adults.

Born in Bristol and now living in Gloucester (facts both cities vigorously deny), she spent many years with her head somewhere else, much to the dismay of family, teachers and employers, before finally deciding to put all that daydreaming to good use and write a novel. Over twenty books later, she still has no idea what she wants to do when she grows up.

JODI TAYLOR

THE MOST WONDERFUL TIME OF THE YEAR

HEADLINE

This collection first published in Great Britain in 2023 by
HEADLINE PUBLISHING GROUP

3

Cataloguing in Publication Data is available from the British Library

ISBN 978 1 0354 1237 2

Typeset in Times New Roman by 11/15pt by Jouve (UK), Milton Keynes

Printed and bound in Great Britain by Clays Ltd, Elcograf S.p.A.

Headline's policy is to use papers that are natural, renewable and recyclable
products and made from wood grown in well-managed forests and other
controlled sources. The logging and manufacturing processes are expected
to conform to the environmental regulations of the country of origin.

HEADLINE PUBLISHING GROUP
An Hachette UK Company
Carmelite House
50 Victoria Embankment
London EC4Y 0DZ

www.headline.co.uk
www.hachette.co.uk

CONTENTS

A CHRISTMAS PRESENT FROM JODI TAYLOR

I was sitting quietly, working on the fifth Time Police book – *Killing Time*; finishing off the Christmas story – *Christmas Pie*; and thinking about *The Ballad of Smallhope and Pennyroyal* – so quite a slack day, as you can see – when Word Came Down from On High. Or from my publishers, as they modestly refer to themselves.

'The new anthology of short stories, Taylor.'

'Yes . . . ?'

'The ones not yet published in print form.'

'Yes . . . ?'

'To be published 1st December.'

'Yes . . . ?'

'We need a little something from you.'

'Actually, I'm a bit hard up at the moment, otherwise . . .'

'Nothing major – we know you're busy.'

'Yes . . . ?'

'An intro perhaps. Or even a very short story.'

'Which?'

'Entirely up to you. Just a little new content for your readers to enjoy.'

'Um . . .'

'Nothing massive, of course. Just a few words.'

'Intro or short story?'

'Well . . .'

'You want both, don't you?'

'Well . . .'

'On what subject?'

'Anything you like. They're mostly Christmas stories so talk about your own family's Christmas traditions. That would be lovely. And then just a teeny tiny story. Not even a full story. A storyette.'

'The only Christmas tradition in my family is when we gather around the table for Christmas lunch and I interrogate everyone as to whether they've bought my latest book. Or, indeed, any of my books.'

'And what's the response?'

'You don't want to know.'

'So that's settled then. Bye.'

So here we are, the third anthology containing all the short stories hitherto not available in print form – St Mary's, the Time Police, and one from Frogmorton Farm – all together in paperback for the first time and entitled *The Most Wonderful Time of the Year*.

Just in time for Christmas.

While we're on the topic of short stories, I'm so pleased the Christmas Day stories have become such a hugely anticipated event. The original intention was to write a story as a small gift from me to my readers and publish it on Christmas Day. And now – ten years later – for many people, it's become a part of their own Christmas tradition.

I must admit I do sometimes feel a little guilty in case there has been mass over-boiling of the Brussels, or – the bane of Pennyroyal's life – lumpy gravy, caused by lack of attention because people are stirring with one hand and reading with the other, although before anyone says anything – it can be done. And I myself have lived with lumpy gravy all my life and it's never done me any harm.

And so, I present to you 'A Storm in a Teacup'.

Enjoy.

PS – I had a bet with myself about how many times I could say 'Christmas' in one introduction. There's a bar of fruit and nut at stake and, reading through, I appear to have come up short.

Christmas. Christmas. Christmas. Christmas. Come here, you little bar of chocolate-flavoured temptation.

A STORM IN A TEACUP

Typically, Dr Bairstow got straight down to it.

'Come in, Dr Maxwell, and sit down. It would appear St Mary's has taken advantage of my absence to trigger an apocalypse. I therefore await your explanation as to the catalogue of catastrophe that was St Mary's Christmas Day.'

'I have none, sir. Just a simple recitation of the facts, after which, I am sure, careful consideration will enable you to see that St Mary's is almost entirely blameless. In fact, the whole thing will turn out to be a storm in a teacup.'

Some people might have described his silence as unencouraging but sometimes silence is golden.

And . . . sometimes it isn't. I pressed on.

'Well, sir – because there are now so many of us at St Mary's and space is something of an issue, we thought we'd solve everyone's problems by erecting a marquis on the South Lawn and . . .'

He blinked. 'The very first sentence of what only one of us will regard as an adequate explanation, Dr Maxwell, and I fear I must already request clarification.'

'The marquis, sir? Or the erection thereof?'

'Can it be, Dr Maxwell, that despite one of the best educations this country has to offer, you are unaware the word is "marquee"?'

'Oh – well, yes, possibly. I always get those two muddled up. Like flammable and inflammable.'

'Is there any possibility of jumping ahead to the arrest of Mr Bashford and the subsequent terrorist alert that ruined Christmas lunch for half the county?'

'Of course, sir. An unfortunate series of events led to the arrest of Mr Bashford and a small – very small – terrorist alert.'

The silence lingered on. Like a fart in a spacesuit.

'I am not prepared to join the dots myself on this one, Dr Maxwell.'

'No, sir. Well, the bald facts – Storm Frances was on her way and it was a windy day. A very windy day and the erection got away from us a little bit. Not entirely our fault, but we didn't anchor the thing down properly.'

'Why not? It seems a basic precaution to me.'

'Crossed lines, sir. Grounds maintenance thought the Security Section had done it and vice versa. Bottom line – no one attached the very large number of concrete weights supplied specifically for that purpose. The wind got up – right up, actually – and off it went. Like a tenticular Mary Poppins.'

'Tenticular?'

'Pertaining to a tent, or tent-like, sir. Tenticular.'

'I bow to your superior knowledge, Dr Maxwell. I believe we had left the marquee . . .'

'Airborne, sir.'

'And causing a certain amount of consternation.'

'Probably, sir. It would appear that many people and animals have a deep-rooted aversion to flying tents.'

'As do I, Dr Maxwell. Especially when they appear to have been launched from St Mary's. But returning us both to Mr Bashford . . .'

'Oh, yes, well – again, sir – not entirely his fault. Eager to rectify the situation – as any responsible organisation would be – St Mary's, as one, shouted, 'To horse – to horse,' piled into all available vehicles and galloped to the rescue.'

'Mr Bashford, Dr Maxwell.'

'Including Mr Bashford. Unfortunately, his car doesn't always function quite according to the promises made in the manual and on the day in question, having reached the Rushford by-pass it . . . well . . . ceased to be. He's had it a long time and although its demise had long been foretold, it was still an upsetting moment, for him, sir.'

'Which he observed by climbing on to the roof.'

'Not as bizarre an action as it first appears, sir. He was seeking a vantage point from which to observe the progress of the marquis across country.'

'Hence the binoculars which caused so much consternation to our security forces.'

'Yes, sir.'

'While clutching his chicken.'

'His *lookout* chicken, sir. Angus was very keen to be included.'

'And at no point did he consider that being discovered, standing on the roof of his car, uttering phrases such as "Target sighted half a mile away and heading north towards Waitrose. Move in. Move in", would cause any sort of consternation among those dedicated to ensuring the safety of our beloved royal family?'

'I think I can safely say that wouldn't have entered his mind, sir. His selfless motivation was the recapture of the errant marquis. As, indeed, it was for all of us. And, frankly, sir, I think someone should be asking the question – why were such a large number of HRHs charging about the countryside, anyway? A bit irresponsible on Christmas Day, I think we can all agree.'

'Certain highly placed members of the royal family were attending – or intended to attend – a Christmas Day service to mark the five hundredth birthday of St Stephen's in Rushford, before going on to visit two orphanages and an elderly person's hospice in the interests of spreading Christmas joy and good-will to all men. Visits which did not occur, of course, due to circumstances I am endeavouring to establish.'

'Not Mr Bashford's fault, sir.'

'I hesitate to take issue with you, Dr Maxwell, but I think even the most incompetent of bodyguards would regard a decrepit vehicle, illegally parked on the freeway constituting part of the designated route, with the driver standing on the roof, complete with binoculars and clutching a chicken—'

'His lookout chicken, sir—'

'To be an occurrence unusual enough to warrant attention. Nor was Mr Bashford's attempt to escape deemed particularly helpful.'

'They startled him and he fell off the roof, sir.'

'He failed to respond when instructed to put his hands on his head and surrender.'

'He was unconscious, sir.'

'And then there was the matter of Angus's subsequent attack, resulting in several dedicated members of the security forces incurring a severe beaking.'

'Angus was defending her master, sir. As any right-minded chicken under the circumstances would. Really, a complete overreaction on the part of the security services. I feel a com-plaint should be made.'

'A complaint *has* been made, Dr Maxwell. I have spent half the morning dealing with it.'

He paused. Here we go.

'Putting Mr Bashford to one side for the moment, we return to the free-flying marquee, by now, I believe, halfway to Rushford, where it stampeded vast numbers of peacefully grazing cows and sheep – according to any number of complaints from local farmers – traumatised a group of worshippers attempting to access St Stephen's, and severely impeded air traffic at the local RAF station where attempts to shoot it down were enthusiastic but unsuccessful, triggering yet another alert on the part of our already overstretched security services. After this small catastrophe, and driven by the strong winds prevailing at the time, I am given to understand the marquee flapped its way towards Whittington where half the residents assumed they were under attack from an unidentified flying object and locked their doors, with the exception of a Mrs Addlepate who immediately offered herself up for . . . probing. The other half of the population, I believe, were too busy uploading the phenomenon to something called . . .' he paused and consulted his notes, 'You Tube. Where it went . . .' he paused again, 'viral. Do I have that expression right, Dr Maxwell?'

'You do indeed, sir. Well done.'

'Leaving chaos in its wake, the marquee was then blown across country to Streetley, where it wrapped itself around the Number Twenty-nine bus, causing the driver to skid off the road and into a small and fortunately very shallow ornamental lake which, sadly for everyone, was heavily populated with over-wintering bird life, all of whom turned on this unexpected threat in something resembling a scene from the famous

Hitchcock film. The driver and passengers were trapped inside for nearly two hours before sufficient man power could be diverted from all the other St Mary's-triggered security alerts, and sent to resolve the St Mary's-triggered avian apocalypse in Streetley. Do you have anything to say to this, Dr Maxwell?'

I slumped. 'Actually, sir – no.'

He flourished a piece of paper. 'An invoice from the tent hire people for their lost marquee.'

'Don't pay it, sir, it's not lost – we know exactly where it is and—'

'It's still wrapped around the bloody bus, Dr Maxwell.' He flourished another piece of paper. 'According to the letter of complaint from the bus company.'

'Do they want it back? The marquis, I mean.'

'No. In fact, reading between the lines of their letter, I don't think they ever want to have anything to do with us ever again. Ever.'

I sighed. 'A bit like the catering company. They packed up and went home, sir.'

'You bring me neatly to my next query, Dr Maxwell. Did this year's Christmas lunch actually occur? And if so – where and when?'

'Actually, sir, it did. Somewhat later than scheduled, but securing Mr Bashford's release took longer than anticipated. However, thanks to the unparalleled talents of Mrs Mack – widely rumoured to be able to produce a six-course banquet for twenty in the middle of the Namib Desert and using nothing but a Bunsen burner and a teaspoon – St Mary's – en masse – sat down for lunch at around twenty-five past two in the morning . . .'

'On Boxing Day, in fact.'

'Time is fluid, sir, as I have heard you say on many occasions. And as to the where – modesty precludes me mentioning that my own not inconsiderable organisational abilities were instrumental in ramming a quart into a pint pot and we dined in the Great Hall and around the gallery. A two-tier configuration, I might say, that lent the whole occasion an air of cosmopolitan sophistication sometimes lacking at St Mary's, and will certainly return next year due to popular request.'

He drew breath to utter. The trick is to get in first. *Attack is the best form of* etc., etc.

'The thing is, sir, and given our somewhat spectacular track record, I really don't think this constitutes an unparalleled disaster and—'

'Given the magnitude of . . . events . . . over Christmas this year, I can hardly wait to hear your personal definition of an actual unparalleled disaster, Dr Maxwell.'

'Well, that would be failure of the chocolate harvest and the sudden and unexplained disappearance of Matt Damon off the face of the earth, sir, but I don't think things are that bad yet.'

'I await your ingenious assessment of our most recent catastrophe with bated breath, Dr Maxwell.'

'Sir, the weather that day was awful – hence the low-flying marquis. Nothing was flying out of the airbase – not on Christmas Day. Not in that wind. Streetley is now a YouTube sensation – the pub's crawling with UFO hunters and doing a roaring trade. Bashford's unfortunate interaction with the security services caused the royal trip to be diverted, thus avoiding the bit of road that later crumbled away due to flooding – you know, where the road runs along the banks of the Rush. We could have had a couple of very soggy HRHs, which would have been embarrassing at best and tragic at worst, sir. Bit of bad planning on someone's part, but all avoided thanks to Bashford's selfless actions. We've even gained our own marquis since the tent people are making us pay for it, the acquisition of which will enable us to expand our range of social events greatly – because those always go down so well locally, don't you think? Really, I don't see this so much as a problem, but rather a series of opportunities. Golden opportunities, sir.'

'You're absolutely right,' he said suddenly. I think both of us took a moment to wonder if we'd somehow fallen into an alternate universe. One where my skills and talents were more widely appreciated. 'This is definitely a series of opportunities, Dr Maxwell. And more importantly – a series of teaching moments.'

He pushed back his chair and stood up. 'You have a three o'clock telephone conference with our deeply unhappy chief constable, a series of placatory letters to write to the Lord Lieutenant, the bus depot manager, Streetley Parish Council, sundry farmers and smallholders, the police, and an RAF station commander, who swears all automatic targeting devices are now pointed directly at St Mary's. Not to mention the disappointed Mrs Addlepate. I myself intend to meet Mrs Brown for afternoon tea at the Copper Kettle in Rushford. Don't just sit there, Dr Maxwell – have at it.'

THE END

Merry Christmas and a Happy New Year to all my readers. Matt Damon – please take care out there.

WHY IS NOTHING EVER SIMPLE?

DRAMATIS THINGUMMY

Dr Bairstow   Director of St Mary's.

Dr Maxwell   Head of the History Department. Parent to
                     Matthew. In *loco parentis* to Adrian and
                     Mikey and the strain is beginning to show.

Dr Peterson   Inching towards the possibility of consider-
                     ing having an important conversation with
                     Miss Lingoss but don't hold your breath.

Mr Markham   What's going on there?

Major Guthrie   His last jump. Surely it won't all end in dis-
                     aster? Not on his last jump.

Chief Tech Farrell   Appearing briefly and mainly in his role as
                     something to do in a dark cupboard.

Adrian and Mikey   Missed the party. Fortunately.

Matthew Farrell   Manufacturing a very important Christmas
                     gift.

Lady Amelia Smallhope	Second daughter of the Earl of Goodrich. Expelled from every top-class establishment that could be bribed to take her. All of whom forecast she would come to a bad end.
Pennyroyal	Former SAS. Crack shot. Explosives expert. Skilled thief. Butler.
Elspeth Grey	Got her mojo back. Yay, Elspeth!
Robert the Bruce	About to be King of Scotland. If he can keep his head.
Henry de Bohun	Sadly doesn't get to keep his.
The Scottish army	
The English army	
Four utter pillocks	Whose lives are about to go right down the pan as soon as the Time Police turn up.

WHY IS NOTHING EVER SIMPLE?

Major Guthrie was leaving us. We all knew he would, sooner or later, but the confirmation was a bit of a blow just the same. He was as recovered as he would ever be. His leg had healed well but not well enough for him to resume his duties as Head of Security. And nothing could replace his lost eye. I believe the Time Police had offered him some kind of cosmetic prosthetic which, typically, he'd declined on the grounds he wasn't Borg, and instead adopted a black eyepatch which he thought gave him a sinister and menacing air but actually made him look like a battered hero in one of those bloodthirsty online computer games. I'd mentioned this and he'd huffed indignantly at me and ten minutes later I'd caught him checking out himself and his eyepatch in the nearest mirror. We never spoke of that moment.

His leaving filled me with dismay. It wasn't that Markham was doing a bad job as his replacement – he was bloody good at the job, actually – it's just that . . . well, Ian Guthrie was Ian Guthrie and we all owed our lives to him many times over.

When he told me that he and Elspeth Grey were taking over the pub in the village, the Falconburg Arms, I was pleased for him because he would be so good at running a pub – and he'd be just down the road should we ever need him. Typically,

Peterson and Markham's thoughts were far more Peterson and Markham-centric. Free drinks for life. Or so they thought.

'Not a chance,' said Ian when they broached this pleasant subject. 'In fact, my business manager –' he nodded at Elspeth, who looked up from her laptop and scowled at them both in a way that made it clear that, while she might have attended the brewery's official Customer Care Course, she hadn't actually believed a word of it in general and certainly not in connection with two customers in particular – 'my business manager has recommended I levy a St Mary's surcharge of at least twenty per cent.'

'What?' demanded Markham.

'Why?' demanded Peterson.

'Oh, all sorts of excellent reasons. Compensation against lost revenue because no one locally wants to share a bar with you lot. A deposit against potential breakages because you know what you're like. But mostly because we're the landlords and what we say goes.'

Peterson and Markham were convinced he was joking. I wasn't so sure. And Leon was certain he wasn't.

Anyway, Guthrie and Elspeth had done their training – although as Peterson said, 'Putting liquid in a glass and handing it to someone – how difficult can that be?' – and now they were all set to go. There was the official opening night – from which St Mary's was banned – and it all went very well, apparently, although there was some St Mary's muttering that we weren't good enough for Guthrie now he had a pub. Which was definitely not true, he said. We hadn't been good enough for him *before* he had a pub.

We were worrying unnecessarily. A week later, as part of our run up to Christmas, we were to have our own official St

Mary's dining-in night. The conservatory in which they served food had been reserved just for us. We responded by turning up in force because, as Markham informed him, they needed the business.

We began with cocktails – which, yes, with hindsight, might have been a mistake. There was a tab running for everyone because none of us could be bothered with money. Indeed, as Ian had cruelly remarked, most of us couldn't count properly anyway. Everyone was colour-coded. I overheard Peterson charging his drink to green and promptly followed suit. I had a couple of margaritas which went down very well, let me tell you, and then we wandered – or lurched – into the conservatory to eat.

The food was gorgeous – they'd hired a new chef – and Elspeth showed she hadn't wasted her time at St Mary's by handing out the dessert menus first because there is nothing more heartbreaking than stuffing yourself on the first two courses and then realising you haven't left room for your favourite pudding. In fact, after I'd given a talk about the Battles of Stamford Bridge and Hastings at a local school recently, one of the teachers had asked me if I had any advice for young people and I'd said yes, always eat dessert first, which I don't think was what she'd meant at all.

Anyway, menus were carefully scanned and dishes carefully chosen. Everyone was in good spirits. We were all here. Even Kal, who had come down from Thirsk. I hadn't seen her since the day she pushed me into the lake, an event she didn't appear to remember at all, telling me I'd been pretty much out of things at the time and I must have imagined it.

It isn't often most of St Mary's is present and uninjured, but at that precise moment we were. All that remained of Dottle's treachery was just a tree stump and a stain on the memory. Peterson had the steam-pump jump under his belt and seemed happier for it. He and Lingoss sat side by side, chatting away to each other and I was pleased for them. Bashford and Sykes sat opposite each other – he with the naked and vulnerable air of a man who has, reluctantly, had to leave his chicken at home and she with the cheerful chirpiness of one whose man has been induced to leave his chicken at home. And I had Leon with me which is always my definition of a perfect evening. And yes, all right, we might have been a little bit noisy, but we had a lot to be noisy about.

I ordered Leon a beer and then another. He commented on my generosity. I smiled benignly and signed the green chit with a flourish.

There were some absentees. Dr Bairstow wasn't here. He tends not to frequent this sort of event, leaving us to let our hair down without embarrassment. It's a shame because it was a good evening and he would have enjoyed himself. It occurred to me that he must sometimes be quite lonely and then someone said he'd gone into Rushford with Mrs Partridge. Everyone said, 'Aww, that's nice,' and Peterson whispered to me that he probably just wanted to be as far away as possible when the obligatory midden hit the inevitable ventilation system.

'Plausibuble denibililility,' he said, wagging a wayward forefinger for effect.

I ordered him another drink and winked at Lingoss whose seemingly casual attitude towards Peterson was fooling no one. Today's hair was a festive red and green.

Mikey and Adrian weren't here, either. Well, they weren't

old enough to drink for a start. Old enough to have built an illegal pod and gallivanted all over the timeline with it, endangering the lives of everyone with whom they came into contact, but not old enough to consume alcohol.

'As if we would ever want to,' Mikey said in disgust. We'd left the two of them babysitting Matthew. They'd turned up at our door, staggering slightly under the weight of pizza boxes and age-inappropriate holos.

Anyway, back to the battering the Falconburg Arms was taking. We ate well. We drank even better, but recent Atticus Wolfe events had rather taken their toll on me and I'd been under instructions from Dr Stone not to make too heavy a night of it, and anyway, neither of us wanted to leave Matthew too long with those particular babysitters, so Leon and I were among the first to leave. We – well, I – staggered into the bar where Ian was waiting for us, all ready to settle the bill.

'Ah yes,' he said, pulling out a tab as long as a toilet roll. 'Green.'

'No,' I said, in some dismay. 'No, no, no. Peterson's green. Not me.'

'Peterson's blue,' he said, consulting a multi-coloured chart of typical military complexity and thoroughness.

'No, he's not. I definitely heard him say green.'

He grinned. 'No, sorry, Max. Far from you charging your evening to him – he's been charging his to you.' He scanned down the list. 'Wow. Someone's had a good night.'

'Do you take credit cards?' I said gloomily.

'What? From you?'

I don't know what was so funny about that. It seemed to me to be a perfectly reasonable request.

9

I turned to Leon who had wandered off and was, for some reason, examining the sign directing people to the Ladies and being of no use whatsoever.

Ian looked down at my giant tab again and said, slightly too casually, 'They're all right, aren't they? Hunter and Markham?'

They were both still in the dining room behind me. That wasn't what he was asking.

I got as far as, 'As far as I know they're both fine,' and then I stopped talking and started thinking. Guthrie and Markham were close friends. He probably knew how things were going better than I did.

'Actually . . .' I said, and stopped and waited for him to leap into hasty indiscretion.

That never works with Ian Guthrie. He just looked at me. I was going to have to say it.

'Actually, he got a letter.' I looked over my shoulder. Leon was further down the hall reading the fire evacuation instructions. A bit of a busman's holiday for him.

Guthrie cast him a glance and then said, 'Is this the one he had back in the summer? After the steam-pump affair?'

I nodded.

He said quietly, 'You doing anything tomorrow, Max?'

'Well, yes, obviously. I'm massively busy. Always am.'

'So no, then.'

'Not really, no.'

'Can you get away sometime?'

I nodded.

'Come and see me. I'd like a quick word.' He raised his voice. 'Now, about this credit card of yours . . .'

I tugged out my wallet, pulled out my credit card, polished

10

it hopefully on my sleeve – as if that would help – and handed it over.

It went through. Both Ian and I were utterly and equally gob-smacked and I whirled Leon out of the door before everyone could discover there had been a horrible mistake somewhere along the line.

We wandered happily up the road back towards St Mary's. Christmas was only a week or so away but the night was quite mild. I didn't even need my gloves.

I admired the pretty golden Van Gogh nimbus around each of the street lights – although that might have been my eyesight rather than actual atmospheric conditions. Or even that last margarita. We held hands – and not just because I might have been a fraction unsteady on my feet. We walked slowly, enjoying a few rare moments on our own, stopping at the little stone bridge over the stream to look at the black water flowing underneath.

I remembered this stream from six hundred years ago when it had been wider and shallower and there was no bridge at all. You got across by hopping from one wide, flat stone to another. Mostly but not always successfully in my case. And there had been bundles of willow twigs standing in the water to keep them supple enough to weave, and up there had been the mill with whatshisname the miller – Robert Stukely – who would rob you blind as soon as look at you, and over there had been the big tithe barns where the harvests were stored. And over there had been Pikey Peter's mother's house . . .

I was wandering happily through the past when Leon, who can be quite frivolous for a techie, suggested pooh sticks. The bridge was well lit at both ends – thank you, Parish Council – and

Leon had his torch anyway. We could easily see well enough to break off a few twigs from nearby bushes. I accepted his challenge and away we went.

He won the first couple of tries because I had some difficulty getting my pooh sticks into the water – I think one went over my shoulder – but I soon found my rhythm and then it was a case of pooh sticks to the death.

We were still at it when some of the others caught us up and then, of course, because St Mary's is very competitive, everyone wanted to play.

Leon and I stepped back and watched their efforts for a while until Leon suggested they might find the game easier and more interesting if they dropped their sticks from the *upstream* side of the bridge. There was a kind of collective 'Ah' of enlightenment, and then they all rushed to the other side. I'm surprised the bridge didn't tip over.

Eventually everyone ran out of sticks and we decided to leave them to it before someone came up with the bright idea of playing pooh sticks with actual . . .

We were just moving away when there were two loud splashes and a lot of cheering and Bashford and Keller floated out from underneath the bridge, flailing and cursing, both locked in mortal combat. We discovered afterwards they'd both been volunteered to be pooh sticks by their colleagues who were taking the spirit of inter-departmental competitiveness just a little bit too far. It was fortunate for them the weather was unseasonably mild and they didn't encounter an iceberg.

Anyway, they were beyond our reach and there wasn't anything Leon or I could do other than abandon them to their fate and go to bed. As we left, I could hear Dieter and Kal wondering if they'd float all the way out to sea and would that be some kind of record?

They didn't, obviously. They somehow made their way into the middle of our lake. No one's ever worked out how they managed that because the stream actually flows *out* of the lake. It was really dark by that time and their pathetic cries for help went unheeded by everyone except Mr Strong, our caretaker, who was locking up for the night. He reported strange noises to the more responsible members of the Security Section who suddenly realised what – or who – it could be and wandered outside to mount a rescue.

Commandeering one of our old rowing boats, they all piled in and set off, torches flickering back and forth across the water. The search took some time and our two pooh stickers would probably never have been found if the boat hadn't actually collided with them both before they completely disappeared beneath the storm-tossed waves, as Cox persisted in calling the lake's placid surface.

There were already far too many of them in the boat to take on any more passengers, so singing loud-and-anatomically-impossible sea shanties, Security towed Bashford and Keller back to shore, taking the scenic route through the pond scum, weed and swan shit.

All was apparently going well until someone thought to look behind the boat and discovered they were being tracked by a dozen or so swans, drawn up in battle formation, necks extended, gliding silently and sinisterly through the darkness. Waiting to pick off the stragglers, as Evans said the next morning, shuddering at the recollection.

There's a kind of unofficial agreement between us and our swans. During daylight hours St Mary's can get up to more or less whatever it pleases – as long as that doesn't include flames, explosions, dogs or music (no idea what the problem is with music – sorry) and St Mary's doesn't intrude on whatever it is they get up to in the hours of darkness. And now we'd broken the treaty. Things were not looking good.

Speeding up, our jolly mariners eventually collided with land and fell out of the boat. They all helped each other up because, as Evans explained afterwards, it was vital not to break ranks. The swans climbed silently out of the water and looked at them. It was at this point that the St Mary's nerve broke and everyone ran. Evans later described it as, 'A text-book tactical withdrawal in the face of avian incursion but with added panic,' and Markham described it as the sort of thing that happened if he wasn't there to keep an eye on things.

Whichever it was, they reached Hawking Hangar only just ahead of either two hundred swans – as Evans later described it – or eight swans, as the slightly less traumatised Mr Strong described it – where they were all rescued by Kal and Dieter who were in pod Number Six for reasons never satisfactorily explained.

Ian and Elspeth later said they were adding a new wing to the dining conservatory on the strength of what they'd taken at the Arms that night and that St Mary's was welcome at any time and to bring our wallets with us.

Dr Bairstow and Mrs Partridge returned from a pleasant night out in Rushford. Neither was soaking wet or covered in swan shit.

Things were very quiet the next day which is always the sign of a very satisfactory night out and I slipped out for a quiet word with Ian.

He was waiting for me at the pub. 'Have you had lunch?'

I shook my head.

He took me into the kitchen, made us both a round of chicken sandwiches and tipped some crisps into a bowl while I made us a pot of tea. We took the whole lot into his little office down the hall. I'd been in here once or twice before. Nothing had changed. It was a nice room with dark panelling and a cheerful log fire. Weak winter sunlight filtered in through the window.

I put a couple more logs on the fire while Ian laid everything out on his desk, saying, 'You eat and I'll talk.'

'This sounds serious,' I said, half-joking.

'It is.'

About to sit down, I stopped. 'Are you sure you want to tell me? Because I'm not sure I want to hear.'

He sat heavily. 'We don't always have a choice.'

I lowered myself into my chair. 'Then why are you telling me now?'

'Because I'm not at St Mary's any longer and someone else should know.'

I put the crisp back on my plate. 'Know what?'

He poured the tea, dropped in a slice of lemon for me and passed it over.

'About Markham.'

It was a good job I'd already put down my tea. 'What about Markham?'

'He might be in trouble, Max. He may need help soon and he may need it quickly. There might not be time for him to explain so I'm telling you now. Don't look so worried – you probably won't ever have to do anything. Just park the information and forget it. With luck you'll never need it. This is just in case . . .'

'In case of what?'

He didn't answer directly, sitting back in his chair and stirring his tea. 'You said he'd had a letter?'

I nodded. 'Yes. He didn't say anything at the time, but it was very obvious he wasn't happy about it.'

'Then they know.'

'Who knows? And what do they know?'

'They know he's disobeyed instructions.'

I was growing cold. This sounded bad. 'What instructions?'

'To keep his head down. To keep his mouth shut. And most importantly, to keep it in his pants.'

I swallowed. 'You mean – not to get Hunter pregnant?'

'I mean not to get anyone pregnant.'

'Why not?'

'Because of who he is.'

I was conscious of great gaping holes opening beneath my feet. Of a few of life's certainties suddenly not being quite so certain.

'He's Markham. Isn't he? For heaven's sake, Ian . . .'

He got up, opened the door, looked up and down the corridor, closed and locked it. Then he crossed to the window, checking it was closed. That done, he returned to his desk, clasped his hands and said, without any emotion whatsoever, 'Markham is the establishment's dirty little secret.'

My stomach knotted. Astonishment. Yes, a lot of that. Fear. Yes, some of that. And anger. 'Don't say that. He's Markham. He's one of the best people I know. He's not anyone's dirty little secret.'

'Calm down, Max. You don't have to tell me that. He and I have been friends for a long time.'

I reached out for my tea. My hand wasn't quite steady and

my thoughts were all over the place. I took a couple of calming sips and said, 'Tell me.'

'I can't tell you much because I don't know much.'

'Tell me what you do know.'

'I know he was still very young when he came to me and yet he'd managed to be in trouble nearly all his life. Whether he was the product of a broken home or the victim of a bad upbringing or anything like that, I don't know. His file was short on personal detail but long on criminal record. He was just . . . when he came to me . . . when he was drafted into the army . . . he was so *angry*, Max. He was lashing out in all directions – hurting others, hurting himself.'

'And you took him in.'

'Yes. I wasn't that keen, I admit. I had a pretty good set of people under me at the time and we'd worked hard together to achieve that and now they wanted me to take this bad apple. But, no one gives you any choice in the army, so grudgingly, very grudgingly, I took him on.

'The first thing I realised was that I'd better ditch that attitude pretty quickly because I was just the latest in a long line of people who hadn't wanted anything to do with him. He'd been shunted from pillar to post and back again. There was one year when he'd had four different homes.

'Yes, I know,' he said as I went to speak. 'But, reading between the lines, he wasn't doing himself any favours at all. People had taken him on with all sorts of good intentions but it never lasted. I decided I'd give him a month and if things didn't get better, then I'd add my name to the long list of people who apparently couldn't be bothered with our Mr Markham.'

He sipped his tea.

'And then I walked around a corner one day and there was our hero having the living shit kicked out of him.'

'Why?'

'Well, no one ever said, but they were an unpleasant bunch of characters and I suspect, with typical disregard for the consequences, our hero had pointed this out to them and they hadn't welcomed his constructive criticism, which was just so entirely typical of his . . . almost a death wish. Sometimes I was convinced he just wanted to cause as much trouble as possible for as many people as possible. Or, it occurred to me, as I stood wondering what the hell I was going to do with him, he was a deeply unhappy young man on a mission to make everyone else deeply unhappy too.'

'What did you do?'

'I yelled at them all impartially; no one was badly hurt so I sent them on their way. I gave Markham twenty-four hours to cool down and then had him in for a chat. I asked him straight out what the hell he thought he was playing at and he said he was making things easy for me.

'That took me back a bit, I can tell you. I demanded to know what he meant and he said he liked me and was therefore making it easy for me to chuck him out. I said what did he think would happen to him if I did that and he said he didn't know and didn't care. It wasn't important. Quite honestly, Max, just in that moment, I've never seen anyone look so lost, so unhappy, so alone, so . . . at odds with the world. It was him versus everyone else. He couldn't possibly win and he was damaging himself in the attempt. I thought about a bird beating its wings against the bars of its cage, hurting itself, bleeding, not understanding what was happening to it . . .'

Ian tailed away.

'Anyway, instead of giving him the traditional stiff bollocking, I actually talked to him. And I made him talk. He's not inarticulate. I listened to what he had to say. I challenged him. I made him think. He soon lost his temper and started shouting – I think that was his favourite way of dealing with everything – but I kept plugging away. We were at it all afternoon. My clerk came in once to see if everything was all right. I don't know what it was that I said to him – Markham – but something must have stuck because slowly, over time, I began to notice his first response to a problem wasn't just to thump the nearest person present. He's not stupid, our Markham. He just needed . . . I don't know . . . I think, over the years, people's responses to his behaviour had been to fence him in, to surround him with a list of things he couldn't do, to make his cage smaller and smaller and I wanted him to see that suddenly, the cage door could be open for him.'

'He started using his powers for good,' I said, oddly touched.

He nodded. 'Exactly.'

'So what *was* his background?'

'Well, there is virtually no information on him for the first ten or so years of his life. At that point he was farmed out to some posh family with whom he didn't get on. I don't know any details. They didn't treat him very well and he went off the rails quite badly. And then from one home to the next, gradually sliding down the greasy pole of unacceptable behaviour. You name it – he was into it. Not drugs or violence or murder – but he was heading that way. And I have to say – a lot of it was his fault. We have to remember, Max, he wasn't always as we know him today. Anyway – and he makes no secret of this – eventually he was offered the choice: the army or prison. He chose the army and came to me – trailing his extensive and imaginative criminal record behind him.'

'I don't understand. Why would he behave like that? Why wouldn't he . . .'

I broke off, slightly unable to believe I'd asked such a stupid question.

Guthrie smiled and sipped his own tea. 'Well, it's Markham, isn't it? I suspect he got fed up with people telling him he should be grateful to them because he was a problem and an inconvenience, so he decided to show them how much of a problem and inconvenience he could really be if he put his mind to it.'

I could identify with that. 'But now he's in trouble again?'

'He was doing so well here, Max. Dr Bairstow gave him his confidence and trust and Markham's more than repaid him. He and St Mary's were made for each other.' He grinned. 'He's a bit of a chameleon, our Markham, haven't you noticed? Adapts himself to whatever's happening around him.'

'In what way?'

'Well, you've noticed his accent.'

'Bristol.'

'He's just taking the piss. He was a Geordie in the army.'

I was gobsmacked. 'You're kidding. Why?'

He shrugged. 'Because he can?'

'But what has this to do with him and Hunter? As far as I know, even the most dangerous criminal is allowed to breed. I know governments are always a bunch of suited control freaks hell-bent on bettering their own lot at public expense, but surely even they haven't yet got around to telling people whether they can or can't have kids?'

20

'I don't know. Perhaps he's part of some social experiment – you know, weeding out the bad by not allowing them to breed.'

'That's . . . that's . . .' I was lost for words.

'It is, isn't it?'

'Why are you telling me all this?'

'Because, as I said, I'm not at St Mary's any longer and I'm worried that one day he could find himself in need of help. Urgent help.'

'What do you want me to do?'

'Nothing. Just keep an eye on things for me, would you?'

'Are you expecting something to happen?'

'I've no idea. He's been keeping his head down and I was rather hoping they'd forgotten all about him. Now, of course . . .' He sighed. 'I'm sorry to lumber you with this, Max.'

'No, it's all right. I think. I'm just a little . . .'

'Taken aback.'

'Yes.' I had a thought. 'Does Dr Bairstow know?'

'Oh yes. I showed him Markham's file.'

'What did he say?'

'He said it was a most unfortunate start to a young life and never mentioned it again. If it was anyone but Dr Bairstow, I'd say he'd forgotten all about it.'

He shifted in his seat. 'If you could have seen Markham when he first came to me, Max. Angry. Defensive. Destructive. Self-destructive. Now look at him. A man with a child on the way who wants only to live quietly and probably isn't going to be allowed to do so.'

'What do you want me to do?'

'Nothing. Just be there. If you're needed.'

I shifted in my seat. 'Ian . . .'

'I know, Max. I haven't done you any favours today. I might have put you at risk as well. Which is why I'm saying – keep this to yourself.'

'Don't worry,' I said. 'I will.' I think I was holding on to the hope that if I never ever mentioned it again then eventually it might slip from my not very capacious memory altogether. Fat chance of that.

Silence fell. I listened to the crackling fire. Felt the warmth from the flames.

'Anyway,' I said, more to push these recent revelations to the back of my mind than because he would have forgotten, 'you haven't forgotten next week?'

'No, indeed,' he said, picking up a sandwich. 'Looking forward to it.'

'You do know it's a record-and-document-only assignment. No interaction. In fact, I forbid you – any of you – to leave the pod.'

'No problem,' he said. 'Don't know if you've noticed but I don't move as fast these days.' He gestured to his eyepatch. 'And I walk into things a lot, as well.'

'Yes, I know. We all think it's hilarious.'

He scowled at me and then picked up a copy of the menu.

'What are you doing?'

'Preparing your bill.'

'What?'

'For lunch.' He nodded at my mostly undrunk tea and uneaten sandwiches.

I drew myself up. 'It was the Battle of Culloden, wasn't it?'

'Bannockburn.'

'No, I'm pretty sure the mission folder says Culloden.'

He replied in purest Caledonian. 'Away, ye wee hinny. Yer bum's oot the windae. Bannockburn.'

I replied carefully and in impeccable English, 'Shut yer yeggie. Yer aff yer heid,' and he was so appalled at this assault on his mother tongue that I was able to escape. But not, however, to have the last word.

I was halfway up the road when the window opened and a voice accustomed to being heard over battlefields and feeding time at St Mary's bellowed, 'Bannockburn.'

I made the Agincourt gesture and ran for it.

As it happened, I never made it to Bannockburn. Well, I did, but not officially. I'm accustomed to encountering obstacles during assignments but rarely beforehand. Today, however, was just Pelion piled upon Ossa.

I'm a mother. Not a particularly good one – no one's ever going to nominate me for the Mother of the Year award – but, after a while, even a bad mother develops certain instincts. You soon realise that too quiet is a hundred times worse than too noisy. Too quiet is sinister. A clean and smiling child should be regarded with the very greatest suspicion and a thorough investigation carried out immediately. Likewise, obedience. An obedient child is a child who's up to something. Obedience is not a natural state for the young. You need to get in and sort things out before events slide, inevitably, towards the catastrophic.

Strictly speaking, Adrian and Mikey weren't mine. They were teenagers who'd turned up one day in their teapot-shaped pod in desperate need of assistance. They were attempting to evade the Time Police so assistance was enthusiastically and successfully provided. They've been living here at St Mary's ever since. Mikey works in R&D, often with Matthew, and Adrian adds colour and variety to Leon's working day in the Technical Section.

Just in case anyone from the Time Police is reading this, their pod very definitely does not reside here. Absolutely not. Never. Because that would be very, very wrong and we at St Mary's are always very careful never to . . . no, I'm sorry – I can't finish that sentence.

It wasn't anything new to see Adrian and Mikey talking together in a corner. It was the *way* they were talking together that aroused my suspicions. Normally there would be laughing, a little bit of shoving, deadly insults exchanged – that sort of thing. But not today. The two of them stood, heads together, talking quietly, all of which was so wrong that my mother senses kicked into overdrive and – yes, I spied on them. No, I'm not ashamed and it turned out to be a bloody good thing that I did.

They'd changed into civilian clothing. Mikey has to change at the end of every working day anyway. It's a rare day in R&D when they're not covering themselves in something unspeakable. Or, worse, covering everyone else in something unspeakable. I still had vivid memories of being pursued around the gallery by R&D-manufactured ever-expanding exothermic foam. Seemingly possessed of a malevolent intelligence – which was more than could be said of anyone else in this unit, as Dr Bairstow had acidly remarked afterwards – it had surged and frothed its way massively around the gallery, swallowing up everything in its path. People fled before it. Except for Bashford who ran the wrong way – typical historian sense of direction – and ended up alone and cornered outside Peterson's office.

His near-end was actually quite moving. Last heard shriek-ing, 'Fly, my pretty one, fly,' he'd attempted to fling Angus to safety over the banisters and into the Hall below. Sadly, Angus has the flying abilities of a brick and she'd been very lucky to be caught by an astonished Mr Sands. As he said later, one minute he'd been concentrating on avoiding certain death by man-eating foam and the next, a gravity-constrained chicken had dropped heavily into his arms.

People had scattered, running for their lives or shooting into offices and barricading the doors behind them. It was like being pursued by a giant Crunchie, said Peterson later as we recovered in the bar. An image that appears occasionally in my dreams.

Anyway, Leon and I had been in the corridor, amicably arguing over the pod schedule, when the giant Crunchie thing kicked off. He looked over my shoulder, shouted, 'Look out,' grabbed my arm and suddenly the two of us were in the airing cupboard. Trapped together in the warm, fragrant darkness. All alone and trying to think of a way to pass the time during what might be the final moments of our lives.

The foam surged along the gallery, wisely stopping short of Dr Bairstow's door, and everyone assumed the danger had passed. Until it began to harden.

It took several hours to chip Bashford free. Fortunately, his head was still above the foam and he was able to converse with his rescuers and enquire after the well-being of Angus, who had not taken kindly to being hurled over the banisters by her idol and was sulking in the kitchen.

Anyway, back to being a mother – as if that's something that ever goes away. The two of them – Adrian and Mikey – had changed out of their working clothes and back into what Adrian often referred to as their battledress. He wore his favourite black jeans and T-shirt with his long, leather coat over the top. He loved that coat and would frequently and dramatically swirl around the building like a villain in a Victorian melodrama.

Mikey also wore jeans, a St Mary's sweatshirt and her truly dilapidated flying jacket, together with her Snoopy helmet and completely unnecessary goggles.

I watched them as they set off down the Long Corridor towards Hawking Hangar. Where we keep our pods.

Just a word of explanation here. Yes, I know it's been a long time coming but it's here now. Pods are our centre of operations. We use them to travel up and down the timeline as we investigate major historical events in contemporary time. Don't call it time travel or Dr Bairstow will probably feed you to the foam.

I stood in a doorway and watched them. I would put money on these two being up to no good. It struck me now – and it should certainly have struck me long before this – that our Adrian and Mikey – long-time fugitives and accustomed to living exciting lives – might well attempt to alleviate their traditional teenage boredom by indulging in a few illicit jumps. Which was no huge problem for me. I'm not sure if anyone's ever noticed but I myself am no stranger to the occasional illicit jump – especially at Christmas. No, the problem lay with the vessel in which they no doubt intended to make said illicit jump.

A mainstream pod wouldn't be a problem – and Leon would almost certainly head them off at the pass anyway. My concerns lay with the teapot. A sentence not quite as surreal as might initially appear. Mikey and Adrian's pod is shaped like a twelve-foot-high teapot. It also has one or two other interesting

26

features – not least the ability to remove objects from their own time, which is very much a no-no and liable to lead to all sorts of trouble with the bastard Time Police – and since we'd told them we'd destroyed the pod and hadn't, we really couldn't afford to attract any attention.

I let them get to the end of the Long Corridor and then set off after them. I'll use the time it takes me to get from one end to the other to explain about us here at St Mary's.

We all belong to St Mary's Institute of Historical Research – a small organisation outside Rushford where we live in peaceful rural seclusion – mostly – and hardly get into any trouble at all. We jump back in time to record major historical events. Sometimes we don't always manage to return successfully, but mostly we do. So that's quite clear, then.

I slipped quietly into Hawking Hangar and waited to see what would happen next. There was no sign of Leon anywhere – I suspected he was in with Peterson and Guthrie, prepping Number Four, all ready for the Bannockburn jump. Where I myself should be right at this moment.

I peered cautiously down the hangar because this was probably something that should be handled with discretion. Which is something I can do when I have to. Number Four was over to my left, easily distinguishable because, in honour of Ian's last jump, someone had stencilled the blue and white cross of St Andrew – the Saltire – on the side.

There was a light on in Leon's office at the far end. I could see Dieter and Polly Perkins bending over a screen, their faces lit from below and actually looking quite sinister. Otherwise, just for once, the place was deserted. Adrian and Mikey had chosen their moment well.

They paused just inside the hangar and then turned off and made their way quietly along the back wall.

I knew exactly where they were going. I slipped in behind them and followed them across the hangar to Tea Bag 2.

TB2 is our big pod. We use it for transporting large numbers of people or plant and equipment. Especially when we're on a search and rescue mission. There's a living area and a toilet that sometimes works, and it's very big and really useful for storing things inside. Such as, for example, an illegal teapot.

This is complicated. Bear with me. We can't use the teapot because as soon as we did, the Time Police would pick up the signature and we'd told them we'd destroyed it. It was part of a deal which they'd broken on their side and we'd broken on ours. Such are the levels of trust between St Mary's and the Time Police. And now, it looked as if our two teapot tearaways had plans that were wrong on so many levels. I didn't know what they were up to, but it wouldn't be good and would almost certainly bring the Time Police down on top of us and then there would be all sorts of tears and trauma. And for us, as well.

I should have expected something like this. Adrian and Mikey were teenagers. The pair of them were geniuses. They'd had the freedom of the whole timeline. They'd come and gone as they'd pleased. Yes, they'd been pursued every minute of every day by the Time Police but it hadn't seemed to cause them any problems. And yes, life here at St Mary's could be exciting at times, but I bet it wasn't half as exciting as their previous existence. I remembered their enthusiasm for bringing down renegade historian Clive Ronan. They'd allowed themselves to be captured by the Time Police and that couldn't have been pleasant for them. Then there had been all the perils of the Cretaceous period and Mikey had nearly been washed away in a flash flood.

Now they were living a quiet-ish life at St Mary's. Dr Bairstow ruled with a light hand and they weren't prisoners but . . . I suspected they were bored. At some point they'd planned this illegal jaunt. I might have been tempted to let them go. They could more than look after themselves. Except for the teapot. The one we were supposed to have destroyed.

I stepped out of the shadows. 'Good afternoon.'

They didn't shriek or panic.

'Bugger,' said Mikey, accepting the inevitable. 'Busted.'

'More than busted,' I said. 'What's going on here? – and I'm supposed to be on my way to Bannockburn so don't mess me about. In fact, I shouldn't be here at all, so make it quick.'

Admitting that was a mistake. I could see their thinking. She's in a rush. We'll fob her off with any old rubbish. Seriously? Did they think I'd never been a teenager myself?

I folded my arms. 'But for this, I have all the time in the world.'

'Well, the thing is, Max . . .'

'Yes?'

'Well, and I can't think why no one has ever done this before . . .'

'Yes?'

'In fact . . .'

Just as we were about to get to the good stuff, I had Peterson in my ear. 'Max, where are you?'

'I need a few minutes. Something's come up.'

'You should go,' said Mikey, generously. 'It's Major Guthrie's last jump and you wouldn't want to miss that.'

Adrian nodded. 'Yes, you'll be late.'

'They'll wait for me,' I said, without any hope at all.

29

Peterson spoke again. 'Max, we're not waiting for you. Get a move on, will you?'

'I'll be there in a minute. Right, you two, what's happening here?'

'Well . . .'

'Stop saying "well".'

'Well, I mean – nothing. Nothing's going on. We're just talking to you.'

I narrowed my eyes. If that didn't work, then I'd smile at them. That always works. People will do anything to stop me smiling at them.

'Obviously I need to narrow the focus of my interrogation.'

'Are you allowed to interrogate us?' enquired Mikey. 'I mean – we're minors, you know. The law doesn't apply to us.'

And there you have their entire attitude to life in a nutshell. I would bet good money they'll still be using that excuse when they're in their eighties. If they live that long.

Peterson was becoming impatient. 'Max, where the hell are you?'

I looked at the two of them grinning at me. Just waiting for me to go away. I came to a decision.

'Sorry, Tim. I'm not going to make it. Go without me.'

That wiped the smiles off their faces. But put the smile back on mine. 'Give my regards to Ian. Have a good trip.'

Peterson was not impressed. 'What's the problem? Max, this is Ian's last jump.'

'Yes, I know,' I said, with a nasty look at the two reprobates in front of me. 'And I'm sorry to miss it but I'll be here when you get back. All ready to review the tapes and point out where you went wrong.'

There was a pause and then Peterson said, 'All right then, if that's what you want. See you later this afternoon.'

He closed the link.

Lights flashed above Number Four's plinth. Moments later there was the familiar wind in my face and then they were gone.

I turned back to Adrian and Mikey. 'Right – I've missed Ian's last jump and now, thanks to you two, I am highly pissed off.'

This was overstating things slightly. I hadn't been that enthusiastic to begin with. Bannockburn was the battle that England lost. It's not that I'm a bad loser – although I am – but we really should have won that one and we didn't, thanks to that dipstick Edward II.

I'm sure I've mentioned him before. The job description for a medieval king wasn't onerous. You kept the realm safe and sired the next generation. Fight and fu—well, you get the drift.

Young Teddy Two managed the next generation part – although he and his wife loathed each other so I bet that was fun – but his main problem was that he was rubbish at controlling his barons.

The whole medieval period was one long, bloody struggle between the king and his lords. Both were vital to the other. The king was the fount from which lands, titles and riches flowed. The barons were vital to the safety of the realm. In return for the aforementioned lands, titles, etc., they maintained the borders. And they were powerful clans. They had to be. The Percys and other northern lords maintained the border against the Scots. The western border with Wales was protected by the Marcher lords – among them, the Mortimers.

31

Roger Mortimer would go on to become Edward's wife's lover and the two of them would eventually overthrow him.

London was a long way off back then; communications were only as good as the weather and the fastest horse, which rendered these families virtually autonomous. Not a problem if you had a strong king who could keep them all in line but definitely a problem if you were weak, ineffective Edward II, over-reliant on low-born personal favourites.

Possibly he was gay. Probably he was gay. And if he'd exercised a little discretion then things probably wouldn't have turned out so badly for him. He certainly wouldn't have been England's first gay king. There was William Rufus, Richard the Lionheart, possibly William of William-and-Mary fame – perhaps even Queen Anne. There's no reason to suppose people in the Middle Ages were any more or less gay than in modern times and he could probably have got away with it if he hadn't flooded his favourite, the despised Piers Gaveston, with expensive gifts. If he hadn't fawned on him in public while tough-as-shit border lords, who needed a firm but light hand, looked on in disgust and laid their plans accordingly.

Gaveston had been safely disposed of and Edward – whose survival instincts were slightly less reliable than Bashford's – immediately took up with Hugh Despenser and his old dad, two utter bastards, who must have made Edward's nobles long for the good old days of Piers Gaveston.

And – for those of you confused by my above rant, we're now back to the reasons I wasn't going on the Bannockburn jump – now I could perhaps spend some time wrapping presents with Matthew. Or rather, since I possess the ability to transform the rectangular shape of a book into an inter-dimensional, Sellotapesmothered, irregular dodecahedral lump of Christmas wrapping paper, Matthew would do the actual wrapping and I would be trusted to hold the scissors and sticky tape. And not to touch anything unless specifically instructed otherwise. I envisaged a quiet afternoon with carols playing and a steadily growing pile of neat packages around our Christmas tree while we scarfed down a plate of mince pies together.

Anyway, back to Adrian and Mikey after that scenic and informative digression. I think it was dawning on them that, like an STD, I wasn't going to go away. Not without some sort of divine intervention. Or antibiotics.

They sighed. 'Well . . . the thing is . . . we're not doing anything wrong.'

'In fact,' said Mikey, apparently struck by a brilliant idea, 'you could say it's our duty to go.'

I folded my arms again. 'And why would I say that?'

'Because – well – we've been invited. We're expected. It would be rude not to go.'

They looked at me triumphantly. Argument over. Whatever their intent had been, their actions were completely justified and I was being an unreasonable adult. I began to feel a very slight sympathy for the Time Police. No need to tell them that. Ever.

'What invite? No one in their right minds would invite you two anywhere.'

'That's hurtful,' said Adrian, hurt. Mikey contrived to look stricken. It's her go-to expression in a crisis.

I unfolded my arms just so I could fold them again. With added menace.

They sighed. Just two misunderstood young people alone

and defenceless in a cruel world. I prepared to make it even crueller.

'The thing is, Max . . .'

'Stop talking about the bloody thing,' I shouted. 'Whatever it is.'

'But you *asked* us,' said Mikey reasonably, effortlessly shifting the blame for everything on to my sagging shoulders. 'You said . . .'

I can't understand why more teenagers aren't justifiably slaughtered by enraged adults goaded beyond human endurance. There should be awards. And an annual dinner. And a rewards system.

'Listen to me very carefully. I'm an historian. I know a hundred and thirty-five ways of killing you without leaving any trace. I know where to bury your bodies so they'll never be found. Just saying. Now, we can do this one of two ways. I can kill you – here and now – quick and quiet – and no one will ever know. Or I can rip you painfully to pieces, smearing your internal organs across the walls and tying your innards in a bow around the light fittings, before going off for the cup of tea I so desperately need. And if by some chance I am apprehended, I shall not only get away with my hideous crime but probably receive a medal and a small reward for services towards ridding the world of two really, really irritating smart-arse teenagers.'

Wordlessly, Adrian pointed upwards to one of the discreetly placed CCTV cameras with which Hawking is infested.

I moved a menacing step closer. '*I no longer care.*'

Nothing happened for long seconds and then, finally, just as I was thinking I was going to have to kill them after all, Adrian

34

pulled out his scratchpad, brought something up on the screen and handed it to me.

It was indeed an invitation. Unbelievably, some idiot had issued these two – sight unseen, obviously – with a formal invitation to some sort of function.

With a plummeting heart, I read the words aloud.

YOU ARE CORDIALLY INVITED TO A RECEPTION FOR

TIME TRAVELLERS

HOSTED BY

PROFESSOR STEPHEN HAWKING

TO BE HELD IN THE PAST AT

THE UNIVERSITY OF CAMBRIDGE

GONVILLE & CAIUS COLLEGE, TRINITY STREET, CAMBRIDGE

LOCATION: 52 12'21'' N 0 7'4.7''E

12.00 UT 28 JUNE 2009

My voice petered away. I looked up. They were beaming at me.

'See,' said Mikey. She pointed at the invitation. 'We're invited.' She seemed to think this made everything all right. 'In fact, we're all invited. Why don't you come too?'

God help me, I was tempted. I was very tempted indeed. Who wouldn't want to go? The chance to meet Stephen Hawking. To talk with him. To see his face as we walked in. To see his face as he clapped eyes on Adrian and Mikey. It would be so worth it.

They were grinning at me. 'There's champagne,' said Mikey, beguilingly.

'Neither of you are old enough to drink.'

'And horses doovers.'

'If you knew what a horses doover was you wouldn't be half so enthusiastic.'

'But Max . . .' she wheedled.

I rallied. 'Where did you get this?'

'It's out there, Max. All over the internet and anyone with a pod can go.' They beamed. Presumably access to the internet and possession of a pod made everything all right.

I shook my head. 'I'm sorry, guys. I'm completely with you on this one, but no.'

'Max . . .'

'No. It's not possible.'

Mikey pointed to the invite. 'But . . .'

'Look – it contravenes the Hundred Years Rule. It contravenes Ian Guthrie's "No jumping back to irritate Professor Hawking" rule and most importantly, the party has already happened and no one turned up. You didn't go to the party. You never got to meet Professor Hawking. It's a shame because I think the three of you would have got on like a house on fire, but no. Believe me, I am sorry, but absolutely not.'

I felt bad. Really, really bad. But no contact with Professor Hawking was just about the first rule I ever learned at St Mary's and one of the few I hadn't yet broken.

They looked so upset that I said, 'Come on. I'll take you for a drink.'

They brightened up.

'Nothing alcoholic.'

They drooped again. I felt like a kitten-murderer but just imagine if I'd missed them. If they'd gone ahead and made the jump. I could just see the teapot materialising in the middle of the room, the two of them throwing out their heavy ladder, hopefully not stunning one of the world's leading cosmologists and Giant Brain. The implications were enormous but thanks to me, would never happen. I'd averted catastrophe. Never mind them – I needed a drink.

So that was how I missed the jump. But not Bannockburn. I didn't miss Bannockburn at all.

Anyway, after all that, just to keep an eye on them for a while and not in the least because I needed a drink, we sat in the bar, talking of this and that, reminiscing about Atticus Wolfe and the Time Police. They regaled me with some of their more hair-raising adventures, all of which confirmed my belief we'd done the universe an enormous favour by removing them from general circulation, and the time passed really quickly.

Too quickly. It was a shock to look at the clock and realise that Number Four's return time had passed more than half an hour ago. And at exactly that moment, Dr Bairstow requested the pleasure of my company.

I said goodbye to the teapot tearaways and trotted up the stairs. Mrs Partridge waved me through.

'Good afternoon, sir.'

'Dr Maxwell, we appear to have a problem.'

For one moment I wondered if he'd heard about Adrian and Mikey's attempt to subvert the course of History, physics, cosmology and the universe in general, but no – we had another problem. Number Four had not returned.

In older, happier days, our assignments were open-ended. We could return any time. Now, however, in these more perilous times, we'd introduced specific return times. If a pod failed to materialise at the designated time, then we could safely assume something had gone wrong. It would appear the Three Stooges had encountered a problem at Bannockburn.

'How late are they, sir?'

'Nearly an hour, now. I am beginning to experience some concern.'

So was I. This was Ian Guthrie, our former Head of Security; Markham, our current Head of Security; and Peterson, our Deputy Director. It seemed unlikely they'd get themselves into difficulties, but this was Bannockburn, after all. It seemed much more likely difficulties had got to them.

I sighed. This is what happens if you let men out on their own without adequate female supervision. They just can't handle it. Guilt kicked in. I should have gone with them. I could have just sent Adrian and Mikey on their way. I could have asked Leon to keep an eye on them. I was Head of the History Department and I'd let them go on their own. One civilian and a couple of idiots. Of course they were going to get themselves lost, injured or dead. And it was my fault.

Dr Bairstow was taking a less pessimistic view. 'I feel sure there will be an adequate explanation, Dr Maxwell. They are probably stranded somewhere unable to return to their pod without assistance.'

I'd forbidden them to leave the pod. I'd suspected at the time they'd ignore that instruction and now look what had happened.

'I'll put together a rescue team as quickly as I can, sir.'

'I think not, Dr Maxwell. Bannockburn is a battlefield. There are around thirty thousand armed men in the vicinity. We could not possibly compete. Therefore, I think, in and out, quick and quiet. A scouting party. Take a look around, locate our people and if you can't immediately retrieve them, jump back here for reinforcements.'

I sat quietly and had a bit of a think. 'In that case, sir, I think I'll take Mr Evans – an obvious choice – and . . .'

I was hovering between Atherton and Clerk when Mrs Partridge entered. 'Miss Grey is here and would like to see you immediately, Dr Bairstow.'

He frowned. I could see his thinking. He wouldn't want Elspeth knowing we were having a problem. On the other hand, Mrs Partridge wouldn't let anyone in without a very good reason.

'Ask her to come in, please.'

Elspeth was pale but resolute. 'They're late, aren't they? Ian said he would ring me as soon as he got back and he hasn't.'

'Good afternoon, Miss Grey. Yes, they are, but not hugely so. Dr Maxwell and I are just considering our options.'

'I'd like to be included in any rescue mission.'

I frowned. I could understand her wish to be included, but I, for one, had several objections to this and I was certain Dr Bairstow would, as well.

There's no nice way of wrapping this up: Elspeth Grey is pod-shy. It's not her fault and certainly no one blames her, but it's the reason she doesn't work here any longer. She and her then partner, Bashford, had been snatched by that bastard Clive Ronan and dropped, defenceless, into the middle of Colchester, minutes before Boudicca turned up to massacre the inhabitants and raze the place to the ground.

We'd got there just in time to pull them out – another illegal Christmas jump – avoided a hundred thousand blood-hungry Brits and an enraged pig – and returned them safely to St Mary's.

Alas for Elspeth, no happy ending. She just couldn't rid herself of the fear that it would happen all over again. Her subsequent assignment had been a bit of a disaster and she'd quietly resigned. No one held it against her. I'm surprised it doesn't happen more often. You could argue that Elspeth was actually the most intelligent person here. You could also argue that she must be really concerned to be volunteering to get back into a pod again.

I looked at her anxious eyes.

'I know what you're thinking, Max, but I have to do this. It's Ian and I'd never forgive myself if . . . I have to stop running away. I have to deal with this.'

'Elspeth, it's not important. There are far more important things in this world than gallivanting up and down the timeline in an unreliable box accompanied by a bunch of lunatics.'

She shook her head. 'I thought if I left . . . started a new life . . . but . . . don't tell Ian . . . but it's not working. It's not St Mary's that's the problem – it's me. I've lost my bottle and everyone knows it. Including me. And everyone's been really nice to me and I don't deserve it. And yes, I'm terrified but I have to get past this. So I can look myself in the eye every morning. I have to do this. I have to get out there and conquer my fears. For Ian.'

I should say no. A few Christmases ago I reunited her and

Ian. I brought them together when everyone thought she and Bashford had been lost forever. And now this was Ian's last jump before what everyone hoped was his long and happy retirement. We've all seen those films where the detective is killed on his last case. The racing driver killed in his last race. The soldier on his last assignment. It's a kind of narrative imperative. And now, here she was . . . Had I brought Elspeth home one Christmas only to lose her during another? And then I looked at her face.

Turning to Dr Bairstow, I said, 'I have no objection, sir. Mr Evans and I can take a quick look around and if Miss Grey is content to remain in the pod, she can monitor the situation from there, give us an overview and warn us of any impending situations. She could be very useful.'

He thought for a moment, staring out of the window, and then nodded. 'Very well, Dr Maxwell. See to it, please.'

We kitted ourselves out in woodland-green camouflage. There was absolutely no point in wrapping ourselves up in contemporary 14th-century gear. For a start, whose side would we choose? Quick, quiet and invisible was the way to go on this one.

I toyed with the idea of taking Leon's pod with its camouflage device but decided against it in the end. In a hazardous situation the last thing you need is to be racing around shouting, 'Where the hell did we leave the bloody thing?' And if we weren't going to activate the camouflage device then there was no point in taking it.

I sighed. Best-case scenario – if they'd obeyed my instructions – and I think we all know how likely that was – they'd be safely inside the pod and we'd be talking about nothing more serious than a minor systems failure. Although don't mention that to Leon. We've never yet had a pod fail, despite, as he often points out, the fragile state in which some of them are returned.

I thought we'd take Number Eight – my favourite pod. We've seen some exciting times together.

We drew weapons – even Elspeth. I took a stun gun, a pepper spray and slapped a small blaster to the sticky patch on my combats.

Evans took the same plus a massive blaster slung over his shoulder. Presumably he was hoping to subdue the Loch Ness Monster at the same time.

Elspeth took two stun guns and a pepper spray.

We surveyed each other outside the pod.

'Everyone all set?' I said.

They nodded.

Leon was just finishing laying in the coordinates. I'd asked for about an hour after their arrival and as close as possible to their landing site. There was a bloody great battle going on out there so I didn't want to have to do too much running around outside the pod.

'All set,' he said. 'Return coordinates laid in as well. Just in case.'

I nodded. Sometimes we have to leave quite quickly and you don't want to spend time calculating the returns. We always set up as much as we can in advance. Plenty will always go wrong and it gives us a couple of seconds' head start on whatever is trying to kill us all.

He smiled for me alone, wished us all good luck and left.

42

'Right then,' I said. 'Off we go. Computer – initiate jump.'

'Jump initiated.'

The world went white.

Well, here we were. Bannockburn, June 1314. The two-day battle which would ultimately result in Scottish independence. There's a bit of a story behind Bannockburn. Well, there's a bit of a story behind most events in History, obviously, but you know what I mean.

The English were occupying nearby Stirling Castle – it being a strategic point for everyone. Edward Bruce – brother of the more famous Robert – was laying siege to it. I suspect it was a bit of a miserable business for both sides – the Scots up to their waists in mud and the English facing the prospect of slowly starving to death – and so the two sides reached a kind of gentlemen's agreement. If the castle wasn't relieved by midsummer, it would be handed over to the Scots without bloodshed.

It is possible that hearing his brother's arrangement – made without his knowledge – that mighty Robert Bruce fetched his younger and much dimmer sibling a mighty thump upside the head, because what Edward had done, in effect, was hurl down a challenge the English king couldn't possibly ignore. A tiny Scottish army that had previously used only guerrilla tactics and avoided formal warfare like the plague suddenly found itself number one on the English summer fixture list.

Once he'd calmed down, however, some brave soul had pointed out to Robert Bruce that he now knew where the English army would be next midsummer and he could therefore lay his plans accordingly. He had time to shape the battlefield to his advantage and he did.

He had pits dug to break up the powerful English cavalry. He revived the fearsome Scottish schiltron – a mass of men welded together with long pikes bristling in all directions, disciplined and well trained and virtually invulnerable to mounted knights. Bruce was a canny man who used the time granted him to skew the odds in his favour.

I called up Number Four as soon as we landed. There was no response. We tried our individual coms. Nothing.

'They're about twenty yards away,' said Grey, peering at the screen.

She was right. Number Four sat at the edge of our small clearing, just to the east of us. Unscathed and undamaged. I only hoped we could say the same of its occupants.

Both pods had landed in the Torwood, situated about half a mile to the south of the Bannock Burn. The English army lay to our right, camped along the Roman road, and the Scots had made their stand on the boggy ground on the other side of the burn, behind their ditches. We had quite a good view from here, which is why I'd chosen it, although tomorrow, when the English would move east to the Carse, less so.

Compared to the Scots, drawn up in four compact schiltrons, the English army must have seemed massive. At least ten divisions, their weapons glinting in a temporary glimpse of the sun, colourful banners and pennants everywhere and heaving with horses, they sprawled across the landscape.

The glimpse of the sun was very short. This was a typical Scottish summer – mild enough but very damp. There was a misty rain in the air. At least no one would have the sun in their eyes or find themselves slowly cooking in their own armour. The downside was that the going was soft. Very soft indeed. I could see puddles of water everywhere. There would be mud on an industrial scale. Actually, until very recently, most of History is mud, blood and pestilence. These days it's greed, corruption and incompetence.

Evans unshouldered his elephant gun. 'I'll go and check the other pod. You two stay here. Keep checking the proximities.'

I looked up. 'There are more than thirty thousand men here today. I'm not sure how helpful the proximities will be but yes, we'll watch your back.'

Elspeth angled the cameras and we watched him approach Number Four. He circled cautiously. He'd left his com open and we heard him call for the door which opened perfectly normally. He disappeared inside. We waited, hoping – no, expecting – to see Markham or Peterson's head appear, demanding to know what all the fuss was about.

It didn't happen.

Evans appeared instead, shook his head and called me over.

'And me,' said Elspeth, getting to her feet.

We checked around very carefully before leaving the pod because we didn't know who else was out there. Well, actually we did, there were thirty thousand of them, and none of them would be feeling friendly.

I sent Elspeth over first, covering her from Number Eight, and then set off myself.

Apart from the lack of people, Number Four looked completely normal.

'The Marie Celeste of pods,' said Evans cheerfully, then remembered Elspeth and shut up.

Everything was working perfectly. Even the toilet, which might have been the one reason someone had nipped outside.

Although, as Evans said, they wouldn't all have gone at the same time. They weren't girls.

The girls in the pod ignored him.

'The external cameras are still running,' said Elspeth, checking over the console. 'Shall we see if there's a clue there?'

I took the other seat and Evans stood behind us.

'Computer – play back external tapes.'

'Playing back external tapes.'

I'd read up on the battle, obviously, so I knew pretty much what to expect and I have to say – apart from the normal troop movements as everyone shuffled into position – not a lot was happening.

'This must be fairly early on,' I said. 'There's no blood or bodies that I can see.'

'Well, something must have happened,' said Evans. 'Something took them out of the pod.'

I felt Elspeth tremble.

'Not Clive Ronan,' I said in an effort to reassure both of us. 'They're none of them overendowed with brains but even they know he couldn't get in. They're perfectly safe as long as they remain inside the pod.'

'It must be something to do with the battle,' said Evans. 'Something unusual or unexpected, perhaps.'

I instructed them to keep watching.

Nothing was happening. Well, there was a lot of milling around, obviously. Battlefields are chaotic places. It's interesting to think I've probably seen more battlefields than even the most experienced general. Concentrate, Maxwell.

'Come on,' I said, talking to the screen. 'What did you see?' And then . . .

'Hang on,' said Evans, leaning forwards.

The English were on the move. A group of about three hundred men detached themselves from the main force and appeared to be trying to get to Stirling Castle.

'I know this bit,' I said, pointing at the screen. 'This is Clifford and de Beaumont. These are the opening moves. The Scots will move forwards to block them.'

They didn't just block them – they charged with such force they split the English line clean in two. Chaos ensued. There was no clear leadership – always a feature of Edward II's reign. Of the scattered English forces, half pushed on to Stirling – the other half lost their nerve, were routed and fled back to the safety of the English lines. We could hear the shouts of derision from the Scottish camp.

While this was happening, the bulk of the English forces were slowly and ponderously on the move. Led by the Earls of Hereford and Gloucester, they headed straight for the Scottish lines.

'They thought the mere sight of their superior numbers would cause the Scots to panic and retreat back into the New Park,' said Grey. I suspected she'd been hearing a lot about Bannockburn over the past few weeks. 'And to be fair, until today, that was their preferred method of warfare. Oh look – here we go.'

The most magnificent figure appeared at the forefront of the English lines. Elspeth focused on his shield. Blue and yellow. Azure, a bend argent between six lions rampant or. The de Bohun family arms. This was Henry de Bohun, riding one of the biggest horses I'd ever seen. The man who famously challenged Robert Bruce to personal combat.

Trumpets rang out from the crowded English lines. We could hear them cheering. Which turned to laughter when Bruce eventually appeared from the Scottish ranks. Whereas de Bohun was fully equipped and armoured and resplendent on his warhorse, Bruce was only lightly armoured and rode a much smaller and lighter horse. A mud-splattered palfrey. A comfortable, lady's ride. Bruce would have used his for cantering from one side of his military camp to the other. Definitely not for charging into battle. We could actually hear the jeers and mockery spreading through the English ranks. They must have thought it was hilarious.

In contrast to de Bohun's full battle rig, Bruce wore only a sword and carried an axe. You could just hear the English thinking – well, this won't take long. What an idiot.

A trumpet sounded again. Light and tinny but clear over our sound system. Before the last notes had died away, de Bohun was off. His great horse reared up, appearing to claw at the sullen sky, fought with its rider for a moment, then lowered its head and thundered towards Bruce, who suddenly looked very small and vulnerable on his little palfrey. We could see great clods of mud being thrown high into the air, dark against the lighter sky.

De Bohun's horse might be huge and powerful but Bruce's was more nimble. And, like its rider, it apparently had nerves of steel, barely batting an eyelid as man and monster thundered towards it. At just the right moment, it stepped neatly to one side. At the same time, Bruce actually ducked under the point of de Bohun's lance, and then, standing in his stirrups, he stabbed upwards with his axe, point first.

It seemed to catch de Bohun under the chin – an unusual

blow from an unusual angle, massively risky, but it paid off. Such was the force of his blow that he shattered de Bohun's head, tearing it clean off his shoulders and sending it soaring high into the air, trailing long ribbons of scarlet blood behind it.

De Bohun's body slumped to one side, frightening and unbalancing his horse, which galloped back to the English lines, reins and stirrups flying. It was met with a stunned and disbelieving silence.

The Scots didn't waste time cheering. Robert Bruce had them all on the attack, smashing into the English forces while they were still ponderously trying to get themselves into position.

We never saw what happened to de Bohun's head.

'Well . . .' said Evans, which pretty well summed up everything.

'Well, I knew he lost his head,' I said, 'but that must have been one hell of an axe.'

And indeed, Bruce's only comment when he returned to his own lines was to lament the loss of his good axe.

Evans opened his mouth to say something and at that moment, the picture trembled. Just very slightly. As if there had been some sort of impact with the pod.

'What was that?' I said, standing up. 'What just happened?'

'Wait here,' said Evans. 'Don't touch the cameras. Don't change the angles.' He disappeared outside.

We watched him on the screen. I saw him appear briefly, glance up and wave and then disappear round the side of the pod.

After a few minutes he was back. 'Max, come and look at this. Careful now. Elspeth, you stay put – just in case.'

I pulled out my blaster and slipped out to join him. Silently he gestured to the side of the pod.

All our pods are much the same. Some are smaller, some are bigger, but they all have the same design: apparently stone-built huts that blend into their surroundings. The stone bit is simply a cosmetic casing. It's fairly robust – although I've knocked some corners off in my time. It's supposed to be fire-proof too, although I did manage to melt it once. The point I'm making, though, is that although the casing has faced some challenges in its professional life, I don't think it's ever had to cope with a diagonal spray of ten or twelve small round holes slanting upwards, straight through the centre of the carefully stencilled Saltire, up towards the top right-hand corner.

There was no mistaking what they were.

'Bullet holes?' I said in disbelief. 'Bullets at Bannockburn?'

Evans nodded, threw a worried glance around and then said, 'Back inside, please.'

'I've checked around everywhere,' said Elspeth as we re-entered. 'They left no messages – no clues – nothing. And there's no response to my calls, either.'

'Let's see some more of the tape.'

What followed consisted mostly of troop movements and a few minor skirmishes. We watched, but our hearts weren't in it and after about ten minutes we blanked the screens.

Evans turned to face us. 'I can think of four explanations.'

'Go on.'

'One – they've removed their earpieces – for some reason that may not necessarily be bad.

'Two – they're out of range. Which is unlikely. They'd have to be several miles away.

'Three – they're physically unable to respond – again for some reason that may not necessarily be bad.'

He stopped.

'Or they're dead,' said Elspeth, quietly.

I caught Evans' eye. 'Unlikely,' he said. 'If it was just historians on their own, then I'd be considering that because everyone knows they're a bunch of overeducated, intellectually stunted idiots with delusions of adequacy, but we're talking about Mr Markham and the major here, so my betting is that if there are any casualties, they'll be on the other side.'

It was a good save. Elspeth looked reassured.

'So,' I said. 'They were present for the duel between de Bohun and Bruce. The camera work proves that. We can see the changing angles and there are close-ups and so on. That would be Peterson's work. Subsequent to that, there's only the one camera operating and that from a single angle. The main events are not even in shot a lot of the time. In other words, the camera was on but no one was operating it. Or even watching the screen. I think it's fair to say they watched the duel and then left. Why?'

'Because the pod was under attack and they went to investigate?' said Evans.

Well, of course they did. Why would anyone remain safely inside a pod when they could get out there and investigate who was spraying bullets around in the middle of a battle on a summer's day in 1314? I'd have been out of the door in a flash.

'I've been reviewing the records,' said Elspeth, still at the console. 'They left the pod nine minutes after the Bruce/de Bohun incident.'

'No record of why?'

'None. The door was open for seven seconds and then closed. It didn't open again until we turned up.'

'Nothing on camera?' asked Evans.

'No, it was pointing the other way.'

'So they went to investigate,' I said, and sighed. So much for not stepping outside the pod.

'What do you want to do, Max?' asked Evans. 'Do we go back and report? Or do we go and check it out?'

They both looked at me.

Going back would waste valuable time if they were in trouble now, right at this moment. On the other hand, returning with more people would make finding them considerably easier. If they weren't already dead. Six of one – half a dozen of the other. I threw it open to the floor.

'Your recommendations, please,' I said.

'We go and look for them,' said Elspeth.

Evans nodded.

I nodded too. 'Unanimously settled then.'

'I've been trying to call them up,' said Elspeth. 'As far as I can establish, their coms are working but they're just not responding.'

'No need to read anything into that,' said Evans, just a shade too heartily. 'It might simply be that they're not in a position to answer and there could be many reasons for that.'

'Yes,' said Elspeth. 'Perhaps they're in a hollow or a cave, or something similar.'

Evans and I very carefully didn't look at each other. 'You're absolutely right,' he said. 'No cause for alarm just yet. Right then. It's you and me, Max. Elspeth, it makes sense for you to remain here as point of contact. They'll probably be back in a minute and we'll have done all this for nothing. We'll leave our coms open at all times. Give us a shout if you see anything. Max – you stay behind me. Don't worry, Elspeth. We'll be back before you know it.'

Our proximities were useless. Well, no, actually they were working perfectly, showing every single one of the thirty thousand men out there.

Our tag readers weren't much better. Over the years we've found the quickest and easiest way to find any missing colleagues is to close our eyes and keep walking until we fall over them. It helps if the rescuees can jump up and down, shouting, 'We're over here, stupid,' and set off a few fizzers as well.

The readers were giving us two readings – one for Peterson and one for Markham – Guthrie had had his tag removed when he left St Mary's – but were declining to tell us in which direction and how far away our missing colleagues actually were. So, helpful as ever.

I tucked myself behind Evans and we moved very slowly and very carefully, flitting from tree to tree, watching where we put our feet and keeping our eyes open. There were God knows how many armed men jammed into these few square miles. Anyone they didn't recognise was an enemy and would be treated as such.

Time passed. We paused at regular intervals to crouch behind trees to try to raise the other team but there was still nothing. We were still in communication with Elspeth, so the obvious conclusion was that our boys were for some reason unable to respond, and that was deeply worrying.

More time passed. The wood itself was silent – there was no

birdsong or woodland noises – and trees deaden sound so the noises of men and horses had dwindled into a distant murmur beyond the trees, from which would emerge a trumpet call, occasionally, or the whinny of horses. The sounds were far off but continuous. A constant reminder of what was happening not that far away.

I began to have a very bad feeling. The further we got from the pod the more nervous I became. There could be a man hidden behind every tree. There could be traps set to catch spies. The area to cover was huge. The two of us could barely scratch the surface. We needed more people and better equipment. I think Evans was feeling the same way because he took a quick look around and then pulled me down into a shallow ditch, whispering, 'Max – I'm not happy about any of this. There's not enough cover and we're too close to the battle lines.'

He was right. We were slightly above and to the south-west of the action but still close enough to see the southern edge of the Scottish lines. As far as I knew no action took place anywhere in the Torwood – no official action, anyway – but there would be troop movements and scouts and we were far more exposed than I was happy with.

'We have to look for them,' said Elspeth, managing to sound angry even over the com. 'We can't just go home.'

'We can come back with more people and cover more ground more quickly,' said Evans, quietly, trying to calm her down.

'And waste more time.'

'He's right,' I said. Listen to me being Mrs Sensible. 'We'll have more tag readers. We'll be able to triangulate much more quickly and easily. We could even stand Bashford on the roof with a loudhailer. What we can't do is creep around in the middle of a battle looking for three people who, if they've got any sense, have climbed a tree and are waiting quietly for a chance to get back to their pod.'

'No!'

'Elspeth, our chances of finding them in this lot are—'

Evans cocked his head suddenly and gestured me to silence. His proximity meter was lighting up like a Christmas tree. Given their uselessness, this generally meant someone was standing about two inches to our right.

I whispered, 'Elspeth – got something. Call you back.'

We worked our way very quietly and slowly along the ditch. The trees were closer together here and there was more cover. Best of all, the almost permanent mizzle had solidified decades of fallen leaves into a wet, dense, but fortunately silent carpet.

At a sign from Evans, we both halted and hoisted a couple of very cautious eyes over the edge.

I didn't see him at first. All credit to Evans because I thought I was just staring at a heap of miscellaneous forest foliage and I wasn't.

The shape resolved itself like one of those 3D pictures. I was looking at a man wearing a sophisticated camouflage suit. A ghillie suit, as Evans later described it. Unbelievably, I was looking at a sniper, lying prone and quietly nursing a long-barrelled, super-sighted, bolt-action sniper rifle.

OK – so not one of my lost boys. Who were still out there somewhere. This was a sniper. The thought kept running through my head. A sniper. There was a sniper here at Bannockburn. In 1314. Suddenly the spray of bullets across the pod made a little more sense. And de Bohun's shattered head as well. A lucky axe stroke – possibly. An armour-piercing bullet – almost certainly.

Evans gestured for me to stay put and I was very happy to do so. He's a grown lad and could easily handle this one on his own. Inch by inch he pulled himself out of the ditch. For a big bloke he moved very quietly, never dislodging earth or leaves, not letting the edge crumble, placing his hands and feet with delicate precision.

Having extricated himself, he paused for a moment, gathered himself and then literally launched himself through the air to land squarely on our would-be sniper.

The impact must have knocked all the air out of the sniper's body. And possibly broken a few of his bones. And crushed a few vital organs, as well. Evans is not small, as I say. At any rate, he put up no sort of fight and quick as a flash, even with the difficulties of getting hold of him in that suit, Evans had him trussed like a Christmas turkey. I was very impressed. I might even remember to tell him so.

I climbed out of the ditch, skidding down the slight slope to where Evans had just finished securing our new friend, and we rolled him over on his back and pulled off his hood to have a better look.

I don't remember his face because the first thing I noticed was the red and white badge of St George on his sleeve. Silly sod. What's the point of doing yourself up to look like a piece of Scottish woodland if you've got St George emblazoned all over your arm? And at Bannockburn, for God's sake. What an idiot.

Besides, it didn't make sense. If they were English, then why shoot de Bohun? His spectacular defeat had pretty much

56

set the tone for the entire battle. The whole thing was one disaster after another for the English. And then I remembered how, at the very last moment, Bruce's well-trained horse had executed that neat side-step and Bruce himself ducked, then suddenly stood in his stirrups to deliver that deadly blow. In my mind I saw the bullet whistle harmlessly past Bruce to shatter de Bohun's head instead.

You see – this is what happens when you try to interfere with History. At the very least you end up bringing about the very thing you tried to prevent. At the very worst you end up dead. Bloody amateurs.

Beside me, Evans went rigid and grunted. I half turned to see what had happened and then he toppled sideways like one of those industrial chimneys, bringing me down with him, driving the air from my lungs and rendering me completely helpless. What the hell . . . ?

Trust me, you never want to find yourself underneath Mr Evans. For any reason at all. The guy weighs as much as the Isle of Wight on a wet day and it's all solid muscle.

Apparently – as I now know – snipers work in pairs. One to set himself up and get the range and angle and do all the other technical bits and pieces, and the other with the spotter scope. I can't think why they don't teach this sort of thing in schools. It's got to be more useful than knowing Lima is the capital of Peru, which I can state, with certainty, is a piece of information I have never, until this moment, had cause to use. They bang on and on about bloody x. And photosynthesis. They even make you knit things, and what an utter waste of time that turned out to be. And yet I don't remember that useful phrase – remember, class, snipers come in pairs – ever being uttered in all the long, dreary years of my schooling. I honestly don't know what teachers find to do all day long.

Anyway, reluctantly setting all blame and recrimination to one side, obviously his partner had turned up, correctly identified Evans as the main threat, taken him out and then used him to incapacitate me. No one functions well with Mr Evans on top of them. That did not come out quite right but you know what I mean.

He was a single-minded bugger. The second sniper, I mean – Evans has all the laser-like focus of cigarette smoke. Completely ignoring his fallen colleague, he secured Evans first because I wasn't going anywhere – trust me, I could barely breathe – and then me second. Showing no compassion at all for sniper number one, he heaved him out of the way, lowered himself to the ground and sighted along the gun.

I wriggled and kicked because suddenly this was serious. Given that he too was wearing the cross of St George, I was pretty sure who his intended target was and this couldn't be allowed to happen. I struggled, but not only had he zipped my wrists and ankles tightly but that great lump Evans was still slowly crushing the life out of me as well.

These men were not amateurs. They hadn't killed us, presumably because that wasn't in their brief. They had their target and they had their objective. Everything else was incidental.

It was bloody embarrassing actually. Two of St Mary's finest – three if you counted Evans twice and many of us do – rendered utterly helpless. The implications were massive. Take out Robert Bruce and everything changed. No charismatic king of Scotland. No Scottish independence. History completely off the rails again. And, most importantly, where the bloody hell were the Time Police? This was exactly the sort of thing they were supposed to deal with. I thought of the number of times they'd appeared on the scene at just the wrong moment and made a bad situation considerably worse – and now that they were really needed there was no bloody sign of them anywhere. Probably off harassing some very nearly innocent historians somewhere else. Not here, anyway, where, just for once, they could be useful.

I couldn't see much – just his hands, camouflaged green and brown like his face. I saw him make a last-minute, infinitesimal adjustment to something and then . . . the world fell silent. I held my breath and waited . . .

And then there was a sound very similar to a large halibut being slapped down on to a marble slab. His hands went into some sort of spasm and then fell limply to the ground.

Behind and above me, a privileged, upper-class voice that reminded me strongly of Miss North said, 'Oh, jolly well done, Pennyroyal.'

A hoarse voice with a strong London accent said, 'Thank you, my lady.'

'Let's see what we have here, shall we?'

'As you wish, my lady.'

I could hear the sounds of people scrambling down the slope. For God's sake – now what?

I saw two pairs of legs and ankles. Boots, combats . . . not much of a clue there and then, thank God, someone heaved Evans off me and I could breathe again.

Well, they weren't Time Police.

Sorry – I can't add anything else to that statement. I didn't know who they were but they definitely weren't Time Police.

59

They were far too quick and efficient for that bunch of nump-ties. And there were only two of them and the Time Police usually travel in fours and – most tellingly – fifty per cent of this pair were female. The Time Police don't really do women. Too difficult for them, I suspect.

I sucked in some grateful air and stared up at the sky above me. Still grey and miserable. Still in Scotland then.

Looking back, there must have been a bloody great battle going on not that far away but I have no recollection of the sounds of it. Whether because we were in a thick, sound-deadening wood or, more likely, because an historian's tiny mind can only concentrate on one crisis at a time, I don't know, but I only remember silence.

I stared at the man now competently zipping the second sniper. I'd seriously lost count of how many of us there were on the ground at that moment. Me, Evans, two snipers ... and still no sign of our own people. What a complete lash-up this was turning out to be. It was definitely time I looked for an office job.

Anyway, back to our possible rescuers. The female was youngish – younger than me, anyway. And tall – taller than me. And thin – thinner than me. And her hair was exactly the same colour that mine used to be. I tried not to hate her on sight and failed miserably.

Her companion was older – perhaps around Leon's age. His white-blond hair was cut short in a rather brutal crew cut. He had hard grey eyes and, frankly, looked much more like a serial killer than serial killers usually do. You definitely wouldn't want your daughter bringing this one home. It began to dawn on me that our situation had not improved by very much.

Evans was still semi-conscious and dribbling so it was all obviously up to me.

I twisted to bring her into view. 'Who are you?'

'I beg your pardon – how rude of us. My name is Amelia Smallhope and this is Pennyroyal.'

I looked over at the serial killer, still competently dealing with the sniper. 'Your hitman?'

'My butler, actually.'

Well, OK, I asked for that. 'No, seriously?'

'Seriously.'

'Your butler?'

'My butler. Can I recommend you get one? If you want to avoid situations like this, I mean.'

'Pennyroyal?'

'That's him.'

'Not Parker?'

'I beg your pardon?'

'Nothing. And you're who, exactly . . . ?'

'Lady Amelia Smallhope,' interrupted Pennyroyal, efficiently going through his prisoner's pockets. 'We should be moving, my lady. The Time Police are almost certainly not far behind us.'

'Of course. And it's nearly time for cocktails.'

'Indeed, my lady.'

'And you are?' She smiled at me.

'Maxwell.'

'And him?'

'Evans.'

'Does he have a first name?'

I wasn't in the mood for this. 'Mister.'

'My goodness, he's a big boy, isn't he? I've always had a

weakness for big men, you know. Things tend to be proportionate. But enough of me.' She gestured at the now ex-snipers. 'I think we'll walk off with these two here. The reward will certainly make all this . . .' she gestured disparagingly at Scotland, 'worthwhile. We'll leave their pod for the Time Police though, just to rub their noses in it.'

I had no fault to find with any of that. Rubbing Time Police noses in anything sounded good to me. And besides, the Elephant of Enlightenment had suddenly fallen from the sky.

'You're bounty hunters? You are, aren't you? You're bounty hunters.'

'We prefer the term "recovery agents".'

Well, bloody bollocking hell. I couldn't believe it. Was it possible those bastards in the Time Police were outsourcing?

She flashed a virtual card at me. I didn't have my specs on and wild horses couldn't have induced me to squint. I assumed it was supposed to be some sort of holographic ID. I was determined not to be impressed.

'And you have to be St Mary's,' she said.

'Not necessarily,' I said, defensively.

She smiled blindingly. She had perfect teeth. 'An inadequate force, inadequately equipped, walking blindly into an unknown situation and making a complete dog's breakfast of everything when they get there? Who else would you be?'

Who else indeed? I stared at them. They hadn't untied us but I didn't think they meant us any harm. I toyed with the idea of asking them about our other team and decided against it. If they'd seen them – alive or dead – they'd have mentioned it. And I didn't want them knowing there were another three St Mary's people out there because that would tip the balance of power in St Mary's favour and they just might decide to do something about that. Starting with us. I wouldn't trust that butler as far as I could throw him.

I tried to divert the conversation away from St Mary's before she started wondering if there were any more of us. 'Actually, you've just described the Time Police.'

Pennyroyal got to his feet. 'And those buggers will be here soon enough, my lady. We should take our prisoners and go.'

'We are not your prisoners,' I said firmly, from my prone and completely helpless position on the ground.

'No bounty on you,' she said regretfully. 'Otherwise I'd beg to differ.'

'So let us go, then.'

'Not taking any chances with St Mary's. You lot do have a bit of a reputation, you know. You're probably not in any danger – the battle's way over there – and the Time Police will be here soon looking for these two. I imagine there will be some witty amusement at your expense but I'm sure they'll let you go eventually. After taking you back to TPHQ for processing, of course. And photographing. And statements. I'm sure it won't be hugely embarrassing at all.'

Craning my neck was painful but I was determined to find out. 'So if you're bounty hunters then who are these two?' I nodded towards their prisoners.

She fetched the nearest one a vicious kick. I made a mental note to dial back on the piss-taking.

'These two? These are members of a particularly witless organisation – trust me, they make St Mary's look like MENSA – dedicated to the promotion and protection of all things English.'

'Oh,' I said.

'They call themselves the English National Liberation Army which they have to abbreviate to ENLA because the majority of them are too stupid to understand polysyllabic words.' She gave them another kick. 'Barely sentient but extremely valuable. The Time Police will pay heavily for these two.'

'Ah,' I said. 'Give them both a kick from me while they're down there, will you?'

'Gladly.' She gave them several, actually. I could only approve this generous gesture. 'These two – ostensibly slightly less stupid than their colleagues – like to think of themselves as "assassins", although most of us shorten the word to just the first syllable. They thought they'd take out Robert Bruce, and guarantee an English victory, thus ensuring Scotland would remain a vassal state of England over the coming centuries.'

Well, isn't it gratifying to be right? Believe it or not, I often am. And that solved the mystery of the shot-up Saltire, as well. They just hadn't been able to resist.

'Wow,' I said. 'No independence. No Stuarts. History all over the place. Good job upsetting that applecart.'

'Thank you.'

I doubt Pennyroyal had ever been agitated in his entire life but he was exhibiting signs of slight concern. 'My lady . . .'

'Yes, Pennyroyal, I'm coming.' She bent over the recovering Evans and smiled at him. 'Shame. Another time, perhaps.'

He grinned blearily back at her, slurring, 'If you're very lucky,' and I made a note to speak to him about inappropriate workplace behaviour.

'Maxwell, I shall say goodbye now and . . .'

No, she wouldn't, because at that moment Elspeth Grey rose

up behind the pair of them like the wrath of God, stun guns crackling with maximum charge, and zapped the pair of them into paralysed unconsciousness. I had forgotten I had said I'd call her back. She must have been nearly out of her mind with anxiety, stifled her fears and ventured forth to find out what was happening.

There was a moment's silence during which Evans and I made a simultaneous mental note never to mention this again.

I pulled myself together first. 'Quick,' I said. 'Cut me free and let's get these two dealt with. They're easily the most dangerous people here today. And that includes the two armies out there.'

Pausing only for a quick recount of unconscious bodies – four and a half so far because Evans was still at the drooly stage – but the day was still young – we zipped Pennyroyal first, paying him the compliment of double ties, then Smallhope, who managed to look elegant even when face down in a Scottish forest. I left Elspeth assisting Evans back into this world and tried again to raise our team.

Nothing.

'We'll leave these two,' I said, pointing to Pennyroyal and Smallhope. 'Make sure they're well secured. I don't know about anyone else but I definitely wouldn't want that butler coming after me on a dark night.'

'What on earth is going on?' said Elspeth, looking around at the bodies on the ground.

'Good question,' I said. 'I think we can assume these two here . . .' I gave the snipers a couple of swift kicks to maintain the tradition, 'were responsible for the death of Henry de Bohun.'

'Given what happened to his head,' said Elspeth, nodding, 'that makes far more sense.'

'Actually, no, it doesn't,' said Evans, who had been examining the sniper rifle. 'This gun hasn't been fired.' He picked up the second sniper's weapon. 'Nor this one. Whoever killed de Bohun, it wasn't these two.'

The implications sank in. There was another team.

'Bloody hell,' said Evans, wiping his chin again. 'Why is nothing ever simple?' Which I thought summed things up very well.

We propped him against a convenient tree. He'd taken quite a hit, after all.

'Right,' I said. 'Back to the pod.'

It was our only course of action. To proceed with our search without a fully functioning Evans would be madness.

Elspeth tightened her lips but said nothing. She'd moved to the top of the slope, watching our backs. Good to see she hadn't forgotten her training.

'What about this lot?' said Evans, gesturing to our prisoners.

'We leave them here. None of this is our business. According to Smallhope, the Time Police will be here any minute. They can sort it all out, including the other team and their pods, too. In fact, this place is going to be crawling with clean-up crews any minute now.'

'In that case, we should definitely go,' said Evans. 'I'm not in the mood to be cleaned up by anyone.'

He bent over the recovering Smallhope and gently moved her into the recovery position. I swear she winked at him.

'Shame,' he said, smiling at her. 'Another time, perhaps. When you're feeling more yourself.'

I made another mental note about inappropriate workplace flirting. 'When you're *quite* ready, Mr Evans.' I tapped my ear to give it one last try. 'Peterson. Markham. Anyone. Where are you?'

'Behind you,' said Markham and the three of them emerged from the trees.

Safe and sound, as far as I could see. And they weren't alone. 'We've brought you a present.'

He gestured to another two ghillie-suited figures, both competently secured with a complicated cat's cradle of their own belts – I recognised the master hand of Major Guthrie from my training days – 'Everything can be used as a weapon, Max' – and blindfolded and gagged with what looked like their own torn-up tighty-whities. I suspected the fell hand of Mr Markham there. And both wore the cross of St George on their sleeve.

'See,' said Evans to Elspeth. 'I told you the damage would be done to the other lot.'

'Oh,' I said, gesturing at their prisoners. 'That's so sweet. You shouldn't have.'

'We grudge no effort.'

'No, you really shouldn't have.' I gestured at ours. 'We've already got our own set.'

'Ah, but these are the ones who shot our pod.'

'Bloody vandals,' I said. 'Leon is not going to be happy.'

'And, rather more importantly, they're the ones who shot the unfortunate de Bohun.'

'Never mind that,' said Elspeth, placing herself in front of Ian Guthrie. 'I'm still waiting to hear why you didn't answer our calls.'

'Didn't know you were here,' said Peterson, tactfully inserting himself between them. 'We thought we heard something crackle once or twice but mostly we were in the wrong place or the wrong time or too busy. When we finally heard you clearly, we were nearly on top of you and it seemed a bit pointless to use our coms then.'

I don't think she heard a word. 'Or why you were all stupid enough to leave the pod at all.'

'They had guns. At Bannockburn. It was our duty to stop them.'

'No, it's the Time Police's duty to stop them.'

We all looked about us at the ostentatiously Time Police-free landscape.

'Well, yes,' said Markham, 'but they're such a bunch of useless wazzocks they'd be bound to screw it up, so we thought we'd better step in.'

No one found any argument to that.

They dropped the two new snipers to lay face down alongside the other two. I carried out another head count. Two plus two plus two equalled six. Sadly, Smallhope and Pennyroyal were now wide awake and glaring.

Peterson bent over them. 'Who are these two?'

'Sorry – where are my manners? This is Lady Amelia Smallhope and her butler, Pennyroyal.'

There was a bit of a silence.

Eventually Markham said, 'And they are here because . . . ?'

'They're bounty hunters.'

'*Recovery agents*,' said Smallhope with dignity.

'And they're after these two?'

'These four.'

68

I counted the snipers by kicking them. 'If we hang on a bit longer, we could be in double figures soon.'

'No, we will not,' said Markham firmly. 'We're leaving. I know you're only historians but even you can't have failed to notice the bloody great battle going on around us.'

A slight exaggeration but I could see his point. There's such a thing as outstaying one's welcome. And Elspeth, taking care to stand near Guthrie, should definitely be taken back to St Mary's as soon as possible. Not least so everyone could see what a hero she had been. She'd left the pod – alone – and come looking for us. That had taken some doing.

'Well, now what?' said Peterson as we prepared to depart with everyone's weapons, because we weren't going to leave those lying around for any contemporaries to fall over. 'Do we just leave them all here?'

'Don't see why not,' I said. 'They were going to leave us.'

'But the Time Police . . . ?'

'Well, these four . . .' I pointed at the snipers, 'are legitimate prey, and these two . . .' I pointed at Smallhope and Penny-royal, 'I'm going to pay them the compliment of saying they're too dangerous to take any chances with. They're probably legit – although that's not our problem. I'm sure the Time Police will soon be here to rescue them.'

I looked down at the two of them. 'I imagine there will be some witty amusement at your expense – because I'll bet you've been witty at theirs on many occasions. I'm sure they'll only put the boot in very gently. After taking you back to TPHQ for processing, of course. And photographing. And statements. I'm sure it won't be hugely embarrassing at all.'

They glared at me.

69

'We should go,' said Markham. He looked down at our prisoners. 'Lovely to meet you all today but we really must be going. Long walk back.'

'Yes,' I said nastily, as we scrambled out of the ditch. 'We can spend the time discussing which bits of "Do not leave the pod" were too difficult for you to understand.'

'They shot at us, Max.'

'And who can blame them. I'm stifling that urge, myself.'

We set off back to the pod leaving four snipers and two bounty hunters. A pretty impressive afternoon's work, I think everyone will agree.

I walked alongside Major Guthrie. 'Ian, I'm sorry to cut this short but I really don't think we should hang around here. There's more going on here than just . . .' I gestured vaguely in the direction I thought the battle should be.

'Than the Scots kicking the English arse?' he said, helpfully.

I glared at him.

He grinned. 'Too soon?'

I persevered. 'I know you'll miss the second day, but . . .'

'It's OK,' he said cheerfully. 'It's not as if we don't know how it ends.'

Evans nodded. 'And I'm bloody sure I don't want to be around when that butler's able to function again.'

Peterson nodded. 'I don't think any of us do.'

I hadn't finished. 'Just think, Ian – we saved Scotland. Your guys missed Robert Bruce and our guys never got around to taking their shot. If those other bastards back there had had their way – that's the ENLA bastards, not the member of the

70

aristocracy and her semi-trained thug – Bruce would have died, and without his tactical abilities, to say nothing of the massive loss of morale, the Scots would have lost. Bruce would never have become king. Scotland would not have become an independent nation. Everything would have been different. We might have been a united nation some four hundred years earlier.'

He frowned. 'Would we? Even if he'd won here today, I don't think Edward would have been capable of holding on to Scotland.'

'He might not but his son would have.'

'Yes, but that means he would have had to concentrate all his attention on Scotland rather than France. Possibly no Crécy and no Poitiers. And even if he'd been successful, I don't think Scotland and England would have become one nation. The English would always have regarded Scotland as a vassal state.'

'And we'd never have had the Stuarts,' said Peterson, turning around. 'Which means that after Elizabeth died . . .'

'Hey,' said Markham from the rear. 'More walking, less talking.'

Barely had he spoken than Evans, who was in the lead, stopped dead. The rest of us remembered we were supposed to be professionals and did not concertina into the back of him.

Gesturing over to the right, he dropped to the ground. We followed suit.

Shit. I thought things had been too easy up until now.

They were on a parallel course with us, about twenty yards over to our right. Eight or ten of them, skinny, badly dressed, damp, muddy, poorly equipped, and heading away from the battle.

Deserters. And English, judging by the direction they'd come from. Fed up with bad weather, bad food and bad leadership, they were going while the going was good. I couldn't blame them. They wouldn't know this – although given how today had gone so far, they might have had an inkling – but English losses tomorrow would be huge. Of those who did survive, many would not find their way safely home. Except for Edward, of course, who, given the way his life turned out, would have done better to have died gloriously on the battlefield.

This bunch crept almost soundlessly through the woods, knives and axes out, very scared and very jumpy.

I crouched behind something bushy and watched them pass.

The good news was that they completely missed us. The bad news was that they were heading in the direction of Smallhope and Pennyroyal. Who were on the ground, trussed and helpless.

I stood up, stared after them, then turned to Markham and whispered, 'We left them tied up. They won't stand a chance. We have to go back.'

Evans shook his head. 'Max, they were going to leave *us*.'

'We're not them.'

'The Time Police will be here any moment,' whispered Peterson. 'Let them do any saving.'

'Tim, it's Christmas.'

'Not here, it's not. It's summer. You can tell by the trees.'

I stared at him, baffled. 'You mean the leaves?'

'No, I mean that grand old Scottish saying: "If you can't see the trees, it's raining. If you can see the trees, it's going to rain".'

I ignored him. 'It's goodwill to all men and all that. You guys go on. I'll catch you up.'

I turned back the way we'd come.

Markham sighed deeply. 'You stay with them,' he said to Evans. 'Get them back to the pods. I'll keep an eye on the daft bat here.'

Evans offered him his big blaster and very, very cautiously, we set off through the vast acres of wet woodland with which Scotland was so generously endowed.

We caught up with them as they were standing over our prisoners, knives drawn, waiting for someone else to make the first move. I didn't blame them. Strange people, strangely dressed. Tied up and left in the middle of nowhere. They'd be deeply suspicious. Would they kill them? Attempt to rob them? If they had any sense at all, they'd leave them there and just keep going.

All four snipers were now making desperate efforts to free themselves. Pennyroyal had rolled on top of Smallhope in an effort to shield her.

As we watched, one of the deserters sidled closer and raised his axe. There were shouts and pleas from the snipers who, while they had no problems with slaughtering others willynilly, seemed to have every objection to having the same done to them. The deserters wouldn't want all this noise drawing attention to them. Three or four more stepped forwards, knives drawn, their intentions obvious.

Shit.

Markham wasted no time in friendly introductions, firing the big blaster at a small bush that had never done him any harm, and which went up in a very satisfactory roar of red flames. I leaped down the slope, shouting and waving my arms and they were so surprised that I was able to stun two of them before they even knew I was there. Two ran away immediately. Two or three hung back, unsure what to do next. The rest stayed to make a fight of it and I left them to Markham. I threw myself down beside Pennyroyal, cutting his ties and rolling out of the way as he exploded into action. Men flew in all directions. Trust me, a pissed-off butler is a terrifying sight. I'd never seen anything like it. He and Markham made a great team. I suspected they were enjoying themselves so I sat down beside Smallhope and regretted the absence of popcorn.

I know it's traditional to say 'When the dust had settled', but this was Scotland, so when the mud had settled, those who could had run away. I counted those on the ground yet again. Two snipers. And another two snipers. Four deserters. Eight altogether. We'd failed to reach double figures which was disappointing. And yes, before anyone starts, I know we're not supposed to injure contemporaries. So put me on a disciplinary. It's a long time since I had a yellow sheet in my file.

'You came back,' said Smallhope. We'd managed to surprise her.

'It's Christmas,' I said, sawing her free.

'Well . . . thank you.'

Everyone was dusting themselves down.

'And,' I said, 'now you have *four* prisoners to deliver. Double the bounty.'

'Very grateful,' said Smallhope.

'Buy me a drink sometime,' I said.

'For God's sake,' muttered Markham, rolling his eyes. 'You'll be inviting them back to lunch in a minute.'

'That's a very good thought,' I said, turning to Smallhope and Pennyroyal. 'What are you doing for Christmas lunch?'

They blinked. 'What?'

'Christmas lunch. Do you want some?'

I don't think they quite knew what to say.

'It'll be good,' I said. 'The food is brilliant and there's a lot of it. Sadly, you'll have to endure the Security Section's traditional rabid reindeer routine but why should we suffer alone?'

'No more chat,' said Markham sternly. 'Back to the pods right now. I'm assuming you two can take things from here?'

Pennyroyal was heaving snipers to their feet. 'My lady . . .'

'Yes, we should be going too. Where's the other one?'

'Which other one?' said Markham, looking around.

'You mean Mr Evans,' I said.

'Yes – the big one.'

'Gone on ahead, I'm sorry to say.'

'Shame,' she said, grinning.

'He's a good lad,' I said. 'Very . . . capable.'

Markham gave me a shove. 'Time to go.'

We went.

'You didn't leave me time to give them our coordinates,' I said as Markham hustled me away.

'If they can't work them out for themselves then they don't deserve Christmas lunch,' he said. 'Now can we please get a move on.'

In among the flurry of medical attention back in Sick Bay, I managed to have a quiet word with Elspeth.

'Elspeth, you were amazing and so I shall say in my report.'

She was almost sparkling. 'Thank you, Max.'

'I have to say this – if you want to come back to St Mary's, it's not too late and I'd be overjoyed to have you.'

She smiled. 'No. Thank you, Max, but no. I still don't want to do it but now I don't want to do it for the right reasons. I don't want to do it because I have something better now. My life has moved on. Rather than because I'm too shit-scared ever to get into a pod again.'

'You're sure?'

'I'm sure. And this is me making the decision this time, rather than the decision making me.'

'In that case, Merry Christmas, Elspeth.'

Deep down, I didn't think Lady Amelia and Pennyroyal would turn up but they did, arriving about eleven o'clock on Christmas morning. They'd obviously done their homework, bringing a beautifully wrapped bottle of something for Dr Bairstow. It would have been wrapped by Pennyroyal, I was certain. No dodecahedral nightmares for him. He'd probably done it at the same time as servicing their pod, cleaning their weapons and producing a four-course dinner. I bet he did flower arranging as well, and spent a happy few minutes imagining the damage he could do with a daffodil.

They were both on their best behaviour. If they were armed, our wands failed to pick it up and we didn't make a big thing of searching them.

Pennyroyal was a huge hit with everyone, demonstrating how to defend oneself single-handed while at the same time making the perfect margarita. I instructed Markham to take notes. He went on to compliment Mrs Mack on her menu and was offered a tour of the kitchen. Matthew was rendered speechless by his conjuring tricks. Even Angus adored him.

We were all gathered in the Great Hall. The tables and

whiteboards had all been cleared away and the usual tasteful St Mary's decorations were dangling from every surface. Our Christmas tree stood tipsily at the foot of the stairs topped by its traditionally lopsided star. Every attempt to replace it with something more modern and in much better condition had been fiercely resisted and last year, Dr Bairstow had formally awarded it listed status. It would now probably survive us all. And speaking of survival, Leon and Dieter had done the Christmas lights this year, thus considerably enhancing our chances of making it alive to Boxing Day.

The Yule Log burned merrily in our massive fireplace, hurling out great gusts of superfluous heat, but it was traditional and we like our traditions here. If you turned down the sound the whole place looked like something out of Dickens. Shutting your eyes helped, as well.

Matthew tugged at my sleeve. 'Have you seen Mikey?'

'Over by the fireplace.'

I watched him set off across the Hall, a carefully wrapped present in his hand. It wasn't very big. I had no idea what was in it.

Very casually, pretending to admire a particularly battered piece of wooden wall panelling, I sidled close enough to hear their conversation. They were talking about cheese and Mikey's lack thereof.

'I know I don't need it any longer,' she was saying, 'but somehow it doesn't seem right, making a jump without my emergency cheese. You know, just in case.'

'Yes,' he said seriously. 'I know.'

She sighed. 'I miss my lucky cheese.'

'Yes, I know. I got you this.'

He handed her the tiny present.

I crossed my fingers that she would know how important this was to him but I needn't have worried.

'Oh, Matthew, this is so kind of you. I'm so excited. I love presents. Can I open it now?'

I decided the next time she wanted to visit Stephen Hawking I would not stand in her way.

He nodded. He was standing very still but his skinny little body twanged with tension.

She carefully unwrapped her present and stared at it.

'It's cheese,' said Matthew, helpfully.

'It's more than that,' she said, smiling at him. 'From now on *this* will be my lucky cheese. Um . . . what's the hole for?'

'To hang round your neck. With ribbon. So you don't lose it.'

'What a good idea,' she said, without a pause. 'Do you think green would look nice?'

He nodded, although I think he'd have nodded if she'd said sky-blue-pink.

Reaching into his pocket, he pulled out a length of green ribbon – I discovered when emptying his pockets later that he had seven different shades of ribbon tucked away – carefully threaded it through the cheese and handed it back to her.

She didn't even blink. 'Brilliant.' She tied the lump of cheese around her neck. 'Thank you, Matthew.'

He nodded shyly, suddenly looking very like Leon when we first met. 'You're welcome.'

Eventually, Dr Bairstow appeared, looking remarkably mellow. Christmas morning, good food, good drink, nothing on fire, no one screaming . . . how often does that happen?

'Good morning, Mr Pennyroyal. I trust my people are making you welcome.'

Pennyroyal straightened up from showing Matthew a card trick. 'They are indeed, Dr Bairstow. Most welcome. I've been given a tour of the kitchens – I have a professional interest, you know – and enjoyed a most interesting half hour with Theresa and her excellent team.'

Theresa? Did he just call Mrs Mack Theresa?

Dr Bairstow looked around the room. 'And the whereabouts of our second guest?'

Markham intervened. 'Mr Evans has volunteered to escort Lady Amelia, sir.' He paused. '*Close* protection, obviously.'

'Ah,' said Dr Bairstow to me. 'One can only imagine the enthusiasm with which Mr Evans has hurled himself into that particular duty.'

I never know whether he's making a joke or not. There's never the tiniest clue. Not even a flicker. No one has ever dared take the risk and I wasn't going to break our record. I murmured, 'Yes, sir,' which he could interpret any way he pleased.

'Mr Pennyroyal, I would like to extend our customary invitation to those who have rendered St Mary's a service. Should you ever require it, there will always be rest and a shelter for you and Lady Amelia here at St Mary's.'

'Thank you, sir. I know Lady Amelia would wish me to express her own gratitude and acceptance of your kind offer.'

Dr Bairstow nodded. As we both moved away, he lowered his voice. 'Worth keeping an eye on those two, don't you think, Max?'

'Absolutely, sir. A very close eye.'

I should perhaps say that Evans, with his usual devotion to duty, kept so close an eye on Lady Amelia that we didn't see either of them until late afternoon on Boxing Day.

It was as I was working my way around the room, looking for Leon so we could go in to lunch together, that I overheard a very interesting conversation.

Markham and Pennyroyal were standing quietly in a corner, both of them far too experienced to stand with their backs to a room.

'Here,' said Markham, handing him a drink.

'Oh, cheers, mate. I would have got it.'

'Nah,' said Markham. 'Too much of a busman's holiday for you.'

They eyed each other for a moment and then Pennyroyal said quietly, 'Do they know?'

Markham's face never changed for a moment. 'No.'

Silence.

'You'll be fine, mate.'

There was another long pause. It would seem neither of them had anything further to say. Thinking the conversation was over, I drifted across to join them. Pennyroyal acknowledged me with a nod. He rummaged in a pocket, took out a smart wallet and extracted a business card.

'You're going to need a job soon. Contact us. We could always do with someone like you.'

He laid the card down on the table in front of us, smiled in a way he probably imagined was friendly and reassuring and wandered off to astound Matthew some more. I heard him say, 'Here, mate, what's this in your ear?'

I looked at Markham. 'Did he just offer you a job?'

He frowned. 'Actually, Max, I thought he was talking to you.'

We stared at each other and then Markham remembered he was supposed to be sticking close to Pennyroyal and I wanted to see what had been found in Matthew's ear – which since it was Pennyroyal could have been anything up to and including a live hand grenade – and we set off after him.

At that moment the front doors were thrown open with a flourish and here were Ian and Elspeth – our other guests of honour, here for their formal dining out.

Ian had been a well respected and highly regarded member of St Mary's. There were a lot of people lining up to shake his hand. One leg would always be shorter than the other, and his hair was greying, but even with the eyepatch he was Major Guthrie and always would be. I waved and cheered with the rest of them.

Dr Bairstow tinkled his glass.

'May I have your attention, please. I'd like to propose a toast – to Major Ian Guthrie, to whom we all, at one time or another, have owed our lives. Veteran of the Civil Uprisings. One of the first people I recruited to St Mary's. Our first Head of Security and, if I may say so, the rock on which we have all leaned.

'Ian, I would like to take this opportunity to thank you for your exemplary service over the years. Many of us are here today only because of you.'

Well, that was true. He'd saved me at Troy. And again at Nineveh. And on countless other occasions. I remembered our constant battles over Outdoor Survival exercises and my avoidance thereof. I remembered his face when we brought back Elspeth and Bashford. So many memories of him. All good.

There was a huge lump in my throat and I suspected I wasn't the only one.

Dr Bairstow continued. 'I know we are all hungry so I shan't keep you any longer, but before we go in, I ask you all, please, to raise your glasses in our traditional toast.' He turned to Ian. 'Major Guthrie, St Mary's thanks you for your service.'

We echoed the toast, our voices ringing around the Hall.

He stood for a moment and then smiled and raised his glass. 'St Mary's – it's been an honour and a privilege.'

THE END

The Ordeal of the Haunted Room

DRAMATIS THINGUMMY

ST MARY'S PERSONNEL

Mrs Farrell
: Whose innocent but unfortunate comment regarding imminent meteorological conditions turns out to be a Good Thing.

Dr Peterson
: An idiot whose inability to remain on his own two feet turns out to be another Good Thing.

Markham
: A reluctant gentleman's gentleman whose encyclopaedic knowledge on how to murder someone and leave no trace turns out to be yet another Good Thing.

Dr Bairstow
: Director of St Mary's. A man who has learned not to enquire too closely.

OCCUPANTS OF HAREWOOD HALL

Mr Henry Harewood
: Owner of Harewood Hall. About to undergo the Ordeal of the Haunted Room. Dum . . . dum . . . dum.

Mrs Letitia Harewood	His wife. Steadfast and sensible.
Baby Jamie	His son. Doesn't do a lot. Obviously . . .
Barnstaple	A substantially built butler, perpetually outnumbered by housemaids and who has learned to react accordingly.
Mrs Trent	Ointment-laden housekeeper.
John and Thomas	Footmen. Useful for heaving an injured Peterson around.
Eliza, Margaret, Millie, Mary, Jane	Housemaids. Founder members of the Mr Markham Appreciation Society. Otherwise, quite sensible girls.
Mr Chance	The second Chance of Chance, Venture, Chance and Spigot – family solicitors.
The Reverend Lillywhite	Tall, grey, probably not a zombie. A pillar of the church. Which isn't half as exciting as being a zombie.

THE ORDEAL OF THE HAUNTED ROOM

The Winter Solstice, 1895. The longest night of the year. The night when anything can happen . . .

Apparently, the whole thing was my fault. I said I thought it was going to snow, Markham and Peterson obediently looked up at the murky sky and Peterson went arse over tit and hurt his foot. How any of that can be laid at my door was a mystery to me and Markham and I held a spirited discussion over just that point until we couldn't hear ourselves any longer for Peterson's ridiculously melodramatic moaning.

'My foot, my foot,' he whimpered.

'Don't be such a baby,' said Markham. 'Let's have a look.'

'Should I get my boot off?'

'Not unless you want your foot to fall off,' I said, which, while an interesting and unusual sight, would not be conducive to the successful accomplishment of our assignment.

Peterson's suggestion as to where I could put my assignment – successfully completed or otherwise – was not deemed particularly helpful.

'Now what do we do?' said Markham. 'It's miles back to the pod and I don't think Hopalong here will make it.'

'I can see roofs through the trees over there,' I said. 'A house or a farm perhaps. I'm sure someone will take us in.'

We heaved Peterson to his feet – well, foot, anyway – and off we set, arguing over whose fault everything was which helped to pass the time.

It wasn't a farm. We passed through a pair of very impressive wrought-iron gates – unlocked, fortunately. There was a crest on the stone pillars, worn almost smooth with age. Markham closed the gates neatly behind us and we strode and hopped our way up the carriage sweep to the posh house at the end of it.

Typically, its rather charming Jacobean exterior had been almost completely overwhelmed by Victorian Gothic turrets and battlements. There was no moat but dungeons seemed a good bet. Nor did any bats hover menacingly over the bell tower, but I couldn't help feeling it was only a matter of time.

Not all was gloom and doom, though. No matter how much the house looked like the setting from one of those children's programmes where pesky kids and their dog thwart the wicked ghosts, warm golden lights shone at several windows so someone was in. Which was just as well because the wind was beginning to get up and there was sleet in it. We were in for some wild weather.

I left Markham supporting our wounded soldier and climbed the steps to ply the knocker with some vigour. Three sonorous booms echoed around the house.

'Bloody hell, Max,' said Markham. 'You made it sound like the last trump. They'll never open the door now.'

It seemed he was right. Time ticked on and no one came. I looked around. The afternoon was darkening and black branches tossed wildly to and fro. This was no time for innocent historians to be abroad. Or us, either.

I was all set to give it another go, but eventually, slowly, the door opened. Narrative tradition demands a sinister butler – with or without a hump – a creaking door, a gloomy hall, cobwebs and somewhere in the darkness, a woman sobbing quietly.

What we actually saw was a stout, mutton-chopped butler, the epitome of respectability, and behind him, a welcoming, well-lit hall. I actually felt a pang of regret. A ghost story would have been nice for Christmas. As Peterson said afterwards, I never learn, do I?

For a moment we all looked at each other and then the butler stepped back, solemnly bidding us welcome.

Fortunately, his employer was considerably less formidable. A tall young woman emerged from a door to the right, asking, 'Who is it, Barnstaple?'

She was sensibly dressed in morning wear – a tailored blouse, high at the neck, tucked into a bell-shaped skirt, fitted over the hips. Her dark hair was dressed high on her head with soft curls at the front. Pretty, practical and fashionable.

'I am endeavouring to ascertain that fact, madam,' he said forbiddingly, never taking his eyes off us. The rain began to come down in earnest.

'Good afternoon,' I said politely. 'I am so sorry to make claims on your hospitality but my . . . brother has suffered a fall and hurt his foot.'

Thus reminded of his injury, Peterson smiled wanly.

'Goodness gracious,' she said, and I made a mental note to dial back my normal bad language before it got me into trouble. 'You must come in. Barnstaple . . .' She gestured to us.

Barnstaple unbent sufficiently to assist Peterson in through the door and settle him in a chair. Within seconds he was surrounded by a bevy of housemaids. Much in the same way that carnivores gather around a stricken antelope. I think there were a couple of footmen in there, as well. While everyone fussed around Peterson – you could see him loving every moment of it – I stepped back and took a quick look around.

We were standing in a large hall, traditionally decorated for its time with gloomy pictures, fussy curtains, and branches of candles everywhere. The colour scheme was dark and sombre. Mysterious shadows jumped in the flickering candlelight although I was inclined to think that was more due to the gale force draughts rather than anything sinister.

Heavy doors opened off this space and the one from which the woman had emerged offered a glimpse of a comfortably furnished sitting room. Interestingly, though, there were no Christmas decorations. Not anywhere. We were only a few days before Christmas. Victorians were usually not subtle when it came to interior decoration so there should be at least one Christmas tree – now very fashionable after its original introduction by Queen Charlotte in 1800 – together with greenery and garlands and ribbons draped over every available surface.

I turned to face our hostess. The mistress of the house, I assumed.

'I am so sorry to have troubled you. I am Mrs Farrell and this is my brother, Dr Peterson, who is, I am sorry to say, incapable of not falling over his own feet. And his man, Markham.'

She smiled politely, glancing at the rain now hammering against the windows. 'It is certainly no afternoon to be outside and I can assure you it is no trouble.'

Well, it wouldn't be for her. She'd have twelve thousand servants downstairs all ready to fulfil her slightest whim. On the other hand, underneath her kind face, her air was distracted and tense. It couldn't be us, surely. We'd only been in the house two minutes.

'My name is Letitia Harewood. This is my husband's house. You are very welcome although you will find us a little distracted at the moment. I think the best thing is to look at Dr Peterson's foot while we can still take his boot off. Perhaps we should cut the laces. Oh, well done, Barnstaple. You think of everything.'

Obviously actually cutting the laces was beneath Barnstaple's dignity – his responsibility ended with producing the appropriate implement. A footman cut the laces and gently eased off Peterson's boot and sock and everyone peered at the affected body part.

'Oh dear,' I said, remembering my role as a member of the weaker sex, barely able to endure the rigours of life without a man to advise me. On the other hand, I'm pretty sure sisters have been giving their brothers a hard time since the world began. 'That looks quite painful.'

'It is,' he said, with gritted teeth. Peterson doesn't bear pain well. You should have heard the carry-on when he was unwell in the 14th century. You'd think no one had ever had bubonic plague before.

There was no getting away from it though, that foot was not looking good. I didn't need field medic qualifications to know feet should not be big, bruised and spherical. Fleshy and oblong is the accepted way to go. With discernible toes.

Several people drew back with exclamations of consternation. Given this was the Victorian age, I half expected a few of them to go off in a swoon. Admittedly one of the footmen turned a little green but none of the housemaids turned a hair. It was Peterson who uttered a pitiful groan, clearly indicating he'd given up the unequal struggle for life and metaphorically turned his face to the wall.

'I'm sure you'll be far more comfortable upstairs,' said Mrs Harewood and Peterson nodded his heartfelt agreement. A housemaid was despatched to light a fire. Another went for hot water and towels. Two footmen were delegated to convey the stricken Peterson upstairs.

'Where is his man?' enquired Mrs Harewood, looking around. There was a momentary pause. Under the cover of my skirts I kicked Markham's ankle.

'I am here, madam,' he said, with dignity. 'Ready to accompany you.'

We set off – Barnstaple regally in the lead, setting the pace. The two footmen – John and Thomas, I think – carried Peterson, followed by Mrs Harewood and me, and finally, bringing up the rear was Markham, that gentleman's gentleman *par excellence*, still indignant over the assault to his ankle and limping slightly and unnecessarily.

She enquired if we'd come far.

'Just outside of Rushford,' I replied, concentrating on getting up the stairs without standing on my skirt or showing too much ankle. 'St Mary's Priory.'

She nodded. I could tell she'd never heard of it.

For those accustomed to the spartan conditions prevailing at St Mary's – and I see I've done my usual thing and gone galloping off into the story without giving anyone a clue as to who we are – start again, Maxwell – we belong to the Institute of

Historical Research at St Mary's Priory, where we investigate major historical events in contemporary time. Do not call it time-travel. Well, you could, obviously, but not unless you wanted to incur the bone-chilling wrath of Dr Bairstow and have more than a fat foot to worry about.

Anyway, the reason we were dancing around on a bleak, cold December afternoon was that we'd jumped back to investigate a Victorian Christmas. Which I suspected would be much the same as everyone else's Christmas except for seventeen-course meals, miserly old curmudgeons undergoing profound personality changes, and the obligatory Christmas ghost.

We'd jumped back to a small town in Rushfordshire 1895, landing just behind the local pub, the Royal Oak – although as far as I knew the Royal Oak wasn't anywhere near us. You know the one – where the future Charles II hid in an oak tree after his father's forces lost the Battle of Worcester. Anyway, we'd left the pod and blithely set off into the afternoon to see what the locals were making of the festive season. Not one hour up the road Peterson had tripped over his own feet and here we were.

Where was I? Yes – arriving at Peterson's room, which was a bit on the sumptuous side. The décor was very masculine – a kind of crimson tartan fabric for curtains, bedspread and cushions. A bright fire was already crackling away as the housemaid, Jane, plied the bellows in an apparent attempt to burn the house down.

Another maid was setting a pitcher of hot water on top of the dresser. Markham entered, reverently bearing Peterson's boot as if it was a holy relic and completely failing to take the whole thing seriously.

'We'll leave you in peace,' said Mrs Harewood. 'Mrs Farrell, will you allow me to show you to your own room? This way.'

'You're very kind,' I said. 'I cannot believe, so close to Christmas, that the sudden arrival of two unexpected guests –' Markham wouldn't count – 'is anything other than a massive inconvenience.'

'I assure you it is not. My husband likes me to run a very hospitable house, and if I say that we are currently entertaining my husband's solicitor and the vicar, I'm sure you will understand why the addition of unexpected guests is no imposition at all.' Her eyes met mine for just a moment. The long-suffering hostess entertaining her husband's less than lively guests. 'And this is your room.'

The door stood open. Housemaids had invaded here, too. This room was decorated in much lighter tones than Peterson's – a soft blue and white. I had a big, deep bed, two bedside tables, a massive Narnia wardrobe in which I had nothing to put, two comfy-looking armchairs in front of another bright fire, and a chest of drawers that was taller than I was – although that's not difficult. A blizzard of small tables had fallen on the room at some point, all of them occupied by thousands of really quite ugly ornaments and baubles. A handsome silver clock ticked on the mantel and three or four fringed rugs had been cast over an already thick carpet. The curtains were drawn and the whole effect was comfortable and welcoming. I looked around. 'This is delightful, Mrs Harewood. Thank you so very much.'

'You are most welcome, Mrs Farrell. I shall leave you to make yourself comfortable. Please ring if you need anything. No doubt you will want to assure yourself of your brother's comfort . . .'

Her tone conveyed her misgivings over her guest's brother's man-servant but that wasn't my problem so I ignored it. 'And when you are ready, I shall be delighted if you would join me for Tea.'

Well, that sounded good.

I took off my hat, tossed it and my gloves on to a chair and unfastened my heavy coat. Mrs Enderby had made it especially for me and it was rather a nice one, actually, dark red, three-quarters length with fashionable leg of mutton sleeves and a fake fur collar. She'd given it a slightly military look with frog fasteners down the front. Underneath I was wearing a close-fitting navy jacket, a high-necked blouse and the fashionable bell-shaped skirt, all similar to the outfit worn by Mrs Hare-wood. I washed my face and hands in pleasantly warm water, only now realising how cold I'd become, tidied my hair and made my way to Peterson's room.

Markham let me in. The invalid was reclining on a mound of pillows, his foot on a cushion with a cold compress laid over. He looked extremely comfortable.

'There you are,' he said. 'I was about to send my man down for some tea.'

I've no idea how his man would have responded to that because at that moment Mrs Trent, the housekeeper, a most respectable lady in plain black, knocked at the door with some ointment 'for the poor doctor's foot'.

The poor doctor accepted this most graciously and demanded tea. Markham scowled at us both impartially and followed her down to the servants' quarters.

I seated myself in an armchair by the fire to dispense sym-pathy. 'You are an idiot.'

'It's swelling like mad,' Peterson said gloomily. 'Do you think I've broken something?'

'That or a bad sprain, which is just as serious.'

'Yes, we could have a problem, couldn't we? They'll offer to send down to the inn for our luggage and there won't be any. Nor any visible means of conveyance. In fact, no one there will know anything about us and at this point the Harewoods will begin to wonder who we are and where we came from. I'm going to have to be well enough to leave tomorrow morning whether I am or not.'

'Let's get some of this ointment on it,' I said, unscrewing the lid and giving it a sniff. 'Perhaps it will help.'

'Or perhaps my foot will fall off.'

'Thus neatly solving all our problems,' I said. 'We can pick it up and return to St Mary's.'

The ointment had a minty smell. 'That's nice,' he said as I smoothed it on. 'Cool. I can feel it doing me good. Put some more on.'

In Peterson's world, more is definitely more. I slathered it on as instructed and was just finishing when Markham returned with a housemaid we hadn't met yet and some tea. I suspected Peterson was the most exciting thing that had happened to them for a long time – I was wrong but I'll get to that – and they were all taking it in turns to come up and have a look at him.

No sooner had she left, however – all flustered because Peterson had smiled and thanked her – than Markham threw himself on to the bed, reclining in a very unservantlike manner. 'You'll never guess what,' he said, his eyes sparkling with excitement. 'Pour the tea, Max.'

I poured them each a cup of tea and returned to the fire with my own cup. 'What won't we guess?'

'Well,' he said, wriggling to get himself comfortable and ignoring Peterson's protests that this was his bed and Markham would have his own straw mattress and half a blanket in an outhouse somewhere. 'While you two were lounging away above stairs, I was in the Servants' Hall getting the low-down on tonight's exciting events. We've really fallen on our feet for this one, Max, although not Peterson, of course – he fell on his arse.'

'I did no such thing,' he said indignantly, sitting up and preparing to argue the point.

'Never mind that,' I said impatiently. 'What won't we guess?'

Markham leaned back with his tea. 'I shall tell you a story.'

Peterson groaned, but I told him he had nowhere better to be, and commanded Markham to get on with it.

'Well,' he said. 'I couldn't believe it to begin with – it's like something out of the pages of a Gothic novel.'

'Well, so are we sometimes,' said Peterson. 'I really don't feel we're in any position to criticise other people over the lack of realism in their lives.'

'What's out of the pages of a Gothic novel?' I said impatiently, because someone has to keep the two of them on track.

Markham grinned wickedly. He looked like a disreputable angel. 'Listen now to the story of . . . *The Haunted Room*. Dum . . . dum . . . dum . . .'

We stared at him.

'No,' said Peterson. 'I don't believe it. An actual Haunted Room?'

'Yes, an actual Haunted Room. Listen, the legend is that,

ages ago, one of the Harewoods was the wrong one. The real heir to the Hall wasn't around – he was out conquering the world or something. His father died and, scenting an opportunity, a younger son turned up and claimed the lot – house, lands, money, everything. Anyway, he was doing very nicely, thank you, and then, seven years later, the real heir returned from whatever part of the world he'd been subjugating and, naturally, there was hell to pay. The imposter was imprisoned in a room here somewhere while they decided what to do with him, but when they unlocked the door the next morning, apparently he'd been unable to face the consequences and done away with himself.'

'So far so normal,' said Peterson, stifling a yawn. 'Probably happened all the time with heirs off discovering diamond mines and circumnavigating the world and dying unrecorded and unknown and people taking their place and getting away with it.'

'Anyway,' said Markham, refusing to be diverted from his thrilling tale. 'The details are a bit hazy. I got them from Millie, who was so excited she could hardly speak, but . . .'

Peterson frowned. 'Who's Millie?'

'The parlourmaid.'

'Is that the same as a housemaid?'

'Good heavens, no – don't even suggest such a thing. Can I continue?'

'By all means.'

'Well, ever since then, before the heir can inherit Harewood Hall, on the night of the Winter Solstice, he has to spend the night in the Haunted Room . . .'

'Dum . . . dum . . . dum,' we chorused.

98

I enquired as to why.

'To prove that he's the rightful heir.'

'No, I mean why the night of the Winter Solstice?'

'Dunno. Because it's the longest night, perhaps, so the ghost of the imposter heir has more time to haunt him?'

'Couldn't he just show his birth certificate or something?' enquired Peterson.

'I don't know. Perhaps they hadn't been invented when this quaint legend was born.'

'What happens if he's not the heir?'

'Then the unquiet spirit of the original imposter will take its revenge and he'll be found as dead as a doornail.'

'Wow,' said Peterson. 'Wish we'd had legends like that in my family.'

'Fun fact,' said Markham, completely oblivious to the lack of enthusiasm usually engendered by his misnamed fun facts.

'Damn,' said Peterson to me. 'I thought we'd got away with it this time out.'

'Fun fact,' pursued Markham, as unstoppable as an historian on her way to lunch. 'The phrase *dead as a doornail* was first used in the 16th century by our old friend William Shakespeare. And again in 1843 by Charles Dickens. Derived from clenching doornails.'

'Can't help feeling that's a rather inappropriate use of the word "clenching",' muttered Peterson. 'Not given the current state of my buttocks after hearing that particular legend.'

'No,' protested Markham. 'It's really interesting. You're hammering the nails into your door –' he mimed hammering a nail the size of a telegraph pole into a door the size of a cathedral – 'and you bend the nails over as you hammer them in, which makes them almost impossible to remove and use again. They're dead. Hence *dead as a doornail*.'

We ignored him. Harsh, but it's the only way.

'So at the stroke of midnight, Henry Harewood will be taken to the Haunted Room . . .' said Markham.

'Dum . . . dum . . . dum . . .' added Peterson. I began to wonder if Mrs Harewood's excellent servants were putting something in the tea.

'I've often asked myself – why does no one ever do anything on the stroke of twenty-five to nine?' demanded Peterson, whom I suspected of slowly being overcome by ointment fumes.

Markham continued. 'Anyway, once inside, he's locked in and there he has to stay, completely alone, until cock-crow or dawn or something dramatic like that, and then they unlock the door and let him out. If he's still alive. And sane, of course. That's why the reverend and the solicitor are here. They have to be present in the house during the Ordeal to prove Mr Harewood's actually done it. Then he can collect the family fortune and everyone lives happily ever after. Except . . .' He stopped.

Peterson held out his cup to me for more tea. 'Except what . . . ?'

'The last incumbent – the present Mr Harewood's father – died. On this night. The Winter Solstice. Last year. While he was actually undergoing the Ordeal of the Haunted Room.'

No one said dum . . . dum . . . dum . . . this time.

'Found dead in his chair by the fire.'

'Torn to pieces by a vengeful spirit?'

'No.'

'Suicide?'

'No, barely a mark on him. A small but deep cut on his forearm that his wife swore hadn't been there when he went in.'

'And that killed him?'

'No – they never found out what killed him. I'm not sure how sophisticated autopsies were then. Fun fact . . .'

Peterson scowled at him. 'You weren't by any chance present when Mr Harewood senior croaked, were you? Only if you were around then, the suicide theory becomes so much more viable.'

'An autopsy carried out on Julius Caesar was able to determine that although he was stabbed multiple times,' I said, absently, 'it was the second blow that killed him.'

Complete silence greeted this interesting remark.

'Hold on,' I said, trying to get the chronology straight in my head. 'Mr Harewood's father must have been quite old when he undertook the Ordeal.'

'Early fifties, I believe. His father, William, Henry's grandad, was in his seventies when he died.'

'And William survived the Ordeal?'

'Well, yes, obviously.'

'So what was wrong with Henry's dad, then?'

'No one knows.'

'And he died actually *during* the Ordeal . . . ?'

'Leaving his son, Henry. The rules say he has to undergo the Ordeal tonight if he is to inherit.'

'Knowing it killed his father.'

'Yes.'

'And they never found out what killed Mr Harewood senior?'

'Well, it was the ghost, obviously, Max. There are about seventy-one housemaids below stairs who will tell you that.'

'But . . .' I said, bewildered. 'Surely he didn't die from a cut arm?'

'No – interestingly, the cut appeared to have been self-inflicted. Although from the blood on his fingers, they thought he might have tried to staunch the bleeding afterwards.'

'*Had* he tried to kill himself?'

'Not unless he'd tried to slash his elbows instead of his wrists. The wound was in completely the wrong place. He was just dead.

'Anyway, Henry'll be locked in the room at midnight tonight and if he doesn't survive the night then the little chap upstairs – that's Baby Jamie, just under a year old – steps up – figuratively speaking – and twenty-one years later, when he's of age, they'll be doing it all again.'

'Wow,' I said, topping up my own tea.

'Although,' he continued, 'to be fair, up until Mr Harewood senior's unfortunate demise, the Ordeal of the Haunted Room had just been a formality. A charming family legend they trotted out at Christmas as the traditional family ghost story. Now, after what happened to Henry's dad, everyone's wetting themselves but being very British about it.'

'Hang on,' said Peterson. 'What's been happening to the estate since Henry's dad's death?'

'Kept in trust until the heir is confirmed.'

'They don't seem to be doing too badly,' I observed.

'Well, according to Jane and Eliza . . .'

'Who?' said Peterson.

'Don't ask,' I said wearily. 'Or he'll be regaling us with details of his new-found friends all afternoon.'

'According to Jane and Eliza, while the estate isn't on its

102

uppers, there's not a lot of money. Only enough for essential estate management and household expenses. Everyone's very upset about it. They're down to less than twenty servants and only seven outside staff. There are grave doubts over whether they'll be able to entertain us in the appropriate manner.'

'We can hire you out,' said Peterson to Markham. 'You can pay our way.'

I sighed. 'We do pick our moments, don't we?'

'It's a gift,' said Markham. 'Few have it.' He looked at Peterson. 'And to think I might have called you a clumsy baboon with all the coordination of a camel on a bike.'

'You *did* call me a clumsy . . .'

'Well,' I said, before the discussion could become too enthusiastic, 'we've got to try and hang around for this. Tim, your foot is far too painful to stand on.'

'It *is* too painful to stand on. I don't think either of you have quite grasped the full extent of my . . .'

Someone tapped on the door. Markham leaped from the bed and became a proper servant again, straightening the young master's bedcovers with the appropriate reverence. For which Peterson would pay later.

Jane was back for the tea tray. Markham carried it down for her and she obviously thought he was wonderful, although, as Peterson said, she probably didn't get out much.

I thought I'd do a little exploring myself, and callously leaving Peterson alone to fester, I set off to find Mrs Harewood.

She was downstairs in the family sitting room, on her knees in front of the fire playing with Baby Jamie. Nanny sat over in the corner, keeping a beady eye on the pair of them and crocheting something lacy with gnarled fingers. Which was a

103

shame because I wanted to gossip, but *pas devant les domestiques*, as Markham would say. And probably with a better accent than mine, as well.

Again, this room was an overcrowded riot of heavy furniture and exuberant patterns. Patterned carpet, patterned curtains – all different patterns, obviously – heavy wooden furniture smothered in lacy coverings, millions of ornaments everywhere, and papered walls plastered with pictures of muddy landscapes and dead animals. Yes, welcome to middle-class Victorian England. But still not a Christmas decoration in sight. Although with this Ordeal thing hanging over them, I could understand that now.

Fortunately, just as I entered, the clock on the mantel chimed four and Nanny and the baby disappeared for their Afternoon Nap. Exactly which of them would be availing themselves of this luxury was unclear.

I sank into a sofa from which, I suspected, I would have great difficulty extricating myself when the time came. Mrs Harewood sat opposite me, plaiting the fringe of her shawl, pulling it loose, then replaiting it again . . . a woman with something on her mind.

She began by asking after Peterson. I reassured her as to his injury and mentioned a couple of other times he'd spectacularly hurt himself, avoiding all reference to the plague, obviously. And the pox, because he always tends to confuse the two.

She said vaguely that was good news and then, her mind obviously elsewhere, repeated herself all over again, which gave me the opening I needed.

'Forgive me, Mrs Harewood, you appear to be considerably distracted and I can't help feeling at least partially responsible.'

'No. Oh, no. Not at all. I'm so sorry, Mrs Farrell – this is not a good time for us, that's all. Nothing to do with your brother's unfortunate accident.'

'I'm so sorry to hear that,' I said, 'but if you'd rather not talk about it . . .'

Nothing ever gets people talking faster than an invitation *not* to talk about whatever is troubling them and, as I hoped, the appearance of a complete stranger whom she would never see again provided her with the ideal opportunity to unburden herself.

Details of the Ordeal of the Haunted Room tumbled over themselves, followed by her anxiety for her husband, her fears for the future and so on. 'I mean, obviously, I'm completely confident that Henry will emerge unscathed, but after what happened to his father . . .'

'But Mrs Harewood, please forgive my asking, but Mr Harewood senior *was* the legitimate heir, was he not?'

'Oh yes. There could be no doubt. He was an only child of an only child.'

'And there's equally no doubt about *this* Mr Harewood?'

'Absolutely none. Henry's younger brother died some eight or nine years ago of an inflammation of the lungs. Something which had troubled him since childhood. Very sad but quite unremarkable. He always had a weak chest, I believe.' She straightened her shoulders. 'However, I am certainly well supported. Mr Chance, our family solicitor, is here – a very capable man – and the Reverend Lillywhite, an old friend of the family and always so kind.' She turned to me. 'I don't like to make light of your brother's misfortune but I must tell you how very grateful I am to have another woman in the house tonight.'

It struck me that telling her wild horses couldn't drag me out of this house tonight might not be the sympathetic and supportive attitude she wanted, so I patted her hand and smiled reassuringly.

'So,' she said briskly, 'shall we have afternoon tea?'

I thought I'd already had afternoon tea but it seemed I hadn't. That had been ordinary tea. *This* was Afternoon Tea.

Barnstaple and two maids wheeled in not one but two tea trollies, laden with doilies, silver teapots, bone china plates, cups and saucers, cake forks, and enough food to feed St Mary's for three days.

'Barnstaple, could you tell Mr Harewood and our guests that tea is ready, please. I think you'll find them in the billiards room.'

'At once, madam.'

Mrs Harewood poured me a cup of tea. I couldn't help noticing it was a different tea service to the one I'd had tea in upstairs. Perhaps they had an upstairs tea service and a downstairs tea service. Just imagine – if they weren't living in such straitened circumstances there might even be a different tea service for every room.

Setting that aside, what we did have were dainty sandwiches cut in the shapes of clubs, diamonds, spades and hearts, very tiny cakes, a whole pile of brandy-snap things, a massive fruit cake fresh from the oven, smelling like heaven and served in the traditional manner with a slice of Wensleydale, some sort of creamy posset, fruit pastries – oh God, I wasn't going to get out of this alive.

I tried to start small and pace myself, but believe me, there was no chance. I even tried to concentrate mainly on the sandwiches, on the grounds they'd be marginally less lethal than the cakes, but my hostess encouraged me to partake at every opportunity. Hospitality was obviously a big thing in the Harewood household.

Speaking of hospitality, two minutes in, Henry Harewood turned up, towing two black-clad figures in his wake.

The Reverend Lillywhite was a tall, thin and cadaverous man. I've never actually met someone with a grey face before – not outside a zombie movie, obviously.

The solicitor, Mr Chance, short and bumptious, was far too cheerful to be a solicitor and his creaking waistcoat was evidence of too many afternoon teas at Harewood Hall.

'Chance,' he said, rolling across the room to shake my hand. 'From Chance, Venture, Chance and Spigot. I'm the second one. What you might call "A Second Chance". Eh? Eh?'

The universe failed to kill me now.

My first thought for Mr Harewood was that he was rather frail-looking for this Ordeal. His fair hair was thin and receding already. He looked very young for his twenty-five years and wore country tweeds, shabby but good. The reverend, obviously, wore clerical bands and Mr Chance announced his profession in a rusty black coat with a wing collar. A watch chain strained across his ample girth. A key hung therefrom.

Henry Harewood greeted me very politely. If he was concerned over his forthcoming Ordeal, none of that showed in his face. If I didn't know better, I would swear he was utterly delighted to hear of our arrival. That the only thing his life had been lacking up to this very moment was the spontaneous arrival of three dubious-looking individuals and none of them with credentials of any kind. Letters of introduction were very

107

important. In such a tightly interlocked society, everyone pretty much knew everyone else, and anyone venturing into a new area would bear letters of introduction, thus establishing them as proper and respectable people with mutual friends. Or, in our case – not. Obviously, we didn't have any letters and they might easily have confined us to the Servants' Hall or even turned us away completely, but fortunately, given the dreadful weather outside, kindness and charity had prevailed.

'My dear Mrs Farrell, I do hope my wife has made you comfortable.'

'Yes, thank you, Mr Harewood, we've been made most welcome. I can only apologise for disturbing you. Blame my brother's lamentable inability to look where he is going.'

Mrs Harewood smiled at her husband. 'I've had some tea sent up to him, dear.' She turned to me. 'If he is well enough to eat, of course.'

I refrained from telling her that even in death Peterson would still be well enough to eat.

The reverend clasped my hand in his clammy claw. As soon as I could, I detached myself from his grasp, picked up my plate to keep my hands out of his reach and prepared to listen.

Conversation was very stilted – polite enquiries after my brother, where were we from, had we any mutual friends or relatives – the usual stuff. I smiled, invented people and places with creative abandon and made a note to brief Peterson later. It would be so typical of him if, after I'd spent an imaginative ten minutes describing last summer with Batty Aunt Jemima at Harrogate, he turned around and told them she'd died ten years ago.

Every now and then the conversation would tail away and

then they would remember their manners and it would all start up again.

'And where was your destination, my dear madam?' intoned the reverend, who had found a space on the sofa beside me, only very inadequately managing to conceal his disapproval of husbandless females roaming the landscape.

'I'm on my way to join my husband,' I said. A fit and proper activity for a wife. Even the church couldn't object to that. 'Mr Farrell is an explorer. At present he's studying the Moche culture in Peru.'

He was horrified. 'You are surely not joining him there? Among the savages? Hardly a fitting place for a gently born female.'

'A wife's place is at her husband's side,' I said primly, embarking on an enjoyable stroll down the highways and byways of hypocrisy. 'No matter the trials or tribulations, my womanly duty is always to my husband,' and spent an enjoyable few minutes watching him struggle with the unreconcilable beliefs that a wife should always support her husband but that the proper place for said wife was in the home.

Determined to find something to criticise, he frowned at me. 'And yet the weather is terrible, Mrs Farrell. What sort of brother brings his sister out on a day like this?'

'Ah,' I said gaily. 'Now that you can blame me for, Reverend Lillywhite. We broke our journey at the inn and I suggested a walk after being cooped up for so long in the carriage. Barely had we gone a mile or so when my brother fell and twisted his foot. I don't think it's broken – just a bad sprain. He will probably be as right as rain tomorrow.'

'You have nursing experience?' he said, with a wary eye on Mrs Harewood lest I contaminate her with these modern ideas.

'A little,' I said, because as Markham frequently explains to Hunter, nursing is no job for a lady. 'Nothing formal, of course, but with a husband, a brother, a son and clumsy friends, I have gained some experience over the years.'

He smiled, but his heart wasn't in it and after this flurry of conversation, things subsided. An awkward silence fell. I chomped away. A prudent historian always eats when she can because she never knows where the next meal will be coming from. Mr Harewood stirred his tea. On and on and on . . . Eventually the silence was broken by Mrs Harewood.

'Oh, for heaven's sake,' she said impatiently. 'Mrs Farrell is perfectly well aware of our circumstances. There really is no need for all this heavy-handed discretion.' She turned to me. 'As you are aware, Mrs Farrell, tonight is the night my husband takes part in a . . . a family ritual, the successful completion of which will lead to him coming into his full inheritance.'

She sat down with a defiant *so there* expression on her face.

I wanted to get them talking about the Ordeal, so I enquired of Mrs Harewood if this was a long-standing family tradition. Which, on reflection, might have been a bit of a mistake.

'Oh yes,' she replied. 'On the first Winter Solstice after . . .'

'Paganism!' exclaimed the reverend and I nearly spilled my tea.

'I beg your pardon, sir?'

'The Roman Saturnalia,' he cried, eyes glowing with a strange and disturbing fervour, 'with its licentious behaviour and overturning of the proper order. The Druids and their heathen sacrifices. And now this – the barbaric ritual with its overtones of darkness and devil-worship – I beg your pardon, ladies – but the violence of my feelings . . . I say again, Mr Harewood – this outdated superstition should find no place in the modern Christian household . . .'

I toyed with the idea of telling him Jesus had probably been born in March and the Christian church had piggybacked their festival on the existing Yule traditions. And probably best not to get him started on Eostre, either. We had enough melodrama without adding an unstable vicar into the mix and besides, little flecks of foam were collecting at the corners of his mouth.

'. . . And the light of the Christian faith pushing back the shadows of cruel pagan practices . . .'

I could feel myself gearing up to compare cruel pagan practices to the compassionate ministrations of the Spanish Inquisition and Mrs Harewood was regarding her husband with a very wifely 'Oh God, now we've set him off again,' expression, when Barnstaple, obviously well versed in the vicar's little ways, earned his pay for the day by offering him an enormous slab of fruit cake and a correspondingly colossal piece of Wensleydale. Rising to that challenge would certainly keep him quiet for a few minutes so I leaped back into the conversation before anyone could have the good manners to change the subject.

'But you are not actually poor,' I said, because, as has frequently been pointed out, I have no tact. I gestured around at their not opulent but still quite comfortable surroundings.

'Oh,' Mrs Harewood said, grasping my meaning. 'The funds allow us enough to keep the estate going.' She cast a dour look at Mr Chance. 'But for such expenses as personal expenditure, Jamie's future schooling and so on . . . my husband is not currently even allowed access to his own money.'

'My dear,' murmured Henry Harewood. 'We have discussed this.'

The Reverend Lillywhite – whom I was really coming to dislike – abandoned paganism and prepared to mount what was obviously his other hobbyhorse – that women were not equipped to understand the law and how it worked. I slung him another slice of cake and a couple of brandy snaps.

Mr Chance was displaying signs of agitation. 'Mrs Harewood, I understand your concerns, but we have been over this many times and I really feel we should not be burdening Mrs Farrell with our private affairs.'

She twisted in her seat to look at him. '*Our* private affairs?'

He blinked under her ferocity and then recovered himself. 'As your husband's solicitor, ma'am . . .'

This was interesting – there was obviously no love lost between these two – and I suspected she didn't love the Reverend Lillywhite either – but unfortunately, I never found out how their little tiff ended because one of the maids, possibly reacting to the overwrought atmosphere, dropped a plate of cakes. The plate fell on to one of the many marble-topped occasional tables scattered around the room as thickly as ants on a jam sandwich.

I don't know about anyone else but I nearly jumped through the roof. Plate and sandwiches bounced off the table on to the carpet and disintegrated. Jane gave a cry and dropped to her knees. To pick up the pieces, I hoped, rather than beg forgiveness.

'It's all right, Jane,' said Mrs Harewood calmly as Barnstaple surged forwards like the Wrath of God. 'Please don't scold, Barnstaple. I think we're all a little on edge today.'

Having picked up the pieces, Jane fled, spurred on her way by Barnstaple's disapproving frown. I suspected he was a much sterner disciplinarian than his mistress.

'I should be rejoining my brother,' I said.

'Of course,' she said. 'Dinner this evening will be at the usual time.' She raised her voice a little. 'We won't change, as a courtesy to Mrs Farrell, but otherwise everything will be exactly as usual, Barnstaple. Exactly as usual,' she added with emphasis.

'Very good, madam.'

'My brother believes he will be recovered enough to join us,' I said, diplomatically translating Peterson's declaration that nothing would make him miss this, even if his entire leg fell off.

'How delightful,' she said vaguely. The gentlemen rose and I left the room.

Peterson was still reclining on a plate-bestrewn bed. 'I have to keep my strength up,' he said before I even uttered a word.

'You're expected at dinner. If you think you can make it.'

'Of course I can.' He gestured at a duck-headed walking stick. 'Donated by the master of the house.'

To pass the time, I took another look at his minty-smelling foot and told him he probably only had an hour to live. We discussed events downstairs – I described Lillywhite and Chance in a manner that wasn't flattering to either of them. I peered out through the curtains – I don't know why because it was pitch-black out there. Peterson discovered a Bible in a drawer in his bedside table and began to read out the good bits. I wandered around, bored. 'Do we know where buggerlugs has got to?'

Peterson looked up from the Whore of Babylon. 'Disappeared under a sea of adoring housemaids, probably.'

'I heard that,' said Markham, entering at that moment. 'And actually, I've been gathering intel. With Barnstaple out of the way they couldn't wait to gossip. I gather your husband's an explorer, Max. Now then,' he added, hunting through the plates in the vain hope Peterson might have left something uneaten, 'this Haunted Room . . .'

'Dum . . . dum . . . dum.'

'Will you stop doing that?'

'What do *you* think?' said Peterson. 'Anyway, what about this Haunted Room?'

'It's located on the ground floor between the library and Mr H's study. Probably a ladies' parlour once upon a time. Now kept locked at all times. For obvious reasons. No one ever goes in there except on the night of the Ordeal.'

'Does anyone know what's inside?'

'According to Margaret – who, to the admiration of her co-workers, contrived to be present on the night of the last Ordeal – and from the quick glimpse she caught as they broke down the door – it's quite a small room. Dusty, obviously. She saw a fireplace with an ornate mantel, one end of a table and what she persisted in referring to as the Armchair of Death because Mr Harewood was sprawled in it, head back, arms hanging, his face a terrible colour, and, I quote, "Quite, quite dead, Mr Markham".'

Peterson frowned. 'He hadn't cried out at all?'

'Nope. And there had never been a problem with the Ordeal before. I gather no one was expecting anything untoward. They locked him in – there was a lot of joking about the ghost – and then they retired to wait in comfort.'

114

'Who's they?'

'Mr Henry Harewood. Not Mrs Letitia, for some reason. Those two cheerful buggers, Chance and Lillywhite. Mrs Victoria, Harewood senior's wife, was present too. She screamed and fainted and Margaret said she never saw any more because Chance slammed the door and told her to look after her mistress.'

'Wow,' I said again. 'Right – plan of action for this evening. Peterson and I will go down to dinner. You'll help Peterson get downstairs. Having done that, make yourself scarce and hang around the Haunted Room . . .'

'Dum . . . dum . . . dum,' said Peterson valiantly.

'. . . to make sure no one's setting up any funny business.'

'And what will you be doing while I'm waiting, all alone in the cold and dark?'

'Eating, drinking, making merry, that sort of thing. I'm sure we'll be able to accompany Mr Harewood to the room to verify he's been locked in. If we can't join you, we'll return to our rooms while you . . .'

'Will continue to sit in the cold and dark making sure no one attempts to interfere in any way.'

'Exactly.'

'Bloody hell, Max.'

'You could warm yourself on a couple of housemaids,' offered Peterson.

'They're very respectable girls,' he said, primly. 'More than adequately chaperoned by Mrs Trent. And besides, have you seen the size of Barnstaple?'

He began to stack plates and cups back on the tray.

We chatted for half an hour. I had forgotten how heavily

115

time lay in the Victorian era. Especially for women. Eventually, I got to my feet and said I had better go and make myself presentable for dinner.

They both nodded, Peterson going so far as to say if I started right now, I might look fairly reasonable by the time they rang the gong.

Back in my room, another maid awaited me. A short bouncy one, this time. They obviously had some sort of maid manufactory downstairs.

'Good evening,' I said. 'And you are . . . ?'

She bobbed a curtsey. 'Eliza, ma'am. Mrs Harewood sent me to make sure you had everything you needed. She says the house is often cold at night and wondered if you'd like to borrow one of these.' She gestured towards the bed where three very pretty shawls had been laid out.

'How very kind of Mrs Harewood,' I said. And because I wanted to keep her on my side, added, 'Which one would you recommend?'

'I think the blue one, ma'am. To go with your dress. And the fringes are very pretty.'

'The blue one it is, then. Thank you, Eliza.'

There was a bit of a pause and then she said tactfully, 'Would you like me to help you with your hair, ma'am?'

'I would indeed. Thank you.'

The hair thing went very well. She managed it much better than I did, piling it all on top of my head and encouraging a few curls to fall over my ears.

Of course, she had two hands and wasn't trying to do it backwards while looking into a mirror. I'd once said to Kalinda Black that I wished I could take my head off and have it on my lap when trying to do my hair and she'd said if she could put her own head in her own lap she wouldn't waste her time doing her hair. She's a very bad person. You don't want to have anything to do with her.

Eliza expressed some surprise at the length and sharpness of my hairpins.

'A lady should never be unarmed, Eliza.'

She nodded, twisting up another piece of hair. 'Indeed, madam, so my granny always said. And I myself always have a hat pin handy.'

'Good for your granny. I hope it worked for her.'

'She had three husbands, madam, so I'm not sure.'

I laughed. 'This is a very nice house, Eliza.'

'Oh yes. My mum was ever so pleased when I got a place here. Very well-respected family in these parts, ma'am.'

She held out the blue shawl and at that moment, the gong sounded.

Markham and Thomas helped our fallen warrior down the stairs. Actually, Peterson did very well. As he said, the prospect of meeting a vengeful spirit who could strike people dead in a locked room was enough to get anyone back on their feet.

Mr Harewood was waiting for him at the foot of the stairs. He and his wife really were the perfect hosts. Introductions were made and Peterson hobbled slowly – and bravely – into the dining room to meet the other guests.

He bowed over Mrs Harewood's hand. 'I really must apologise for thrusting myself on you in this manner,' he said.

She had herself well under control. 'Not at all, Dr Peterson. We are delighted to have this opportunity to welcome you to

Harewood Hall. Such good fortune we were nearby when you had your accident.'

'Indeed,' said Peterson. 'I am a stranger to this part of the county, ma'am. Have you lived here long?'

The clock struck the hour as he was seated on her right hand. Everyone paused in the middle of seating themselves and stared. A nice little Victorian tableau. Then the chimes ceased and everything started up again. I was placed with Mr Harewood at the head of the table. Mr Chance and the reverend occupied the middle ground.

'The family has been here for just over two hundred years, I believe,' she said, answering Peterson's question. 'We held for the king in the Civil War and were rewarded with this estate.'

'A pleasant part of the world,' observed Peterson as the first course was served. Clear soup with a distinct taste of sherry. Quite nice, actually, but the first thing I realised was that it wasn't actually that long since I'd enjoyed a very substantial tea. On the other hand, everyone else was about to tuck in and I rather felt I had the honour of St Mary's to uphold, so I tucked in too. I stopped listening and concentrated on not slurping or spilling it down my front.

Dinner was tense but at least this time no one dropped anything. Possibly in an effort to push back the shadows – both real and imagined – Barnstaple had caused too many candles to be lighted. The wind outside was strong, the heavy curtains moved constantly and the draught caused the flames to flicker. To me, every face took on a gargoyle-ish quality.

Barnstaple and John waited on us, which rather limited the topics of conversation. We ran through the normal stuff – the weather, the harvest this year, the forthcoming Boxing Day meet at the Royal Oak, the doings of the dear queen, the vicar's Christmas Day sermon. They gossiped a little over their neighbours, although only very discreetly in the face of Mr Lillywhite's disapproving silence. I wondered if there was anything of which the Reverend Lillywhite did approve. Apart from a free dinner, of course.

'A doctor?' said Mr Chance to Peterson, as the plates were cleared. 'Are you a medical man, perhaps?'

'Historian,' said Peterson as his dish was taken away.

'Hence his inability to remain on his own feet,' I said and everyone laughed very cheerfully.

The clock struck the quarter hour as the fish was served. I had no idea what it was. The fish, I mean. Not salmon and not prawns – that's all I can say. Freshly fried in butter and served with a creamy sauce. Rather tasty, though.

'Just outside of Rushford,' I said in reply to Mr Chance's query as to *exactly* where I hailed from. I suspected he was by no means as amiable and good-natured as he appeared. Those dark eyes were very shrewd. 'St Mary's Priory. Do you know it at all, sir?'

'I have never visited that part of the county,' he said which was a relief because I'd been half expecting him to do the '*Oh, do you know so-and-so?*' trick and I never know whether to say yes or no.

'Although,' he continued, 'I believe there are some very interesting Roman remains near Rushford.'

Everyone stiffened in case mentioning the Romans set the reverend's pagan phobia off again, but fortunately he was immersed in his fish.

Chance also could eat and talk at the same time. He should

119

apply to St Mary's. Although I had to say there would be Fat Chance of that.

Did you see what I did there? Told you the universe should have killed me when it had the Chance. Behave yourself, Maxwell. And possibly drink less wine.

Reverend Lillywhite's appetite was impressive. How anyone could remain that skeletal with what he put away was a mystery. As far as I was aware there was no Mrs Lillywhite – unsurprising – so he might only ever eat when he visited his parishioners. Personally, I'd have locked the doors, turned out the lights and pretended to be out. Or converted to another belief system. I watched his little hands scuttle across the table. Like white spiders.

Dinner was very leisurely. Nothing was rushed. I wondered if everyone was as conscious of time ticking away as I was. The half hour sounded. This time, no one looked at the clock.

The entrée followed. I was beginning to flag but Peterson's appetite appeared unimpaired so – challenge accepted. Roast beef, stewed mutton and a capon were all served, each with numerous side dishes. I spared a thought for Markham, concealed out there in the hall somewhere, clutching a stale crust as he watched all these dishes go by. Although, knowing him, his harem of adoring housemaids would have ensured he was adequately nourished before he set out.

I had made up my mind to decline the dessert – I was well and truly stuffed and I thought such restraint would make me look elegant – but they wheeled in a raspberry cream and several cheesecakes and my resolve crumbled. I did lay off the wine, though. I was going to have enough difficulty staying awake as it was. Mr Harewood partook fairly freely, however, and I really couldn't blame him. The handsome marble clock on the mantel was chiming the quarter hours with frightening regularity and every time it did so the conversation would die away to pick up again moments later. The hour of the Ordeal was approaching.

At last, Mrs Harewood smiled at me and we ladies withdrew to let the men get on with their carousing. Barnstaple was just wheeling in the most massive cheeseboard I'd ever seen in my life – and they'd be passing the port around as well. I just wanted to lie down and go to sleep for a week or so. I was convinced I'd never need to eat again. No wonder they all wore corsets.

Mrs Harewood paused in the hall. An icy draught swirled around my ankles. I shivered. She was right, the house was chilly. I pulled my shawl around me.

'There will be a good fire in the sitting room,' she said. 'Do go in. I shall just check on Baby Jamie and then I will join you.'

'May I come too? He's such a lovely little boy.'

I think she was grateful not to have to go alone and I wanted a better idea of the layout of the house, so we set off up the stairs which were wide and shallow with an intricately carved balustrade curving up the wall. But it was so cold. Even the heavy chandelier swung gently, making the shadows dance. I felt the atmosphere thickening around me. I shivered again and concentrated on the peacock-blue-and-gold carpet. There was hard, bright colour everywhere in this house.

Mrs Harewood carried a lamp, even though the landings were well lit. Our footsteps were silent on the thick runner but more than once I stopped to look behind me . . .

The nursery was on the top floor. At some time during its

history, a number of tiny attic rooms had been knocked into one and the sloping roofs made it cosy. Nanny was still crocheting by the fire and Baby Jamie was fast asleep in his crib, his little fists clenched over his head. The wet nurse/nursery maid – Annie – was working her way through a pile of darning. Both got to their feet, curtseyed, and then sat back down again. There was a cheerful fire, plenty of coal in the scuttle and a good supply of candles. Thankfully, in this little haven of light, warmth and security, no clock ticked the moments away. All was peaceful.

'Everything is under control, madam,' said Nanny in her comfortable voice. 'We'll ring if we need anything – although we won't – and Thomas says he will come at once.'

'You are not to leave Jamie.'

I had the impression it wasn't the first time she'd said that today but Nanny nodded imperturbably. 'Not even for a second, madam.'

'And don't let anyone in. Not before dawn, anyway.'

'No, madam.'

Mrs Harewood peered into the crib for final reassurance. The light from a nearby lamp illuminated her features. Anxiety was etching deep lines across her young face.

'Thank you, Nanny. Lock the door behind us.'

'I shall, madam. Good night.'

I was quite sorry to leave the warmth and security of the nursery and I was certain Mrs Harewood would be as well. I suspected only her duty to her husband was keeping her from spending the night with her child.

The tall grandfather clock in the hall was just striking ten as we came down the stairs.

Downstairs the servants were preparing for the Ordeal. Maids rustled past, building up the fires and lighting lamps in every room. Branches of candles and oil lamps stood everywhere. Every nook and cranny was to be ruthlessly illuminated. Pairs of servants would be stationed on every floor. Every door, every window was locked. There would be no hiding place anywhere in this house tonight. Unless, of course, something was already inside the house, in which case, I couldn't help thinking, we'd locked it in with us.

Outside, the wind howled and rain lashed the windows. It was a dark and stormy night . . . But to be honest, I didn't think anything would happen. I honestly thought that Mr Harewood senior's death was just a blip. That he had succumbed to something that the medical profession of the time had been unable to identify and the fact that he had died on the night of the Ordeal was just unfortunate. Or perhaps he had somehow managed to commit suicide in some unknown manner and arranged for his body to be found in the Haunted Room to spare his family the shame and scandal. Suicide was still illegal in this time. Anyone failing in their attempt could look forward to a spell in prison.

This family wasn't fabulously wealthy – not by fabulously wealthy standards – but now I knew what I was looking for, there were signs of . . . not poverty, but careful expenditure everywhere. Some carpets were a little threadbare in places. The linen had been carefully darned. There would be money made available if they could prove it was for the benefit of the estate but nothing for their own personal use. I wondered if perhaps they were living off Mrs Harewood's dowry. On the other hand, the servants easily outnumbered the family, and threadbare or not, their house was comfortable, and they were obviously getting by. Given what had happened to Mr Harewood's father, why would they put themselves through all this? In the end, I came straight out with it and asked Mrs Harewood, who hesitated.

'I'm sorry,' I said. 'That was very impolite of me.'

'No,' she said. 'I think if it was just us, then perhaps we might not choose to undertake the Ordeal. Our personal needs are very simple. But Jamie's future is at stake. And remember, until recently, the Ordeal had been just a quaint little family ceremony. A ghost story to be told around the fire at Christmas. Chilling at the time and then the lights go up and it's quickly forgotten as we send round the rum punch. But for Jamie's sake – he must come into his inheritance when the time comes.' She smiled at me. 'Every parent wants to give their child the best they can, don't they?'

Not always, in my experience, but I smiled and nodded because there were enough storm clouds building on her horizon without me telling her that there was a very good chance young Jamie might not survive long enough to undertake the Ordeal anyway. I worked it out in my head. He'd be nineteen in 1914. And if Henry was still around, then he'd be in his midforties. I couldn't remember the upper age limit for being called up. If Baby Jamie didn't make it through World War I then this might be the last ever Ordeal of the Haunted Room.

I blinked and returned to 1895. Back to Mrs Harewood. The clock was just striking half past ten. Not long now.

'Are you able to tell me about the last time? Mr Harewood's father? Obviously, you weren't present then.'

'No. Henry was, of course. And the reverend, Mr Lillywhite. It's part of the conditions that two independent witnesses attend the Ordeal so Mr Chance was here, too. He's been our man of business for years. And his father before him.'

'So everyone here will know what to expect?'

'They will. And here they come now. And Barnstaple with the tea.'

Oh, dear God – more food and drink.

Everyone served themselves this time. Leaving the men gathered around the fire and talking shooting, Mrs Harewood and I retreated to the other end of the room.

'Do you feel able to tell me exactly what will happen? How does this work?'

'Well,' she said nervously, beginning to fiddle with her shawl again. 'The only way in and out of the room is through the door. The windows were nailed shut years and years ago. The door is solid and there are three locks. Henry has one key. Mr Chance has one and Mr Lillywhite has the third. All three must be used together in order to gain access.'

I wondered if that was the key on Chance's watch chain.

She swallowed. 'Once inside – and I dread to think what sort of state the room will be in because no one can ever enter it – we'll make him as comfortable as we can. Barnstaple will set a fire and light the candles and then, on the stroke of midnight, we . . . lock him in and leave him there.'

Her voice trembled. The clock struck a quarter to eleven and I tried to distract her. 'How will he pass the time?'

She tried to smile. 'Well, he will have his books so it's perfectly possible he won't even notice where he is. And a decanter, and Mrs Trent will send something up for him to eat, and so, apart from the dust and dirt, for him, it may not be so different from a normal evening.'

'Doesn't it worry you, having a locked room in the house?'

'To be honest, Mrs Farrell, until my father-in-law's death, I rarely thought about it. Now . . .' She sighed and stared into the fire.

I didn't want to, but politeness compelled me to say, 'Mrs Harewood, it occurs to me this is a family matter and we are intruding. Would you prefer us to go to our rooms and leave you in peace? At least it would relieve you of your obligation to entertain your guests.'

She seized my wrist. 'Oh no. Please, I will admit I was a little vexed that today of all days you should . . . but since Mr Chance and the reverend were here anyway, I now find I am very grateful for your company. It is so pleasant to meet some people whose lives are not overshadowed by this . . . ritual.'

'Will you wait up all night?'

'Well, I shan't sleep of course – not once Henry enters that room – but I shall retire to my chamber . . .' I suspected she didn't want to have to entertain Chance and Lillywhite through the long night and I didn't blame her in the slightest, 'and then, I suppose, we just . . . wait.'

And that was just what we did. Mr Lillywhite clasped his hands and closed his eyes. I suppose that's the advantage of being a vicar – people never know if you're praying or whether you've just dropped off after another heavy meal.

The clock struck eleven. I counted the strokes. I think we all did. In an hour's time . . . We sat and watched the hands on the clock inch their way towards midnight. The clock struck half past eleven. All conversation had long since ceased. We sat in silence for a few minutes and then, suddenly, evidently unwilling to hang around any longer, Mr Harewood slapped his knees and rose to his feet.

'I can bear this no longer. Let's get it over with, shall we? Is everything ready, Barnstaple?'

Barnstaple ceased to tidy away the tea things and looked across to his master. A candelabrum stood on the table at his elbow, lighting his face from below. For a very fleeting moment, he was no longer the comfortable, conventional butler, supervising the staff with quiet efficiency. Just for one moment, in the flickering candlelight, his face was full of shadows and mystery. And then it was gone and he was Barnstaple again. 'Everything is ready, sir.'

'Then off I go.'

It took a while for them to organise themselves. I simply picked up my shawl and draped it around my shoulders. I've always believed in travelling light. We trailed out of the room. The whole house blazed with light. They must have lit every chandelier, every sconce, every candelabrum, every oil lamp. Shadows had been banished. It must have taken them ages to light this lot.

Mr and Mrs Harewood led the way. He clutched an armful of books, saying over his shoulder, 'An excellent opportunity for me to reread the *Iliad*, Chance.'

Mr Lillywhite frowned. I suspected he felt it would have been more appropriate for Mr Harewood to have armed himself with the family Bible, and he might have been right. Given the size of most of them I reckoned it could do some real damage if wielded in anger.

Messrs Chance and Lillywhite followed the Harewoods and

they in turn were followed by Barnstaple and a gaggle of housemaids bearing all the various pieces of kit deemed essential for the coming Ordeal. Peterson, leaning heavily on Markham, limped behind them and I trailed along at the back. My traditional position in the scheme of things.

As Markham had said, the room was on the ground floor, next to the library. It would have been on the east side of the house so I could easily see it being a favourite place for ladies to sit in the mornings. Although not any longer.

We halted outside a door indistinguishable from any of the others. I was rather disappointed there were no bloody handprints around the handle, or any deep gouges in the wood as a terrified occupant had clawed at the door, driven mad by terror. Although as Peterson later pointed out, they would all be on the inside of the door, Max, wouldn't they, you idiot?

There was, however, a brand-new lock. To replace the one from Mr Harewood senior's Ordeal, presumably. When they'd broken down the door and found him sitting there . . .

Mr Harewood clutched his half dozen books and Barnstaple supported a silver tray with a decanter, a glass and several covered plates of food barely sufficient to keep a normal man on his feet for a week. John carried a box of kindling, two housemaids had brought a coal scuttle each, and an excited-looking Eliza was burdened with a dozen or so long candles.

There were three locks on the door just as Mrs Harewood had said. One at head height, one above the door handle and one below.

I heard the big clock in the hall begin to strike a quarter to midnight.

There was a moment's silence and then the solicitor, Chance,

128

stepped up. 'We must not be late. If you are ready, Mr Lillywhite.'

From the look on his face, the reverend was neither willing nor able. He was, however, ready. Wearing what could only be described as his 'I am among pagans' expression, he stepped up to the door.

Reaching up, he inserted the key in the highest lock, which turned with little effort. I suspected Barnstaple had been round with an oil can and feather. Withdrawing the key, the reverend stepped back to make room for Mr Chance – who was not smiling, just for once. He copied the vicar's actions, opening the lock below the handle.

They both stepped back and finally it was Henry Harewood's turn. Handing his books to his wife to hold for him, he took out his key and inserted it into the final lock. The sound of it turning was very loud in the silence. Withdrawing the key, he tucked it into his breast pocket. I assumed the three separate locks with their three separate keys were to prevent any unauthorised access to the Haunted Room. Or unauthorised egress as well. Henry might have a key but he'd be unable to get out of the room if the other two refused to use theirs. I had a sudden thought. Would they let him out if he begged them? I could picture a terrified Henry Harewood clawing at the door, screaming to be released, and a smiling Chance refusing to budge, saying, 'It's for your own good, my dear sir. Only another six hours to go . . .' while the reverend intoned a psalm in the darkness.

The door swung silently open. Darkness yawned at us. There was a cold, damp breath of air in our faces that was suddenly very unpleasant. Our candles flickered and shadows jumped across the wall. One of the maids shrieked. Not to be left out, another one or two others screamed as well. Disappointingly, no one swooned.

Henry Harewood raised his candle high. I think anyone would have forgiven him a slight tremor but the light shone steady and strong. Without hesitation, he crossed the threshold and stepped into the room. The rest of us remained in the doorway, peering in.

I couldn't see much – Barnstaple was substantial, even for a butler – but the dim light revealed a thick coating of dust over every horizontal surface. No footprints showed. Nor fingerprints, either. Every surface was completely undisturbed and it was very obvious that nothing had been moved and no one had entered this room since the last Ordeal. The faded curtains had not even been drawn back from the windows. I could imagine everyone scrabbling to get Mr Harewood senior out of the room as quickly as possible, slamming the door behind them. Keeping whatever lived in this room safely contained behind the door. I looked around. Was it watching at this very moment? Watching us from the shadows? Waiting for us to leave, when it would have Henry Harewood to play with during all those long hours until the sun rose again?

I could hear the rain still lashing against the window panes behind the curtains. The rain hadn't let up for one moment since our arrival. Despite the high wind whistling in the chimney, the curtains were quite still. Unusually for a house this age there was no draught here. The windows were indeed tightly sealed.

This had clearly once been a very pleasant room but now, sadly, was musty, fusty and dusty, which I thought sounded like three cartoon characters, and it occurred to me that possibly I had had too much wine at dinner after all.

A sofa which would normally reside by the fire had been pushed under one of the windows. A long table, thick with dust, would have been ideal for reading, dressmaking, bonnet trimming, husband hunting, watercolours, or any of the pastimes deemed suitable for Victorian ladies by Victorian men.

A delicate chandelier hung overhead and the central square of carpet – where not covered in dirt – showed a pattern of garlanded roses. With what would, no doubt, have been a pretty view out over the gardens, I could see it would once have been a lovely room. But not tonight. Tonight it made no attempt to welcome the intruders.

The mirror over the mantel was spotted with age and threw back distorted versions of ourselves. Everything in here felt not quite right. Just a little off. And very, very cold. I could see Henry Harewood's breath clouding in the damp air.

He walked slowly across the room, holding his candle high. A number of us followed on behind him. I have to say – I wasn't that keen to enter but I'd never hear the end of it if I didn't, so I followed Peterson and Markham into the room.

John peeled off to begin clearing the remains of the old fire and laying the new. None of the maids would come in – they clustered outside, nervously peering around the doorjamb, squeaking and jumping at every loud noise.

Mrs Harewood also refused to enter. She stood outside with the maids as Barnstaple deployed his forces. John was laying the fire with professional speed. Barnstaple was laying the table – because of course Mr Harewood hadn't eaten anything for two hours, which was probably illegal in middle-class

131

Victorian England. He spread a crisp white cloth across part of the dusty table – because he had standards, obviously – and began, slowly and meticulously, to lay the table. Napkins, plates, forks . . . Bringing a breath of normality to the situation. Whatever horrors gathered in the corners of the room, Barnstaple was checking the maids had packed the right forks.

The solicitor, Chance, prowled around, checking the windows, and finished eventually at the mantel, where he took up a position that would enable him to observe everything. The reverend stood by the table with an expression of stern determination.

John took a spill from the jar on the mantel. Lighting it from a candle, he applied it to the fire. A small, unenthusiastic yellow flame ran along a splinter of kindling. It was touch and go whether the fire would light. He was already reaching for another spill when, finally, it caught.

The footman plied the bellows like a madman before the flames changed their mind, presumably. I was certain lighting fires wasn't usually part of his job and he just wanted to be out of this room as quickly as possible.

Looking back through the door into the warm, brightly lit, *normal* world beyond, I could see the maids had all retreated to a safe distance. I suspected Mrs Harewood's servants had divided themselves into two camps – those who wanted to see what was happening here – from a safe distance, of course – and those who couldn't even be dynamited out of the Servants' Hall tonight.

Mr Harewood surveyed the old armchair close to the fire. The one in which his father had died. 'I think, Barnstaple . . .'

'Of course, sir.'

He made a gesture and John ceased his work with the bellows. Together the two of them removed the armchair to a dark corner, bringing up another from the other side of the room. I personally wouldn't have done that. The thought of that old chair, with its former occupant, staring at me, unseen, from that dark corner . . . while the shadows gathered . . . I wondered if it had occurred to anyone there might be two ghosts in this room now.

However, Mr Harewood seemed happy enough, arranging it just so before the fire and thumping the cushions. A cloud of dust arose. He stepped back, coughing.

'Henry,' said his wife reprovingly from the doorway. 'Your coat.'

He smiled faintly. 'Sorry, my dear.' But she had brought another welcome breath of normality to the room. Or perhaps it was just the fire warming things up.

Barnstaple was lighting the candles around the room. Was it my imagination or were they not making any difference? I could imagine the resentful shadows fighting back. This was the night of the Winter Solstice. This was *their* night.

Peterson, Markham and I were clustered out of everyone's way, just inside the doorway. We watched Barnstaple set a small table alongside the chair, dust it fastidiously, and place the decanter and glass on the top. The fire was blazing nicely and if you didn't know the purpose of this room and couldn't smell the must, then everything would be lovely.

'Well,' said Henry cheerfully, looking around. 'A good fire, books and wine. I think I shall spend a very comfortable night.'

Mr Chance looked down at his grimy hands, grimaced, and pulled a handkerchief from his pocket. Wiping his hands, he regarded the dark smudges with distaste. Looking up, he saw me watching him, lifted his chin defiantly and tossed it into the fire. 'Shall we look at our watches, gentlemen?'

I was pleased to see he had a slight struggle removing his watch from his tightly straining pocket. I suspected our Mr Chance visited Harewood Hall rather frequently. On the Off-Chance of a good meal, perhaps. OK, I promise I'll stop now.

Peterson and Markham had remained nearer to the door. I knew if anything was to happen, Markham, at least, wouldn't miss a trick.

'Gentlemen,' said Mr Chance, softly. 'I make the time six minutes to midnight.'

'And I,' said Mr Lillywhite.

Mr Harewood fumbled for his own watch. 'And I.' He walked over to his wife. 'Don't wait, my dear. Go back into the warm. I shall see you before you know it.'

Mrs Harewood took an audible breath, stepped into the room and took her husband's hand. 'Do you have everything you need, Henry?'

'I do indeed.' He patted her hand.

She lifted her chin. 'In that case, my dear, I shall wish you a very good night.' Her voice was firm and her glance didn't waver.

He kissed her cheek. 'Goodnight, Letitia. Sleep well.'

She took one long, last look around the room – just a con-scientious wife making sure her husband had everything to make him comfortable – bade us all a general goodnight and withdrew. Slowly and without running. I admired her restraint.

Mr Chance began to move towards the door. 'Do you have your key, Mr Harewood?'

He patted his breast pocket. 'Quite safe, Chance.'

'Please remember, Mr Harewood, under no circumstances can the door be opened before the end of the Ordeal. That is very important.'

Henry Harewood nodded.

For a moment I thought Mr Chance would say something else – something comforting, perhaps, but after a long pause he said only, 'Remember, Mr Harewood, to lock your side of the door.'

'I shan't forget.'

The Reverend Lillywhite bowed formally and followed him out, very carefully not touching anything in case he caught a nasty dose of paganism.

We all listened as Mr Harewood locked the door from his side. As he finished, the clock in the hall began to toll midnight. The time of the Ordeal was upon us.

I watched Chance lock the door and pocket his key. I watched Lillywhite lock the door and pocket his key. Having done so, they seemed at rather a loss as to what to do next.

Peterson yawned and said it was time for him to go to bed as well and that seemed to be a signal for everyone to shuffle their feet and disperse to a muttered chorus of goodnights.

Markham had already disappeared but I would bet good money he wasn't far away.

The house was completely silent as I helped Peterson back to his room. Mr Harewood was locked in for the night and come what may, no one would let him out before morning.

Eliza was waiting for me in my room. It would seem that in addition to the shawl, Mrs Harewood had also loaned me a

135

nightdress and wrapper. Not a froth of lace and ribbons, I noted, but something sensible in light wool. I sighed. At what point in my life had the universe deemed me unsuitable for frivolous nightwear and decided that wool was to be my lot henceforth? But it was a very pretty pink and, watching the curtains billow slightly at the windows, I was certain I'd be grateful for the warmth.

Eliza was very helpful with the corsets – which made me glad I'd gone with contemporary underwear. Uncorseted women were an affront to God and society. And she wouldn't let me take down my own hair, either. She busied herself tidying my stuff away, spinning it out as long as she could. I suspected she didn't want to walk back to the Servants' Hall on her own. Eventually, even she couldn't linger any longer.

'Shall I leave the candles burning, ma'am?'

'Yes, please, but take one for yourself if you need it.'

I climbed into bed for the look of the thing. It was soft and the sheets were warm. She'd obviously been at them with the warming pan. She turned at the door and bobbed a curtsey. 'Goodnight, ma'am.'

'Goodnight, Eliza.'

She closed the door quietly behind her.

I waited five minutes for her to get clear. The clock on the mantel said twenty past twelve. I pulled on my unglamorous but warm dressing gown and eased open my door. Believe it or not, such scandalous behaviour was probably the most hazardous part of this night. Peterson was only across the landing but brother or otherwise, anyone caught creeping into a bedroom not their own in these times would be out on their ear before the shouting stopped. I stood for a moment, listening carefully.

I had my story ready. If anyone appeared, I thought I had heard my brother calling. But there was nothing. No sinister footsteps. Not even a mouse scratching behind the wooden panelling. The landing was well lit by a large candelabra at each end and another at the head of the stairs, and there were no hiding places.

I slipped out through the door, closing it quietly behind me, and ghosted across to Peterson's room. He was alone. Markham, I guessed, was still concealed downstairs, watching for foul play.

Peterson was wearing gaily striped PJs in blue and white, which is not a sight to encounter unexpectedly. I did not reel but that's only because I'm supposed to be a highly trained professional. 'Good God, you look like a convict.'

He smoothed the front of his PJs and looked down at himself. 'I thought I looked quite dashing.'

'First things first,' I said. 'Let's have a look at your foot.'

Actually, it looked much better. Still black but the swelling had greatly subsided. A tribute to the housekeeper's ointment, I said. A tribute to his superior constitution, he said.

'I'm fine,' he continued, bravely. 'As long as I keep my foot flat and don't flex it, it hardly hurts at all.'

'Good,' I said, losing interest. It had only been a polite enquiry anyway. I'd have said good if it had actually fallen off and I'd accidentally kicked it across the floor.

'What do you think will happen?' he said, leaning back on his pillows.

'Honestly?' I said. 'Absolutely nothing.'

And then we heard it. Coming from below. A dull, pounding noise. And a voice shouting for help.

I ran across the room, wrenched open the door and then remembered Peterson.

'Go,' he said, struggling to get off the bed. 'Don't wait for me.'

I ran out into the corridor. All the candles were still lit. Nothing had changed. I don't know why I thought it would. Only about half an hour had passed since we'd left Henry Harewood to face his Ordeal in the Haunted Room. I headed for the stairs. The pounding was louder now and I could hear the words.

'Help. Help. Let me out. For God's sake, let me out. I can't . . . I . . .'

I flew down the stairs, the frantic shouts ringing in my ears. Chance and Lillywhite were emerging from the sitting room. The reverend's face had turned from an unhealthy grey to chalk white. It wasn't an improvement.

Markham was at the door, rattling the handle. 'Unlock the door, Mr Harewood,' he shouted. And then to me, 'We have to get him out.'

I could hear Mrs Harewood's voice coming down the stairs. 'Henry? Oh my God, Henry. What is happening?'

'Get him out,' shouted Markham again, pushing the Reverend Lillywhite towards the door in a very disrespectful manner.

Lillywhite hesitated. 'I don't think you quite understand . . .' He stood close to the door. 'Henry, my boy. Just hold on. This means so much to you. Think of your wife and child.'

The voice grew fainter. 'Let me out. Can't . . .'

'You heard him,' I shouted, wheeling on the vacillating vicar. 'Let him out. Before it's too late.'

Yes, I know what you're thinking. We're not supposed to

meddle. We're supposed to let events take their course. Record and document only. Never interfere. I think it fair to say that for most of us at St Mary's, this still needs some work.

The pounding on the door was becoming weaker. Mrs Harewood arrived in a hurry. Elbowing the reverend into the middle of next week she began to batter at the door.

I seized the reverend's coat lapel. *'Give me your key.'*

He was outraged. 'Madam, I . . .'

'Give me your key or I'll knock you senseless and take it from your unconscious body.'

He recoiled. Literally. And yes, I know I'll never go to heaven but have you seen the sort of people who qualify for heaven? Seriously? You want to spend eternity with people like that?

With trembling fingers, he pulled out his key and handed it over. Chance, eyeing me as if I was some sort of madwoman, was already holding his out to me.

'It's no use,' shouted Mrs Harewood. 'Henry has the other!'

By now, Barnstaple and the two footmen had joined us. At the other end of the hall, the maids fluttered around the servants' door, hands to their mouths, white and frightened. Some of them were crying. Eliza, however, was brandishing a rolling pin.

And then, the pounding ceased. In the sudden silence, something slithered down the door. I heard the thud as it hit the floor.

'Henry!' screamed Mrs Harewood. The maids all screamed too. She threw herself at the door, slapping the panels. 'Henry. Open the door. Use your key. Henry!'

There was only silence from the other side of the door. Mrs Harewood was very nearly hysterical.

139

'Perhaps, Mrs Farrell,' said the reverend stiffly, removing my hand from his lapel, 'your time would be better served attending to Mrs Harewood.'

'No, I don't think so,' I said. 'Stand aside, sir.'

Peterson arrived, hobbling down the last few stairs. 'I'll see to Mrs Harewood. Markham – get that door open.'

I handed him the keys, but if Henry hadn't unlocked the door from his side, they'd be useless. They'd have to break the door down. Again.

He hadn't. Markham turned both keys but nothing happened. The door refused to budge. And time was ticking on. There was now no sound at all from the Haunted Room.

I looked at Markham. I think we both suspected the same thing. Mrs Harewood was beyond speech just at this moment so I enquired of Barnstaple whether gas lighting had been installed in the room.

He blinked at the question and then shook his head. 'No, Mr Harewood would only consent to gas in the main rooms downstairs. He felt . . .'

That was all I wanted to know. If the room was filling with gas and there were all those candles . . . and that blazing fire . . . then we'd have abandoned poor Henry and concentrated on evacuating the building. Especially Baby Jamie upstairs. But there was no gas. Whatever dangers awaited us, being blown to pieces was not one of them.

Markham was eyeing our resources. Barnstaple was big and heavy. And John was a sturdy lad. In a couple of years, he too would have achieved the traditional butler silhouette.

'Break the door down,' he said tersely.

It was a solid door. In films and holos, doors fly open if the hero so much as gives them a stern glance. This one put up a fight. The two men threw themselves at it again and again, seemingly making no impact at all. I was about to suggest someone try to batter their way through the windows from the outside when, with a great splintering of wood, the lock tore away. Several housemaids screamed but disappointingly, no one swooned.

The door should have burst open, but this one moved only a few inches and then rebounded off something on the other side. Markham shoved John aside. 'He's collapsed on the other side of the door. Push.'

He, John and Barnstaple put their shoulders against the door and heaved.

Mrs Harewood was sobbing loudly, wringing her hands and calling her husband's name, but there was only silence from inside the room. Henry Harewood lay unconscious on the floor, but what if there were something else in there with him . . . ?

I looked around. Not far away stood one of those disgusting elephant's feet, a useful receptacle for a number of umbrellas and walking sticks. I ran over, seized something substantial, ran back again and stood ready, stick raised high. If there was anything waiting to burst out of that room then it was going to have to get past me.

The three of them heaved again, pushing Mr Harewood's body along the floor as the door opened until it came to rest against the carpet from where it refused to budge. Markham squeezed through the gap. Not for the first time, I gave thanks he was quite small.

Seizing him under the arms, he dragged Henry away from the door. Barnstaple and John surged forwards.

Markham held up his hand. 'No, no. Stay out.'

They cast fearful glances around the room, obviously expecting the worst, but I'd seen Henry Harewood's face. I took a deep breath and ran into the room.

Wrenching aside the curtains, I averted my face and used my stick to bash away at the window panes. They were small and there were a lot of them but I got there in the end. Cold, harsh air billowed into the room.

'Now,' said Markham to John, waiting in the doorway. He seized Henry under the arms and John grabbed his feet. Together, they carried him from the room.

'Dear God,' shuddered Mr Lillywhite, looking down at Henry's face. 'The devil walks tonight.'

Standing over by the windows, I took the opportunity to have a good look around.

Nothing much had changed. The fire still burned with a bright, orangey glow so nothing had come down the chimney. At some point, Henry'd poured himself a glass of wine but not touched it. Likewise, the plate of food was uneaten. Until I got to them, the windows had all been sealed shut. The curtains had been laden with dust. The candles still burned in their sconces. And there were no gas jets in the room. I looked up at the ceiling. I'm not sure what I expected to see but it wasn't there anyway. I looked down at the floor. A dusty parquet, with footprints showing where we'd burst in, and a trail of them to the armchair and the fire; but the rest of the dusty floor was undisturbed. Wherever I looked there were absolutely no clues at all.

The Reverend Lillywhite stood at the door, still apparently reluctant to enter in case he became contaminated. Mr Chance,

142

a lawyer to his fingertips, had taken up his favourite position at the mantel.

I went to stand by him, saying quietly, 'What happens if Mr Harewood dies?'

He pursed his lips. 'Well, when Mr Harewood senior was discovered, we resealed the room and waited until the next Winter Solstice after his death.'

I nodded. 'Which was just one year. But if this Mr Harewood dies, it will be a much longer wait for Baby Jamie, however.'

'Indeed.' He frowned heavily. 'I'm not sure the estate will be able to stand it.'

'It's best Mr Henry doesn't die, then.'

He pursed his lips again and nodded.

Behind me, Mrs Harewood, much calmer now we had her husband out of the Haunted Room, was instructing them to carry him to the family sitting room. She led the way. I could hear housemaids scurrying hither and thither under a volley of instructions. The reverend trailed after them, leaving me, Chance and Peterson.

Mr Chance leaned against the mantel and closed his eyes. 'It has happened again,' he said faintly. 'I don't believe it.'

'Neither do I,' I said.

He opened his eyes. 'I fail to take your meaning, Mrs Farrell.'

I said nothing.

He narrowed his eyes, suddenly a much less cheerful chappie than a couple of hours ago. 'Who are you?' he said. 'Where do you come from? Who are your people?'

'I told you. Rushford. St Mary's Priory. My husband is Leon Farrell – the famous explorer.'

'But you are travelling alone.'

'With my brother.'

His eyes narrowed further as he stared from me to Peterson and back again. 'I can see no resemblance.'

'Well, thank heavens for that,' said Peterson, quite unkindly, I thought. Brothers.

'I think, Mrs Farrell,' said the solicitor, 'that you should attend to Mrs Harewood.'

'Yes,' said Peterson. 'I'd feel much more confident of Henry's survival if you were in the same room as him, Max.'

Chance looked up. 'What do you mean by that, sir?'

'He'll be all right for the moment,' I said. 'Markham won't let him out of his sight.'

Peterson said nothing.

Eliza appeared in the doorway with the cheerful chaplain behind her. 'Oh, ma'am . . . sirs . . .' She bobbed a curtsey. 'Mr Markham asks if you could join him at your earliest convenience, ma'am.'

I was pretty certain Markham's exact words had been *tell her to get her arse in here.*

'How is Mr Harewood?' asked Peterson.

'They say he is still living, sir.'

'I'm on my way,' I said, and lifted my dressing gown out of the dust.

'And I,' said Peterson, 'will perform the most vital function of all and guard this room.'

Mr Lillywhite drew himself up. The phrase *pillar of the church* took on a whole new meaning. 'I really don't think that is at all necessary. There's nothing of value in here.'

'I'm not so sure,' said Peterson. 'But I'll stay anyway. Just in case.'

Chance bustled towards us, saying importantly, 'As the family representative, I should be the one to take charge here.'

Peterson smiled gently. Those who think he's just a nice bloke with hair like a haystack don't usually find out he's not until it's too late. 'Charge is already taken,' he said, quietly.

Chance bridled. 'And who are you, sir, to assume . . . ?'

'Someone with no vested interest of any kind,' said Peterson. 'An unexpected arrival. A neutral observer. Now, if no one minds, I'll just . . .' He pulled up a chair and sat down with a sigh of relief.

At some point, Barnstaple had also returned. Putting these unfortunate occurrences behind him he was, once again, the perfect butler. 'May I bring you any refreshment, sir?'

Peterson shook his head. 'No, I'll just sit quietly here. I think everyone has grasped that this room is dangerous, but just in case anyone has any ideas about nipping in and out while everyone's back is turned . . .' He tailed off and smiled amiably at everyone.

Chance beat me to the sitting room but once at the doorway, politeness prevailed and he stepped aside to allow me to enter first. They'd stretched Henry Harewood on the sofa. I could see at once . . . his face . . .

Someone – Markham, I guessed – had commanded them to open the windows. The curtains billowed in the wind and heavy rain pattered on to the rather fine table underneath. No one took any notice. It felt good to feel fresh air on my face again.

Mrs Harewood, a sensible woman and excellent mother, had already removed her husband's coat, collar and tie and was busy chafing his hands.

'Brandy,' she cried, looking wildly around.

'Thank you,' said Markham. 'I don't know about anyone else but I could certainly do with one.'

It took a moment for her to grasp what he'd said and then she straightened up, all ready to annihilate him on the spot.

I moved up behind her. 'Please, Mrs Harewood, attend to your husband. I promise, you may safely leave all this to us.'

She turned to me. I felt so sorry for her. She was frightened, bewildered and in agony for her husband. The last thing she needed was her social order undermined by a scruffy individual most famous for the frequency with which his internal system offered accommodation to a record-breaking number of parasites. Tapeworms, hookworms, flukes, ringworm – unpleasant things that burrowed blindly – Markham had provided five-star accommodation to them all. None of which Mrs Harewood needed to know. She was groping for words and I took advantage of her speechlessness.

'Mrs Harewood, please. This was not an accident.'

'You mean . . . ?' She looked around. 'There are . . . it was . . . supernatural after all?'

'Good heavens, no, madam,' said Markham, cheerfully. 'Just normal, deliberate, human deceit.' He poured her a brandy and passed her the glass. 'Just a sip.'

She chugged it back like a professional and handed it back to him. Even Markham looked astonished. I felt proud of my gender although I didn't dare look at the reverend.

I watched her thoughts rearrange themselves. 'Are you

146

telling me . . .' she said, 'it was in the decanter? Someone –
here in this house – poisoned my husband?'

'Yes,' I said boldly. 'Someone here tonight meant to kill
your husband.'

She was struggling. 'But this is . . . this is monstrous. It
can't possibly be true. I can't . . . I won't believe it. Are you
suggesting that I . . . ?'

Markham and I exchanged glances. By suspecting the
decanter, Mrs Harewood had just ruled herself out. Not that I'd
had any suspicions of her anyway.

Mr Lillywhite approached. 'Mrs Harewood, madam, this
has been a trying night for you and these people – whoever
they are – are not helping by making these baseless accusations. Allow me to ring for your maid. You will feel much
happier in the peace and quiet of your own room.'

'Don't be so silly,' she said, drawing herself up. Personally,
I thought he was lucky not to get the decanter around his
lughole. 'How could I be happier in my own room when my
dear Henry lies . . .' She couldn't go on.

I suspected that never in his life had anyone called the Reverend Mr Lillywhite silly. Not to his face, anyway. He bridled.

'My dear madam, I simply meant . . . the delicate state of
your nerves . . . this unfortunate occurrence . . . and now these
preposterous accusations . . .'

'Yes,' said the solicitor, nastily, warming his bum at the fire.
'Please feel free to repeat these preposterous accusations in
front of witnesses.' He gestured around the room. 'Two professional men – if I may count myself so – a butler of unimpeachable
reputation,' he paused for a quick headcount, 'three maids and
a footman. If you dare to repeat those accusations, Mrs Farrell,

I shall have no other recourse than to a court of law. If, of course, you can persuade anyone to give credence to anything so trivial as the utterings of a female.'

Behind him, Markham slipped from the room.

'Oh,' I said easily, chugging back a brandy myself, because why not? 'I don't anticipate any difficulties. The law will listen to me.' I smiled that smile. The one that winds everyone up. 'Mrs Harewood, if you will grant me the liberty of instructing your servants, I believe we can have all this cleared up in only a few moments.'

On the sofa, Henry Harewood stirred. His wife flew to him. 'Henry.'

He tried to sit up. 'Oh, my head.' He became aware of his surroundings. 'What? Why am I here? What has happened?'

I bent over him and felt for his pulse. 'There was an incident, Mr Harewood. You are perfectly safe now. I am sure your head is splitting but you will recover much more quickly if you lie quietly. Please be assured my colleagues have everything in hand. Barnstaple, would you be kind enough to place yourself in the doorway. And perhaps John, too. It would be unfortunate if anyone felt the need to leave prematurely.'

Barnstaple looked to his mistress, who nodded. The two of them placed themselves just inside the doorway, shoulder to shoulder. I was reminded of Gandalf. '*You shall not pass!*'

'Do not let anyone leave this room. You may, however, admit my colleagues who are standing behind you at this moment.'

Markham and Peterson re-entered the room. Peterson was carrying the vase of spills from the Haunted Room. He placed it quietly on the table and sat down.

I bent over Mr Harewood and felt for his pulse again. 'Sir, Mr Harewood, are you able to tell us what happened to you?'

He endeavoured to sit up and Mrs Harewood propped some cushions behind his head.

'I locked myself in,' he said, his eyes taking on that glazed look they do when people are trying to recall something. 'I heard the other keys turning. I tugged at the door – just to assure myself it was locked. I heard Mr Chance's and Mr Lillywhite's footsteps die away and knew I was now alone.'

He continued, more strongly now. 'I took up a candelabrum and examined the room. Dust was everywhere and it was obvious no one had been in there since . . .' He choked. Mrs Harewood held a brandy to his lips. '. . . Since my father's death.'

I was watching him closely. Normally you look to see a person regain their colour but Henry Harewood was losing his. His hectic flush was slowly dying away.

He was continuing. 'Having assured myself I was completely alone, and drawn by the warmth of the flames, I seated myself by the fire and went to pour some wine.'

'It *was* the wine,' cried Mrs Harewood. 'I knew it. Henry, the wine was poisoned.'

'Please pardon my contradiction, madam,' said Markham, 'but it was not.'

Henry shook his head. 'It doesn't matter – I didn't have time to drink it.'

He chugged back some more brandy and Markham said, 'Continue, sir.'

Henry stared at Markham for a moment, obviously attempting – as so many had done before – to ascertain exactly who this person was and what did he think he was playing at, while not being so discourteous to his guests as to point out their servant's impudence. A real social conundrum but I've learned just to go with it. He – Markham – usually knows what he's doing. It amuses him to play the clown but trust me – he's not.

'Well, I opened my book. The *Iliad*.' He smiled ruefully. 'I've been meaning to enjoy Pope's translation again but there never seems to be the time.'

His eyes clouded.

'Henry!' said his wife sharply, obviously long accustomed to recalling her spouse from whichever academic hinterland he'd wandered into.

'Yes, my dear,' he said absently, and then, more strongly, 'yes. Well, I opened my book and almost from the first page the lines seemed to dance before my very eyes. I felt an over-whelming desire to relax, to lean back, to close my eyes and fall fast asleep.'

I exchanged a glance with Markham and Peterson. Peterson had laid his hand protectively on the vase. Barnstaple and John continued to stand motionless and forbidding. The Argonath.

'I have never felt so tired. No matter how I struggled, my lids were heavy. My breathing slowed. My head was so thick. I could no longer remember where I was. Or even who I was. I just had to sleep.'

His wife buried her head in his shoulder. 'Oh, Henry.'

'Now, my dear.' His movements were a little uncoordinated but he did his best to pat her in a reassuring manner very similar, probably, to the way he would calm a gun-shy spaniel. 'I am here now. It's all over.'

Mr Chance looked up from the fire. 'Sir, it is my unpleasant duty to inform you that since you did not complete the Ordeal, it is, unfortunately, not all over.'

'Oh, be quiet,' cried Mrs Harewood. I was really getting to like her. I could just see her in a green and purple sash campaigning for women's suffrage in the decades to come. But back to the plot.

Mr Lillywhite, looking still more unhealthy, even for a member of the undead – sorry, clergy – stammered, 'Forgive me, Mr Harewood, but I must ask – were you conscious of any . . . any pagan presence at all?'

Harewood laughed. 'My dear sir, I was barely conscious. I felt as if my whole body were being dragged backwards into the dark. A tiny voice was shouting at me to rouse myself, to leave the room forthwith, but my limbs were too heavy. I could not move them. I could not resist in any way.'

'But you must have, dearest,' said Mrs Harewood. 'We heard you banging on the door. We heard you shouting to be released. Do you not remember that?'

He passed his hand over his forehead. 'I am not sure. I have no recollection. I suppose I must have.'

I looked at his hands. They were unmarked and perfectly clean. I remembered the solicitor Chance's grubby paws, but for Henry there had been no bruising and his fingernails were intact. These were not the hands of a man who had pounded on a door, shouting for his life.

'Mr Harewood,' I said. 'Out of curiosity – how did you rouse yourself sufficiently to alert us to your predicament?'

Yes, I really was talking like a heroine in a Victorian melodrama. Any moment now I would be saying, 'There's just one thing I don't understand . . .' thus enabling the big strong hero to explain everything to the little woman.

'Well,' he said, blinking. 'It was the damn— the strangest thing. I felt myself going and then – so strange – a searing pain in my left arm.'

I felt the hairs on the back of my neck lift. 'Please, can you show me?'

Obligingly, he rolled back his shirt sleeve and there, two inches below the inside of his elbow – an angry red burn. That had to have hurt. No wonder it had roused him.

I stared at it. Markham stared at it. Peterson stared at it. Three of St Mary's finest, trained to deal with every emergency known to man – and quite a few that haven't been invented yet – and we gawped like idiots.

Eventually, I said, 'That looks painful.'

'It is,' he said, rolling his sleeve down again. 'But Mrs Trent will have an ointment for it. She usually does.'

'You should be grateful,' I said. 'The pain, however caused, was sufficient to bring you temporarily to your senses.'

He nodded. 'I pulled myself out of the chair. I knew this was no normal slumber. Nothing – *nothing* could have induced me to sleep – to close my eyes, even – in that accursed room. Holding to the furniture for support, I managed to propel myself towards the door. All the time I could feel my strength ebbing away and my senses sliding into darkness.'

'And yet you managed to batter at the door,' said Mr Chance, a slight note of scepticism in his voice.

He shook his head. 'I have no memory of that. I am surprised I could even lift my arm.' He smiled at his wife. 'And then I opened my eyes and found myself here.'

152

He looked around the room. We watched the realisation dawn. 'The Ordeal . . .'

'Is not important right now,' said Mrs Harewood, firmly.

'Is not important at all,' said Markham. 'You will want to take legal advice, of course, but I don't think anyone is going to quibble over this year's Ordeal. You'll get a free pass, I think.'

Mrs Harewood twisted to look at him. 'Who *are* you? Really.'

'He's my brother's manservant and we're all perfectly normal people,' I said, telling one of the biggest lies of my career. 'We are exactly who we claim to be. Chance passers-by. My brother sustained a genuine accident and we sought shelter in your house. That we arrived tonight is only a coincidence. We have no connection in any way to your Haunted Room. Which is *not* haunted, by the way.'

Another untrue statement but now was not the time to mention that something had burned Henry's arm. Something had pounded on the door.

'But . . . but a man died in there,' cried Mr Lillywhite. 'I was there. I was present at the time. I saw it all. A man died without a mark on him.'

'Except for a small but deep cut on his left arm?'

'Yes.'

'You said my husband had been poisoned,' cried Mrs Harewood. 'Is it possible his father was as well?' A thought evidently struck her. 'Was the poison somehow introduced through the cut on his arm?'

Mr Lillywhite appeared distraught. 'Madam, I cannot feel that this is a conversation at which you should be present. Your distress must be overwhelming.'

'No,' said Mrs Harewood simply. 'But my patience is rapidly coming to an end. Why . . . ?'

'Ah,' said Peterson, at the table. 'I think we can answer that question. With your permission, of course, Mr Harewood.' He held up the vase of spills he'd brought over from the Haunted Room.

'What are you doing with that?' enquired Mr Chance, sharply. 'That is estate property. Give it to me.'

'No,' said Peterson. 'I don't think so.'

'My dear man, I am the family solicitor. We have been with the family for decades and after the unfortunate circumstances this evening . . .' He stopped.

'Go on, Mr Chance.'

'Please do not make me say this in front of Mrs Harewood.'

'Say what?'

'Well, I'm very sorry to have to announce this here and now and in front of everyone, but Mr Harewood has not completed the Ordeal, has he? I am, therefore, with enormous regret, unable to allow Mr Harewood to assume full control of the estate.' He turned to Henry Harewood. 'My dear sir, never have I been more reluctant to carry out my duty.'

'So, to be clear,' said Markham, interrupting him. 'Access to the Haunted Room is by means of three different keys, and one of each is held by you, the reverend and Mr Harewood himself.'

'That is so,' Lillywhite said, puzzled. 'So no one person can access the room. Not on his own.'

'That is correct,' said Chance. 'That is how the Ordeal was designed. No one person can access the room and every part of

154

the Ordeal must be confirmed by at least two independent witnesses.'

'And no one can gain entry between the Ordeals?'

The reverend shook his head. 'No, it is always kept locked.'

Mr Chance was impatient. 'I have said this several times. No one single person can carry out the Ordeal.'

Markham was thoughtful. 'So, anything placed in the room during Mr Harewood senior's Ordeal would still be there today.'

The room was suddenly very still.

Henry Harewood was struggling to rise from the sofa. 'I don't understand. What is this about?'

'My dear sir,' said Mr Lillywhite, bending over him. 'Please do not exert yourself. You have experienced a terrible ordeal. I believe I have, on several occasions, warned of the perils of this unchristian . . .'

Harewood knocked his hand away. I had a feeling the vicar's dining days at Harewood Hall were over with.

Peterson pulled the vase of spills towards him and looked at it. I looked at it. Markham looked at it. Everyone looked at it.

It was just a normal little vase. Cheap, white and narrow, holding around a dozen paper spills. You know what I mean. Unwanted paper, torn vertically, rolled up and used to light lamps, fires and candles. Every Victorian room had a jar of them on the mantel.

'I don't understand either,' said Mrs Harewood stoutly. She left her husband to join the group around the table. 'What is so special about this vase?'

Markham once appeared onstage at Shakespeare's Globe theatre. He played the Ghost in *Hamlet*. Because he's an actor, you know. We didn't hear the end of it for years and years and now, just as we'd thought it was safe to go back into the water, his thespian talents were waking to a second spring. He walked slowly to the table and picked up the vase.

'Nothing,' he said. 'Absolutely nothing.'

And to prove it, he pulled out the spills and hurled the vase to the floor, where it smashed into pieces. Tiny fragments of china flew through the air. The maids screamed in alarm. Disappointingly, no one swooned.

Mr Chance recoiled. 'Are you mad?'

'The jury is still considering its verdict,' said Markham.

'Then why?'

'The vase is unimportant,' said Markham. 'But to a dying man, trapped in a locked room with only minutes left and no means of communication, these spills were the only paper in the room.'

'But I don't understand,' said Mr Harewood. 'What could he have possibly wished to communicate?'

Motionless, Markham waited until every eye was upon him. The pause thundered on and on until it became almost unbearable and then . . . his big moment . . .

'The name of his murderer.'

The word *sensation* didn't even begin to cover it. For a very, very long time no one moved. No one spoke. Everyone stared at Markham. And then at the spills. And then back to Markham again.

And then, with a sudden roar, the windows blew wide open. The curtains billowed across the room, dragging themselves across a small table and sending a tray of glasses flying. A heavy gust of rain blew into the room. The decanter lay on the floor, brandy slowly seeping into the carpet.

The through draft was making doors slam in the hall outside. As if whole platoons of poltergeists were out on a pre-Christmas works outing. The reverberations caused a picture to slither down the wall and crash to the floor, evoking more shrieks and screams from everyone. We were like a haunted house on steroids.

Everyone stood frozen – whether from the shock of Markham's pronouncement or the fear of something prowling around the house trying to get in, I couldn't tell. I looked around the room. Everyone's face registered shock or fear or complete incomprehension. Mrs Harewood gave a faint cry, took two paces backwards, collided with a sofa and sat down in a hurry. I didn't blame her.

Surprisingly, Mr Lillywhite was the first to speak.

'Nonsense,' he said in what I assumed was his pulpit voice. 'I have never heard such utter nonsense. This man has no idea what he is saying. Who are you to burst in here making wild accusations? I beg you, Mrs Harewood, please do not allow whoever these people may be to distress you any further after the unfortunate events of this evening. I suppose Christian duty precludes us from expelling them forthwith into this dreadful weather.' From his expression I guessed doing his Christian duty was a bit of a struggle at the moment.

'Speaking of which,' I said, 'I think we can close the windows now. Now that the fresh air has revived Mr Harewood, there is no point in the rest of us catching pneumonia.'

No one moved so I crossed the room and closed them myself,

shutting out the wild night. Abruptly, the sound of wind and rain subsided. I pulled the sodden curtains across the windows for good measure and picked up the decanter. There was still a good amount left. When I looked around again still no one had moved.

Mrs Harewood swallowed. 'Is there . . . I would like . . . no, I *demand* an explanation. What is happening here?' She looked at Markham. 'You have been very free with your accusations. Now back them up with evidence.'

Technically, it was my assignment, but now was not the moment to push myself forwards. I suspected my credibility with both the church and the law was fatally compromised anyway and likely to remain so for the foreseeable future. I nodded at Markham to continue.

He looked around the room. Mr Chance still clung to his position of dominance with his back to the fire. Barnstaple and John still stood, poker-faced, at the door. The maids had clustered together in the far corner. They looked terrified but I bet wild horses couldn't have dragged them out of this room. The Reverend Lillywhite had taken refuge behind the sofa. Whether to protect the Harewoods or himself was not clear.

Markham cleared his throat. 'Let us proceed traditionally and begin at the beginning. Mr Harewood senior did not survive the Ordeal of the Haunted Room. He was discovered dead, and I've been told his face was mysteriously congested and everyone assumed a stroke or fit of some kind. There was not a mark on him apart from a small cut on his left arm, just below the elbow, which had bled but not substantially so. Certainly not enough to cause his death. I do not know if an autopsy was carried out . . . ?'

Harewood shook his head. 'No. The scandal . . . the gossip . . . My mother died shortly afterwards. She never fully recovered. She always said everywhere she went there were looks and whispers. No one would visit us. We could barely get tradesmen to deliver.' He tailed away.

'That was very unfortunate,' said Markham, 'but I think you will agree those weren't the only consequences of that night.'

'No.' He cast a look at Chance. 'My father had failed to complete the Ordeal and his full inheritance couldn't be released.'

Chance spread his hands. 'My dear Mr Harewood, as I explained at the time . . .' He gritted his teeth. 'And several times to Mrs Harewood subsequently – my hands were tied. I had no choice.'

'And I am assuming,' said Markham, 'that, as tonight, Mr Harewood's body was removed from the Haunted Room with all speed?'

The Reverend Lillywhite nodded.

Chance flushed. 'There was such turmoil. Such shock. We did not know what to do. There was Mrs Harewood to attend to. The doctor to summon. The maids were in hysterics. Chaos reigned and somehow . . .'

'And the Haunted Room?'

'Secured by Barnstaple the moment we left. In case . . .' Chance stopped. *In case anything escaped* were the words not spoken.

'Never mind that now,' said Mr Harewood, turning to Markham and Peterson. 'You said my father was murdered. Who? Who murdered him? I demand you tell me immediately.'

Lillywhite drew himself up. 'This is preposterous. I cannot think what these people could possibly be suggesting.'

'I am suggesting,' said Peterson and suddenly his tone was not so pleasant, 'that Mr Harewood senior was a man of courage and resource. Realising he was dying . . . realising who had killed him and why . . . he improvised. Recognising he had only seconds of life remaining to him, it was vital he convey the identity of his murderer to the world. He had nothing upon which to write until his eye alighted on the spills so close to hand. He broke a glass, nicked his arm and inscribed the name of his killer, in his own blood, on one of the spills we see here tonight and, in his dying seconds, replaced it in the vase on the mantel.

He took a breath. 'Mr Harewood, the name of the person who killed your father has been sitting, undiscovered, in the Haunted Room since the last Ordeal. Unknown to anyone. Even the murderer.'

Chance stared at the spills in Markham's hand. 'Are you saying . . . ?'

Markham nodded. 'We are indeed, sir. If we examine these – now – in front of witnesses – we shall solve the mystery of the Ordeal of the Haunted Room. Everyone here tonight – with the exception of Mrs Harewood – was present at the last Ordeal.' He looked up mischievously. 'Shall we take a moment to speculate on the identity . . . ?'

'Oh, just do it,' cried Mrs Harewood. Obviously a woman happy to rush into action without a thought for the consequences. I wondered if she could possibly be an ancestor of mine.

'And,' continued Peterson remorselessly, 'if we solve the murder of Mr Harewood senior then we solve the attempted murder of Mr Henry Harewood tonight. After all, this is a quiet

160

neighbourhood, and it seems unlikely there would be two ruthless, conscienceless murderers within the parish.'

'Someone tried to kill Henry,' said Mrs Harewood, flatly. She said it again, and from the conviction in her voice, I knew she believed us. 'Someone tried to murder my husband.'

Markham nodded. 'Yes, Mrs Harewood, I am afraid so. Now, shall we find out who . . . ?'

He seated himself at the table and very slowly began to unroll the first spill. It was blank. Then the second. Blank again. Every eye was upon him. The only sound was the faint rustle of paper as he unrolled one spill after another and laid it flat upon the table.

Five more to go. Then four. Then three.

With only two spills remaining, the murderer's nerve broke. Sprinting across the room he made for the nearest window, wrenched at the curtains and scrabbled for the window catch. So fast did he move that just for a moment we were all taken unawares. It was Barnstaple, the true hero of the evening, who moved like lightning. Kicking aside a footstool, he seized the killer by his coat-tails as he fumbled at the window. Spinning him around, he bunched a massive fist and swung. The murderer flew through the air, crashing into two or three of the many knick-knack-laden tables scattered around, shattering them in the best dramatic traditions and then lying very still.

Mrs Harewood rose to her feet in vengeful fury. Women weren't much educated in this time and she therefore enjoyed the advantages of not having attended Harrow or Eton, and not having had the principles of fair play drilled into her. She had no hesitation therefore in playing her man while he was down

161

and spent an enjoyable minute adding several swift kicks to the murderer's current difficulties. It would, at this stage, have been perfectly proper for her husband to remonstrate with her over such unwomanly behaviour but strangely, he did no such thing. Finally, out of breath, she desisted.

The murderer lay prone on the floor. Panting, Mrs Harewood stood over him and I had no doubt that should he manage to escape her wrath there was always Barnstaple behind her, just waiting for another opportunity. In other words – there was No Chance of escape.

I have got to stop doing that.

Unwisely, the Reverend Lillywhite bent over her. 'My dear Mrs Harewood, such unchristian actions can only be caused by the profound pain and anguish you must be suffering. That you should have to witness such violence . . . I recommend a period of quiet reflection in the sanctuary of your own room while you remember your female responsibilities.'

Actually, excitement had brought a flush to her cheeks, her hair was severely disarranged and I thought she looked very pretty. I could see her husband thought so too. She tucked a piece of hair behind her ear. 'Oh, do be quiet, Lillywhite.'

It seemed safe to assume Harewood Hall donations to the restoration of the church tower would be considerably reduced this year.

Markham bent over a deeply unconscious Chance. 'Very neat. Well done, Mr Barnstaple.'

Barnstaple thrust his bruised knuckles behind his back and bowed to his mistress. 'I do beg your pardon, madam.'

'Not at all,' she said gaily. I suspected the brandy. 'Your master and I are greatly in your debt, Barnstaple. How did you guess what he would do? I confess he took me completely by surprise.'

Barnstaple bowed again. 'Mrs Trent and I are responsible for a great many young people below stairs, madam. Most of them of the female persuasion. We have learned to expect the unexpected.'

'Good heavens,' murmured Mrs Harewood, and wisely probed no further.

Leaving us all with this startling insight into life below stairs, Barnstaple was already supervising the removal of their former man of business. If the lock hadn't been shattered, I suspect they would have locked him in the Haunted Room . . . dum . . . dum . . . dum . . . yes, we're back to that again. Live with it.

'The silver room, I think, madam,' he said to Mrs Harewood as he and John manhandled him out of the room. 'Both door and lock are substantial. And later this morning, first thing, I shall despatch John to notify the authorities.'

'Thank you, Barnstaple,' she said, and proceeded to pour herself another brandy. I had one too. We females need every assistance we can get to see us through the harsh rigours of life.

As soon as the door had closed behind them, she turned back to Markham who had, in the last ten minutes, against all the odds, managed to make himself socially acceptable.

He grinned at her. Slowly she reached out and unrolled the remaining spills.

All were blank.

She stared at him, bewildered. 'How did you know Mr Chance was the murderer?'

'I didn't,' Markham confessed. 'Sorry.'

Henry Harewood was now sitting up properly. 'So, my father wasn't . . . ?'

'Yes, I'm afraid he was. And I believe his last action was to leave the name of the man who had murdered him.'

'But,' he said, bewildered. 'They're all blank.'

Markham pulled an apologetic face. 'Yes. Sadly, I suspect it was written on the spill John used to light the fire.'

Both Harewoods stared at him.

Peterson was already pouring them a brandy.

I had another one too.

Eventually, Mrs Harewood was able to find her voice. 'But why?'

'I think you will find, madam, that Mr Chance's administration of this estate has not been as . . . meticulous as it might have been.'

'In other words, he's been helping himself. For quite a long time, I suspect,' said Peterson, helpfully.

Henry Harewood looked up. 'And my father suspected?'

'I think so. Your grandfather was possibly not as able to monitor his affairs quite as he would have wished . . .'

'Yes, he was unwell. His heart. His doctor had instructed him not to exert himself.'

'So Mr Chance was, to some extent, unsupervised.'

'Very possibly. He and my father . . . did not work well together.'

'Really, you know,' said Markham, 'the whole thing was just too easy for him. I don't expect he could help himself.'

'Yet help himself he did,' concluded Mrs Harewood, tightly.

There was a pause. I made myself comfortable and waited, because I knew someone would say it sooner or later. I was not disappointed.

164

'But I still don't understand,' said Mr Harewood. Behind him, Markham and Peterson high-fived before taking their seats at the table and preparing to answer questions. 'How did he do it? How did he kill my father – and very nearly me – without leaving a trace? *Were* we poisoned?'

'Gassed,' said Markham.

He shook his head. 'Impossible. There is no gas anywhere upstairs. We keep it for the public rooms only. And I would have smelled it.'

'Not that type of gas,' said Peterson.

'Carbon monoxide,' said Markham. 'I suspect nickel tetracarbonyl – and before anyone asks, it nearly happened to me once. An accident,' he added in what he probably thought was a reassuring manner. 'It's a colourless, odourless gas. Quite undetectable in this instance. And quite painless.' He looked at Henry Harewood. 'You would simply have gone to sleep and never woken up.'

He shuddered. 'Like my father.'

'Somehow, your father had an idea what was happening to him. Not the technical details, of course. He didn't know how, but he did know who and he did know why. I suspect he contemplated writing it on the table beside him, but that would have been too easy for Chance to wipe off when he burst into the room and so, with his last strength, he wrote his murderer's name and concealed it in the only place possible and prayed it would one day be discovered.'

'Chance must have been *desperate* to ensure the Ordeal wasn't safely completed.'

'Yes. When the Ordeal failed again, the room would be locked up and control of the estate would remain his for

probably the next twenty years. Until Baby Jamie grew up –
and he, Chance, would almost certainly be dead by then. And
if he wasn't – well, young Jamie would simply have been the
latest to fail the Ordeal.'

'But we were all there,' interjected Mrs Harewood. 'In the
room with him. And he couldn't have entered the room beforehand. How could he possibly have achieved it without anyone
seeing?'

'Right in front of our very eyes, madam. He very artistically
dirtied his hands and wiped them on his handkerchief, in which
he had already secreted half a dozen small phials of the sub-
stance in question. He then threw his handkerchief into the
back of the fire. The impact broke the phials and the heat slowly
released the gas through the fabric, giving him plenty of time
to vacate the room. The effects would be felt by Mr Harewood
in under thirty minutes and death would follow very shortly
afterwards.'

'Can you actually *prove* any of this?'

Markham pulled out his own handkerchief and unfolded it,
revealing three tiny pieces of smoke-blackened glass. 'Dr
Peterson found these in the back of the fireplace.'

'How ever did you guess?'

'The colour of the flames, madam. The gas makes flames
turn orange. And the livid colour of your husband's face. And
there were several references to Mr Harewood senior's com-
plexion as well.'

'But,' said Mr Harewood, obviously about to ask the question no one had an answer to. 'How did I burn my arm?'

Markham has made a career out of plausible answers for

implausible events. 'Perhaps, while you were so light-headed and unsteady, you fell and burned your arm on the fender.'

'In that case, how did I find the strength to get up again? And through my shirt and coat . . .'

'Alas, sir, I cannot help you there.'

'If it is of any comfort, Mr Harewood,' said Peterson. 'I don't think anyone in this family will ever have to complete the Ordeal again. I suspect that after formal charges are brought, the remaining members of Chance's firm will be only too happy to agree to a legal waiver of the Ordeal of the Haunted Room. The scandal would do them no good at all. And the conditions are too perfect for embezzlement. The estate could have been under his sole control for years to come.'

'There would have been nothing left,' murmured Mrs Harewood.

Mr Harewood took her hand. 'There may not be much left anyway.'

'Unimportant,' said his wife, firmly. 'We will take what is left and rebuild. We are young and we have each other.'

They gazed fondly at one another.

'Well,' said Peterson, pulling himself to his feet. 'I don't know about anyone else, but I'm feeling quite tired. If someone could remove the brandy from my sister's reach, we'll take ourselves off to bed.'

Mrs Harewood stood with him. 'I don't know how we can ever thank you, sir.'

He smiled. 'There is no need, ma'am. You were kind enough to offer us the hospitality of your house. It was the least we could do. My foot is now very much recovered and you will have Christmas to prepare for. We will depart after breakfast, if we may, and leave you in peace.'

I don't know how anyone else slept that night but Victorian beds are surprisingly luxurious and comfortable. I sank into a warm soft slumber and was awoken at a respectable hour by an excited Eliza, who reported Mr Chance had been removed by the constable and was on his way to Rushford for the next assizes.

We breakfasted well. Faced with two long rows of chafing dishes, we accepted the challenge. I worked my way through devilled kidneys, kedgeree, scrambled eggs, the best sausages ever, bacon, kippers, ham and cold beef. But not the porridge. Followed by fresh bread, creamy butter and apricot jam. All washed down with, in my case, steaming hot chocolate. I told Peterson that if we were going to have to carry him then I would need my strength.

Unnecessary, as it turned out. They offered us the carriage. As Markham said, we'd now had the complete Victorian experience and could return confident in the knowledge of a job well done.

The coachman dropped us outside the Royal Oak. We helped Peterson down and thanked the coachman. He tipped his hat and pulled away. We watched him down the street until he turned off for Harewood Hall and was out of sight.

'All right?' I said to Peterson.

'I think so,' he said bravely, but he wasn't. He'd been fine last night in bedroom slippers but resuming his boots had not done his foot any good. He hadn't said anything because it really was essential we cleared off before the authorities began their investigations.

The pod was parked about a quarter of a mile behind the inn. We strolled through the bustling stable yard, with sweating horses being led away and new ones being harnessed. Passengers stood gulping coffee in the few minutes between changes. Grooms and ostlers raced back and forth. I wondered how much busier the yard would have been before the railways.

Behind the extensive stable blocks stood a maze of anonymous buildings, barns, storerooms, carriage houses and so on, and behind that a cultivated area and orchard, behind that a patch of waste ground bordered by a wood and behind that, finally, our pod. Normally, just a hop, skip and jump, but after about fifty yards, the sweat was pouring off Peterson.

'It's not much further,' I said, worried for him. He was looking very pale.

'I'll go on ahead,' said Markham to me. 'You two stay here and I'll be right back with something painkilling.'

'Hurry,' I said because it was starting to rain again.

He disappeared into the murk.

I leaned Peterson against a tree like an old plank and we waited.

Nothing happened. A fine rain fell on us. We sheltered under the tree as best we could.

'The silly bugger's lost,' said Peterson impatiently. 'I should have sent you, Max, except your sense of direction is even worse than his and you'd be in Reykjavik by now.'

'Interesting about the wound on Henry's arm,' I said, to distract him. 'Exactly the same place as his father's.'

'Yes,' he said. 'And if Henry was virtually unconscious then who pounded on the door?' He shifted his weight to ease his foot. 'It would seem the so-called Haunted Room just might have been after all. Just by a different ghost to the one expected. With a slightly different agenda. One come to save – not kill.'

The rain really started to come down. The feathers on my bonnet began to droop. Rain ran down my face. I began to brood. I think it was the injustice of it all. We were heroes. We'd Saved the Day. And here we were, up to our ankles in the mud, the cold, the wet, and thoroughly pissed off about it. And my feet were freezing. Where the bloody hell was Markham?

'Right,' I said, giving Peterson my muff to hold. 'Time for action.'

He looked uneasy. I think he thought I was going to amputate his foot. 'What are you going to do?'

'This.'

Reader – I carried him.

Well, for about three feet anyway and then I collapsed and he fell on top of me and then Markham turned up and laughed for an unnecessarily long time.

Back at St Mary's, I don't think Dr Stone could understand why, when he asked if we'd eaten or drunk anything contemporary during this jump, we fell about laughing. We paid for it, obviously – two days in Sick Bay and then it was off to see Dr Bairstow to regale him with details of our exciting, if unscheduled, adventure.

Our reports lay on his desk in front of him. Occasionally, he would peer at one of them, highlight a detail, and then sit back as if he couldn't quite believe his eyes.

'I notice you have, all of you, headed your reports *The Ordeal of the Haunted Room*.'

The words dum . . . dum . . . dum . . . were very definitely not uttered. Not this time.

He sat back. 'You appear to have achieved quite high levels of direct interaction on this assignment. May I draw your attention to the importance of the *record and document only* aspect of our assignments?'

I think the silence was answer enough.

He sighed. 'You were directly responsible for saving Henry Harewood's life.'

We nodded. We were.

'Without you he would have died.'

We nodded. He would.

'And you are directly responsible for the solicitor Chance losing his.' He looked up. 'He would have hanged, you know.'

I thought about trying to get away with saying that surely one would cancel out the other, so, overall, you know, problem solved, but decided against it.

'Frankly,' he said, sounding slightly disappointed, 'I find myself astonished History didn't strike you all dead on the spot.'

I pulled out my scratchpad. 'Well, actually, sir, it's possible there might have been a very good reason for that.'

'Really?' he said, suddenly interested. 'Do you think we could persuade History to pass it on? I frequently find myself quite *desperate* for a reason not to strike you all dead on the spot.'

His staff chose to believe this was one of their employer's little jokes.

Sometimes I break things to him gently and sometimes I just hit him smack between the eyes with it.

'We've been doing some research, sir,' I said, opening up a data stack, 'and I have to tell you it's much worse than you think.'

He closed his eyes.

'I'm afraid, sir, our actions have had the most enormous ramifications.'

He did not groan because he was Dr Bairstow, but I could see it was close.

I pressed on. 'According to my information, Henry Harewood served with distinction in WW1. As did his son, Jamie, who became a major in the Glosters. Both of them survived the conflict. And, as you can see, Mrs Harewood wasn't idle, either. She opened Harewood Hall as a nursing home for wounded soldiers and airmen. She became a competent and efficient nurse who almost certainly saved several of her patients' lives. Her daughter, Jennifer Harewood, married one of them. And if you look, sir . . .'

He opened his eyes.

I twirled the data stack. 'Jennifer's daughter, Harriet, was parachuted into France in 1943.'

He closed his eyes again – as if the axe might fall at any moment. 'Again, Dr Maxwell – with this sort of impact on the timeline – how are any of you still alive?'

I paused. Because now it was time for the biggie.

'It gets even worse, sir. Harriet's great-great-great-greatish granddaughter fought in the Civil Uprisings.'

'Forgive my asking, Dr Maxwell, but how do you imagine this information is making things any better?'

'I suspect you may be worrying unnecessarily, and as a conscientious employee, it is my duty to alleviate your anxiety, sir.'

'Given your anticipated abbreviated life expectancy, Dr Maxwell, may I urge you to get to the point.'

I beamed.

'The thing is, sir . . .'

He sighed. 'Ah – another phrase that never bodes well. I am beginning to wonder if I was perhaps a trifle over-optimistic in authorising this month's wages bill. It seems unlikely any of us will live long enough to collect it.'

Markham spoke up. 'She was a pilot, sir.'

'My concern over whether we shall live long enough to get to the point has led me to lose track somewhat. Of whom are we speaking now?'

'Harriet's great-great-great-greatish granddaughter, sir.'

'The pilot.'

He nodded. 'That's the one, sir.'

He sighed again. 'And what of this pilot?'

I looked out of the window. The setting sun streamed through the windows, making my eyes water. In my mind's eye I saw it as Mrs Mack had described it. Coming fast and low, out of the sun, hanging in the sky, big and black in its own shimmering heat haze, rockets armed and ready, massive rotors chopping the Thames and flinging spray about as it hung over Barricade Bridge, waiting to end everything. The pilot, helmeted and anonymous. No one ever knew who she was. And then, unaccountably – pulling up and disappearing back into the sun. The moment that changed everything.

I hit him with the punchline.

'She flew Leviathans, sir. In the Civil Uprisings.'

His office was suddenly very quiet.

He sat for a moment, then turned and stared out of the

window as I had done, perhaps seeing what I had seen, remembering as I remembered, and then reached out his hand and flattened the data stack.

'It would seem, Dr Maxwell, that no good deed ever goes unrewarded.'

'I like to think so, sir.'

'In that case, I feel I may – cautiously – resume my plans for next week.'

'If we are all spared, sir.'

'Thank you, everyone. I think that will be all.'

A Merry Christmas from St Mary's and a peaceful and prosperous New Year.

THE END

AUTHOR'S NOTE

I wrote this St Mary's short story and then, about three months later, in the middle of the night, I had one of those moments. I got out of bed and firkled around my bookshelves for my ancient copy of *Hag's Nook* – a wonderful detective story by John Dickson Carr. I couldn't find it anywhere, which, since it's a tiny flat, was annoying. I bought another copy, read it through and realised there are some echoes of his classic tale in my own.

My first instinct was to pull the St Mary's story and put the whole thing down to being a general disaster magnet. However, John Dickson Carr is a great literary hero of mine and so I'd like to present this year's St Mary's Christmas escapade as an homage to him and his amazing locked-room stories. (Also, as my agent, editor and daytime-self pointed out, the similarities between the two are nowhere near as great as I imagined at three o'clock in the morning . . .)

Thanks to Nigel the Chemist, who was very helpful about the best way of killing someone in 1895 and getting away with it. And knew how long it would take. And knew all about writing your murderer's name in blood. Another one who has to delete his browser history on a regular basis.

THE TOAST OF TIME

DRAMATIS THINGUMMY

Lady Amelia
Smallhope

Second daughter of the previous Earl of Goodrich and sister of the current E of G. Organiser of extravagant Christmas presents. Very successful bounty hunter. Sorry – recovery agent.

Pennyroyal

An alleged butler. Currently toiling over a turkey. Ditto with the recovery agent thing.

Markham

You'll never guess what he's got down his trousers.

Maxwell

Definitely not considering catering as an alternative career. Rubbish at buttering toast.

Mrs Mack

Former urban terrorist and one of the leaders of the Civil Uprisings. Now Head of Kitchen Services at St Mary's – a much more hazardous occupation.

Ellen, Sally, Janet, Kim, Edna, Terry and others	Kitchen staff grappling with an unexpected colleague.
Dr Dowson	Locked out of his own Library, would you believe?
Mr Evans and his Magnificent Security Team	Modelling the very latest in gardening gear – to the massive appreciation of some of the Parish Council.
Mrs Partridge	Keeping her cool as all around her lose theirs.
Captain Hyssop	Yes – her again. The scourge of the Security Section and sadly still at St Mary's.
Commander John Treadwell	Whose meeting with the Parish Council is about to take a typically St Mary's turn for the worse.
Mrs Huntley-Palmer	Proud owner of the soon to be TWOCed not-as-classic-as-Dr-Bairstow's-Bentley Bentley. Representing the Forces of Darkness – or the Parish Council, as they're usually known outside of St Mary's.
The Rev Kev	Keep pedalling, Kev. Eyes front and place your trust in the Lord.

Miss Peek Miss Frean	Also members of the Parish Council. The acceptable side of the Forces of Darkness. Recipients of more horticultural insight than they bargained for but bravely soldiering on. Bless them.
Major Guthrie	Ex-St Mary's but having no success in leaving them behind. His secret cellar is not as secret as he thinks it is.
Elspeth	His strangely shaped partner.
Various unexpected Christmas guests	Hush – they're a secret. Have to kill you now.
Various shady characters	Or 'Naughty People Easily Translated into Ready Cash', as Lady Amelia refers to them.
The Time Police	Arriving just a fraction too late in this instance but jolly useful for tidying up loose ends and allowing the author to get on with the story.
A ram	Not on Markham's Christmas card list. Very prepared to stand his ground against two of St Mary's former finest.

Various lost treasures	One of which spends most of the story down Markham's trousers, which is no way to treat a legend.
Mrs Huntley-Palmer's not-as-classic-as-Dr-Bairstow's-Bentley Bentley	Enjoying a brief moment of fame.

AUTHOR'S INTRODUCTION

It was the title that came first for this one. I thought *The Toast of Time* had rather a nice ring to it. True, it doesn't have much to do with the story, but I never let that stop me.

I wanted to write a story that brought everyone together for Christmas. A bit of a tall order given that Max was separated from St Mary's both geographically and temporally but I've done my best. All the old favourites are here – and some new ones, too. Lots for you to get your teeth into.

SPOILER ALERT – Not only is Pennyroyal eventually able to remove his arm from the turkey, but we even find out what Markham is keeping in his trousers.

Merry Christmas to you all.

THE TOAST OF TIME

It was the toast that started it. Markham and I were making toast. Or rather, I was making it and he was in charge of the buttering because, apparently, I don't butter all the way into the corners. Once I would have argued fiercely. I would probably even have held him down while I demonstrated just how much butter it is possible to get into even the most remote corner – and not necessarily using a piece of toast, either. Or even butter. But that day I just couldn't be bothered.

He finished buttering, passed me back the appropriately garnished baked bread product – without looking what he was doing, obviously – and I reached out for it – without looking what I was doing, obviously – and rather like the British Relay Team, we dropped the baton at the crucial moment and the toast crashed to the floor. Butter-side down, obviously, because toast doesn't know any other way.

Both Markham and I stared at it. I, because butter-side-down toast just about summed up my life at that moment, and Markham . . . well, I've no idea why he does anything, let alone stares at a piece of toast.

Neither of us moved. The rain smacked against the windows, the kettle switched itself off, the toast obviously wasn't

185

going anywhere unaided, and Markham and I were watching it go nowhere.

Markham sighed. 'Once again the Toast of Time falls butter-side down.'

I nodded. Of course it did.

We might be there still if Pennyroyal hadn't come in.

'Well, pick it up,' he said. Pennyroyal runs a tight ship, and random slices of toast littering the spotless kitchen floor were never going to be his favourite thing.

I bent to pick it up while Markham wiped up the butter.

I looked around. I was pretty sure the five-second rule would apply so I blew on it, cut it neatly in half and buried it at the bottom of the pile. No one would ever know.

Markham brought over the teapot and I wrangled the plate of toast on to the table.

Pennyroyal accounted for the top layer.

Markham moved more quickly than me and snaffled the next tier.

Which just left me and the gravity-damaged bottom level.

I sighed and slathered it an inch thick with marmalade because everyone knows marmalade kills ninety-nine per cent of all known germs. Dead.

We ate in silence.

For anyone wondering about the cause of my depression, it was that time of the year again. The time of jolly and holly and Christmas pudding and carols and arguments and bickering and presents and goodwill.

And families.

This would be the first time for ages that I'd been away from St Mary's for Christmas. I don't know how Markham was feeling about that but I really wasn't in a festive mood at all. *Au contraire*, as our French friends would say.

I missed Leon. I missed the way he smiled for me alone. The way he looked for me whenever he entered a room. And I missed Matthew. Especially our nightly battles over face-washing and teeth-cleaning.

I even missed St Mary's. The lunchtime scrum. The noise. The smells. And continually having to step over an unconscious Bashford. Or Roberts and Bashford glaring at each other over a grinning Sykes. Or Sands and his never-ending knock-knock jokes. Even Angus crooning happily from the top of a cupboard.

Normally, at this point, I'd go on to describe St Mary's, what we did, warn people against saying 'time travel' in Dr Bairstow's hearing, talk about the pods without mentioning the word 'cabbage' in every sentence and just generally bring people up to speed on how things stood at the moment.

But not this time.

For a start, Markham and I were no longer at St Mary's. Neither was Dr Bairstow – whose whereabouts are, at present, a closely guarded secret to be dealt with at another time. Along with Mrs Brown. I can only say they're not at St Mary's. And that's it. That's all anyone's getting from me.

Back to me and Markham, living wild and free on toast.

Smallhope and Pennyroyal had given us a home. A very comfortable home. There was good food and plenty of it. And excellent pay and conditions, together with lots and lots of rules to break, bend or completely ignore, but nothing could compensate for not being at St Mary's any longer. And, worst of all, we'd both of us lost our families. Leon was out there somewhere, jumping up and down the timeline, keeping Adrian, Mikey and Matthew on the straight and narrow, possibly assisted by Professor Penrose but more probably not. And Hunter and Baby Flora were safely hidden away from the world. Markham saw them occasionally – not as often as he would like to, I suspected – while I hadn't seen Leon since I left St Mary's.

But, we were here and we were safe. We shouldn't complain. We had a roof over our heads and a certain amount of job satisfaction as we apprehended various lowlifes (lives?) who thought it would be a good idea to conceal themselves in another time to escape the attentions of the Time Police, but failed to take into account the Magnificent Markham and Maxwell – bounty hunters.

Sorry – recovery agents.

I really didn't have a thing to complain about. Compared to how badly things could have turned out, everything was fine – it really was. But so dejected were Markham and I that neither of us could be bothered to argue about whose turn it was to clear away the breakfast things and load the dishwasher. We just got up and did it in silence.

'It's like a wet weekend in here,' said Pennyroyal, rummaging in his briefcase.

I looked out of the window at the rain. He wasn't wrong. It was indeed a wetter weekend in here than it was out there.

'Perhaps this will cheer you up,' he said. 'New assignment for you,' and dropped a file on the table.

We looked at it. 'Anything interesting?' said Markham, poking it with his finger.

'Depends,' Pennyroyal said. 'Take a look and tell me what you think.'

Markham opened up the file. Lady Amelia and Pennyroyal always preferred paper to electronics. Their home was as secure as they could make it but there was always the chance of something unexpected erupting through the door and catching them in the act, so paper was their preferred way to go. That way one of them could shove the evidence in the range while the other launched a small nuclear strike at their unwelcome visitors. No – I'm not joking.

'Where did you get this?' asked Markham.

'An announcement on the Dark Web,' Pennyroyal said. 'Useful place if you know where to look.'

According to the single sheet of paper in the file, a Flying Auction was to be held. That was it – no other details. Just the announcement and two long lines of coordinates at the bottom of the page.

I stared at it. 'What on earth is a Flying Auction?'

Pennyroyal was pouring himself a coffee. 'Flying Auctions are markets of no fixed abode. They simply occur as and when required. They are an established way of disposing of items that can't be widely advertised. Or even advertised at all. This one purports to be selling historical artefacts.'

'*Fake* historical artefacts?'

Pennyroyal grinned. 'Not if we're very lucky.'

'So would we be buying? Selling? Observing?'

Pennyroyal shook his head. 'In these sort of circumstances, Lady Amelia always favours keeping our plans fairly loose. A fast and flexible approach enables us to take advantage of sometimes rapidly changing situations.'

'Ah – gotcha,' said Markham. 'Make it up as we go along.'

'Yes. We appreciate this is the first time for you two, and if

189

you feel it would be wiser to limit your ambitions to something fairly modest then that is entirely up to you. On the other hand, of course, you might well encounter a set of circumstances from which it would be criminal to walk away empty-handed.'

You had to admire his use of the word criminal.

'Well, let's go and see, shall we?' said Markham, picking up the file, and we moved into the room next door, leaving our host to his coffee. This was the closest thing Pennyroyal and Smallhope had to an office. There was a data table, scratchpads, reference material, writing stuff – and an industrial-strength shredder probably robust enough to shred both me and Markham in the not-unlikely event of our hosts deciding they were tired of our company and needed to dispose of the bodies.

I fired up the data table and laid in the coordinates as Markham dictated them.

We double-checked the lat and long and viewed the result with equal astonishment and amusement.

'Cheeky buggers,' said Markham. He nodded with his head at Pennyroyal's end of the farmhouse. 'Do you think he knew?'

I nodded. If someone told me there was nothing Pennyroyal didn't know then I'd believe them.

The coordinates translated to a decrepit old country house just outside of Rushford. Somewhere remote and that had been empty for some time. You would know it as the future Institute of Historical Research at St Mary's. The date was November 1921.

'Standard procedure,' said Pennyroyal, coming in to view the result and to have a bit of a laugh. 'They choose somewhere out of the way and forgotten, give it a bit of a temporary tart-up, invite a few select punters and auction off a ton of very dodgy gear.'

'Does that mean some of it's fake?'

'No – as often as not the stuff is all genuine. It's the acquiring of it that is the dodgy bit.'

'Stolen?'

'Yep. Looted. Pillaged. Smuggled. Just generally nicked. Can't be sold on the open market, obviously – hence the Flying Auction.'

'What sort of very dodgy gear?' I asked. 'What can we expect to see?'

'Could be anything. Quite often you don't know until you get there.'

I gestured to the twirling data stack. 'Isn't that a bit of a risk? Publishing the where and when, I mean.'

Pennyroyal shrugged. 'Got to get the punters in somehow. This was only up for thirty minutes last night. You have to be quick. Any longer and some sort of virus comes winging its way through your system and your whole electronic life collapses around your ears.'

I nodded. Yes, Major Ellis – then Captain Ellis – of the Time Police had once explained that particular tactic to me.

'You have to know where and when to look,' Pennyroyal continued. 'I had a bit of a tip-off. Someone owed me a favour. The trick will be to get in and out of the auction before those Time Police buggers track it down.'

'So where did the organisers get whatever they'll be selling?' asked Markham.

'No idea, but it won't have been legal.'

'Specific instructions?' said Markham.

He shrugged. 'Don't get caught.'

Smallhope and Pennyroyal are not in business out of the goodness of their hearts. Making money is their prime objective. Something to which neither Markham nor I objected because – as I always said – they're not my rules so why should I bother? And we were making a fair bit of money as well. When all this came to an end – *if* all this ever came to an end – then both Markham and I would find ourselves quite well set up for the future, which would certainly be useful if we had to make a fresh start somewhere else. I sometimes wondered what our chances were of ever enjoying a normal life again. To which Markham would invariably reply that we'd hardly enjoyed a normal life before, so there wasn't a lot of difference really, was there?

He would also like to point out that I haven't explained where we were, what we were doing and why, so here goes.

Obviously, we're not at St Mary's any longer. I was sacked after falling out big time with the new Director, Commander Treadwell, then head-hunted by our charming hosts, before going on to break Dr Bairstow out of a secure government establishment. As you do. It had been a lively couple of months.

Markham and his family had quietly disappeared before the authorities could take it into their heads to do more than sack him, and here we both were, earning a dishonest crust. Although where here *is* isn't quite clear. Nor are we in our own time, which is a source of grief to Markham because his baby daughter can't join him here. And Leon's busy with his own problems – which, since they involved controlling Matthew, Professor Penrose, Mikey and Adrian, would be extensive.

We're living in a large farmhouse – aptly named Home Farm – along with Lady Amelia Smallhope, who is a genuine member of the aristocracy – sister of the current Lord Goodrich, I think – and Pennyroyal, her butler. And bodyguard, thief and thug as well, and who could probably kill you in a million different ways while mixing the perfect margarita at the same time.

They'd offered us both a job and so far, it was going quite well. It turns out that there are a significant number of people who, having made their own time too hot to hold them any longer, relocate to the past, together with a dozen or so big bags of gold, to spend their days in peace and prosperity, living off their illicit gains. In some cases, they simply pick up where they'd left off, but in a different century. A whole new time and place to exploit and terrorise. But not for long, however, because Markham and Maxwell are on the job now. We zoom in, overpower the illegals by whatever method seems good at the time and then hand them over to Smallhope and Pennyroyal who, in turn, present them to the Time Police in return for a very handsome reward. A very handsome reward indeed. Pennyroyal then deducts expenses and we split the rest between us. Yes, Markham and I really weren't doing too badly at all.

One day I knew I'd be reunited with Leon and Matthew, but even so . . . This was my first Christmas away from St Mary's since I'd gone to work there. There was no reason why we wouldn't have a perfectly pleasant Christmas here, but . . . well, it wasn't home.

On the other hand, neither Markham nor I were on the streets. Or in prison. Or dead, so there was no real reason for my mood. I sat up. I had a living to earn and I should get on with it.

Where was I? Yes – back to the plot. If that's what you want to call it. Our loose brief. Arrive, sum up the situation, bring back anything that could be translated into cash. Don't get caught. Have a good day.

Markham and I went off to select our costumes.

The costume room is next door to the office. The costumes are arranged on racks, more or less chronologically. The majority of outfits appeared to be from the 1800s onwards. I guessed not many people ever wanted to be relocated to the Middle Ages. It's by no means as picturesque as the entertainment industry would have you believe.

My instinct was to wear something from 1921, but as Markham pointed out, that wasn't really necessary, was it? No contemporaries would be present at the auction. We could both wear ordinary clothes and be comfortable, just for once.

'We don't want to be too distinctive,' said Markham, rifling through a rack of clothes ranging from Roman and Greek tunics, European doublets, Tudor and Stuart silks and satins, huge Georgian skirts, Regency breeches, Victorian frock coats, sharp 1920s suits, fringed flapper dresses – I held my breath because you never know with him – mumsy 1950s housewife stuff, and even a few mod outfits from the 60s, including the classic Mary Quant Mondrian dress which I actually quite fancied myself. 'Never make it easy for people to describe you to the authorities,' he continued. 'Simple, good quality, tasteful. A bit like me, really.'

'You once went through an entire assignment dressed in pink,' I said. 'I hardly think that marks you out as an expert on quiet good taste.'

'It was *rose*,' he said, hurt.

'It was eye-catching,' I said. 'And that was without the giant feather in your hat.'

He disappeared into another rack of clothes, muttering as he went.

In the end, I went for a rather nice pair of black trousers, a white shirt, a khaki jacket and a casual scarf, loosely knotted. Scarves are good. They can double as bandages, slings, or blindfolds. You can tie people up with them, or use them to carry away your loot. At a pinch you can even wear them, although for some reason, only Frenchwomen seem able to achieve that effortlessly nonchalant careless look. I laboured for nearly thirty minutes over my effortlessly nonchalant careless look and in the end Markham did it for me.

He himself was simply dressed in a leather jacket and dark jeans. We surveyed ourselves in the mirror.

'Looking good,' I said.

He smirked. 'We're Markham and Maxwell – bounty hunters.'

'Recovery agents,' I said gently.

Our pod was parked around the back. The perfectly genuine farmhouse had a perfectly genuine farmyard at the rear. A couple of people came in every day and did farming things while Smallhope and Pennyroyal got on with the business of living dangerously but making a lot of money at the same time. There were barns, stables, sties, all with various bits of agricultural equipment scattered around. Real chickens pecked in the yard – something which always caused Markham some disquiet because he's not completely at home with the animal world.

The big building to the left – accessible from the house in case we ever needed to make a quick getaway – was, ostensibly, a barn, but actually it was the rural equivalent of Hawking Hangar. Our pod was in there – actually it was Leon's pod, but currently enjoying temporary new ownership. It was usually neatly parked alongside our employer's slightly larger pod and connected to the power supply by thick black umbilicals. Pennyroyal was very keen on any pod being ready to go at a moment's notice.

I was surprised they had only the one pod – what happened if they needed to split up, for instance? – but Markham reckoned they had one other at least, carefully tucked away somewhere else that we didn't know anything about. Thinking about it, that made sense.

Ours was the only one here today because Lady Amelia was off doing her Christmas shopping. Why she couldn't have taken the car like a normal person was never satisfactorily explained. Perhaps she was avoiding London's notorious parking problems. I don't know whether Harrods provided parking for their customers but I could just picture her pod occupying a premium spot while she herself zipped around, credit card in one hand, margarita in the other, buying up half the shop.

I think out of kindness to me and Markham, she and Pennyroyal had declared this Christmas a 'no gift' zone (something with which I'd been happy to comply – I'm not sure what would constitute the perfect gift for a wayward member of the aristocracy and her thug of a butler), so I assumed it was her family for whom she was shopping. And Christmas food, of course. Pennyroyal had produced an extensive list of delicacies without which Christmas could not possibly proceed.

A sneak peek had revealed our Christmas would be enhanced by:

Every bottle of claret in the western hemisphere. That would be Pennyroyal. He's very partial to the occasional glass.

Three rivers' worth of salmon – smoked and otherwise.

Hand-shot venison – what? Is there any other way? Unless our Caledonian cousins have taken to pursuing deer across the highlands with a trebuchet. On the other hand, it's Caledonia – anything is possible.

A vast quantity of esoteric cheeses including Stinking Henry. A cheese so pungent that the law required it to be served underwater for the safety of society.

Icelandic tea bags – don't ask me what that's all about.

Organic sprouts – yeah, like that renders them any more acceptable.

The world's most expensive coffee – yuk. Sticking three noughts on the price does not render coffee any more drinkable, people.

Twiglets – Pennyroyal again.

Two gross of macaroons – although I might have misread the quantity.

Hand-picked peanuts – what was the alternative? Feet-picked?

Château Cusheeyonne's world-famous champagne – obviously. To be read with a French accent. Obviously.

Two boxes of Pennyroyal's specially designed Christmas crackers – one hat, one joke, one hand grenade, presumably.

Taylor and Edwards's Magnificent Self-Igniting Christmas Pudding with free fire extinguisher.

And a turkey hand-reared exclusively on the finest corn and

so free-range it had apparently been on a walking tour of the Lake District.

Well, shopping for that lot should keep Lady Amelia occupied for a while.

Our pod – well, my pod – all right, Leon's pod – looked very small in the vast space of the barn. That's partly because it is very small. It's a single-seater with some unusual features. Markham and I both fit inside quite neatly, although once I'd had four people and a ton of boxes and crates in there and things had been more than cosy.

The barn was chilly. I called for the door and we entered the pod. We carried nothing personal and we certainly weren't armed because that would be asking for trouble. We had our invitations to the auction, of course, printed off by Pennyroyal, without which there was no chance of getting in, even if we promised to buy everything in sight. Apparently, they contained some kind of hidden code that would sort the goats from the sheep. I had a perfectly genuine credit card in the name of Smallhope tucked in an inner pocket, because who would attend an auction without the means to purchase something, and just in case there was any trouble and we had to prove who we were to the authorities, Markham and I both carried Smart-Cards, each disguised as a small business card, on which our fake names were neatly inscribed but with a hidden hologram, the reading of which by a Time Police scratchpad would identify us as acting under their authority. For any other authority we'd have only our wits on which to rely. So, as Pennyroyal said, completely on our own, then.

I have to say, this being on the dodgy side of the law business is excellent. I can really recommend it. There was no tedious checking each other over for inadvertent anomalies, no uncomfortable clothing, no hours of boning up on the appropriate subject matter – you just strolled into your pod and went. So that's what we did. We strolled into our pod and went.

Early November, 1921. The war had been over for three years but there still weren't a lot of men around in the village. They hadn't built it yet, but there would be a war memorial up by the church to the eighteen men who hadn't come home again. That's a lot for a small place like this. I often wondered how they would have felt if they'd known that thirty years later, they'd have been inscribing yet more names on the memorial. That the War to End All Wars actually hadn't.

Gloomy thoughts for a gloomy day. It was autumn out there. Chilly and damp. I could see dew-drenched cobwebs hanging in the hedgerows and the grass was beaded with moisture.

We'd parked in the field behind the Falconburg Arms. A number of grubby sheep peered curiously as we exited the pod.

'There's a ram,' said Markham, nervously. He and the animal kingdom don't love each other, as I say. I looked forward to seeing him being beaten up by the kitten that young Flora would inevitably demand.

'It's that time of year,' I said. 'Just make sure he doesn't see you as competition and you'll be fine.'

'Fun Fact,' he said, taking care to walk on the non-ram side of me.

Markham and his allegedly Fun Facts are one of the great curses of the modern world. The secret is not to let him get started. 'I don't care. Just keep your eye on Big Boy over there.'

He was big, too. And his horns were impressive. He stared at us and stamped a warning hoof.

'No,' said Markham. 'Listen. This could be useful. Did you know that if a ram backs away from you it isn't because he's intimidated but simply because he's lengthening his run-up?'

'That was your Fun Fact?'

'No – my Fun Fact is that if that happens then we should walk towards it.'

'Walk *towards* it?'

'Yes. And don't run. He'll think you're charging and respond appropriately.'

'And if that doesn't work?'

'Wave a stick. They don't like that.'

'Bugger,' I said, looking at our stickless state.

The ram stamped its foot again. All its wives had stopped eating to watch the entertainment.

'I think it's going to charge,' said Markham. 'Stand your ground.'

'No – you stand your ground. I'm off.'

He grabbed my arm. 'No – don't do that. Just stand still and then, as it rears up on its hind legs, you step smartly to one side.'

'You do know you're insane, don't you?'

'The important thing is not to run, Max. These things can hit thirty miles an hour. Can you?'

Since I couldn't, I tried to stand behind Markham. Since he was trying to stand behind me, we were going nowhere.

The ram snorted a funny snorting sound. We were going to die.

'OK,' said Markham. 'If all else fails then one of us should wrestle it to the ground.'

'What?'

'Grab its horns and wrestle it to the— hey, wait for me.'

We ran. At speeds of very nearly thirty miles an hour in my case. The ram watched us with contempt then lowered its head and continued eating. As did its many wives.

'Well, that was embarrassing,' said Markham, clambering over the gate to stand beside me.

'Not for the ram,' I said, dusting myself off and looking up and down the main street.

There was a great deal more commercial life going on than in my time. Apart from the Falconburg Arms I could see at least two more pubs, together with some kind of all-purpose shop with its contents spilling across the path outside, a bakery, and what looked like a haberdasher. Milk and meat must come round on a cart, I reckoned. The most modern building was a garage with a single solitary petrol pump at the top of the hill. Markham craned his neck.

'What are you doing?'

'Trying to see how much they charge for petrol.'

Men do this. Football, beer and the price of petrol. Incomprehensible, but the best thing to do is let them get on with it.

Not all the little cottages were occupied. A good many were still boarded up. Perhaps they'd been abandoned during the war and for some reason the inhabitants never returned. The Great Slump wouldn't happen until the late 1920s, but here in rural England, the post-war depression was already biting.

There were no street lights. The hedges bordering the road were untrimmed. I don't know what the road was made of. Most of it was covered in a lethal mixture of mud and fallen leaves. The trees were bare, silhouetted against the sky, and there was no colour anywhere in the world.

There were no people about, either. Such men as had returned from the war would be working, either in the fields or in Rushford. Women would be in the home and the kids in school. Everyone in their proper place.

The bridge over the stream was a rickety wooden affair that didn't look capable of supporting the weight of a car. Or even a laden wagon. We picked our way across very carefully. There was definitely no road on the other side. A muddy track, badly rutted by wagon wheels, led up to St Mary's, very visible between the bare trees.

The day was cold. Not one of the bright and frosty days. This one had a chill that struck right through to my bones. No wonder sheep were so bad-tempered, living in a muddy field in these temperatures. Perhaps we should have parked closer, but caution – and Pennyroyal – had advised keeping the pod a safe distance away. Should the Time Police appear and attempt to arrest us all, we didn't want our pod swept up with all the others.

St Mary's had that blind look common to empty houses. The windows were shuttered but both the gates were open. One was hanging off its hinges so it probably wouldn't have shut anyway. Between weeds and potholes, the drive was barely visible. I wondered when someone had last lived here.

We'd been careful, but others hadn't been so cautious. Or, more likely, too lazy to walk that far. Two or three small rectangular boxes were parked in the long grass on what we'd come to know as the South Lawn.

'There's another two under the trees over there,' said Markham. 'And I reckon there'll be some more round the back.'

I began to do some calculations in my head. Say an average

of two people per pod, five pods that I could see, probably more. Lady Amelia always charged top whack for her bounty, saying that if we didn't put a high price on our services then how could we expect anyone else to do the same? So that was a possible ten people – minimum. A lot of people. And that didn't include those running the auction. Although how two of us would manage ten people was a bit of a mystery. Never mind – we'd think of something. There was a lot of money parked here.

I grinned at Markham. 'Are you thinking what I'm thinking?'

He grinned back again. 'Seriously, Max, we were born to do this.'

We carried on slowly up the drive. St Mary's looked truly decrepit. There were things growing out of the chimneys. The stonework was crumbling quite badly. In fact, two heavy wooden buttresses were pushing it upright in one place, and everything was stained with rainwater because the gutters and downspouts had been pinched for the lead. It would be horribly damp inside. I never before realised how much work Dr Bairstow had had to do to make it habitable – or nearly habitable. And even after all his work, there was always something falling down. Or off. Or in. Although, to be fair, this was quite often not unrelated to events within St Mary's itself. Professor Rapson's dandelion wine had blown out the windows. The kitchen and admin staff had brought down the lantern roof in the Great Hall. Frozen chickens had demolished the Library. To say nothing of dead dogs flying through the windows, runaway monoliths, exploding rocks . . .

I was quite unprepared for the sudden and unexpected attack

of homesickness coming out of nowhere. I don't know why, because I was actually far more comfortably housed at Home Farm. It was warm, there was plenty of hot water and the food was good. I wondered what St Mary's was doing now. How were they getting on without me? Very much better, probably. Rosie Lee, my alleged PA, always claimed History Department efficiency soared when I wasn't around.

I snuck a glimpse at Markham to see how he was taking being back at St Mary's, but his face told me nothing. It never does if he doesn't want it to.

Hands in pockets, we strolled slowly up the drive, getting the lie of the land. No one else was in sight. The whole place looked completely deserted. We'd got this far unchallenged. I began to wonder if we were in the right place.

Markham nudged me. 'Bet you never thought you'd be doing this when you got up this morning?'

'No,' I said. 'We're very, very naughty people.'

'We certainly are,' said Markham. 'We're the Pros and Cons.'

I sighed. Every time I thought he'd forgotten that stupid name . . . he hadn't. He'd wanted a team name, he said, and since he'd done a bit of time here and there, that made him a Con. Short for convict, he would explain, convinced that if I could only see the joke, I'd adopt the team name with enthusiasm. He was always trying to get me to disguise myself as a prostitute so I could be the Pro part. It was never going to happen, but you can't fault his perseverance. Well, you can, and I was going to fault it with a clip round his bloody ear one day if he didn't give over.

On the other hand, Combat Wombat – his second choice – hadn't met much favour either – especially from Pennyroyal, whom I suspect has a very specialised sense of humour. Me bleeding to death at his feet would probably evoke a merry chuckle. Combat Wombat did not.

I had an idea Markham would never give up on Pros and Cons and that he'd be repeating his arguments ad infinitum, which is never fun, but at least it kept him off the Fun Facts – which, as you will have observed, are even worse.

'Fun Fact,' he said, as we approached the steps.

'Oh God . . .'

'Do you know,' he said, ignoring me, 'this is exactly how St Mary's looked the first time I clapped eyes on it.'

'Did you have any idea what you were getting into?' I asked.

'Nope. Did you?'

'None at all,' I said. 'I thought I'd come for a research job.' I stepped back and looked up. 'The house certainly looks deserted. Do you think we've come to the wrong place?'

'No.'

'How do you know?'

'Other than all the pods scattered around the place, there's a very modern security camera concealed behind the pediment.'

'Excellent,' I said, which, I admit, is not the normal reaction to finding oneself under surveillance, but it was good to know we were in the right place.

'Microphones?'

'Doubt it,' he said, shaking his head. 'Too much faff for only one afternoon. Plus there's too much background noise. Wind and whatnot.'

'I can't see any more pods,' I said. 'Do you think there'll be any hidden up in the woods?'

Markham frowned. 'Possibly, but I suspect these will be people too posh to walk.'

'*We're* walking.'

'We're not posh.'

'They don't know that.'

'We're eccentric.'

I nodded. 'OK. I can do eccentric.'

'Eccentric is my middle name,' he said.

'No, it's not.'

'You don't know that.'

Peterson would not have wanted me to miss this opportunity. His lifelong quest to discover Markham's real name occupied much of his waking hours. And as Deputy Director of St Mary's, it wasn't as if he did a lot of work anyway. Cunningly, I said, 'I don't even know your *first* name.'

'No, you don't, do you?'

And now we were at the front door, having walked up the drive, having a natural conversation and behaving perfectly normally. Which, trust me, is the best way to do it.

We broke off as the doors opened before us. I saw two men, both adhering to the 1920s setting. They were dressed in dark jackets, grey striped trousers and very nearly terminally shiny shoes.

'Hello there,' said Markham cheerfully. 'Are we in the right place?' He flourished his printed invitation which was immediately scanned.

The secret is not to watch anxiously, worrying about whether or not you'll pass muster, but to fix your attention elsewhere. We turned our back on whatever they were doing because it wasn't important and of course we'd get in, and surveyed the remains of the once and future South Lawn.

'I bet this was a nice place once,' remarked Markham.

I nodded. 'Shame to let these old places go but I suppose no one wants to live in them any longer.'

'No,' said Markham. 'Only idiots would live in a place like this.'

We turned back again.

'Everything OK?' said Markham, holding out his hand for the invite.

'One moment, please, sir. This is a polite request for you to surrender any weapons voluntarily.'

'Not armed,' he said sunnily, which was perfectly true. Unless we'd brought Pennyroyal's portable armoury with us, we'd never be able to match the sort of firepower our hosts – whoever they were – could probably muster.

We were wanded anyway, which displayed typical levels of trust between punters and puntees.

They stepped back. 'Everything is perfectly in order, sir and madam,' said Retainer One, not relinquishing our invite but imprinting a barcode on the back of Markham's hand. 'This will grant you access to all the parts of the building deemed safe. For your own safety, sir and madam,' he imprinted another barcode on mine, 'please do not deviate from the safe areas. Some parts of this building are in a fragile condition.'

'Be awful if you had to dig us out before we'd had the chance to buy something expensive,' said Markham.

'Our thoughts exactly, sir.' Retainer Two handed us a glossy catalogue. I couldn't wait to see what was being offered, but first things first.

Retainer Two continued. 'Ahead of you is the Great Hall where the auction will take place in . . .' He consulted a lovely old-fashioned fob watch. They really had spared no expense.

'Twenty minutes. Refreshments are being served in the old dining room to your right. The artefacts are currently being displayed in the Library should you wish for a closer look, although each item will be brought through into the Great Hall when its turn comes. Is there anything else with which we can assist you?'

'Toilets,' said Markham promptly, because climbing out of the toilet window is always number one choice for a quick exit.

'First floor, sir. Ladies to the right, gentlemen to the left.'

'Thank you,' said Markham. 'All ready, dear?'

He offered me his arm. I'd like to say I seared him to the bone with a single glance but he never notices that sort of thing. I've no idea how Hunter copes with him but she seems to do quite well. Speculation on her methods has been varied, imaginative and fruitless.

We were approached by a man dressed as a waiter and offered a glass of champagne each. We're not supposed to drink on the job but I took a sip anyway. Just for authenticity, you understand.

Markham tucked his catalogue away. 'Let's go and see if it's the real deal, shall we?'

Mindful of the ever-watching cameras, I nodded enthusiastically, and was quite proud of myself for remembering to ask our waiter where the Library was, and off we went.

My first thought was, thank God Dr Dowson couldn't see the state of his beloved Library. For a start, part of the ceiling had come down and R&D hadn't even moved in yet. All the bookcases were empty. In fact, there wasn't a book in sight anywhere. Some of the shelving had come away from the walls, bringing the plaster down with them and exposing the wooden lathes. There were holes in those too. The windows were boarded up so at least the swans wouldn't be joining us. The lights were on but I could hear the sound of the generators in the distance, so the building hadn't yet been wired for electricity. Actually, it was all a little bit sad.

'Over here,' said Markham, taking my arm, and we went to inspect the merchandise.

Well – was all I could say. In fact, I'll say it again. *Well*.

'Bloody hell,' said Markham, transfixed.

'Excuse me,' said a voice behind us because we were blocking the way. We stepped aside and I led Markham to a quiet corner where Dr Dowson's desk normally sat, whispering, 'If even a fraction of this is genuine . . .' and had to stop because the implications were mind-blowing. If this was typical of Flying Auctions, then I was going to be recommending to Smallhope and Pennyroyal that we move into this area full-time. The display was gobsmacking – and that's a technically correct historical expression. Absolutely gobsmacking.

I took another sip of champagne because – *well*.

We made our way slowly around the room. Anticlockwise.

'Fun Fact,' whispered Markham and I just knew he was about to explain the origin of the word widdershins, but at that moment, my brain was concentrating on the glories on display.

Directly in front of me, resplendent behind a transparent but no doubt very effective security shield, stood an exquisite golden, glimmering panel, very carefully lit to bring out the detail. Markham dragged out his catalogue, but if this was what I thought it was, then we were looking at a panel from the famous Amber Room. It was staggeringly beautiful. I had no

209

idea whether it was genuine or not – it looked genuine, but the best fakes always do. On the other hand, given the nature of naughty people for whom the timeline is just something to plunder, it might well be the real thing. I had no way of telling, but if it was . . .

The Amber Room was part of the Catherine Palace, built in the 18th century at Tsarkosoye Selo near St Petersburg. The palace was stuffed full of gold-gilded mirrors, mosaics, carvings, ornaments, furniture and so forth, but was most famous for the massive amber wall panels in one of its rooms – hence the name, the Amber Room. Tsarkosoye Selo was captured by the Germans in 1941 and the Amber Room was disassembled and taken back to Germany, after which it was never seen again.

As you can imagine, the panel was attracting a great deal of attention. I could hear gasps and soft cries of amazement. Markham and I stood a little to one side, ostensibly admiring the panel, but in reality, checking out our fellow punters. Of whom more later.

A little further on stood what looked like a great stone sarcophagus. Heaven knows how they'd got it in here. Actually, heaven knows how they'd managed to get it out of its original resting place. I couldn't see it going anywhere without a ton of heavy-lifting gear. Or some kind of anti-grav device so beloved of sci-fi writers. A carefully printed notice nearby proudly informed us we were looking at the Sarcophagus of Menkaure.

'What do you think?' murmured Markham.

I pretended to flip through the catalogue. 'Well, the sarcophagus was originally looted from the Pyramid of Menkaure – that's the smallest of the three Cairo pyramids – and loaded aboard the merchant ship *Beatrice*, which sank on her way back to England, taking the sarcophagus with her. Given the size and weight of it, it's unlikely to have been reclaimed from the bottom of the sea, even if anyone knew where it actually sank. A fake, I should imagine. Or they've somehow obtained a genuine sarcophagus and called it Menkaure's to jack up the value.'

'Or,' said Markham, 'given the dastardly deeds of Time Pirates . . .'

'Really,' I said, turning to look at him. 'That's what we're calling them now? Time Pirates?'

'Yeah,' he said, excitedly. 'I've always wanted to be a Time Pirate. Haven't you?'

I rolled my eyes.

'Yes,' he said, thoughtfully. 'If it was me, I'd have half-inched the thing before it even got on board the *Beatrice*. The fact that the ship foundered before the theft was discovered was just a piece of luck.'

I stared at the lump of inanimate matter in front of me. And then the sarcophagus, as well. 'A possibility, I suppose.'

'A probability, I would have thought,' he said. 'What's next?'

The next exhibit was tiny. We had to wait for people to move away before we could get close enough to see for ourselves. Two fragments of papyrus covered in faint, light brown symbols or handwriting. Markham consulted his catalogue.

'Oh, this is interesting. Greek texts from the Hidden Library of Ivan the Terrible. Know anything about those?'

'Wow,' I said, peering more closely and trying to see if I recognised any of the symbols. Ivan's Hidden Library was supposed to have contained hundreds of ancient Greek texts – it was famous for them, in fact – and here were just a couple of

211

fragments. I had visions of laughing Time Pirates – bugger, now he'd got me at it – tearing the texts into fragments and selling each piece separately. I gritted my teeth. These bastards were going to hell.

We moved on. 'A jewelled star of the Order of St Patrick,' said Markham, reading the carefully handwritten sign. 'Stolen in 1907 and never seen again.'

'Until now,' I said, moving on. 'Oh my God.'

The next exhibit was jaw-dropping. A copper scroll retrieved . . . good word . . . *retrieved* from Qumran and supposedly giving specific details of the exact location of the massive hidden treasure referred to in some of the existing scrolls. 'Bloody hell, Markham.'

'Hush,' he said, taking my elbow and moving me on towards a waiter bearing a silver platter. 'Have a vol-au-vent and calm down.'

I did both – one more successfully than the other.

We both recognised the objects on the next table. Three bejewelled golden eggs, each in a transparent display case and snuggled in a nest of purple silk. 'Fabergé eggs,' I said. 'These could well be genuine' – as if I'd know any different – 'there are still a number of eggs unaccounted for, I believe.'

'Three less now,' said Markham, thoughtfully.

I opened my catalogue. The first egg – only about four inches tall – was described as the Alexander III Commemorative. The surface was enamelled in a beautiful greeny-blue with an almost metallic sheen. The exterior was divided into squares and diamonds by precisely placed jewels, each with a central design, in tiny, winking precious stones. It was exquisite and must have taken months of eye-straining work.

'This is one of three eggs made to commemorate Tsar Alex-ander III,' I said, reading from the catalogue. 'Every egg contained a surprise and this one contained a tiny golden bust of Alexander himself. I wonder if it's still inside.'

Markham was staring thoughtfully and said nothing.

The next egg was the largest at nearly nine inches high. 'The Royal Danish,' I read aloud, 'containing miniatures of the King and Queen of Denmark.' I stared at the beautiful pale blue and white object in front of me, its jewels sparkling even in the current not very good lighting. 'Wow.'

'There's an elephant on the top,' said Markham, critically. I don't know what he had against elephants but I suspected one would have got the better of him at some point in his life.

The third egg was labelled the Nécessaire. 'Designed as an etui,' I read.

'A what?'

'An etui. It contains – or did contain – miniature women's toilet items. No, hang on – women's miniature toilet items. I'm surprised you didn't know that.'

'You're reading that out from the catalogue, aren't you?'

'Maybe.'

We gazed in awed silence at the glittering bejewelled egg, nestling in its silk nest. Sapphires, emeralds, rubies, diamonds – it was superb. One of the most beautiful things I'd ever seen.

'This one survived the Revolution,' I continued, 'and was last seen officially in 1952.'

There was no reply from Markham. He was staring at the eggs. No – actually he was staring at the transparent boxes containing the eggs. Each was in its own case so I suspected each egg was to be sold separately.

'What are you thinking?'

'Nothing. Nothing at all.'

'Don't believe you.'

'If you steal something from someone who has already stolen it in the first place, then is it actually stealing? I mean, you're not depriving the rightful owner, are you?'

'A tricky conundrum, but possession is nine tenths of the law,' I said.

'Exactly what I was thinking. Shall we move on?'

We moved on. Up until this moment, everything I'd seen had been beautiful, magnificent, spectacular, or a combination of all three. Not this time. 'Bloody hell, that's ugly.'

Markham clutched my arm. 'That's the Jules Rimet Cup.'

'The what?'

'Your ignorance is astounding.'

'Hey . . .'

'It's the World Cup.'

'The what-what?'

He sighed in an unnecessarily exaggerated manner. 'It's the Jules Rimet Trophy. Presented to winners of the World Cup.'

I must have looked blank.

'Football, Max.'

'Oh. Sorry – I thought you were talking about something important.'

'No, if a country won it three times then it was theirs to keep.'

I peered at the object in question. 'As a punishment? A warning not to do that again?'

He ignored this. 'It was presented to Brazil permanently and then it was nicked from Rio de Janeiro in 1983. Never found.'

'You can see why. Who would want that on their mantel-piece? Not when you could have the Sarcophagus of Menkaure.'

'You're so weird,' he said. 'Let's move on, shall we?'

We moved on. All the years I'd worked at St Mary's and I'd never had any idea the Library had ever housed anything like this. Damp and dilapidated it might be at the moment, but there were all sorts of stunning artefacts housed here today. I've never seen such a treasure trove. Not outside of a museum, anyway. There were fragments of fossils, including, suppos-edly, a piece of Peking Man. We spared that a brief glance and then I touched Markham's arm. On a small table, propped against the wall, stood, supposedly, Michelangelo's *Leda and the Swan*.

'Bloody hell,' I said, staring, unable to believe my eyes.

'Bloody hell,' said Markham, for completely different rea-sons. 'How the hell did that ever get past the religious censors? Is that swan doing what I think he's doing? Is it suddenly very hot in here? It's a miracle the paint didn't melt.'

I moved him on. Before he melted.

There were various fragments of scrolls and papyrus, including, apparently, work by Sappho; some small statues res-cued from Nimrud before parts of the city were destroyed by ISIS; what looked like a parliamentary mace – from Victoria, Australia, according to the catalogue; and any number of swords.

Including one in particular.

Unlike the gleaming, fairly modern-looking weapons lying around, this was a dull, badly nicked affair, with loose leather threading around the hilt. I stared for a moment. Given where

215

we were and the supposed quality of the artefacts on offer, this was . . . intriguing.

I consulted my catalogue.

It's not polite to hyperventilate in public. Sadly, my efforts not to hyperventilate in public nearly caused me to explode. I did manage to stay on my feet but I might have experienced just the faintest tremor.

I was looking at Durendal. The legendary sword of Roland. Durendal.

Originally forged by Wayland the Smith, maker of weapons and armour to gods and heroes, it was supposedly presented to the young Charlemagne by an angel and later given to Roland, who was one of the twelve legendary paladins of Charlemagne. At the Battle of Roncevaux Pass, Roland held the rear, enabling Charlemagne's army to retreat to France, and doing massive damage to the Saracens, including, I think, the Saracen king and his son. Legend says Roland and his men routed the hundred-thousand-strong army.

Roland was killed and there are several versions of what happened to Durendal. Some say Roland attempted to destroy it by repeatedly clashing it against the rocks, but the sword could not be broken. The monks of Rocamadour claim he flung it into a deep ravine where it still lies – although not any longer if I was looking at the real thing. Some say that he fell, mortally wounded, and his last act was to try to conceal the sword beneath his body.

Whichever story was true, there was a possibility I was looking at the actual sword of Roland. Durendal. As with all the other exhibits, this one was securely encased in a transparent box, but I was able to walk all around it, getting as close as

216

I could. At one point I was so close my breath was actually steaming the case. A security guard coughed and I moved back on wobbly legs. This sword could be genuine. It looked genuine. Imagine if it was.

Markham took my arm. 'All right?'

I nodded, unable to speak. And that doesn't happen often.

I looked at it again. Old. Tired. Battered. Torn from its resting place. The place where its master had left it. Doomed to end its days in a vault somewhere, possibly never to see daylight again. It didn't seem right, somehow.

I looked around, torn between *Oh my God, this stuff is amazing* and *Oh my God, these people deserve to be torn asunder by angry horses*. And whether I meant the people running the auction or the punters themselves, I couldn't say. Who is the greater criminal? The person who supplies the demand or the person who creates it?

The people here looked respectable enough – I bet at least half of them were pillars of their communities. Business-suited men. Impeccably turned-out women. All crouched gloatingly over what was nothing better than plunder. They were no better than the grave robbers of Ancient Egypt.

There were real treasures here – treasures that belonged to the world – that should be available for study and research. They'd been ripped from their context – and don't get me started on what so-called lesser treasures would have been destroyed during the process – and were about to be snapped up as an investment by people whose souls were made of the sort of hairy gunk normally found at the bottom of a grease trap. I should do something.

I looked around. In addition to the two very superior

gentlemen on the door, there were two more similarly dressed and acting as ushers, six highly visible security staff inside with an unknown number outside, two stately waiters, and another unknown number of catering staff doing a sterling job somewhere because the refreshments were excellent. All were men, all were very polite and professional and, I suspected, all were armed to the teeth. We wouldn't be single-handedly arresting this little lot.

We left the Library and split up to get the lie of the land. Or looking for the toilet, as it's known if you get caught.

The Ladies' restroom was on the first floor – up the familiar rickety and uncarpeted stairs – Bashford would do himself a real injury if he fell down these – and just down the corridor from my old office. I resisted the temptation to go and look.

Internally, St Mary's was in a pitiful state. All the windows were shuttered. Most of the doors were locked. Plaster was falling from the walls and the smell of damp was very strong up here. I know there were generators outside but I had no idea how the organisers had managed to get a water supply – probably better not to ask – so I gave the facilities a miss and headed back downstairs again to the Great Hall.

Markham was waiting for me at the bottom, just as a little bell tinkled. People began to move towards the rows of chairs that had been set out.

The Flying Auction was about to begin.

The ushers locked the doors and, interestingly, a paragraph on the back page of the catalogue informed us no one was allowed to leave until the auction was concluded. Even after they'd purchased their items of choice, everyone had no option but to stay put until the end. A sensible security precaution – and, I suppose, there was always the chance another item would unexpectedly catch their eye.

There were eleven other customers excluding me and the embryo Time Pirate at my side. Only two were women. One was the traditional Lady in Black. She sat slightly apart, her wide-brimmed hat shading her face. Completely pointless because she chain-smoked throughout the entire proceedings – despite murmured protests around her – and was so wreathed in smoke you couldn't make out her features anyway. I've no idea how the auctioneer knew whether she was bidding or not but that was his problem. The other woman was fur clad and elderly. She kept her attention solely on her catalogue and appeared only interested in the supposed works of Sappho.

The men were more difficult to place. They all wore suits of either dark grey or black. Markham and I were easily the most casually dressed people there, and that included the staff. I think three of the suits had come together – they all seemed to know each other, anyway. They sounded German or maybe Austrian. Some of the others seemed to know each other, as well – there was a great deal of handshaking and some back-slapping. They probably met at this type of thing quite often.

Markham and I split up. A greater chance of one of us getting away should things go tits up, said Markham. And for God's sake, don't bid for anything by mistake.

One of the waiters held a chair for me. I was off to the right – Markham to the left. I suspected the major bidders – the ones from whom they expected to make big money – were seated front and centre. However, the chairs were very comfortable with – ta dah! – cupholders. I placed my mysteriously empty glass in the appropriate holder where it was immediately topped up again. Seriously, I could get used to this.

I settled myself and then looked around. There were still two or three empty seats so possibly some people hadn't turned up or had changed their minds. I could see two guards at the front door, wearing neat black suits and earpieces. They probably carried enough weaponry to invade a medium-sized country. Presumably their function was to keep us in and everyone else out. There was no Long Corridor because Hawking didn't exist yet, so the only other exit from the Great Hall was through the kitchen. Another guard stood there. I knew there were two more in the Library, guarding the merchandise. Another one stood at the foot of the stairs. So that was the six accounted for.

The two waiters flitted about, either refilling glasses or brandishing trays of elegant snacks. We were encouraged to partake freely so I did, because you don't want to be rude, do you?

I glanced casually around and Markham had vanished. Nowhere to be seen. I didn't dare peer too closely. There was no shouting so presumably he hadn't been caught yet. Whatever he was doing.

I made a business of scanning through my catalogue and marking up items in which I might possibly be interested, all the time keeping my eyes peeled for him. Whatever he was doing. I sighed and began to plan our possible escape. Out through the kitchen seemed quickest and easiest, although I wasn't optimistic.

A bell tinkled and the auction began.

The auctioneer – a tall, cadaverous man in formal morning wear who looked like an undertaker but had the most melodious voice I'd ever heard – took up his position at the podium set up outside the Library, checked his catalogue, straightened his sleeves, ran an experienced eye over the expectant crowd, and began.

'Good day, ladies and gentlemen. Today's auction will be conducted in English. I believe most of you are comfortable with that language?' He paused. No one disagreed. 'The currency will be pounds sterling. Conversion charts can be provided on request.' He paused again. No one took him up on the offer.

'Before we begin, there are just a few tiny housekeeping details to address. As old friends will already be aware, the doors will be locked for the duration of the auction. I can assure you this is solely for reasons of security and absolutely not because we intend to hold you all to ransom afterwards.'

He paused again for the uncertain laugh. I made sure to smile at his jolly jape while thinking, shit . . .

'Just to reassure you all – in the extremely unlikely event of a fire, please remain calm and our staff will escort you quickly and safely to the nearest exit.'

In common with every meeting I'd ever attended, no one took a blind bit of notice of the important information designed to save their lives in an emergency, instead shifting impatiently in the seats and rustling their catalogues.

'And finally, as always, you will be required to surrender your catalogue on leaving. For obvious reasons. And now, if everyone is ready – we shall begin. Can we have the first lot, please.'

We started with the small stuff. Fossils, tablets, scrolls and such. I suspected the Amber Panel would be the climax of the afternoon. The pace was brisk. Each item was brought in and displayed on two big screens set up each side of the room. Anyone who wanted a closer look was invited to do so although no one was allowed to touch. That done, the auctioneer would name the opening bid and off we would go. Bidding was fierce and fast. There were, obviously, no telephone or internet bids. If you wanted to bid, then you had to be here in person to do it.

Bids were tremendously discreet. No one waved their arms around like a windmill. Half the time I had no idea who was bidding, but presumably the auctioneer, standing on his temporary dais outside the Library, had an excellent view of his audience.

I sat very quietly, hands firmly clasped in my lap, and hoped Markham – wherever he was – was doing the same. The cost apart, we'd never get a giant, inadvertently purchased sarcophagus home in the pod.

On completion of each sale, the artefact in question was taken to a separate room – part of what would be Wardrobe one day – presumably to be packaged and paid for. The ushers would have the next item up on display even before the first one had cleared the room. There would be murmurs of either congratulation or disappointment and then everyone moved on to the next lot. The whole thing was slick and well organised. These people were really professional. So fast were they that the first three to four items sold in under five minutes.

I looked down at the catalogue again. The final paragraph advised us that once the Flying Auction was over, guests were requested to vacate the premises no more than thirty minutes after the sale of the last item. I calculated the whole thing would be over and done with in less than two and a half hours. If they hadn't received any sort of tip-off, the chances of the Time Police nailing any of this little lot were remote. All the better for Smallhope and Pennyroyal, of course. And Markham and Maxwell, too.

My attention, which had been wandering as I watched the crowd, was suddenly caught. The next item had not appeared as smoothly as it should have done. In fact, it hadn't appeared at all. The air of expectancy gave way to concern. This was obviously unprecedented. People began to crane their necks towards the Library. Had something gone wrong? I too was gazing around with a worried expression, only I was looking for Markham. Who was nowhere to be seen. I sighed. Here we go.

A guard appeared at the auctioneer's side and whispered urgently. As I watched, more armed guards moved suddenly in front of the doors. Which were locked, anyway.

The auctioneer, whose face showed no expression at all, turned back to the murmuring customers.

'Ladies and gentlemen, many and profound apologies. This auction is at an end. No more items will be offered for sale this afternoon. I regret to inform you that we have a thief in our midst.'

Well, that was a bit rich considering who it was coming from.

I looked around again. Definitely no Markham in sight and I think we all know what that meant. He could be in the bog, of course, but it was much more likely he'd been in the Library. Being a naughty boy.

Things suddenly looked very ugly indeed. Black-clad security staff stood at every door. More were emerging. A lot more than I'd originally noticed. I wondered if they'd been outside watching for intruders. The punters were murmuring angrily among themselves. Outrage and 'Do they know who I am?' were only seconds away.

The auctioneer drew himself up to his full height. 'Ladies and gentlemen, regrettable though such a step might be to us – nay, repugnant, even,' he paused, suddenly looking considerably less benign than a minute ago, 'you will all be searched.'

'We will not,' said a man behind me. Other people nodded in agreement. I had no issues with being searched, but heaven knows what Markham could have hidden in his nooks and crannies. Always supposing you could find someone foolhardy enough to approach his nooks and crannies without special equipment.

The auctioneer wasn't having any of that. 'Willingly or unwillingly, you will be searched. If you do not cooperate, you will be held down and searched, a procedure you will not enjoy. Now, we can do this the easy way – or we can do it these gentlemen's preferred way, which is with lots of public groping and all the unpleasantness that will entail.'

There was a lot of angry muttering. One or two people stood up, clearly intending to head for the doors. They'd be turned back and things would get ugly. Time to establish my credentials as a good girl. I stood up. 'You may begin with me.'

The auctioneer bowed gravely. 'Thank you, madam. Your cooperation is greatly appreciated.'

I was taken into the Library, now half empty of treasures, although the big stuff was still here. The two other women trailed along as well. It would seem that women were to be searched in here – men in what would one day be Wardrobe.

I tried to see which artefact could be missing but the layout was different now that some items had been removed and it could have been anything. Except for the sarcophagus, the amber panel and *Leda and the Swan*, all still very visible.

The search was manual, carried out by a man because there were no women on the staff. He was thorough but professional. The groping threat might have been just that – a threat. On the other hand, of course, I might now be outside the accepted parameters of groping eligibility.

He certainly knew what they were looking for, even if I didn't. At his request, I handed over my jacket. He went through the pockets and then patted me down in a general sort of way, but it was very obvious that whatever he was looking for, I didn't have it. I suspected they'd checked their own footage and knew I hadn't moved from the auction area. It wasn't a strip search – I was wearing clean underwear, should anyone be curious – and it certainly wasn't a rubber gloves job, either.

They did Chain-Smoking Lady at the same time. I was interested to see they'd managed to persuade her to desist for a few moments, though I have to say the haze appeared to be permanent.

Eventually he was done with me and muttering, 'Thank you, miss,' he passed on to his next victim – the fur-bedecked matron who gave him to understand she had boundaries and crossing them would result in the loss of his front teeth. Disappointingly, she didn't say how that would be accomplished and I was ushered out before I could see how her search went.

Everyone was presented with a glass of champagne on

225

completion of the search. I took my glass and circulated, listening to the outraged comments around me.

Markham had mysteriously reappeared. I have no idea from which direction he'd emerged. No one has worked out how he does that. He was now standing just inside Wardrobe, waiting in the men's line, three from the end, hands in his pockets, looking bored.

I tried to keep my face expressionless. Would he have had a chance to stash the stuff or was it still on him?

Casually I made to wander over – there might be an opportunity for him to pass whatever it was on to me, now that I'd been done, so to speak, but a guard very politely turned me aside. For precisely that reason, I suspected. The guard wasn't unpleasant. In fact, everyone was very polite. Mind you, for the amount of money some people were splashing out, they should be.

Markham twitched me a frown. Bugger. He hadn't managed to shed his load. Now what?

His line was inching forwards. He was the next one to be searched. I had only a minute to think of something. I was just contemplating setting fire to the place – my go-to procedure in times of crisis – when there was a shout from outside, a bang that sounded very like an explosion, and a sudden impact on the doors as something big tried to gain access.

Everyone – punters and puntees – stood frozen. Including, it has to be said – me. Because I knew what this was. Sinking under the weight of stolen goods he might be, but suddenly, Markham was no longer the issue. Because if this was who I thought it was, then we could kiss goodbye to our profit margin and commission this afternoon. To say nothing of brief but thoroughly unpleasant treatment at the hands of the Time Police.

I had only seconds to think of something. I flung a quick prayer in the direction of the god of historians and just for once – it worked. I was damn near dazzled. Because I'd had a Brilliant Idea. A staggeringly Brilliant Idea. Stonking even by my standards. All I would need was a ton of luck and balls of steel. Stand back everyone and watch Maxwell Save the Day.

Without thinking – a very valuable character trait, trust me – I ran up the wobbly stairs to the half-landing. Glancing at my watch – because I had to get this right – I pulled out my SmartCard and held it high, at the same time shouting, 'I am an accredited representative of the Time Police and you are all under arrest. Your pods are impounded and all stolen property seized by me.'

And suddenly found myself looking down at every gun in the western hemisphere. Unimportant, as it turned out. Barely had I finished speaking when the outer doors exploded inwards with an enormous crash and suddenly there were armoured men everywhere shouting at us to put our hands in the air and get down on the ground.

I don't know if you've ever tried that, but it's bloody near impossible – not without bruising your knees quite badly, anyway.

The bloody Time Police were here. Useless pillocks that they usually were. But not today. Today I was very pleased to see them.

They were fully helmeted so I couldn't see their faces. I couldn't read any of their names either but I didn't think I recognised any of them. Which, I hoped, meant they probably wouldn't recognise me, either. They strode around in typical Time Police mode, pushing people in all directions and shouting at the tops of their voices. I couldn't see outside, but I didn't mind betting the South Lawn was covered in pants-wetting black pods. Arrested by the Time Police. Oh – the embarrassment of it all.

I was grabbed by some sapling with the name Rosen imprinted on his chest. 'You're nicked.'

'No,' I said, 'I'm not.'

You're not supposed to argue with the Time Police. They don't like it. He pulled out his sonic. I was seconds away from not having clean underwear any longer.

'I'm one of you,' I said. Not words I ever thought I'd have to utter again. 'This is my ID. Do you have some higher form of life to which I could show it?'

He didn't sonic me but I'm guessing it was close.

Very, very slowly, because I think I might have managed to annoy him, I offered him my SmartCard – the one with the magic hologram authorising the bearer to act on behalf of the Time Police when the occasion warranted, etc., etc.

He stared suspiciously. At least I assumed that was what he was doing, I could only see myself reflected in his shiny black visor. I compounded the danger I was in by using my reflection to check my lipstick was OK. Personally, even I'd have shot me.

He ran my card through his scratchpad and it bleeped. He nodded and reluctantly – very reluctantly – stepped back. I made sure I retrieved my SmartCard because Pennyroyal had been very explicit on the subject of lost cards.

The officer in charge, a big bloke, even for a Time Police gorilla, started giving orders for the transfer of prisoners. Time to act. And while everyone was concentrating on me, they weren't concentrating on Markham and whatever he was up to.

'Not so fast, young feller,' I cried, trotting across the Hall and channelling Lady Amelia as hard as I could go. 'I think you'll find this is our collar. I and my team tracked them down. We followed them here and arrested them, and their pods, and their stolen property. Ergo – our collar. Our bounty.'

I flashed my SmartCard again, really quite enjoying myself.

He loomed but I wasn't in the mood to be a loomee. 'How many of them are you claiming you arrested?'

'All of them.' My gesture encompassed the entire room. 'And I've already officially impounded the really rather impressive stash of goodies in the next room. And their pods outside. I'm awfully glad to see you, of course, because I'm really not sure how we'd have got all this lot back to TPHQ, so I'm grateful for your assistance. Nevertheless –' I flourished my card again – 'my collar, sunshine.'

One or two punters, possibly under the mistaken impression that sticking with me would enable them to escape the Time Police, nodded vigorously.

'If you collect the security footage –' I gestured to the cameras – 'you'll see that I arrested everyone here at 1529 hours, and you entered the premises at 1530. I'm happy to let you take them into your custody now, of course, because you'll be saving me all that tedious paperwork.'

I scribbled a receipt on the back of my catalogue and handed it to him. 'If you could sign my docket, please. Thank you so much, Captain. The prisoners are officially all yours. We'll be off now and leave you to take all the credit. To which you are welcome, with my goodwill. Toodle-pip.'

Markham was standing behind him, innocence radiating from him in waves. He smiled politely at the officer, holding up his own SmartCard. 'Good afternoon, officer. When you're ready, ma'am.'

It wasn't that easy, of course. They had to go through the footage first, but there I was, large as life – slightly larger, actually, because the food at Home Farm was very good – wreathed in the rosy glow of slightly too much champagne, single-handedly arresting the entire room and impounding their pods and stuff. I stood patiently while all this happened because my concern now was getting myself and Markham out of their clutches – not least because the wannabe Time Pirate standing beside me was riddled with stolen property.

Eventually and very reluctantly, they let us go.

'Slowly and without running,' said Markham as we left the Hall and headed out through the front doors.

Just to be on the safe side, I waited until we were down the drive, out of the gates and halfway to the village before asking, 'What did you get?'

'Two of the Fabergé eggs. Valuable and portable.'

'And priceless.'

'And that.'

'How did you . . . ?'

'Well, their security was very good as far as it went, Max. Those display boxes were uncrackable and I didn't even try. Sadly, the silly sods didn't think to screw them down because, well . . . why would they? I magicked away the two smaller ones.'

'How?'

'Sleight of hand. I just tossed them under the table. Hidden by the fancy hangings. Mind you – I had to pick my moment and I had to be quick. One minute there – the next minute gone.'

'But wasn't there some sort of alarm?'

'As I said, Max, their security wasn't as good as it looked. Mind you, I don't know what else they expected. Everything was powered by generators. Their greatest strength – holding the auction in the past – turned out to be their biggest weakness. The bulk of their power went on lighting, heating and refreshments. And the cameras, of course.'

'Didn't they pick you up on camera?'

'Well, there was a fair bit of agitated milling around when someone said they'd seen a rat.'

I regarded him suspiciously. 'Who said they saw a rat?'

'A genuine error,' he said, looking hurt. 'I think it was that woman's fur thing actually, but the lighting was very bad.'

'They'd have rumbled you sooner or later. Good job the Time Police did turn up.'

'Yes, they've done us several massive favours today, haven't they? And the best thing is they don't even know it.'

'Let's have a look then.'

He looked shifty. 'Ah.'

'Oh God . . . what have you done?'

'No, no, everything's fine – it's just that when the Time Police turned up, I grabbed the opportunity to stash the stuff in case they took it into their heads to search me.'

'You idiot – I had everything well in hand.'

'Well, I didn't know that.'

'You should have. I always have everything well in hand.'

'How can you say that? I've never known anyone have anything less in hand than you.'

'Says the bloke who stole two priceless eggs and then lost them.'

'They're not lost. I know exactly where they are. It's just a case of . . . going back and getting them.'

'Are you insane? The Time Police will be all over St Mary's.'

'They won't find them.'

'You hope.'

'They won't know they're missing.'

'They will if they match their haul against the catalogue. Missing – two Fabergé eggs.'

He shrugged. 'I took a chance. If the Time Police do find them then we're no worse off. If they don't . . .' He grinned.

'Well,' I said, doubtfully. 'You might get away with it. They were very small. I suppose you could argue they're the sort of thing that could easily be mislaid.'

'Um . . .' He looked even more shifty.

'Oh God – what now?'

'Well, it was just lying there. It seemed too good an opportunity to miss.'

'What was too good an opportunity to miss?'

'The sword. You know – the one you quite liked.'

The world swam before my eyes. I clutched his arm. 'Durendal? The sword of Roland? You stole the fabled Durendal?'

'I did indeed. If I wasn't before, I'm certainly a legend now.'

'Don't you have to be dead before that can happen? Because if so I'm happy to oblige.' I was struck by a thought. He looked remarkably sword-free. 'Did you stash that too?'

'No. Too big.'

Oh God. 'So, where is it?'

'It's fine,' he said. 'Everything's fine. Absolutely fine.'

'*Where is it?*'

I knew the answer even as I asked. He was walking strangely, even for him.

'Down my trouser leg.'

I can't tell you what images flashed through my mind because these stories are supposed to be suitable for young people.

'Which leg?'

'Can't you tell?'

'Don't tell me the eggs are down there, too.'

'Of course not. They weren't big but I couldn't keep them on me so I shoved them behind one of the bookcases.'

'What?'

'What's the problem?'

'Well, I don't know. I thought you'd have buried them. Or found a secret panel or something.'

'I had seconds to dispose of some of the hottest property in History. And it's only supposed to be temporary. I'll retrieve them somehow later on.'

'So, you shoved two priceless artefacts down an unknown hole where something unpleasant could happen to them, and another down your trouser leg where something unpleasant is certain to happen to it.'

Markham grinned. He does this. He does the most outrageous things and when you attempt to point out the outrageousness of the things he's done, he just grins at you, and after a while your brain shuts down and you find yourself agreeing that his actions were entirely and completely reasonable, and well done, Markham.

'Nothing wrong with the inside of my trousers.' He shook his leg like an inaccurate drunk on a Saturday night.

Unpleasant image aside, I was horrified. 'You're kidding. It's the sword of Roland. It deserves a bloody sight better than having all your private bits within nestling distance. Good job it's not still sharp.'

He grimaced. 'Yes, it is.'

'A good job?'

'Still sharp.'

I ignored any potential damage to his nether bits. They'd once survived a thorough scalding – they could handle this. 'The eggs. Which bookcase?'

'Second one from the end on the left. They'll be fine. Lots of reasons they might not still be there in our time, of course. Renovation, rebuilding and all that. They could have been found any time since 1921.'

'True – although we've never heard anything.'

He grinned. 'No, we haven't, have we? I'm a bit optimistic about this one, Max. But I'm not risking taking this bugger through time.' He slapped his leg and then winced. 'Not with all these Time Police bastards around. I'll just stash this some-where and then we'll jump forwards and do a bit of sneaky retrieval, shall we?'

We were nearly back at the pod. I have to say I was surprised how well our pod blended into the general landscape. There were strange little huts all over the place, knocked together out of old bits of wood, sacking, mismatched bricks and stones – anything anyone could lay their hands on. Everyone in the village seemed to have at least one for animals, wood, farm stuff, fodder, old furniture, and so on. Our pod was just one of many.

'What will you do with the sword?'

'I thought I'd bury it or shove it inside a tree or something.'

'What sort of tree?'

'I don't know. And none of them have any leaves right now, which makes it even more difficult. I'll have to mark the tree somehow.'

'With what?'

'A sign or something.'

I had a cunning thought. 'Your initials.'

He blinked. 'We'll need a big tree.'

'Yeah.' I waited a moment and then said, casually, 'You'd better tell me what they are in case you don't live long enough to retrieve it.' And waited, because this would be something to report back to Peterson. If I ever saw him again.

'What – all of them?'

Now I blinked. 'How many have you got?'

'Initials?'

'Yeah.'

'Altogether?'

'Yeah.'

There was a lot of heavy breathing and finger counting. I held my breath. This was it . . .

'One.'

He might have had a sword down his trouser leg – that was his story anyway – but he still moved too fast for me to get to him, disappearing into the woods in search of an appropriate tree.

I made my way back to the pod for a nice cup of tea. It had been quite an exciting day.

And it wasn't over yet.

On Markham's return, there was a certain amount of discussion between us. This is St Mary's speak for a bit of an

235

argument. But no bloodshed. Bloodshed is defined as a *brisk* discussion.

'I've set the coordinates for exactly the same place,' I said. 'Ian won't squeak if he sees our pod in his back field.'

Markham nodded. 'Date?'

'Last summer,' I said, and braced myself for argument.

'Why then?'

'Well, we don't know how long the Time Police will occupy the building. And although we know St Mary's is empty now, we do know it'll become a school very soon. We could try to gain access then, but I think the chances of getting in unnoticed would be remote. After that, it's requisitioned as a hospital during the Second World War and the last thing we need is to be dancing around a semi-military establishment in wartime without any official ID. We know it was empty afterwards, but I can't help feeling that if the organisers of the Flying Auction had been able to gain access then, then they would have done so, because at least it would have been wired for electricity. So I think the best thing for us is to jump back to our own time, last summer – because we weren't there then – but if we are caught, then I have lots of plausible explanations.'

Talk about over-explaining.

He was very unimpressed. 'Such as?'

'Sorry? Such as what?'

'These plausible explanations of yours. What are they?'

'I haven't thought of them yet,' I said with dignity.

'And suppose someone else has got there first and the stuff disappeared years ago?'

'Well, I don't think that's happened. We've heard nothing.

No headlines about unexpected treasures discovered in obscure country house libraries. All the bookcases are still original, so for all we know they just replastered the walls, shoved the bookcases back against them and filled the shelves up with books again.'

'Can't help feeling a lot of that is wishful thinking, Max.'

'I'm not the one who shoved two priceless Fabergé eggs in a hole in the wall.'

'I made an executive decision,' he said with dignity.

'Look – if they're not there then, we'll jump back to, say, the 1960s.'

'The place could be full of hippies,' he objected.

'Well when, then?'

He remained silent.

I tried again. 'Look, it makes sense to go back to our own time, not least because if we are caught there isn't actually a reason why we shouldn't be there. All right, I've been sacked, and there was a certain amount of "never darken my door again", but that's only something to worry about if I'm actually caught. And why would I be? No one's more familiar with the layout of St Mary's than me. Come on – don't tell me we can't outwit Treadwell. And we can certainly run rings around Hyssop.'

He still didn't say anything.

'And it's *not* because I want to go back to St Mary's.'

'I didn't say it was.'

'Well, don't, because that's got nothing to do with it.'

'I never said it did.'

I glared at him.

He said nothing and I thought I'd got away with it and then he said brightly, 'And Leon might be there.'

Now I said nothing.

We landed in exactly the same place. Except we were in a different century. And a different time of year because now it was summer. And a different time of day. And there were fewer fields, less livestock and more houses. And no ram. Otherwise – not a lot different.

'Can you remember where you left the sword?'

'Of course I can,' Markham said indignantly. 'It was only ten minutes ago.'

'Then let's go.'

We set off across the fields, parting at the edge of the woods.

'Right,' I said. 'I'll get the eggs and you get the sword because you know where you left it.'

He was staring at the leaf-laden trees. 'It might take me a while. Things will have changed. The tree will probably be dead.'

'If you can't find it then you can't find it. We're no worse off.'

'True. Try to stay out of trouble.'

I laughed and he shot off into the woods.

I didn't hang around either. There were security cameras dotted throughout the grounds, although I knew from experience that early morning was the best time to sneak around. The night watch would be yawning and writing up their logs and the day watch would be stumbling down the stairs on their way to their breakfast bacon butties.

I checked my watch. Just after six in the morning. This had to be a move calculated with military precision. I was standing behind the bin store in the car park. Birds everywhere were singing the 'Hallelujah Chorus' and really putting their backs into it. The sun shone. The grass was damp with dew. Everything was peaceful and . . .

I could hear it coming. I tensed. I had to get this just right. I wouldn't get another chance. Deep breath, Maxwell.

The bread van appeared around the corner. Five minutes past six on the dot, pulling up at the back door. The driver jumped out and began to unload. Now. Before the back door opened.

Bashford never locks his car. He lives in hope of it being stolen. He once left it unlocked in the middle of Rushford with a bottle of whisky on the front seat as an incentive. Returning three days later he was dismayed to find the car still there. And the bottle of whisky. To be absolutely clear – Bashford's car is never going to be stolen. Ever.

I opened his car door, slammed it shut and strolled over to the bread-van driver as if I'd just got out. We were just a pair of unfortunate sods whose jobs required them to do this crack-of-dawn stuff.

I gave him a grin. 'Do you want a hand, mate?'

'Oh. Cheers.'

He passed me over a tray of croissants. I shuffled into position so that when someone opened the back door, I was standing behind the driver with the tray obscuring most of my face.

'Morning,' he said cheerfully and I followed him in. As far as the driver was concerned, I was with St Mary's and lending a helping hand out of the goodness of my heart. And St Mary's would think I was just a slightly-more-smartly-dressed-than-usual deliverer of baked goods.

The familiar smell hit me as I crossed the threshold. Dust, old stone, damp, yesterday's lunch. Some things never change.

I strode boldly down St Mary's back passage. Don't bother – all the jokes have already been made – and into the deserted kitchen. I plonked the tray on a handy worktop and pushed off before the kitchen assistant on earlies could catch sight of me. I think it was Ellen, but I was so busy making sure she couldn't see me that I didn't really see her, either.

I shot out of the kitchen, through the empty dining room, and out into the Hall. It was only as I was weaving my way through whiteboards and tables and stacks of miscellaneous historical paraphernalia – things really hadn't got any tidier since I left – and was halfway across the room that I realised I hadn't thought to bring any tools. Never mind, I'd think of something. I always did.

Not this time. I should have realised as soon as I saw the doors were closed. No one ever closes our Library doors – they're too big and heavy. Normally, we hook them back against the wall. Not today, however. And not only were they closed – they were locked.

Bloody, bloody Treadwell. We never had this bother when Dr Bairstow was in charge. Although, on reflection, the culprit was more likely to be that waste of good oxygen, Hyssop – our new Head of Security. Towards whom I harboured a great deal of ill will – and she didn't love me, either. It was so like her to lock things up at night. I looked around. All the doors were closed. Wardrobe, Matthew's former classroom, everything. Everything was locked away. I'd never have got in the building if I hadn't come in with the bread. That had been a stroke of luck. Which had now run out. And I couldn't stand here forever; people would be coming down for breakfast. As all sensible people do in a crisis, I headed back to the kitchen.

It *was* Ellen. She was going around switching things on, filling the water boilers and so on. She had a radio on and something cheerful was making enough noise to cover any sounds I was making. I waited until her back was turned and then shot into Mrs Mack's office, pulling the door almost closed behind me. I knew I wouldn't have long to wait.

Nothing much had changed – including Vortigern the cat, sprawled across her desk like a prolapsed bolster. In fact, I was pretty sure he was in exactly the same position as the last time I'd seen him. I wondered if perhaps he was dead and no one had noticed, so I poked him – just to make sure.

He wasn't.

I sucked my finger and left him alone.

I heard Mrs Mack call a greeting to Ellen, bang something around on a metal surface and then she pushed open her office door. Bearing in mind she'd once been an urban terrorist I very carefully didn't creep up behind her. She could kill me with an egg cup. And probably would.

I said quietly, 'Good morning.'

She stiffened, but fortunately remained egg cupless. She turned slowly. 'Max?'

'The one and only. How are you?'

'Surprised. Actually, on second thoughts, no, I'm not. Why are you here?'

'I'm up to no good and I need to get into the Library.'

'You'll be lucky. Hyssop keeps the keys now.'

'Even yours?'

She grinned. 'Not after I'd dragged her out of bed at four-thirty in the morning for six days on the trot.'

'You get up at half past four in the morning?'

'Not after she gave me back my kitchen keys.'

I was enormously cheered to find someone else making Hyssop's life hell.

'When will the Library open?'

'Not until eight o'clock.'

Shit. Shit, shit, shit. I'd hoped to be long gone by then.

'Can't Dr Dowson let me in?'

'He doesn't hold his own keys any longer.'

I said, more to myself than to Mrs Mack, 'She's going to have to go,' but she nodded agreement just the same.

'I can't hide you away anywhere, Max. Unless you're prepared to stand in the cold room all morning . . .'

'Nope,' I said, struck with a Brilliant Idea. 'I'll hide in plain sight. Give me an overall. I'll do the toast.'

'Oh dear,' she said. 'Will you really?'

A little harsh, I thought.

She handed me an overall – I never found out whose – and one of those white hats. Fortunately, my hair was still quite short – courtesy of Martin Gaunt, of whom I try not to think because the bastard cut my hair. He actually cut my hair off. All right, yes, I was breaking Dr Bairstow out of his establishment at the time, but that's not the point. The bastard cut off my hair. All of it. Although obviously I'm over it now. Obviously. Anyway, I was able to tuck it all away quite easily. I pulled off my scarf and jacket, shrugged on the overall, and thus anonymously clad, I sallied forth on major toast-making duties.

Actually, I didn't have to do much at all. St Mary's has a giant toast-making machine and all I did was feed bread in at one end and take the finished product out of the other. Endlessly. I honestly had no idea St Mary's ate so much toast. And they weren't even all here. According to Mrs Mack, Sands was leading a team to 17th-century Edinburgh – something to do with James VI about to become James I – and Roberts had taken the rest off to Denmark. To investigate the assassination of Harald Greycloak. All of which was good news. I love the History Department dearly but I couldn't help feeling their absence considerably enhanced my chances of getting through this unnoticed.

A big stroke of luck though – Hyssop had despatched her own security people to go with both teams. They were all out, leaving our own people in charge of building security. This was excellent news. I could easily see Evans or Keller munching their way through a pile of superbly prepared toast and carefully looking in the wrong direction as I snuck past.

'It's not good though,' said Mrs Mack as I rammed in yet another ten slices of bread. She looked over her shoulder and made sure we both had our backs to the serving hatches because the dining room was beginning to fill up. 'Evans' people have barely been on a jump since you left. Hyssop makes sure only her own people get the good stuff. Our lot are hanging in there – Evans sees to that – but they're getting bored. Sooner or later . . .' she tailed off.

Yes. Sooner or later they'd start to drift away and then we'd just be left with useless Hyssop and her useless band of useless troglodytes.

I seriously toyed with the thought of telling her Dr Bairstow was still alive. That he'd be back one day. And Markham, too. But I couldn't; I couldn't give Dr Bairstow away. So I lowered my voice and said, 'Well, I'm here to walk off with something valuable right from under her nose, if that's any consolation.'

'It is.' She looked over my shoulder. 'Take that toast over, will you?'

The kitchen had filled up. There were six of us now on breakfast duties – Sally on eggs, Mrs Mack mixing something in giant bowls, Kim doing the tea, Terry doing the bacon, Janet pouring orange juice, Edna on sausages. I wished I was on sausages. I suddenly realised I was hungry. I should have availed myself of more refreshments at the Flying Auction. I sighed. Was I beginning to lose my historian skills?

I don't know if Mrs Mack did it on purpose, but I arrived with the extra toast at exactly the same moment as Peterson turned up at the counter. There was no time to pull my hat down or turn away or do anything, really. I think it's fair to say he was as surprised as me. We stared at each other for long seconds and then he smiled and said, perfectly normally, 'Two slices, please.'

I shoved some random toast at him. 'Everything OK?' I asked, and if people wanted to assume I was talking about the toast then that was fine by me.

'You were at my wedding,' he said quietly, apparently making the hard choice between Marmite, marmalade or jam.

'Me and my monkey,' I said cheerfully.

He selected marmalade. 'Where is he?'

'Up in the woods doing unspeakable things to trees with the contents of his trousers.'

He stepped back. 'Oh my God – that's something my mind is never going to be able to unsee.'

I looked at him from under my hat. 'How are you?'

He grinned. 'Surviving. Felix keeps me sane.'

'You chose a good one there.'

'I did, didn't I. You here long?'

'No – I'm gone in a little while. Have you seen Leon?'

'Once. Have to say he was looking a bit frayed around the edges. I think his crew had been giving him some grief.'

'Well, if you see him again, can you say . . .'

'I can, yes.' He paused. 'Max, for God's sake . . .'

'It's all right – we'll take care.'

'I was going to say, please could you pass the butter.'

He was lucky he didn't get it thrown at him. He grinned, winked and turned away. I deposited the toast in the rack, grabbed a slice for myself and pushed off.

I couldn't leave the kitchen until Hyssop unlocked the Library and she obviously wasn't going to do that until Dr Dowson turned up. Typically, just for that one morning, he was late. I suppose he thought that with all the History Department out on assignments, he'd re-catalogue something, or play with his card indexes, or even just have a bit of a snooze in the little-used 'Political Ethics' section. Nothing he needed to be on time for, anyway. Time ticked on and there was no sign of him.

Fulfilling St Mary's almost insatiable desire for toast took me a very long time. I was knackered at the end of it. At some point Commander John Treadwell himself came down. I kept my distance and managed to avoid him by getting stuck into the mountain of washing-up at the big sink in the corner.

'I thought we had giant machines for this,' I said to Mrs Mack, waving my hose around.

'We do. This is the stuff that won't fit. Get on with it now.'

I worked side by side with Ellen and Terry for an hour or so. I don't know what Mrs Mack had told her people but they accepted me without question. We even had a refreshing mug of tea together. I've long had the suspicion Mrs Mack recruits from the criminal classes. They once blew up St Mary's using nothing but flour power. I personally wouldn't cross any of them.

They angled me so my back was to the dining room and the hat and overall rendered me almost completely invisible. It was hard work, though. I decided to be much nicer to the kitchen staff in future. Not that I'd been particularly brutal before – and I always said thank you when I took my plate back, for instance . . . and then I realised it was very possible I might never come back here again. Not unless something amazing and unexpected happened. And then I became depressed all over again. The only good thing was that Leon and Matthew weren't here. I hadn't seen my family for quite a while now and lovely though it would have been to spend even a little time together, I don't think it would have done me much good.

And then – finally – Dr Dowson turned up.

I let him eat his breakfast in peace because twenty minutes wasn't going to make a lot of difference. He and Professor Rapson sat at a table in the corner, arguing amiably together. I was alternately scrubbing something sticky at the sink and trying to reassemble some piece of esoteric kitchen equipment I'd foolishly taken to pieces to clean and hopping with impatience at their slowness. Eventually, though, they got up and made their way towards their respective places of work.

I was heading after Dr Dowson when bloody Treadwell turned up out of nowhere and stood talking to Hyssop. Right outside the bloody Library. There was no way I could get past them. And I couldn't hang around in the Hall either.

I could go out and around the building and try to climb in through the Library windows, but if they were locked for some reason then I might not be able to get back into the building again.

'I don't know what to do,' I whispered to Mrs Mack. 'Why can't he just bugger off somewhere? Dr Bairstow never came out of his office. Why can't Treadwell do the same?'

'Well, he can't stand there for much longer,' she said. 'He has a Parish Council meeting at ten. We're doing the refreshments now.'

I recoiled. 'He feeds them? Isn't that a bit like feeding gremlins after midnight?'

She rolled her eyes and went away.

I spent the next half hour laying out plates and doilies and fancy biscuits. Since Treadwell had turned up to replace Dr Bairstow, everything had been costed down to the last penny and saving money was his – Treadwell's – first priority. I couldn't help feeling he could have saved a bit by:

(a) serving cheaper biscuits

or

(b) serving no biscuits at all

or

(c) buggering off somewhere else and taking Hyssop with him.

Just saying.

I was arranging the biscuits in an artistic pattern – lemon, chocolate, vanilla and so on – when I looked up to see Evans and his team go past the windows, dragging various pieces of gardening equipment with them.

I squinted and craned my head to see where they were going. 'What are they doing?'

It was Mrs Mack, busy turning tiny cakes on to a cooling tray, who answered. 'Those members of the Security Section not actually out on assignment or guarding the building are seconded to . . . other jobs.'

'What sort of other jobs?'

'Gardening – which is probably where they're off to at the moment – or handymanning – fixing things or moving furniture around. That sort of thing.'

'I can't see them being happy with that.'

'They're not. In fact, the whole bunch are rather fed up at the moment.'

'I can imagine. It's a miracle they're even still here.'

'They're waiting for you to come back, Max. You know – the once and future historian.'

I shook my head. 'That might never happen.'

'You shouldn't doubt yourself.'

I shook my head again. 'It's Christmas where I am. Or will be in a couple of days. There's no Leon. No Matthew. No St Mary's. No home.' I tailed away.

She dropped another tray of cakes on the stainless-steel top. 'St Mary's is like having the pox – you're never really free of it and it affects your life choices forever. And home is wherever you happen to be at that moment. You know that.' She passed me the Oven Gloves of Comfort. 'Can you take those biscuits out of the oven for me, please. We need to get a move on.'

She was right. I couldn't hang around here all day and I still had to get into the Library. On an impulse, I asked her if she had a crowbar I could borrow, and do you know, she did, and while she was fetching it, Treadwell and Hyssop cleared off.

I plonked this very useful-looking implement – clearly labelled *Property of the Kitchen Department* – on to my trolley, covered it with a cloth and trundled it into the Library, which was deserted except for Dr Dowson working quietly at his desk.

He looked up as I and my trolley clattered through the doorway, saying, 'Ah. There you are.' He showed no surprise at all. 'I was certain we hadn't seen the last of you, Max. I told that old fool upstairs you'd be back. For one reason or another.'

'Dr Dowson, sir, could you make yourself scarce for ten minutes?'

'I could do, but why?'

I pulled out my crowbar. 'I'm very sorry but I'm going to have to vandalise one of your bookcases.'

'Oh – you've come back for them, have you?'

It took a moment to register but then I very nearly dropped the crowbar in shock. 'What?'

'Second bookcase on the left? That was you, was it? I can't think why I never guessed before.'

'What was me?'

'Two rather nice Fabergé eggs? That was you?'

I think, for a moment, I might have felt a little dizzy. 'Dr Dowson . . .'

'Oh, no cause for alarm, Max. They're quite safe.'

'You found them?'

'Oh yes.'

'When St Mary's was refurbished?'

'No – actually, not until the time that old fool upstairs tried to kill us all with frozen chickens.'

Ah yes, the professor's rapid chicken-firing gun experiment. There had been substantial damage.

'They're still here?' I think up until this moment I hadn't really believed that could be possible. 'Where?'

'In an archive box on the top shelf in my office. Covered in very authentic dust and marked *Library Classification Notes ARS to TIT*. Perfectly safe. I've been keeping them for the day we'd have to bribe someone or pay a ransom or bail you out of prison. May I suggest you continue to leave them where they are?'

I shook my head. 'Sorry, sir, I have a Greater Purpose.'

'In that case, come through.'

We moved into his cluttered office and he carefully closed the door behind us. 'Do you know how much these things are worth, Max?'

'I have a vague idea. Thank you for looking after them. And can we not say anything to anyone.'

'You can trust me. And the old fool upstairs as well.' He pulled out his wooden ladder and began to climb. 'We're the Guardians at the Gate, Max.'

He passed down an archive box. I settled it carefully on the desk, and, still not quite believing they were here and safe, whipped off the lid.

There they were. Two small but exquisitely jewelled Fabergé eggs, still in their protective display cases. When I think of everything that had happened at and to St Mary's over the years . . . fires, explosions, invasions, frozen chickens . . . It was a bit of a miracle they were still intact.

I stared thoughtfully. Wisely, Markham had avoided the biggest egg, the Royal Danish; these two were much more portable. If I could get them out of their cases they would fit very nicely in my pocket. *If* I could get them out of their security cases. I picked one up, looking for the release mechanism.

Dr Dowson read my thoughts. 'Oh – that's easy enough, Max. Any competent librarian can undo a security case with nothing more than a paper clip.'

I wrinkled my nose. 'I don't think so, sir. These are very high-end and . . .'

There was a click and one case sprang open. A fraction of a second later, the second followed suit. Never underestimate the skill set of a chartered librarian.

Feeling extremely stupid, I very carefully lifted the first one from its case and eased it into my left-hand pocket, where it sat – heavy but safe.

This is just a small point but well worth making, I think. Ladies – never, ever find yourself wearing a garment with no pockets. You'll have nowhere to stow your stolen Fabergé eggs.

A moment later the second was in my right-hand pocket. They were very heavy. I hung a Tea Towel of Concealment from each pocket and replaced the box lid. 'Thank you, Dr Dowson. I'd better be off now. Don't want to be caught with these in my possession.'

Markham's voice sounded suddenly in my ear. 'Have you got them?'

Dr Dowson was replacing the box on the top shelf but I turned discreetly to one side anyway. 'Yes. Have you?'

'Can't find the bloody tree.'

He couldn't find a tree in a wood. Typical. 'Keep looking.'

'I *am* keeping looking.'

'I'll come and give you a hand.' I turned to Dr Dowson. 'I have to go. Thank you for looking after them.'

'Our pleasure, Max. I'm not going to ask what you're doing with them. Give my regards to Mr Markham.'

I opened my mouth to say I hadn't seen him for months, gave it up, and said, 'I will. Take care, sir.'

I replaced the unused crowbar and trundled my trolley back across the Hall – carefully not catching anyone's eye – and back into the kitchen.

Mrs Mack was waiting for me. 'All right?'

I went to take off my overall. 'Fine, thank you. I'm off now. Your crowbar's on the trolley. Thank you for your help.'

She started to say something but I'd stopped listening. I was staring out of the window, unable to believe my eyes. Although I could believe my eyes. That was the problem. Because now I'd have to gouge them out and burn them.

Actually, it was a good job I *was* staring out of the window because that daft bat Hyssop chose that exact moment to stride into the kitchen demanding to know if the refreshments for Commander Treadwell's meeting were ready. I jumped a mile and pretended to do something with some piece of culinary equipment I later discovered was a ricer, which came as a complete shock to me because I thought it looked like something with which you could separate cats from their nadgers. Still – what do I know?

Our relationship – mine and Hyssop's – had been short but full of incident. She and her team had wrecked the Babylon assignment, shown themselves incapable of grasping the basic principles of St Mary's, indirectly been responsible for me being sacked – although to be fair, that had been mostly me – and generally meddled with everything and everyone, and then saved my life when the idiot Halcombe and his mate Sullivan were about to either rip my arms off or shoot me. Whichever came first.

So, as I say, mixed feelings. I had no idea how I should react to her or she to me, so I kept myself well hidden. Just to be on the safe side.

I heard Mrs Mack say, 'Of course,' in the tone of voice she uses to Fascists when they try to invade Cardiff, and fortunately for both of us, Hyssop, continuing with her Woman on a Mission morning, strode back out again before she could clock me, still staring, paralysed, out of the window and wondering if I would ever be able to unsee . . . things . . . again.

In my own defence, I did struggle. A prudent historian – never met one of those – but as I say, a prudent historian would seize the moment while everyone's attention was elsewhere – as it very soon would be – and shoot out of the door to assist her colleague in his search for a tree in a wood. Fortunately, prudent historianism never happens to me.

'I'll take them up,' I said to Mrs Mack, meaning the refreshments, obviously, and not the things outside the window.

Mrs Mack stared at me. 'You?'

'Yeah.'

'Why?'

'Look out of the window.'

She did.

Mrs Mack led the troops who threw the Fascists out of Cardiff. She made the final stand on Barricade Bridge. She faced down a Leviathan. Nothing fazes Mrs Mack. Today, she reeled.

'Max . . .'

'Yeah,' I said.

'Max . . .'

I pointed to the calendar. She squinted and reeled again. 'Oh my God – that's an actual thing?'

'It's underlined twice,' I said.

'I thought someone was just having a laugh.'

I pointed out of the window again. I think she would have liked to close her eyes but sometimes your body parts just won't do as they're told.

I asked her where the trolley was for Treadwell's meeting.

She gestured blindly. I checked everything over and added an extra pot of boiling water because he was going to need all the refreshments he could get.

She still hadn't moved. 'Max . . .'

'Someone has to inform Commander Treadwell,' I said, 'and trust me, I will scramble over the cold, dead bodies of my former colleagues for the opportunity to do it myself.'

She still hadn't moved.

I patted her on the shoulder. She was tough. She'd get over it.

I took the goods lift to the first floor, humming a cheerful tune as I went. And, because the lift is slow and you have to pass the time somehow, I snaffled two lemon biscuits and a chocolate fondant cake on the way up. And then a fairy cake because they were still warm. And then I thought Markham might like one so I popped another into my pocket. Then I thought he'd never miss what he'd never known, and ate that one too.

I brushed off the crumbs, straightened my hat, checked my tea towels were secure and arrived at Treadwell's office.

I don't think Mrs Partridge is capable of anything so pedestrian as a start of surprise but she certainly raised an eyebrow when she saw me.

'Trust me,' I said. 'I come in peace.'

And up went the other one. Then she waved me through.

'You should come too,' I said, as she got up to open the door for me. 'You really won't want to miss this.'

Treadwell looked up with a beaming smile which, I think, we can safely assume was because he thought I was the Parish Council. I've never seen a smile disappear so quickly. It was like watching the Cheshire Cat being hit by a truck. Not being anything like as classy as Mrs Partridge, he executed several starts of surprise. I suspected I was the last thing he expected to see that day.

'What are you . . . ?'

I banged into his desk with the trolley because I'm not good at controlling things with four wheels and there was a tinkle of overturned crockery. Mrs Partridge frowned, although it wasn't the best crockery so no great disaster.

I said, 'Sorry,' and scrabbled to right the cups again.

I finally had the satisfaction of knowing I'd caught Treadwell on the hop. I could see him trying to work out why I was here, why I was dressed like that, and what the bloody hell was going on. And lastly – but definitely not leastly – that the Parish Council would be walking through his door any moment now.

'What are you doing here?'

I ignored his question, pouring myself a cup of tea. I offered one to Mrs Partridge because I'm polite, but she shook her head.

I picked up another biscuit and rearranged the ones still on the plate in the hope no one would notice they were looking a little thin. Very thin, actually, since I'd had more than half of them.

I sipped my tea and said casually, 'Would I be right in thinking you thought you'd get more value for money from the non-Hyssop part of the Security Section by ordering them to do a few odd jobs when things are quiet?'

'Possibly,' he said, a little stiffly, I thought, but interestingly, he made no move to contact Hyssop to have me thrown out.

I hadn't finished. 'And would I be right in thinking it's the third Thursday of the month, which means it's the day for your monthly meeting with the Parish Council?'

'Possibly,' he said, still unwilling to commit himself, although everyone knew it was.

I glanced at the clock. Three minutes to ten.

'Do you remember one of your many complaints about St Mary's was that it was almost completely unaware of the world around it?'

He'd pulled himself together. 'Is there some point to your maunderings, Kitchen Assistant Maxwell?' He'd always been a sarcastic bugger.

I was grinning fit to bust. 'And fourthly – and possibly most importantly – are you aware that today is actually . . .' I paused, all the better to build up the suspense, '*World Naked Gardening Day*? And yes, that is a thing. It's on Mrs Mack's calendar downstairs.'

I saw him open his mouth to tell me not to be so ridiculous, close it again, struggle to take in the implications and then, all of a sudden, push back his chair and move to the window.

I joined him because there was no way I was missing this.

256

Mrs Partridge hadn't even bothered to try to account for her presence and was standing at the other window. Evans was marching his team smartly down the drive. A neat squad of six, all in military formation, garden implements at the correct angle across their chests.

They were all correctly kitted out with goggles, gloves and steel-toe-capped workboots, everything legal required for the safe operation of all those strimmers, scythes, axes, pitchforks and chainsaws, presumably. A sight to gladden any health and safety officer's heart. Although from up here, they rather gave the impression they were about to wage war on a small country.

The most striking aspect of their appearance – for me, anyway, I can't speak for anyone else – was that they were all stark bollock naked. With the main emphasis on the last three words in that sentence.

I don't know what was passing through Treadwell's head just at that moment – probably a desire to kill us all and take refuge in the pub – and as he struggled with the situation, the gates opened to admit a small convoy of cars. The Parish Council had arrived.

First – as always – was Mrs Huntley-Palmer, who swept in through the gates in her not-quite-as-classic-as-Dr-Bairstow's-Bentley Bentley – a source of continual resentment for her, which Dr Bairstow had never done anything to alleviate, often handing Markham his keys and asking him to ensure his car was strategically parked next to Mrs H-P's in the car park.

She slowed for a moment as though unable to believe her eyes – although the evidence was dangling there for all to see – and then she sped up. Scattering gravel in all directions, her not-quite-as-classic-as-Dr-Bairstow's-Bentley Bentley screeched to an illegal halt outside the front doors. I caught a brief glimpse of her struggling to get out.

Up next was the vicar, the Rev Kev, pedalling sedately through the gates on his ancient bike and a little flushed on a hot day like this. I'd met him once and he seemed quite a nice bloke despite his calling. He rode past, waving at Evans, did a bit of a double take and then pedalled faster, his eyes fixed sensibly on the drive ahead of him.

Two other cars – occupants unknown – slowed and then slowed some more and then sped up.

The final car, a battered old Austin even more ancient than its owners, contained Miss Peek and Miss Frean, who didn't mess about. There was none of this girlie slowing down for a better look. They actually stopped and got out.

Treadwell met my eyes. I gave him my best *nothing to do with me* look – because it wasn't, just for once – and started slinging plates and cups on to the briefing table. Once I'd got everything nicely arranged, I helped myself to the last chocolate biscuit and headed for the door.

The last I saw of Miss Peek and Miss Frean, they were being greeted by Mr Evans, who's a lovely lad and always very respectful towards elderly ladies. He stood to attention and threw them one of his best salutes, which I think both ladies very much appreciated, and then they all clustered around the rose bed – not too closely in some cases – presumably to discuss the curse of aphids and how to rid oneself of the pesky little buggers.

Mrs Huntley-Palmer was just surging through the front doors as I walked back around the gallery. I could hear her demanding to know the whereabouts of that Treadwell person and not to fob her off, so I didn't even try, pointing politely and informing her he was in his office and very much looking forward to explaining St Mary's latest gardening initiative. Then I headed for the goods lift and laughed all the way back to the kitchen.

I was just sneaking through the door when Markham Spoke. Before anyone says anything, he's the one insisting on the capitals – don't blame me. Apparently, they lent emphasis to his Quest. I asked if that was the one where he'd spent a couple of hours shoving his arm up dead trees and he got very huffy, banging on about badgers, stinging nettles, sinisterly rustling undergrowth, man-eating squirrels and heaven knows what else. Anyway, among all the complaints, self-congratulations and vivid descriptions of the perils he had survived, it would seem he'd found the sword.

I said, speaking of peril, had he ever seen Evans naked, and there was a thoughtful pause which I used to shut down my com. By this time, I was back in Mrs Mack's office, where I handed over her hat and overall and thanked her politely for her hospitality. She thanked me for my morning's work, warned me never to consider the field of catering as an alternative career, and tactfully averted her eyes as I transferred a fortune in Fabergé eggs into a Tesco carrier bag.

The Great Hall was empty – obviously. As was Wardrobe. I suspected the normal occupants had developed a sudden interest in gardening. I shot out of the front doors and down the steps just as Markham sidled around the corner. He was walking strangely again so I guessed the sword had been returned to its original hiding place.

I grinned at him. 'Whosoever draweth this sword from these trousers will . . .'

'. . . will not survive the experience,' he said.

'You can barely walk. How are we going to get back to . . . ?' I stopped because he was leaning against the Bentley and grinning at me and it wasn't pretty.

The penny plummeted. 'You . . . that's Mrs Huntley-Palmer's . . . oh my God, that's brilliant.'

'Isn't it?' he said smugly. 'And imagine the reasonable explanations Treadwell's going to have to come up with.'

'With you every step of the way,' I said, 'but for God's sake, become rightwise king of all England and remove that sword before you inadvertently cut off your own todger.'

I averted my eyes while he rummaged.

'Hold that,' he said, thrusting something unpleasantly warm at me. I made him bundle it up in his jacket.

The car was unlocked. Mrs Huntley-Palmer had been in far too much of a hurry to get to Treadwell to bother about tiny things like that. She had, however, taken the keys with her.

No one was in sight. And I was pretty certain that while faces lined the windows of St Mary's, no one was looking at us. Trust me, if you've got six naked men showing you the best way to eradicate greenfly, you have precious little attention for a spot of Grand Theft Auto happening just over there. We snuck into the car and closed the doors very quietly.

'Are we going to hot-rod it?'

'For the last time, Max – hot-wire. Hot-*wire*.'

'Is it important?'

'No more important than knowing the Saxons won at Hastings.'

I opened my mouth and then shut it again.

I don't know what he did but the engine roared suddenly into life. Markham shoved it into gear and we raced off down the drive, tooting the horn for dear life. Past Evans and his team who waved like madmen. Past the near delirious Misses Peek and Frean, as they immersed themselves thoroughly in the unique horticultural experience that is St Mary's, and out through the gate, straight down to the village.

As getaway dashes go, it was only a couple of hundred yards, but as Markham said, it was the gesture that was important. 'It's this one, isn't it,' he said, primly obeying the Highway Code, indicating left and pulling into Mrs H-P's overdecorated cottage with its twee gables, immaculately landscaped gardens and historically inaccurate windows.

She'd left her garage door unlocked, so I nipped out and threw up the door. Markham pulled in smoothly and switched off the engine. He took a minute or two to wipe off our fingerprints and exited the car. I pulled the door back down again.

'She'll have reported us to the police by now,' he said, giving the door handle a final wipe. 'There'll be lots of activity and searching – she's a local JP so she won't give them any choice – and after a while, someone will think to look in her garage and with luck, assume she's losing her marbles and possibly arrest her for wasting police time. Score one for Dr Bairstow in his continuing battle against the evil wiles of the Parish Council.'

'That's . . . diabolical.'

'Yep,' he said, clutching his sword like a mini Arthur on his way to Mount Badon. 'Fancy a drink?'

We crossed the road to the pub which was very quiet at that time of day. 'This is no good – they're not open yet,' said

Markham. He stood in the reception area, shouting, 'What ho, mine host.'

I asked him what had happened to standards.

'It's Christmas,' he said, indicating the bright summer sunshine outside.

'Oh God,' said Guthrie, appearing through a door. 'Go away. We're closed.'

'No, you're not.'

'We are now.'

'Give us a drink and we'll go.'

'How about I don't give you a drink and you go anyway?'

'How about you give us two drinks and we don't implicate you in the theft of Mrs Huntley-Palmer's classic-but-not-as-classic-as-Dr-Bairstow's-Bentley Bentley?'

'How about half a glass of water between you in the car park and then you bugger off?'

'Don't you want to see what I've got in this bundle?'

'No.'

'Or what Max has in her carrier bag?'

'No.'

Elspeth appeared. 'What's going on? Hey, Max.'

Both Markham and I stepped back. I said, 'Elspeth? Is that you?'

'Well, of course it is,' said Guthrie. 'Who did you think it was?'

'She's a different shape.'

'So will you be if you don't bugger off.'

'Congratulations,' I said to Elspeth. 'You look amazing.'

She beamed. 'I am amazing.'

'Is he still making you work?' demanded Markham, darkly.

'Heaving beer crates and things around. Do you want me to have a word?'

'No, he's not and no, she doesn't,' said Guthrie. 'And why are you still here?'

'We need help,' said Markham, crumbling into piteousness.

'I've said that for years. Go and get it.'

I dropped the carrier bag on the reception desk because it was becoming heavy.

Elspeth peeked inside. 'Ooh – pretty.'

Guthrie groaned. 'Elspeth, don't look. They'll seduce you to the dark side.'

'Too late,' said Markham. 'Can you pop these in your secret cellar for us?'

'What secret cellar?'

'Your secret cellar.'

'I don't have a secret cellar.'

'Yes, you do. It's an ancient pub. They all had secret cellars to hide the smuggled brandy and rum from the Revenue. You know: "Brandy for the Parson, Baccy for the Clerk".'

'What?'

' "Watch the wall, my darling, as the Gentlemen go by." '

'You're insane. Give that here before someone sees it.'

I just had time to snatch up the smaller egg – the Nécessaire – as Guthrie disappeared the sword and the other egg. After which we had a shot of something powerful to settle our nerves – Elspeth had orange juice – and we were shown the door.

Markham clutched Guthrie's arm, hissing, 'Keep it secret. Keep it safe.'

'Bugger off and never darken my door again,' said Guthrie

amiably and I couldn't help feeling that if he'd been Frodo Baggins then the entire Mordor jaunt would have proceeded down a very different path.

We made our way back to our pod, still patiently waiting for us in the sunshine. At least the solar power levels would have been topped up which would be one less thing to do when I got back.

I checked everything over carefully, because mistakes happen when you're tired. And I was tired, but at least we had a couple of days off ahead of us. Good food – because Pennyroyal doesn't produce any other sort – lots to drink, and an opportunity to put my feet up for a bit. I told myself this would be a very enjoyable holiday and I wasn't going to miss the madness and mayhem of a St Mary's Christmas at all. Not one little bit.

We landed with only the tiniest bump – because I'm not Peterson. I shut everything down while Markham checked some of his more remote areas for post-sword trauma. I gave him the egg to hold while I set everything to charge, then we decontaminated and left the pod.

Pennyroyal had forgotten to leave the lights on in the barn. I sighed. It was only a little thing but . . . oh, I don't know. We fell over each other trying to plug in the umbilicals but we got there in the end.

'Come on,' said Markham. 'It's freezing in here. Let's get inside.'

'Have you got it?'

'Of course.'

'Please tell me that's not down your trouser leg as well.'

'I am a possibly married man,' he said, primly. 'And you definitely are a married woman. The contents of my trousers are my own concern.'

'I cannot think of anything that interests me less than the contents of your trousers.'

By this time, we were at the door and fumbling for the keypad. Markham banged in the code and finally we were inside. Light and warmth were all around us and we made our way to the kitchen.

Lady Amelia had returned in our absence and was enjoying a post-Christmas-shopping drink. An island of margaritaness in a sea of up-market shopping bags, hampers, beautifully decorated and beribboned gift boxes and the like. She was obviously exhausted, poor thing.

Pennyroyal was doing something to a very large and very naked turkey. For the avoidance of reader trauma, I should emphasise that the turkey was already dead. Although if it wasn't, it very soon would have been after what Pennyroyal was doing to it.

'Hello there,' Lady Amelia cried. 'How did it go? Successfully, I hope. Let me pour you a drink while you regale us with tales of your triumph.'

'It didn't go too badly,' I said, sitting down. 'The Time Police turned up, sadly . . .'

'Arseholes,' she said. 'In fact, sodding arseholes. I hate it when they do that. Did they whip everything away before you had a chance to . . . ?'

'Yes,' I said, gloomily. 'When we left, they were loading up one of their big pods. Illegals, punters, stolen property, pods . . . they got the lot.'

'Well,' she said, bravely downing the rest of her drink. 'Never mind. We can't win them all.'

'We won this one though,' I said, gently laying my catalogue/receipt in front of her. 'We got the lot. Everything. Everyone. I was able to arrest the entire room and officially impound the contents a fraction of a second before the buggers came through the door.' I pointed to the receipt. 'Signed, sealed and delivered. By a certain Lt Rosen himself. Time Police verified. Official. With the whole thing recorded and over twenty witnesses, the Time Police had no choice but to agree. It was quite a moment. Even better, the bounties and rewards should be yours as soon as you present your receipt.'

Lady Amelia was jubilant. 'What a haul! Oh Frabjous Day! Pennyroyal, come and look at this.'

Pennyroyal dragged himself away from his own private festival with the turkey at the other end of the kitchen. He flicked me a glance and just for a moment I thought he was going to smile. 'Indeed, my lady.'

'Artefacts, perpetrators, punters, pods, the lot. Wouldn't be surprised if we didn't have to work for the rest of the year.'

'It is late December, my lady. We wouldn't have worked for the rest of the year anyway.'

'Well, you know what I mean. Bit of a party-poo this evening, I think. Lots to celebrate. Colleagues' efforts to reward. Bounties to calculate and gloat over. Undrunk margaritas to rectify, and so on.'

'Yes, my lady.'

Markham joined us at the table. 'You know you told us we weren't doing gifts this Christmas?'

She nodded. 'I do. Not terribly fair on fifty per cent of the team, I thought. Besides – Christmas, you know . . . no families and . . .'

Markham heaved the jewelled Nécessaire out of his pocket and laid it gently on the table in front of her. 'Yeah,' he said. 'We're not that good at doing as we're told. Merry Christmas to you both.'

Both Pennyroyal and Smallhope lead adventurous lives – even by our standards – and it takes a lot to astonish them but we managed it now.

Pennyroyal withdrew his arm from the turkey again and Lady Amelia actually put down her glass.

'Bloody bollocking hell,' she said. Not sure from where she picked up that particular phrase but just a gentle warning to all that I've copyrighted it.

The egg sat quietly on the kitchen table. Scores of tiny jewels winked in the soft overhead lights. The little object glowed in the warm kitchen, making everything else around it – especially me and Markham – look shabby and second-rate.

We didn't touch it – although why I thought it would fall apart now after everything that must have happened to it in its life was a bit of a mystery. We just gently circled the table, viewing it from all angles.

I think it's accurate to say they were gobsmacked – the pair of them.

'I don't know what to say,' she said, eventually. 'I genuinely don't know what to say.'

'We thought it would cover our board and lodging for a few weeks,' said Markham, helpfully.

'I rather think you might be understating its value,' she said. 'A month, at least.'

She sat back down again and picked up her drink.

'By the way,' said Markham to Pennyroyal, 'the lights are out in the barn. Do you want me to take a look?'

'Nah,' he said, looking at Lady Amelia. 'It'll wait.'

There was a silence. I looked from one to the other. 'What?'

Pennyroyal sighed and withdrew his arm yet again. 'Never going to get the bloody turkey done at this rate. Now, my lady?'

'Now,' she said, decisively. 'Follow me, everyone.'

We followed her along the corridor towards her own private quarters at the end.

'We thought we'd open up the old sitting room,' she said. 'It's got a lovely fireplace and lots of room to spread out in. We'll need to put up some decorations, of course, because it's looking a bit gloomy at the moment, and do the tree, and bring some logs in, but that shouldn't take too long. Oh, and we'll need to clear it out first. It's a little cluttered at the moment.'

She flung open the door and stepped back.

I saw Leon. And Matthew. And Hunter, sitting on a sofa. No Flora, because you can't take babies out of their own time. Well, you can, but trust me, it's a world of pain and grief if you do.

I saw Dr Bairstow and Mrs Brown together by the fireplace. I saw Adrian and Mikey over by the tree ransacking a box of Christmas decorations and Professor Penrose wrestling with the Christmas lights – well, there was a catastrophe just waiting to happen.

I just had time to take it all in before Markham pushed past me to get to Hunter. She stood up, laughing. 'I've come to take you home for Christmas. Flora's waiting to see her daddy again.'

The next minute I was in Leon's arms. He said, 'Merry Christmas,' and then Matthew was there, as well.

'Mum, I built a machine that makes tea and biscuits at the same time.'

'Well, good for you,' I said, not panicking in any way because I'm a mother and my duty was clear. 'Does it work?'

'No, but Uncle Penrose says it will one day.'

I looked around suspiciously. 'Where have you left Uncle Markham's assistant?'

'R2-Tea2? It's in the barn. Uncle Pennyroyal wouldn't let me bring it inside.'

I grinned at the suspiciously blank-faced Uncle Pennyroyal. This was why the lights had been off in the barn. So we wouldn't see TB2 parked there.

There were greetings and hugs and drinks – together with a bloody great jug of margaritas for which I had to fight Lady Amelia – and someone lit the fire without incident and Mikey and Adrian started to put up the Christmas decorations and no one fell off the ladder – and there were jokes and laughter and everything was lovely.

At the height of the noise and chaos, Hunter and Markham got up quietly and went out of the door.

I followed him out into the hall. Hunter was putting on her coat.

'Are you both going now?'

'Yeah,' he said. 'Have a great Christmas.'

'You too.' I hugged Hunter. 'Lots of love to little Flora.'

Markham took my hands and smiled. 'Merry Christmas, Max.'

Hunter grinned. 'He'll be back before you know it.'

'Oh God – really?'

'Ready?' said Pennyroyal, coming through the door. They followed him down the passageway. I opened the door back to the sitting room and when I looked back, they'd gone.

I settled myself in the crook of Leon's arm and recounted the day's adventures. Dr Bairstow especially seemed very taken with my story, particularly the bit about Mrs Huntley-Palmer's nothing-like-as-classic-as-his-Bentley Bentley, which he made me repeat several times. With all the appropriate actions.

Leaving Leon supervising the Christmas lights – thus considerably enhancing Home Farm's chances of seeing Christmas Day unignited – I went out to the kitchen to talk to Pennyroyal and see if I could help with supper.

'Nah,' he said, pricking sausages with what looked like a kukri. 'You've had a busy day. I can manage.'

'OK,' I said. 'After the holidays are over, can you and I have a word?'

He looked up at me. 'Problem?'

I shook my head. 'Idea.'

'OK.'

Adrian brought in more logs for the fire. Under Professor Penrose's instructions, Mikey and Matthew finished decorating the tree. Again, no one fell off the stepladder.

I had another margarita.

Then I took Leon upstairs to show him our room, which took an astonishingly long time considering it wasn't a large space. And then, having given everything a very thorough inspection, he insisted on doing it all again, because, he said, you couldn't take any chances with these old buildings. If it hadn't been sausages for supper, we might have been there all night.

Eventually, with all the fires going, all the lights on and darkness relegated to outside where it belonged, we assembled around the table for a Christmas Eve supper of jacket potatoes and sausages. The curtains were drawn, the turkey was in the oven, good smells prevailed, and there was a fresh jug of something tasty nearby. Leon held my hand under the table in a manner that led me to believe there would be more room inspections after supper.

Dr Bairstow tinkled his glass and stood up. 'With your permission,' he nodded at Lady Amelia, 'I would like to say a few words. Firstly, to thank our hosts for their generous hospitality.'

'Hear, hear,' we all said, raising our glasses.

Lady Amelia waved this aside. 'We enjoyed your hospitality last year. It seemed only fair that this year it was our turn.'

He continued. 'Never has the phrase *living in interesting times* been more appropriate. And we are living in uncertain times too. None of us knows where or how we will be living this time next year. Our lives have been overturned. We are scattered. We are apart – but we are St Mary's and therefore we are never alone. I believe we may take comfort in small things. For instance, we are together, here and now, and one day, we will be together again. Family and friends will be reunited. And so, I would like to take this opportunity to say to you – and to all the friends of St Mary's, wherever they may be at the moment – whatever the world throws at us, we shall prevail. I am convinced of it. Here's to us. A very Merry Christmas and a Happy New Year to all.'

THE END

SANTA GRINT

ROLL CALL

TIME POLICE PERSONNEL

Commander Hay   Has had a Brilliant Idea.

Captain Farenden   Unsuccessful reindeer obtainer. On the other hand, he does meet a kindred spirit. Watch this space . . .

Major Callen   Manages to avoid any direct involvement. Smart.

Major Ellis   Is not about to have the best day.

Lt Grint   It's all his fault. Everything is his fault. Even Jane thinks it's his fault.

Lt North   Reluctant enabler.

Officer Curtis   You can't teach children to eat jelly by numbers. I'm sorry, but you just can't.

Officer Rockmeyer	Failing to fulfil the function of four fully trained sheepdogs.
Lt Fanboten	Concussed but does have a mountain named after him so not all bad.
Officer Schultz	Ventured too close to the koi pool and never seen since.
Officer Oti	Dubious sleigh-bell duplicator.
Officer Parrish	Member of the by now legendary but for all the wrong reasons Team 236. Phallic balloon creator.
Officer Lockland	Grint's partner in crime. Has a bit of a revelation in the garden shed.
Officer Farrell	In plain clothes again. Can be seen from space.
Miss Meiklejohn	Artificial snow manufacturer. Failed artificial snow deliverer.
Officer Kohl (Socko)	Reluctant Santa Claus.
Time Police helicopter pilot	Refuses to give his name for fear of retribution from the Union of Helicopter Pilots and Associated Trades.

Officer Hansen	Appearing in his alter ego of one-legged reindeer.
Officer Varma	Can hardly believe she's risked her life going out with Team 236. AGAIN.
Commander Hay's box of emergency tissues	A second outing!

MORE NORMAL PEOPLE

Tiffie	Sad. So sad. Her only friend is a toad.
Mr Fluffy	Aforementioned toad.
Fiona	*Princess* Fiona. And don't you forget it.
Simon	Going to the seaside as soon as his legs are mended. His mum says so.
Receptionist at the Little Petals Residential Childcare Community for Exceptional Children	Bit of a mouthful. No one gets it right.
Francis of Assisi	Who's she?

Raffy and Jugs	Not Brain of Britain material.
Ruth Wedderburn	Simon's mum. Illegal? Not illegal? Immaterial, really. Smallhope and Pennyroyal have her in their sights.
Lady Amelia Smallhope	Hello again!
Pennyroyal	Her alleged butler.
Raymond Parrish	Possibly beginning to regret his son's burgeoning sense of responsibility. His *expensive* burgeoning sense of responsibility.
Ms Steel	Instigator of the psychic link connecting all PAs throughout the universe. And benefits from a rather nice bottle of wine, as well.

Author note to self: write books with fewer characters in future.

SANTA GRINT

The story doesn't really begin here, but it's as good a starting place as any.

It was Captain Farenden's habit to withdraw to his own office and give his commanding officer a few minutes' peace at the end of their working day. On this occasion, however, and in anticipation of his commanding officer's reaction, he had carefully left their connecting door ajar.

Commander Hay closed her last file, shut down her data table, and reached for her very excellent coffee, freshly brewed in her very excellent new coffee machine which, for some reason never adequately explained, had been installed in Captain Farenden's office rather than her own. She switched on her screen. It was her habit to watch the early evening news broadcast – partly to keep herself up to date, but mostly to discover whether everyone else's day had been as bad as hers.

Closing her eyes, she sipped slowly, relishing the end of an unexpectedly peaceful day. The internal difficulties of last year, while not exactly melted away, had certainly retreated to a safe distance. For the time being. Life, she felt, had improved to the extent that, even after all this time, the unfortunate combination of the Time Police and the partial destruction of quite a large area of the formerly respectable London borough of Mile End no longer featured quite so prominently in the headlines.

Life, however, having lured her into a false sense of security, now prepared to pounce.

This news station liked to end the daily bulletin on a happy note. To brighten the unremitting gloom, they said. The *And Finally* snippet was carefully selected to imply that never mind all the crap just regurgitated for the benefit of the viewing public, there might – just might – be hope for the human race after all, that there was no need to go off and end it all just yet, and look at this adorable skateboarding duck.

Captain Farenden grinned to himself and waited.

'And finally,' chirped the newsreader. 'They're calling him *The Time Police Officer with a Heart*. In an organisation not known for its humanitarianism, one single Time Police Officer has surprised us all.'

Captain Farenden began an internal countdown.

Ten.

Nine.

The silence from Commander Hay's office was absolute.

Seven.

Six.

The newsreader's voice continued. Unfamiliar words such as '*Heart-warming . . . Compassion . . . Kindness . . .*' filtered through the open door.

Four.

'*Hope . . .*'

Two.

'*Benevolence . . .*'

One.

'While no one knows the name of this Good Samaritan, all indications are that the Time Police have finally taken on board the barrage of criticism provoked by their actions in Mile End last year – actions which resulted in widespread damage to property and threat to life – and are even now moving towards a more . . .'

And . . . Lift-Off.

'*What the fire-truckity fire truck? Charlie?*'

Captain Farenden got up and carefully arranged his face. 'You called, ma'am?'

'No, I bellowed. What the fire-trucking . . .'

'Can I gather you've just seen the news, ma'am?'

'*The Time Police officer with a heart?*'

'Yes, ma'am.'

'I don't employ people to have fire-trucking hearts. I employ them to be hard-nosed bastards dedicated to keeping the Time-line straight. Who is this pillock? They didn't give his name.'

'Well, ma'am . . .'

'Have him shot and thrown into the river. And then fish him out and do it again.'

'Well, ma'am . . . actually . . .'

'Come on – spit it out.'

Captain Farenden paused. Unkind people might have said he was savouring the moment. 'Lt Grint, ma'am.'

She sagged back in her chair and then recovered. 'You had me going there for a moment, Charlie. Good one.'

'No, ma'am. It was Lt Grint.'

She sat up again. 'They said he was overcome with compassion.'

'Yes, ma'am.'

'Concerned with the welfare of those less fortunate than himself.'

'It's a news bulletin, ma'am. I don't think they concern themselves overly much with facts.'

She reached for her paper knife. 'Bring me Lt Grint. Now. I intend to close my eyes and when I open them again, I want to see him standing in front of me. With a more than adequate explanation.'

'To be fair, ma'am . . .'

'I have no intention of being fair, Charlie. Get him up here now.'

'He's in a briefing right at this moment, ma'am. If you could wait fifteen minutes . . .'

'How the hell did this happen? I mean – Team 236 – yes. I wouldn't put anything past those three idiots, but Grint . . . ?'

'Well, ma'am, you'll remember, there was a fair amount of grief arising from the damage we did in Mile End.'

'You mean when we displayed exceptional bravery and determination against overwhelming odds, and a heavily out-numbered Team 236 rescued a prominent member of those bottom-feeding, shit-spewing incompetents we're supposed to regard as a functioning government?'

'That is certainly one way of looking at it, ma'am. Many prefer to describe it as demolishing her house and those of her neighbours, destroying the road outside, damaging private vehicles and generally frightening the living daylights out of the honest, God-fearing citizens of Mile End.'

'Didn't we leave the sewers intact?'

'We did, ma'am.'

'Make a note, Charlie. Next time – take out the sewers first. Give them something to really complain about.'

'So noted, ma'am.'

She sighed. 'I still fail to see what any of this has to do with a certain recent news bulletin.'

'Well, ma'am, again, if you remember, there was a meeting at the end of November . . .'

Cue flashback music and wavy images.

Commander Hay, her adjutant, Captain Farenden, and Majors Ellis and Callen were sitting around her briefing table. The Senior Officers' meeting was drawing to a close. It had gone well. No one was dead. No one was even bleeding. Commander Hay carefully closed her last file. Major Ellis pushed back his chair.

'Before you go, gentlemen . . .'

Recognising the signs of a commanding officer keeping the best to last, Major Ellis sighed, returned his seat to upright, closed his tray and prepared to assume the brace position. Commonly known as putting your head between your knees and kissing your arse goodbye.

His suspicions were well founded.

'It would seem, gentlemen, that after Major Callen's dramatic and slightly overenthusiastic helicopter rescue at Mile End earlier this year – and to try to persuade the government to bear its share of paying for the repairs – it has become necessary to improve our reputation a little. Project a more friendly, compassionate image. I intend, therefore, that next month – December – the Time Police will hold a children's Christmas party.'

She sat back to await results.

Major Callen blinked. 'What children? We don't have any children. None of us do. It's Number Seventeen in the *Big*

Boys' Book of Time Police Rules and Regulations. Didn't we all take a solemn oath not to contaminate the gene pool with Time Police DNA?'

Commander Hay waved her hand vaguely. 'Orphans, then. I believe there are some living almost next door.'

Unwisely, Captain Farenden intervened. 'With respect, ma'am, you may be thinking of the dogs' home.'

'Well, it's nearly Christmas so there are sure to be some orphans knocking around somewhere. Find them and bring them here for a Christmas party.'

Correctly foreseeing to whom this particular task would fall, Captain Farenden allowed himself a small sigh. 'Do you have any particular age range in mind, ma'am? Babes in arms, pre-school, junior?' He paused and braced himself. 'Teenagers?'

'Good God, no. No one other than teachers or police officers voluntarily engages with teenagers.'

'Parents?' murmured Major Ellis.

'Not if they can help it. No – go for the quite young, Charlie. They're to be mobile and able to toilet themselves but not old enough to answer back or possess offensive weapons.'

Captain Farenden made a brief note. 'Yes, ma'am. Will you be calling for volunteers to assist in these . . . festivities?'

'I can't think of a quicker way of emptying the building. Inform *all* personnel they will be expected to volunteer. Cancel everyone's leave just to be on the safe side. Operational requirements aside, I want every officer you can muster. A traditional format, I think. Fancy dress. Games. With prizes. Jelly. Lots of jolly holly everywhere. Carols. Festive joy.'

Ignoring the blank looks on her colleagues' faces, she added, 'I'm sure you all know the sort of thing. Allocate everyone a specific task to ensure no one tries to wriggle out of their responsibilities. Inform everyone that biting children is probably against the law. Show them how to smile. Get the press involved. Lots of lovely publicity. Pictures of warm and fuzzy Time Police officers everywhere, all entering into the spirit of Christmas. And make sure everyone is well aware of the results of my displeasure.'

Observing the stunned expressions of Majors Callen and Ellis, Captain Farenden leaped into the breach, saying faintly, 'Yes, ma'am,' and shut down his scratchpad before things could get any worse.

Commander Hay gestured. 'Off you all go, then.'

Three weeks later, the magnificent atrium had been cleared of all things Time Police – any temporal crisis would have to wait now until after the New Year – and glum-faced officers were less than enthusiastically pinning up hastily acquired Christmas decorations. There was a certain grumpiness in the air. This was *not* what they had signed up for. Many of them had refused to vacate their comfort zone and, far from wearing fancy dress, were still in uniform. As a concession to the season of goodwill and, more importantly, having been commanded to be so – they were unarmed. Commander Hay had issued her first royal decree regarding the potentially fatal combination of small children and lethal weapons. Being gunned down by a bunch of excited ten-year-olds was not how she wanted the Time Police to be remembered.

In response to her second royal decree, officers had bitten the bullet and were wearing either Santa hats or reindeer antlers. Or, in the case of Lt Grint – neither.

Officer Curtis, burdened with a fine set of scarlet reindeer antlers, demanded to know what the fire truck all these crush barriers were for. 'Are we building a barricade? Battersea is certainly the right place if so.'

Rockmeyer shook his head. 'It's to keep the little buggers away from the koi.'

A tinsel-bedecked Lt Fanboten peered into the depths of the award-winning, architect-designed koi pool with its spectacular waterfall. The proud centrepiece of the magnificently landscaped atrium. 'I've always meant to ask – should koi carp have teeth?'

He was joined by Officer Curtis. 'Actually, sir, we think they might be piranha.'

'Ah – that would account for a lot. Did we ever find Officer Schultz?'

Luke Parrish, proud member of Team 236 – or *those idiots*, as they were professionally known – was balancing precariously on a wobbly stepladder and doing something cruel and unusual to balloons. His teammate, Jane Lockland, stood patiently at the bottom, festooned with useful implements and offering helpful, constructive and wholly disregarded advice.

Luke sighed as another balloon exploded under his gentle handling. 'For fire truck's sake, Jane. Why are we even here?'

'Well, I'm here because I'm a nice person and I volunteered. You're here because Major Ellis ordered you to be here in revenge for you giving him lip over . . .' She paused. 'Well, everything, really.' She looked around. 'I see your blonde from Logistics is here.' She paused again. 'Oh look – and there's your brunette as well. This should be interesting.'

Luke applied himself again to his astonishingly phallic arrangement of balloons. 'Calm yourself, Jane. I'm keeping

286

them at opposite ends of the atrium. With luck, they'll never know.'

Jane stared up at him. 'You do know women talk to each other, don't you?'

'Well, obviously, but if they're not talking about *me* – which most women are for most of the time – then it's just knitting patterns, or make-up, or fretting about what they can do to attract my attention.'

'Go on,' said Bolshy Jane. 'Kick that ladder away and watch him split his skull open on the marble floor. You'd enjoy that and everyone deserves a treat at Christmas.'

Fortunately – or otherwise – she was distracted by Luke demanding to know why Matthew wasn't there. 'How did he get out of this?'

'He didn't. He and Mikey are setting up the artificial snow drop.'

'Great idea. We bury the little buggers in artificial snow and then swear it was an accident. Love the thinking behind that one. Hey, look, your boyfriend's here. He must be really keen. Or perhaps he's just stopped in for a snack. You know – a couple of kids, lightly grilled. Just to keep him going until supper.'

'I'm going away now,' said Jane. 'Good luck with the ladder.'

Lt Grint stepped out of the lift, took one look around and immediately tried to get back in again. His way was blocked by Commander Hay who had come to check on the progress of her brainchild. 'Not so fast, Lieutenant.'

Grint gestured back over his shoulder. 'I've just remembered something . . .'

'No, you haven't.'

'Ma'am . . .'

'Do I need to take out my gun and tell you to get on with it?'

'Why does it have to be us?' said Grint, seriously aggrieved at the injustice of it all. 'The SAS are much nicer than we are and would do this so much better.'

'Drawing my weapon in three, two, one . . .'

Alone and unarmed, Grint turned to face the foe.

Around him, officers for whom Ebenezer Scrooge simply hadn't been trying hard enough were wrestling with tinsel, paper chains, golden stars and – despite being banned by the Geneva Convention – glitter.

An inadvertently sparkly Officer Rockmeyer demanded to know what he could possibly have done to deserve this.

Curtis shrugged. 'Because it's Christmas. You know – goodwill towards all men.'

'What exactly does that mean?'

'It means we smile as we shoot people. Season of joy and all that.'

'I'm always joyful when I'm shooting people. I don't need Christmas for that.' Rockmeyer paused. 'Do you think Parrish knows his balloons look like giant scrotums?'

'Scrota.'

'What?'

'Scrota – plural of scrotum.'

'It's not.'

'It is.'

'How do you know?'

'Lt North told me.'

'Under what circumstances could you possibly be discussing scrotums with Lt North?'

'SCROTA, stupid. Not SCROTUMS. Oh, good afternoon, Commander.'

An hour later everything was ready. The atrium looked unfamiliarly Christmassy. Balloons hung festively from every surface capable of bearing their weight. Matthew tilted his head to one side and squinted. 'Is it me or do those balloons look like giant . . . ?'

'No,' said Jane quickly.

'It's just that if you squint . . .'

'Then don't squint.'

'Wow, will you look at the size of that,' said Bolshy Jane, squinting for dear life. 'Has he modelled it on himself, do you think?'

'I'm not even looking,' said Jane. 'My only consolation is that most of the dear little kiddies won't understand.'

'You don't have a lot to do with children, do you?' sighed Bolshy Jane.

Three long tables ran down the centre of the atrium, looking festive and bright, covered with red tablecloths adorned with Christmas trees and beaming Santas.

'Good idea – red won't show the blood,' said Bolshy Jane.

'Will you please shut up.'

The tables were laid with paper plates and cups all decorated with cartoon characters – most of whom Jane didn't recognise – together with plates of sandwiches, sausage rolls, bowls of crisps, jugs of fizzy drinks, jam tarts, fairy cakes, mince pies, slices of Christmas cake, and bowls of quivering jelly in garish primary colours – not a piece of fresh fruit in sight.

'Great,' said Bolshy Jane. 'We can send them all home with scurvy.'

A giant Christmas tree stood at one end of the atrium, sporting a red and white colour scheme, most of which, on closer inspection, turned out to be red and white Time Police 'Do Not Pass This Point – Danger of Death – Scene of Crime' tape, although someone with an artistic flair – Officer Curtis blushingly admitted his guilt – had worked it up into a really rather attractive display of bows and festoons.

A hastily assembled throne sat beneath the tree, surrounded by amateurishly wrapped presents. Girls' presents in pink on the left, boys' wrapped in blue on the right. The Time Police worldview is very traditional.

Almost unanimously, Officer Kohl – Socko to his friends – had been nominated as Father Christmas. The only two dissenting votes were from Officer Kohl himself – obviously – and Luke Parrish, who had nominated Lt Grint for this honour. Lt Grint had personally destroyed the ballot paper and only with difficulty been restrained from destroying Officer Parrish as well.

Father Christmas's grand entrance was scheduled after games and food. Even the Time Police knew not to do things the other way around. Lacking access to any reindeer despite all his best efforts – and that was an afternoon Captain Farenden wouldn't forget in a hurry – the Time Police would deliver Santa in their smaller helicopter. Sadly, the pilot had refused to wear antlers. Or dress as an elf. Or play Christmas carols over the loudspeaker as they landed, because, he said, he had his image to think of. Such actions would, he said, be regarded as bringing helicopter piloting into disrepute and subject him to disciplinary action by the Union of Helicopter Pilots and

Associated Trades. When asked what sort of trade was associated with helicopter piloting, he had declined to reply. He and Father Christmas were currently in a holding pattern over Kew Gardens. They had, however, happily consented to their call sign being designated as Slay One.

Suspended from the ceiling high above, a number of cunningly slung tarpaulins held the Mikey-manufactured artificial snow which, according to its creator, would drift slowly and softly over the atrium, giving the whole scene a delightfully festive air. In this she had been ably assisted by Officer Farrell, who had unaccountably failed to mention that a similar effort at St Mary's some years ago had unfortunately resulted in self-igniting snow, an unforeseen conflagration, and delighted children – because after some years' experience of annual Christmas parties at St Mary's, local children's expectations were high and rarely disappointed. The resulting inferno had been followed by mass evacuation and the spectacular arrival of the fire brigade, who had eaten all the mince pies.

Lt Fanboten tilted his head, listening to his com. 'The bus has arrived. They're heeeeeeeeere.'

'How many?' enquired Ellis, noting that Major Callen appeared to have completely vanished.

'Only thirty, sir.'

Time Police officers who had cheerfully charged into quite minor skirmishes where they were outnumbered more than ten to one had drawn the line at putting themselves in a position where they were similarly outnumbered by small humans. A three-to-one approach had been favoured. In favour of the Time Police.

The doors opened to admit a very unmilitary straggle of small children, of varying sizes, shapes, gender and race. They halted uncertainly. The Time Police instinctively assumed Defensive Position Number Three. Both sides eyed the other.

They say that cats can unerringly pick out the one person who hates and fears them, and will then happily spend the entire day lovingly entwined around that person's neck. A similar gift is enjoyed by young children. Within seconds, a subgroup of two small humans had identified their prey and moved in.

Lt Grint stared down at the two little girls. It was very possible he had never seen so much pink in all his life.

'I'm Tiffie,' said the first one. 'I'm sad.' She held up something brown and warty. 'This is Mr Fluffy.'

'That's a toad,' said Grint, far out of his social depth but clinging to this one indisputable fact.

Tiffie clutched at Mr Fluffy, who appeared to be enjoying the process. 'He's my friend. My only friend.'

Grint had no difficulty believing a kid clutching a toad had few friends.

Another little girl tugged at his trouser leg. 'My name's Fiona. I'm a princess.'

'Um,' said Grint.

Tiffie grinned gappily. 'Will *you* be my friend?'

Grint dragged his attention back to Tiffie. 'Um . . .'

His trouser leg was subjected to further assault. 'You have to call me *Princess* Fiona.'

'Um,' said Grint, desperately looking around for assistance.

None materialised. He was on his own in a sea of pink.

'Can you lift me up?'

Princess Fiona held up her arms.

'And me?'

Tiffie held up one arm. And a toad.

Unable to think of a good reason why not, Grint crouched and rose again, one pink-clad small human in the crook of each arm. And a toad.

Everyone in the Time Police mentally ditched images of a vomit-covered Major Callen as their favourite screen saver for something involving Lt Grint and a lot of pink. And a toad.

'Hey.'

On the grounds that his day couldn't get any worse, Grint looked down.

A small boy looked up at him.

'Um,' said Grint.

'I'm Simon.'

'Um . . .' Aware he was festooned with little girls – and a toad – Grint shrugged. 'No arms left, kid. Sorry.' And noticed, too late, that Simon was on crutches.

Simon shrugged back. Grint noticed that in addition to the crutches and the sullen expression, Simon hadn't bothered to remove his coat and woollen gloves.

'He's got bad legs,' announced Tiffie.

'Bad luck,' said Grint.

'Yeah,' said Simon.

Their conversation might have progressed further but the situation was taken out of both their hands as Grint found himself submerged in a tidal wave of pink questions.

Fiona pointed at the tree. 'What's that over there?'

'A Christmas tree.'

'Why is it tied up?'

Grint sighed. 'It's decorated.'

Tiffie pointed to the barriers. 'Why can't we go over there?'

'The fish will eat you.'

293

'Do you like my dress?'

'Um . . .'

'Do you like my dress better than Fiona's?'

'*Princess* Fiona's. And no, he doesn't. Do you?'

'Um . . .'

Simon was grinning at him. Mercifully, at that moment, the first game was announced. Musical Chairs. Tiffie and Princess Fiona were lowered to the floor. Grint was handed Mr Fluffy to hold. The music started up. The game began.

Lt Grint was not the only member of the Time Police to stand stunned. The competitive instincts of the under-elevens are very strong. At one point there was a pitched battle for one of the remaining chairs. The last little boy was eliminated and led away, weeping copiously. Princess Fiona and sad little Tiffie glared at each other over the final chair. Blood was in the air.

'Do something,' said Commander Hay, nudging Major Ellis.

He stared at her in horror. 'I'm not going out there.' He looked around the atrium, although what he could be seeking was unknown.

'What are you waiting for, Major?'

'I'm looking for North or Varma.'

'Why?'

'I'm a member of the weaker sex.'

'Move it, Major.'

Major Ellis made an executive decision and strode into the arena, handed both little girls a prize and instructed Curtis to begin the second game and to be quick about it. Once again, both children and Time Police assumed battle positions.

Party Piñata was a success. Pin the Tail on the Donkey was not and made even more inroads into Time Police medical

294

supplies than the infamous Mile End incursion. Which had involved a helicopter. And several rocket-propelled missiles.

Then came the three-legged race. At their request, and not without major misgivings, Grint lashed together what he suspected would be the unstoppable combination of sad little Tiffie and Princess Fiona. It was only as Grint was depositing Mr Fluffy next to the jelly – for safekeeping, he told himself – that he remembered the third member of his new . . . for want of a better word . . . team.

Grint looked down at Simon. 'You up for this?'

Simon looked down at his crutches and then up at Grint. 'What do *you* think?'

'Do you want a prize or not?'

Simon scoffed. 'How?'

'Trust me, kid. We're going to win this. Come on.'

Without waiting to see if Simon followed on, Grint made his way to the starting line, where a harassed Rockmeyer was failing to fulfil the functions of four fully trained sheepdogs.

'Um . . .' said Rockmeyer, eyeing Simon's crutches.

'Hold these,' said Grint, handing them to him.

'Um . . .' said Rockmeyer, but it was too late.

Officer Curtis was addressing them through the medium of a loudspeaker. 'On your marks. Get set. Go.'

Watched by open-mouthed officers, Grint seized Simon, tucked him under one arm and galloped to the finishing line.

'Well done, kid,' he said, lowering Simon to ground level again.

Rockmeyer handed Simon back his crutches. 'Great technique.'

The winning team was presented with a small cup by a grinning Commander Hay who, foreseeing a time when a little blackmail might prove useful, urged Captain Farenden to record this happy event.

Tiffie glared at Simon. 'You cheated.'

'Yeah, but the kid on crutches gets away with it every time.' He looked up at Grint. 'That was so cool.'

'Hmm,' said Grint, uneasily aware that some might not consider him a good role model for impressionable young people.

Tiffie tugged at his trousers again. 'What's your name?'

'Grint.'

'No, your first name?'

'Lieutenant.'

Since Lt Grint suspected six-year-old girls possessed the interrogating skills of Officer Varma, he was greatly relieved when a bell rang somewhere, and everyone traipsed off to eat.

Except Simon.

Grint looked down. 'You not hungry?'

'I . . .'

'What?'

'Need to go to the toilet.'

'Oh. Right. Over there.'

'Need someone to hold my crutches.'

Grint sighed. 'Come on.'

Entering the facility, Simon stared at the urinals, which had been installed to cater for the needs of men – most of whom were considerably over six feet tall – and which were, consequently, at near chin-height for an undersized ten-year-old.

Grint sighed again and lifted him to the appropriate elevation. Which should have solved the problem, but owing to a slight miscommunication, one of them emerged with wetter boots than when he had gone in.

Nor was that their only problem. They were the last to approach the tables and all the seats were taken. One of them by Mr Fluffy.

'I'll shift him,' said Grint.

'No, don't. She'll scream the place down and I'm not hungry anyway.' He looked around. 'How much longer, do you think? Before we can go home, I mean.'

Grint was surprised to find that someone was enjoying the afternoon even less than he was.

'Wait here,' he said, parking Simon perilously close to the koi. 'And for God's sake, don't put your hand in the water.'

He returned a minute later with an enormous plateful of food. Jelly jostled sausage rolls. Cakes balanced precariously on sandwiches.

'Wow,' said Simon. 'Are you allowed to do that?'

Grint was puzzled. 'It's on a plate. What more do you want?'

'Well, in the home, you can't have cake until you've eaten your bread and butter.'

Grint, whose only experience of orphanages was through the medium of *Oliver Twist*, was unsurprised to hear this.

'Just start at the top and work down,' he said. 'That's what I always do. And here's a Time Police tip – always eat dessert first.'

'Why?'

Belatedly, Grint realised that *because you never know what might burst through the wall and rip out your guts before you get a chance to finish your meal* might not be entirely age-appropriate under these circumstances, and decided to go with the equally anarchic, but slightly less horrifying, 'Why not?'

Simon nodded at this seemingly acceptable answer.

Grint contemplated the carnage currently occurring at the

tables. No force in the world can withstand a pack of hungry under-elevens. Officers struggled to keep up with demand, but it was hopeless. In an effort to minimise the mess, Officer Curtis was attempting to persuade his charges to eat by numbers.

'Right,' he said, in what the Time Police would consider to be an officially encouraging tone. 'On one – lift spoons . . . On two – no, not yet. Wait until I . . . OK, let's try again, shall we? On one – oh, you already have . . . All right – moving on . . . On two – no, no, no, we've done that. That was on one . . . No, I'm not saying on one again. I'm saying we've done on one . . . Yes, I know you're all holding your spoons. Let's just . . . On two – take a spoonful of jelly and . . . well, never mind that – it'll wipe off . . . Yes, I can see yours is green . . . No, it's all the same . . . Yes, it is. Green tastes just the same as red . . . Yes, it *does*. Look . . . Why are you crying? . . . No, I'm not eating your jelly, I'm just showing you . . . Look – here's more jelly. And it's red . . . But you wanted red. Stop crying. Please . . . Look, just swap your jelly . . . With him . . . Yes, you . . . Because yours is green and she doesn't like red any more . . . Right – everyone sorted? . . . No, don't put down your spoons. No – definitely don't eat it with your fingers . . . God, that's gross – use a spoon, for God's sake . . . Why are you crying? Why are you all crying?'

'We'll stay here, I think,' announced Grint hastily, and they seated themselves on the low wall around the pool. 'What do you want first?'

Simon considered. 'Sausage roll.'

Grint handed him one and then wondered if he should also have brought plates, napkins, a knife, spoons and God knows what else. 'You eating in those gloves?'

Simon handed them to Grint. 'Can you hold these for me?'

Grint shoved them in his pocket. 'Nice gloves.'

'My mum gave them to me. Just before she went away.'

Grint frowned. His instincts told him this was an important piece of information, but Simon had closed his lips as if determined to say no more.

'I thought you were an orphan.'

Simon shook his head. 'I'm a temporary orphan. I've got a mum.'

'Where is she?'

Simon shrugged. 'Dunno. But she's coming back. I know she is.'

In Grint's childhood world, *going away* had meant either prison or death. Sometimes both. 'When?'

'Very soon. Because she's taking me to the seaside. After my op, we're going to see the sea.'

'Op?'

'To make my legs work properly. Then we're going to the seaside. She promised. When my legs are better. I've never seen the sea. Have you? What's it like? She said we'd go soon. To the seaside, I mean.'

The little voice went on and on. From one extreme to the other. From barely saying a word, it would now appear that Simon was unable to shut up. Grint, watching the big Time Police clock ticking away the slow seconds, opened his mouth to say, 'Give it a rest, kid,' then caught a glimpse of Simon's face and changed what he'd been about to say. 'Have another sausage roll, kid.' And made the discovery that kids can talk and eat at the same time. If you didn't mind flaky pastry going everywhere.

'And she said if we had a pod, we could jump to when my legs were better.'

'Really?' said Grint, suddenly as focused as a gun dog on a plummeting pheasant.

'Or a jetpack so I wouldn't have to walk.'

Grint relaxed. 'Or wings.'

Simon nodded. 'That would be so cool.' He eyed the enormous Time Police officer sitting alongside him. 'Have you got wings?'

Grint shook his head with genuine regret.

After the games and food came the carols. Everyone was to assemble around the still-standing Christmas tree. The Time Police have a procedure for unfamiliar situations. Assemble your team, assess the situation, proceed accordingly. Grint therefore assembled his jelly-smeared team – including Mr Fluffy – calculated the distance to the nearest exit, caught Commander Hay's eye, and sighed again.

The opening carol was 'Away in a Manger'.

'*Away in a manger,*' warbled Tiffie and Princess Fiona, channelling charming cherubs like champions.

'*No crib for a bed,*' rumbled Grint, causing Luke Parrish to edge behind the Christmas tree for a minute or two. Just to pull himself together again.

And then it was present time. The doors were flung wide.

Officer Rockmeyer, who had been rehearsing his line for the last week, inflated his diaphragm and prepared for his big moment. His attempt to discuss motivation and backstory with Officer Curtis had not gone well and so, at various intervals, his colleagues had been treated to:

'Oh. Goodness. I *think* I can hear someone important coming.'

'Oh. Goodness. I think I *can* hear someone important coming.'

'Oh. Goodness. I think I can hear *someone* important coming.'

'Oh. Goodness. I think I can hear someone *important* coming.'

'Oh. Goodness. I think I can hear someone important *coming*.'

Summing up his audience today, however, he made the wise decision to go with, 'OhgoodnessIthinkIcanhearsomeone-importantcoming,' before someone was trampled.

This was the cue for Officer Oti to shake a Mikey-assembled contraption, supposedly in an attempt to simulate sleigh bells, although she had her doubts.

One of the coconut shells issued to Officer Hansen to simulate the clip-clop of reindeer hooves had suffered an unfortunate mishap. The subsequent and singular clop . . . clop . . . clop – which so resembled a one-legged reindeer using his last strength to drag himself home for a final, tragic glimpse of his loving family at Christmas – was so heartrending that several of the little kiddies wept, and even Officer Curtis suffered an unexpected lip wobble.

'The best thing about orphans is no parents to complain,' said Commander Hay, producing her box of emergency tissues and instructing a tiny tot to blow. There not being a great demand for tissues in the Time Police, the box had spent many years in the darkness of her bottom drawer alongside the emergency brandy. Which tended to have a much shorter and more exciting life cycle.

'Ho. Ho. Ho,' roared Officer Kohl, stunning thirty small children, their helpers and his colleagues into terrified silence.

Each child was duly presented to Santa, who demanded to know – in a manner modelled on the interrogation technique of Officer Varma – whether they'd been naughty or nice.

Every single child perjured their soul and swore they'd been nice, except for Simon, who scowled and said he'd been naughty, temporarily terrifying Father Christmas who, foolishly, hadn't anticipated this response and had no back-up plan. It was later agreed he'd recovered well with an impromptu, 'Never mind that, what would you like for Christmas, little boy?'

'New legs so I can go to the seaside.'

'Ho. Ho. Ho,' said Socko desperately, handing Simon a present. Simon took it politely and limped away. Only Grint noticed he never opened it.

The final part of the afternoon was the snow, designed to fall gently on wondering upturned faces entranced by the magic of it all. And on the orphans, as well.

Mikey pulled out the remote and pressed the appropriate control. Sadly, one of the tarps snagged, thus causing a considerable amount of not-as-light-as-you-might-think snow to be deposited in one giant clump, lightly concussing Lt Fanboten, who had the misfortune to be standing beneath it at the time. Everyone cheered as he was stretchered away. Princess Fiona demanded they do it again.

And then the party was over. Slightly stuffed and sticky orphans were escorted off the premises. The tables were cleared away and battle-hardened Time Police officers drifted off for a stiff drink and a bit of a lie-down. The artificial snow was found to have solidified into an immovable mound that had, when mixed with the lifeblood of Lt Fanboten, welded itself to the floor. Where it remained until April. Officers simply worked around it. The formation of a new ski division was mooted on the grounds it was a pity to waste such a wonderful opportunity. Someone – Luke Parrish – planted a small flag on the top, and there it remained until the day Lt Fanboten – possibly seeking revenge – lost patience with continually having to divert around this seemingly immovable obstruction, opened fire with his blaster and Mount Fanboten – as it had become known – melted away. Which was both good and bad. Good in that the Time Police had a large portion of their atrium back again, and bad because the stink of burning snow was so pungent they had to close the building down for the rest of the day while it was dealt with.

The New Year came and went. Lt Grint – as so many had done before him – formed a series of New Year's resolutions. The first of them – not kicking the living shit out of Luke Parrish at least once a day – seemed so doomed to failure that he couldn't be bothered to waste any time on it and so moved on to the second – a daily run around Battersea – something on which he embarked with enthusiasm all through January, February, and a good part of March, as well.

The weather warmed. Daffs bloomed. The trees were covered in a greenish fuzz and Lt Grint, rummaging through his wardrobe one day, discovered Simon's forgotten gloves still stuffed in his pocket. He stared at them for a long while, then picked up the gloves, put on his jacket and went out.

He must have run past it nearly every day and never noticed it before. A large, shabby building set back from the road. So bleak and forbidding was the exterior he had automatically assumed it was either an ex-nuclear bunker or a religious establishment of some kind dedicated to the worship of one of the less forgiving deities. Which didn't narrow the field much.

Such gardens as were visible weren't untidy, but certainly bore the signs of more than their fair share of wear and tear. There were scuffed patches in the grass, a knotted rope hung from a tree branch, and there wasn't a single flower in sight. A battered sign by the gate informed him – in very small lettering, so as to get it all in – that he was standing outside the Little Petals Residential Childcare Community for Exceptional Children. Grint remembered Simon and his crutches. Tiffie and her only friend, Mr Fluffy. Fiona insisting she was a princess. He looked up at the blank windows and chickened out.

And again the next day.

On the third day, after work, he planted himself in Jane's path and suggested a stroll through the park. Puzzled but compliant, Jane changed out of her uniform and accompanied him.

That he had a destination in mind was apparent, but she said nothing. Not even when they found themselves outside the Little Petals Residential Childcare Community for Exceptional Children.

'Oh,' said Lt Grint, in apparent surprise. 'Look.'

Jane obeyed. 'Isn't that where . . . ?'

'Yes,' said Grint. 'And I still have Simon's gloves. He will need those. I must return them.'

Jane cast him a thoughtful glance but agreed that yes, now that winter was over, Simon would need his gloves back and Grint should definitely return them.

The reception area-cum-administrative office was marginally more cheerful than the outside. Accustomed as she was to the Time Police colour scheme of vibrant beiges and greys, Jane halted just inside the door, her eyeballs assaulted by every colour of the rainbow. Reds, blues, yellows and greens were everywhere. Jungle animals stalked the walls, peering suspiciously through once emerald-green foliage and scarlet flowers. By the state of them, the animals, flowers and foliage had been there for some considerable time. The walls were so heavily pockmarked that Jane would not have been surprised to hear a battle had been fought on the premises. The floor covering had been selected for its hard-wearing properties and would certainly skin alive any orphan unfortunate enough to fall on it. A hard bench ran along one wall, with a box of very shabby toys pushed underneath. These were toys at the very end of their life cycle. And the room was chilly. Jane suspected the heating was on as seldom as possible.

A pair of scuffed wooden doors led to what Jane suspected was the orphanage proper.

A well-wrapped woman was seated at the reception desk, typing busily at an ancient laptop. Jane noticed her fingerless gloves. Six or seven filing cabinets crowded the walls. An antique photocopier stood in the middle of the room where it could cause maximum inconvenience to anyone attempting to access the cabinets. Everything was spotlessly clean but cramped. Jane suspected the Little Petals Home for Residential Children, or whatever it was called, had long since outgrown its home.

The receptionist looked up and smiled. Her name badge read *Emily Caldicott*. 'Good evening. I'm afraid we're closing in a moment. Do you have an appointment?'

Grint pulled out his ID. 'Time Police.'

She glanced at it and continued typing. 'Yes?'

Grint paused. In his experience, the magic words *Time Police* nearly always produced some sort of effect – either good or bad – and the situation would proceed accordingly. He'd

never actually encountered disinterest before, and his reper-
toire of follow-up phrases was correspondingly slim.

'Gloves,' prompted Jane.

'Yes.'

Silence followed.

'Gloves?' said the receptionist.

'Yes.' There was another pause. Grint remembered his
words. 'We held a Christmas party.'

The woman stopped typing. 'Oh yes – now I remember. You
did. Did one of the children leave their gloves behind?'

'Simon,' said Grint.

'Oh, yes. He would. Such a naughty boy.'

'Not his fault,' said Grint. 'He gave them to me to hold and
I forgot them. I've brought them back.'

'How kind. Thank you.' She paused, probably expecting
Grint to produce said gloves.

He shifted uneasily. 'I hope he didn't get into trouble for
losing them.'

She sighed. 'Young Simon is in so much trouble these days,
lost gloves wouldn't make the slightest difference.'

She held out her hand for the still-non-appearing gloves.

Grint frowned. 'He was having an operation.'

'Yes, that's right.'

Grint frowned again, seemingly at a loss what to say next.

Jane intervened. 'I hope everything went well.'

'Yes, yes. He recovered very nicely.'

'Well, that's . . . nice.' Jane turned to go.

Grint didn't move. 'How did he enjoy his trip to the seaside?'

'What trip was that?'

'He told me he was going to the seaside. With his mother. After his operation. He didn't actually talk about anything else the whole time.'

The woman's face tightened. 'She never came for him. And now . . . if you don't mind, I have to help serve up supper. We're somewhat short of space so we have two sittings.' She made gestures towards the front door.

Grint remained exactly where he was. Jane could have told her she was wasting her time. 'What happened? To his mother, I mean.'

'She never turned up,' repeated the woman. 'As far as I know, she hasn't even contacted him.'

Jane was horrified. 'You mean she just . . . ?'

'Abandoned him. Yes.'

'But he did have his operation?' persisted Jane.

'Yes, he did.' She paused. There was obviously more.

'But . . . ?' said Jane.

The woman pursed her lips. 'He doesn't try. Doesn't try to help himself. Doesn't try to get on with the other children. Doesn't try at anything, really. He's always been a difficult boy, but now . . . he's rude and sullen and won't make any sort of effort at all. The other children won't speak to him. We're looking at other . . . more suitable facilities for him. Ones better suited to his needs.'

'His needs,' said Grint flatly. 'All he needs is his mother and a trip to the seaside. I appreciate you can't magic up his mother, but surely someone could have taken him on a day trip and . . .'

The woman bridled. 'We do have other children here besides Simon, you know.'

'Of course you do,' said Jane, elbowing Grint in the ribs before they could add the distinction of being thrown out of an orphanage to their service records.

Grint surprised everyone. Including himself. 'I'll take him.'

'What?'

'I'll take him since you can't be bothered.'

She flushed. 'It's not a case of not being bothered.'

'Good. Trot him out tomorrow and I'll take him to . . .'

'I can't release a child to you.'

'Why not?'

'Well, for a start, I don't know who you are.'

'I'm a Time Police officer,' said Grint who frequently found this sentence simply melted away most of life's little difficulties.

'I don't care if you're Francis of Assisi.'

Grint had no idea who she was.

'Now, if you don't mind, I need to lock the doors and help get the children ready for their supper.'

Grint regarded her steadily.

'Look, we're all sorry for Simon. We don't know where his mother is. If she doesn't show, then there's nothing we can do except try to help Simon as best we can. And we have tried. Are trying. He's hurt and angry and we're doing our best for him, but our other children have needs too.'

'We understand,' said Jane quickly. 'It's just such a sad story.'

'One of many,' Emily Caldicott said and, deploying a technique the Time Police themselves might have envied, herded them firmly towards the doors. Seconds later Grint and Jane found themselves on the other side, listening to the bolts being thrown. A few seconds after that, the lights went out.

'Come on,' said Jane, leading him back into the street.

'You go on. I'm going for a walk.'

'No, you're not,' said Jane firmly. 'You're thinking of doing something stupid and you'll be caught and then Simon will never go to the seaside.'

Grint looked down at her.

'Well, you're planning something,' she said. 'I can tell.'

Grint shifted his weight. 'No, I'm not.'

Jane made a noise indicative of disbelief.

'I'm not.'

Jane folded her arms.

Grint sighed. 'It was just a thought.'

'It's called kidnapping and people don't like it.'

'I would have brought him back.'

'You'd be finished in the Time Police. After you came out of prison.'

Grint retreated to his default state and said nothing.

'These people are professionals. They know what they're doing.'

Reluctantly, Grint nodded.

'And his mother might still come back.'

'Yes.' Striving for the appearance of a man finally convinced by these compelling arguments, he said, 'Shall we go and get something to eat?'

Grint was very thoughtful on his return to TPHQ. Fortunately, since he was habitually taciturn, no one even noticed, let alone commented. Jane was initially suspicious, but a couple of slightly hairy assignments – during which things had gone as badly as things normally went for Team 236 – diverted her attention and the matter of Simon and his trip to the seaside slipped to the back of her mind.

Not so Lt Grint, who, after nearly a fortnight of careful thought, made his way to the Records section and Lt North, where he made his requirements known and braced himself.

North surveyed him for a disconcertingly long moment. Grint reminded himself he had seniority and technically outranked her and that he was a Time Police officer and therefore afraid of no one. Except, possibly, Lt North. And, now he came to think of it, Officer Varma. Not forgetting Commander Hay, of course. Other than that – absolutely no one.

'Just to be clear,' said North. 'You want me to trace a woman – name and address unknown – mother of Simon – surname unknown – who disappeared from an unknown location on a date also unknown.'

'Yes,' said Grint, pleased to find his instructions had been so clear. With so little to go on, he had worried there might be a problem. 'How long do you think it will take?'

'A year – perhaps two.'

'Oh,' said Grint, taken aback. 'Well, that's . . .' Just in time, he remembered Lt North's habit of shooting people just to make her point, and changed what he had been about to say. '. . . Disappointing.'

'Do you have anything else for me to go on? With which assignment is this connected? Perhaps I can pick up something from there?'

'Um . . .' said Grint.

She fired up her data table. 'Just the reference number will do.'

'Um . . .' said Grint.

North stared. 'Are you asking me to do this off the books?'

'No,' said Grint defiantly, and very wisely left it at that.

'I'm sorry – I can't. If you had more for me to work with, I might be able to do something, but at the moment I wouldn't know where to start, especially since I wouldn't be able to conceal my enquiries among our day-to-day stuff. Not that I would need to do so, after your convincing assurance this is all completely above board.'

Grint's shoulders slumped. And then unslumped. 'The Christmas party.'

'This Simon came to the party?'

'Yes.'

'Well, that's better. I can access the security clearance list for his surname. That's going to make a big difference.'

'I'll come back in an hour.'

'You'll come back when I tell you to.'

'How long?'

'As long as it takes. Your time will be best spent acquiring a gift appropriate to the illegality of what you've asked me to do. Now go away.'

Two days later, he found a handwritten note in his pigeonhole. Good. No electronic trail. Just a name and address.

Ruth Wedderburn. Last known address – 4 Marine Terrace. Rushby.

At last – things were really looking up. Two problems solved at the same time. He could combine reuniting Simon and his mother with the long-awaited trip to the seaside.

What could possibly go wrong?

The Time Police are not overgenerous with high days and holidays. Since very few officers are encumbered with friends and

311

family, this is not usually seen as a problem. Jane's actions, on finding herself with free time, were usually to tidy her room, check over her uniforms and, if time permitted, go out and enjoy a little personal shopping in the sunshine.

Today, however, was a beautiful spring day, and to spend all of it inside would be a sin – Jane's ideas of sin were characteristically moderate – so she picked up her bag and exited TPHQ. Entering the nearby underground station, deliberately designated Terminal Time Police to discourage inadvertent disembarking, she used her ID to obtain the free travel to which she was entitled and stepped on to the escalator.

A very familiar figure stood some ten steps below her. She opened her mouth to call his name and wave but just as she did so, he turned his head and spoke to someone concealed by other commuters. Someone very much shorter than the other commuters.

Simon.

Jane's heart grew cold. He hadn't . . . Surely he hadn't . . . He couldn't possibly be so . . .

Alas – he could and he had.

Lt Grint and Simon stepped off the escalator together and headed towards the platform. Jane abandoned all thoughts of shopping and followed on, easing herself through the crowd. If she could somehow intercept them . . . use the time before the next train turned up to persuade them to return . . . before any real harm was done . . . while everything could still be explained away . . .

Sadly for these sensible plans, the train pulled in as she emerged on to the platform. The crowd surged forwards and Jane lost sight of them both. She jumped into the carriage anyway, craning her neck for the very distinctive shape of Lt Grint, who had made his way down to the other end. Jane grabbed a handy seat that gave her a good view of him, mentally apologising to any pregnant women in the carriage, and never took her eyes off either of them.

She couldn't get any closer – people were embarking and disembarking at every station. Even when they changed at Tottenham Court Road, the crowd was too great for her to reach them. She would have to wait until she could grab them at the end of their journey, somehow dissuade them from whatever madness the two of them had planned, and return them – Simon in particular – whence they'd come. They could say they'd found him wandering in the park. Or something. Anything. Jane was quite astonished to find she was prepared to lie like stink to protect Lt Grint. And Simon, obviously. The truth could only lead to Grint being dishonourably discharged, arrested, imprisoned, and possibly a guest appearance on the sex-offenders' register. He was ruining his life. What the fire truck did he think he was playing at? She was surprised at the hot anger and panic roiling around inside. Grint, of all people.

She followed them off the train at Paddington and caught up with them before they could access the hyperloop platform.

'Hey.'

Grint was horrified. 'Jane?'

Jane went straight to the point. 'What the f— on earth do you think you're doing?'

'Nothing,' said Grint, too surprised by her sudden appearance to think of an acceptable lie. Actually, he wasn't sure there was an acceptable lie. Not that the truth – *removing a small boy from his place of residence to take him to the seaside for the purposes of pleasure* – was any sort of improvement. On balance, he'd stick with 'nothing'.

'Are you insane?'

'No,' said Grint, pleased to be able to answer this one truthfully.

'You have to take him back this very moment and just pray no one has noticed.'

'They won't,' said Simon with confidence. 'They'll just be pleased I'm not hanging around moping or winding up the other kids. Believe me, it'll be hours before anyone notices I'm gone. And even then, they'll just think I've wandered off round the park to see the parrots and the peacocks again.'

Jane struggled to regroup. 'Why would they think that?'

'Because that's what I've been doing for the last week. So people would get used to me not being around.'

Jane wheeled on Grint. 'You *planned* this?'

'Well . . . yes . . . of course we did. Planning is the most important stage of any operation and . . .'

'*Not in this instance.*'

Grint could only remain silent in the face of such folly.

Jane tried to calm down a little.

'You have to take him back. Simon, you have to go back.'

'No,' said Simon simply.

Jane couldn't decide which of them to shake first.

'Simultaneously?' suggested Bolshy Jane.

Wild ideas galloped through Jane's mind. Should she scream? Attract attention? Make a scene? She could accuse them of trying to kidnap her. That would certainly get all of them shunted somewhere out of public view. Once there, she could claim it was all a misunderstanding and she was Grint's girlfriend . . .

'You *are* Grint's girlfriend,' reminded Bolshy Jane, exasperated.

. . . And then she could tell them the whole thing was just a silly row and the authorities would send them all home – embarrassed but probably unarrested.

'Not your best idea, sweetie,' said Bolshy Jane, and Jane had to admit it wasn't.

'Actually,' continued Bolshy Jane – Jane made a mental note to visit MedCen – should she ever again have that opportunity – and request medication to make the voices go away. Or, failing that, earplugs – 'Actually, sweetie, your best course of action might be to let them go. The chances are that Grint will be able to get Simon back unnoticed. Probably. Perhaps. And even if he can't, the home won't want the scandal of people knowing you can just walk in and scoop up an orphan any time you like. They're not fashion accessories, you know.'

'I think you should go with them,' said Wimpy Jane. Jane was completely unsurprised the voices in her head had started ganging up on her. Why wouldn't they?

'And why would I go with them?'

'Chaperone.'

She hadn't thought of that.

'We need to go,' said Grint. 'Our train's due.'

They both looked at Jane. Who looked back. Crunch time. What should she do?

Everything in her power to prevent Grint ruining his life was the answer to that one.

She looked again at their faces and groaned. Fire-trucking hell.

An hour and a half later, they alighted at Rushby. It was a pretty station. Tubs of bright flowers had been placed around the entrance and a nearby plaque proudly announced the station had been awarded Best of Class in its category for the third year running.

Jane considered fainting. Grint would pick her up – she hoped – and she could claim she was too ill to go on. Surely then he'd escort her home again.

'I wouldn't bank on it,' said Bolshy Jane darkly.

Simon disappeared into the gents' toilets and Jane seized the opportunity to interrogate Lt Grint as to his intended plan of action.

'So, he doesn't know his mother's here,' she said when he'd finished.

Grint shook his head. 'No. I thought if she wasn't – or if she'd moved on – or something – then . . .'

'Yes?'

Grint shrugged. 'At least he'll have seen the sea.'

Bolshy Jane rolled her eyes.

Any further discussion was prevented by Simon appearing from the toilet and raring to go.

The station was situated at the top of the town. They stood on the pavement and looked at the award-winning view.

'I can see the sea,' shouted Simon. The first signs of excitement Grint had ever seen in him. 'Look – there's the sea. Wow – it's so big.'

It's such a lovely day, thought Jane in despair. Had it been raining cats and dogs, she might have been able to persuade them to come home. She went to say something to this effect and then caught the expression on Simon's face. He was still the sad, pale child she remembered, but today his eyes shone with excitement and anticipation. Only a monster would deprive a little boy of his first sight of the sea. She could faint later.

And it was indeed a beautiful view. The sun sparkled on the bright blue sea. A few boats with brave red sails scudded about in the water. Fishing boats were clustered in the pretty harbour, more or less enveloped in a crowd of screaming seagulls. A gentle sea fog misted the horizon. She couldn't see much of the town itself, only lots of red roofs, bright in the sunshine.

The streets were very steep and many of them were narrow and cobbled. Grint looked down at Simon. 'Let me know if you can't manage.'

It was very apparent Simon would drop down dead rather than admit such a weakness.

Jane sighed. Apart from them both breaking the law in a very specific and limited way, there was always the possibility Simon might not be physically ready for this and they could be setting back his recovery. Or causing a relapse. Suppose he slipped and broke one of his newly mended legs. What then? And she couldn't even think about how to handle his possible reunion with his mother.

Grint turned to look at her over Simon's head and smiled. 'Thank you for coming.'

Jane refused to be won over. 'We will be discussing this for an hour or so at the first opportunity.'

Grint nodded gloomily. 'I thought we might.'

They made their way slowly through the streets. Now that she *was* here, Jane would have liked to peer in one or two shop windows – after all, shopping was what she had set out to do this morning – but it was very obvious Simon wanted to get down to the sea as quickly as possible.

'I can smell it,' he declared, his face flushed with excitement.

'Or flushed with sunstroke,' muttered Wimpy Jane. 'Or

317

flushed with fever because he's done too much too soon. We really shouldn't be doing this.'

'Too late now,' said Bolshy Jane cheerfully. 'Ooh – is that candyfloss?'

Jane was consulting a local You Are Here map. Marine Terrace wasn't far. They had plenty of time. And it put off the moment . . .

She and Simon both stared meaningfully at the candyfloss stall and then back at Grint, who sighed and disappeared towards the stall while Jane and Simon wandered along the seafront to look down on the beach below. They could hear the soft hiss of the waves. Gulls paddled at the waterline. The breeze tugged at Jane's hair. She was aware that with only very little encouragement, she might enjoy herself.

'Can I go for a paddle later?' asked Simon.

'Don't see why not,' said Jane, coming to the conclusion that one of them at least should get some fun out of the day before the axe fell.

'Cool,' said Simon. 'I've never paddled before. Or had candyfloss.'

'Neither have I,' admitted Jane.

Bolshy Jane laughed. 'Sweetie, if we stop to list the many, many things you've never experienced, it'll be time to go home before we've finished. You've never had candyfloss, you've never paddled, you've never had a boyfriend before, you've never had . . .'

'Enough,' said Jane.

Lt Grint, meanwhile, arriving at the head of the queue, requested three sticks of candyfloss. Carefully – and not entirely convinced the stuff didn't have flesh-eating properties – which would account for the colour – he made his way back to his travelling companions.

Who were already eating candyfloss.

'Well, this is very generous of you,' said Jane, pulling off a huge lump with her fingers, 'but we haven't finished the first lot yet and I don't think Simon should have so much sugar.'

Grint looked at Simon who had candyfloss in his hair, his ear, between his fingers and down the front of his hoodie. It must have taken him a good few minutes to get himself in that state. And then he looked back at the three sticks of candyfloss in his hand and Jane and Simon polishing theirs off in front of him.

'Jane, where did you get that?'

Jane stopped eating, looked at her own candyfloss, then at Grint, then at the candyfloss he was holding, then at the stall, and then back at Grint again.

'From you. You bought it.'

'No, Jane, I didn't.'

'You *did.*'

'When?'

'About five minutes ago. You had three sticks of the stuff. You handed Simon his, and said, "Don't get it all over yourself and, more importantly, don't get it all over me."'

'Then what did I do?'

Jane was silent for a long time and then said quietly, 'You walked back over there.' She pointed to the vendor.

'Then what happened?'

She frowned. 'I . . . don't know . . . I . . . You were standing here. With more candyfloss.'

Grint made to set off back to the stall. Jane caught his arm in alarm.

319

'No, no, wait. Stay here. I don't think you should go any-where. Stay with us.'

Grint dumped his candyfloss in a nearby bin. Jane followed suit with hers. Simon showed absolutely no inclination to do anything so ridiculous.

Grint and Jane looked at each other. 'OK,' said Jane. 'You're scaring me now.'

'I'm scaring myself as well.'

'I'm not scared,' said Simon, a long strand of pink stuff hanging from his cheek. He looked like an amateur snake whose skin-shedding had not gone quite according to plan.

Grint edged himself closer to Jane, who in turn, nudged Simon into the space between them and took his hand. 'Physi-cal contact at all times,' he said.

Jane nodded. 'Do you think . . .'

'I don't know. It might be a natural Time fault. You do get them occasionally, left over from the Time Wars, but I've never heard of anything in this area before. Or – and this would be my first choice – someone's up to something, temporally speaking. We should check this out.'

'No, we should leave.'

'Why?'

Jane indicated Simon.

'No,' said Simon firmly. 'We should definitely stay and check it out. Here. By the sea. And you can buy me another candyfloss. Or a hot dog.'

'Kid, you'll be ill.'

Simon grinned pinkly. 'Yeah.'

'We should call it in,' said Grint.

'As soon as we do that, they'll know where we are,' said Jane.

Simon finished the last of his pink fluff and lobbed his stick into the bin, at the same time eyeing the discarded candyfloss speculatively.

'Don't even think about it,' said Jane warningly.

Simon shook his head. 'No, listen. We should definitely check it out. Whatever it is. Cos then you've got a reason to stay here. You're investigating. And if you solve it, then you won't be in trouble, will you? See, no downside.'

Grint stared at him. 'Do you know anyone called Parrish?'

'No – don't think so. Do you?'

Jane drew Grint slightly aside. 'Look, there's an easy way out of all this. Let's take Simon to his mother. She can ring the home and tell them he's safe with her. No one's going to read anything sinister into your actions if the first thing you do is hand him over to his mother – *probably* won't read anything sinister into your actions – and once Simon is with her, *then* we can investigate this anomaly, sort everything out, and hope it goes a long way towards mitigating our sins.'

Grint smiled slightly. 'Thank you for calling them *our* sins.'

'You said Simon has no idea his mum might be here?'

'No, haven't mentioned it – just in case she's moved on again or something. I thought we could take a casual stroll, knock on the door and see what happens. Simon's never lived here so he won't be suspicious.'

'Suppose she doesn't want to know? Suppose she has actually abandoned him?'

'I'll go first and check things out.'

Jane nodded. 'OK. You tell him now while I try and clean him up a little. This pink stuff is really sticky.'

Jane produced a tissue and scrubbed as Grint leaned against

the railings and endeavoured to manage expectations. 'Listen, kid – see those steps? Yeah, the steep ones. We thought we'd take a walk up there and look at the cottages at the top.'

'Then can I have a hot dog?'

Grint shrugged. 'Yeah, why not?'

Marine Terrace was a tiny row of fishermen's cottages set halfway up the towering cliffs and separate from the town. Simon held tightly to Lt Grint's hand as they tackled the steep steps. Interesting choice, thought Jane, trying not to pant.

Number Four was, astonishingly, the fourth cottage along. Very bright and cheerful with its painted cream walls and blue door and windows, but somehow impersonal. A holiday let, thought Jane.

She halted and stared. 'That's a little worrying.'

Grint nodded. 'It is. Stay here.'

The front door was standing wide open. There might be nothing sinister in that, but nevertheless, Grint approached with caution and tapped politely.

Jane eased Simon behind her and took up a position a few yards away.

Grint stepped inside, straight into a tiny front room with an old-fashioned black fireplace. Shelved alcoves stood to either side. They were empty. There were very few personal items in the room and some of them were on the floor. A small table near the door had been overturned.

Grint frowned. Had there been a struggle? Or had someone been in a hurry to leave and knocked it over on the way out? He trod silently into the kitchen. Stairs led up to the bed-rooms. Turning back, he gestured to Jane, still waiting near the front door.

'I'm going to check out upstairs. Wait inside until I give the word.'

Jane nodded.

Standing just inside the door, they listened to Grint's heavy footsteps overhead, crossing from room to room and then back down the stairs again.

Simon looked up at Jane. 'What's happening?'

'We're not sure,' said Jane. 'Let's just wait, shall we?'

Grint reappeared, holding something. He crouched in front of Simon, which brought their eyes to more or less the same level.

'Simon – is this you?' He held out a small, crumpled photo. A younger Simon sat next to a young woman with short, bubbly curls and Simon's eyes.

Simon's mouth dropped open. Slowly he reached out and touched the photo. 'That's my mum. And me. She keeps this in her handbag. In her purse. Next to her driving licence.' He stared at Grint. 'Does this mean my mum lives here?' He looked past Grint at the toppled table. 'Is she . . . ? What's happening? Where's my mum?'

'She looks lovely,' said Jane reassuringly. 'What's her name?'

'Ruth. Has something happened to my mum?'

'We don't know,' said Jane, gently taking the image. 'Let's go back outside and you can tell me all about her and then we can start looking.'

Grint stood up. 'The important thing is not to get upset. She wouldn't like that. All right?'

Simon stared up at him, his eyes huge.

'You shouldn't worry too much, kid. I'm wondering if your mother bumped into the table and knocked it over. Perhaps she hurt herself and she's gone to the doctor.'

'But the front door was open,' said Simon, his lip quivering.

'She was in a hurry to get to the surgery, I expect. The thing to do now is to be brave. I know you can do that because the lady at the home was telling us about you. Yeah, I know you're a bit different from the other kids, but that's good. And well done for not being what people expect you to be. Sometimes you just have to say to people, "No, this is how I am. Live with it." And after a while, they will leave you alone.'

Jane could easily imagine Grint's childhood being one of solitary defiance.

Simon nodded and reached for the image again. Grint took Jane aside.

'Two bedrooms – both occupied,' he said quietly. 'Women's stuff in one – men's shaving stuff in the bathroom. Three toothbrushes. No signs of a struggle upstairs. No blood.'

'OK,' said Jane, watching his face.

He lowered his voice. 'There's a big bolt on the woman's bedroom door.' He paused. 'On the outside.'

'Oh dear,' said Jane. 'That's not good.'

'I shouldn't have done this, should I? I've just made things worse for Simon.'

'Not necessarily,' said Jane. 'If something has happened, then at least we can raise the alarm.'

'But why? Is Ruth Wedderburn someone special?' Grint had a sudden inspiration. 'Simon, do you remember when we were talking about your mum? At Christmas? What does she do?'

Simon looked up from the image. 'She makes things.'

'What sort of things does she make?'

'Things – you know.'

Jane had a thought. 'Do you know who she works for, Simon?'

324

He shook his head.

'Did she perhaps tell you not to say?'

He shook his head again, suddenly miserable. All his sparkle had disappeared. Grint's right, thought Jane. We've only made things worse.

'I don't really know what she makes,' said Simon. 'She doesn't talk about it much. I want my mum. This isn't our house. I want to go home.'

Jane put her arm around him, saying to Grint, 'We can't stay here. Well, *we* can – he can't. If we're going to look into this, we need to take him somewhere safe. Police station, perhaps.'

Grint lowered his voice. 'Jane, when he was at the party, he told me his mum talked about making him a pod.'

Jane stared. 'Oh.'

'I didn't take any notice at the time because he went on to talk about a jetpack. And I think I mentioned wings as well, but the point is . . .'

'A pod,' said Jane, in a hollow voice. 'And a possible temporal anomaly. It's not rocket science, is it?'

'No, it's Temporal Dynamics.' He sighed. 'Take him back, Jane. To London. I'll handle things here.'

'I'm not leaving you.' She looked around. 'We really need to call this in.'

'We need to get Simon out of here first,' said Grint.

'I think it's a bit late for that. The Time Police will want to talk to him – you know that. We might as well all wait here.'

Grint shuffled his feet. 'The game's up, Jane, isn't it? I'm sorry to have got you into this.'

'It was my choice,' said Jane firmly. 'I could have gone back to the home and reported you, you know.'

'And now you're as implicated as I am.'

'Yeah . . . well . . .'

Grint pulled out his com and went into the kitchen. She could hear his voice through the half-closed door.

Simon was staring around. 'Something horrible has happened to my mum, hasn't it?'

Jane crouched beside him. 'We don't know that.'

'That's why she didn't come for me. Is she dead?'

'No,' said Jane, with as much confidence as she could muster.

'I spoke to Ellis,' said Grint, reappearing through the door. 'He already knew we were here. The home's made a complaint. A team's already on their way. ETA ten minutes. They're coming by helicopter. More discreet. We're not to touch anything. Let's wait outside. We can walk down to the beach. You can have your paddle. Would you like that, Simon?'

Simon shook his head. 'No.'

Grint put his hand on Simon's shoulder and looked at Jane. 'I've made a complete balls-up of this, haven't I?'

'No,' said Jane. 'Something is going on here and no one would have known anything about it if it wasn't for you.'

'Jane – I'm . . . sorry.'

'We'll talk about it . . .'

His mouth turned up. 'When we both come out of prison.'

Jane cast a quick glance at Simon. 'If it turns out his mum does have some expertise in certain areas and that has brought her to the attention of someone . . .'

'Who?'

'Could be anyone. Big business. A bunch of loonies.' She paused. 'Someone like Henry Plimpton . . .'

326

Grint peered through the window. 'There's a garden shed – I'll just check it out before we leave.'

Opening the back door, he set off across the overgrown lawn towards the perfectly ordinary wooden shed. He reached for the handle and then stopped. Faintly, through the door, he could hear a quiet buzzing. Or droning. That wasn't good. Not good at all. They should leave.

Now.

Grint spun around and began to run.

Straight into a taser.

Jane saw the two men as they came past the window. Instinctively she pushed Simon behind the armchair in the corner and gestured for him to keep quiet. Once he was out of sight, she shoved the chair as far back as it would go. Simon wrapped his arms around his knees, closed his eyes and held his breath.

He heard Jane say, 'Who are you? What do you want?'

Then came the sounds of a slight struggle – the table went over again – and Jane being hustled away. The back door banged. Other than a clock ticking somewhere, there was silence throughout the house. An empty silence rather than the silence of someone waiting for him to emerge. Or so he hoped. What should he do? Run? Or stay where he was? If they came back for him, he'd be discovered in seconds.

Simon squeezed out from behind the chair, got to his feet and listened. Still nothing. But for how long? Suppose the door opened and they grabbed him the way they'd grabbed Jane?

Panic washed over him. Everyone had gone. He was all on his own. What should he do? Simon very badly wanted someone to tell him what to do. Taking a deep breath, he yanked open the front door and ran blindly. Along the path. Down the steps. Faster and faster. Faster than he'd ever run before. His legs hurt but he couldn't stop. He mustn't stop. He had to . . .

He never saw the man at all. Not until he ran straight into him, bounced off the railing and sat down hard on his bottom.

Grint awoke to the smell of creosote and compost and found himself face to face with a giant green snake. Someone had taken the opportunity to swap his arms for his legs and vice versa. Nothing appeared to be working properly. A common symptom of over-tasering. Unsurprisingly, it took a lot of juice to put someone like Grint on the ground.

He appeared to be lying on a hard concrete floor. The long green snake thing resolved itself into a garden hose, which was a relief. Grint had no huge objection to forty-foot-long green snakes, but no one ever wants to find themselves eyeball to eyeball with one while lying bound and helpless. Compost, creosote and a garden hose. He was in the garden shed.

The next thing he saw was Jane, tied to one of those cheap plastic chairs people use in the garden. That must be why he was on the floor. They'd never have been able to squeeze him into one of those things. Even supposing it could bear his weight. Jane didn't look particularly comfortable. On balance, Grint reckoned he was better off on the floor.

The only good news in this somewhat catastrophe-laden day was that Simon didn't appear to be present. Although Grint's view was somewhat limited, and for all he knew Simon had been stuffed into a bag of compost.

A large pair of boots filled his vision. Grint regarded them with misgiving. Boots plus face frequently equalled pain.

The buzzing in his ears resolved itself into voices. Two voices. Two people. Or a ventriloquist, possibly. He squinted up at Jane, who frowned and very fractionally shook her head. Which could mean he wasn't to speak. Which was OK with him. Or possibly that Simon wasn't here. Which was good. Or that she couldn't get free. Which was bad. Or that he should just stay where he was until the situation resolved itself and a clear course of action emerged. Which suited Grint just fine. His arms and legs were still AWOL.

'This is shit,' a man's voice was whining. He sounded very young, late teens – possibly early twenties. And he was very unhappy about something. 'Just shit. I tell you, something's not right. You shouldn't of touched it. Any of it. Look at all those red lights. And what's with that fog? She didn't say anything about fog.'

'She didn't say a lot of things.'

She being Ruth Wedderburn, Grint presumed.

'And neither did he,' continued the whiney voice. 'I reckon we've been stupid to get involved in this. Let's just piss off while we can.'

'He won't be happy with us.'

'Then he should be here, shouldn't he? He's gone. She's gone. This thing's gone haywire. And now the sodding Time Police are here. We should go while the going's good. Walk out the door and don't come back.'

The slightly older voice cut in. 'Look – we'll find her. She can't have got far. We'll bring her back, make her fix it, and job done. We sit back and watch the money roll in.'

'Yeah? If you ask me, we'll see precious little of that. In fact, I bet that's where he's gone. He's off doing a deal right now and we won't see a penny. And now there's these two here and they're fucking Time Police.' He dropped his voice to what he thought was a whisper. 'They've seen our faces, Raffy. The best thing we can do now is to run. And don't look back.'

There was a short silence, during which Raffy, presumably, was considering his options. Grint could still hear a low droning noise, which he was pretty sure wasn't the effect of being tasered. Actually, that was a point. He tried to squint down his own body. Involuntary bladder voiding was a well-known symptom of tasering. Not something he'd want Jane to witness, obviously. Nothing felt warm and wet. Not that that meant he was more kindly disposed towards his captors. There would be payback later on. Something for everyone to look forward to.

In the meantime, Whiney-voice was continuing. 'And I dunno what you did but now it won't switch off. And the field output's in the red, which even I know isn't good, man. We really need to get her back here. She's the only one who . . .'

There was an unmistakeable note of panic. Grint lifted his head to try to see what was happening.

'Shit – he's awake,' said Whiney-voice.

'Check he's still secured,' said Raffy.

'You check. I'm not going near . . .'

'Just do it, will you? Taser him again if he gives you any trouble.'

A dark shape loomed.

Grint glared. Which did not appear to have any noticeable effect.

Something dropped on to his face and from there to the floor. He swivelled his eyes and focused. His ID.

'So – you're the bastard Time Police,' said the voice.

'I've called it in,' said Grint thickly. 'They'll be here at any moment.'

As he had hoped, Whiney-voice defaulted to instant panic mode. 'Told you. I told you. It's all gone tits up and Joe's disappeared and we'll be carrying the can for all this. I can't afford to be caught again. And neither can you. Not with your record.'

Raffy responded in sudden temper. 'Shut up. Just shut up.'

Sound advice. Without meaning to, Whiney-voice was spewing helpful information with every word. Officer Varma frequently maintained that a successful interrogation could easily be conducted from any location and in any position – including on the floor, it would seem. He now knew there were at least three of them, including the absent Joe. That they'd built some sort of equipment – or rather, Ruth Wedderburn had. Under duress probably, given the bolt on the bedroom door. Had she escaped? And now, whatever she'd built wasn't behaving itself. And Joe, whoever he was, wasn't here. Had he gone after her? Grint tried to flex his arms and felt the plastic ties bite even more deeply into his wrists.

Whiney-voice hadn't finished. 'Raffy. Why are they here? We ain't done nothing wrong.'

Grint could tell from the sound of his voice that Raffy was grinning. 'Kidnapping . . . ? Coercion . . . ? False imprisonment . . . ? Yeah, we ain't done nothing wrong, have we?'

'That the Time Police would be interested in, I mean. What are they here for?'

Grint flashed Jane a glance. She was sitting quietly in her plastic chair, looking her usual unthreatening, slightly nervous self, but like him, she would be listening to every word.

So what *was* going on here? These two – possibly three – men had forced Simon's mum to build something for them. Given the anomaly at the candyfloss stand, some sort of Time-manipulation device, presumably. And yet neither man considered Grint and Jane's appearance to be connected with whatever they'd been up to. Not surprising, really. In Grint's experience, every illegal was always convinced they hadn't done anything wrong.

The next stage – inevitably – would be for these idiots to decide the best way forward was for them to dispose of unwanted and unwelcome Time Police officers and continue with their plans for the day. He could only hope Simon had had the sense to raise the alarm and wasn't just paddling quietly in the sea and enjoying his day. Grint's thoughts turned to methods of escape.

As TPOs, Jane and Grint were tagged. All officers were. A basic precaution. Even the idiots at St Mary's were tagged. In fact, one of the idiots, given her propensity for unscheduled disappearances, was the proud possessor of at least seven tags – three of which she knew nothing about. Either their captors were not aware of standard Time Police precautions or hadn't realised the implications.

The good news – and suddenly it *was* good news – was that Ellis and a team were on their way. North could furnish them with Ruth Wedderburn's address. They might even be here already. They'd find him. Sadly, they'd find Jane, too, but he could lie about that. He'd tell them he'd forced her to come. Against her will. That she was an innocent party. Except Jane would tell the truth. She always did. He sagged. There really was no good way out of this. But first things first . . . Time to continue his interrogation.

The same idea seemed to have occurred to Raffy, who

nudged him with his boot. 'What are you doing here? What do you know?'

'Nothing,' said Grint honestly.

Grint had been right. Boots plus helpless Time Police officer equalled a great deal of pain. He curled up as best he could, but a kick to his knee sent agony lancing up and down his leg. His breath hissed. He told himself it was good they were mostly leaving his face alone. Because they needed him to be able to talk. On the other hand, if he didn't say anything – how long before they started on Jane?

Who was forcing herself to sit perfectly still and watch.

'Sweetie,' said Bolshy Jane very quietly. 'He's doing his bit, but I think the next part has to be up to you.'

Jane nodded. She'd come to that conclusion herself. Although physically, she was as helpless as Grint. What was she supposed to do?

The answer came almost immediately. What was it everyone always said about her? *You don't look like a Time Police officer.* And they were right. Despite nearly two years' service under her belt, Officer Lockland still presented the appearance of timid Jane trembling in the shadow of a grandmother who no longer existed.

'I am Jane Lockland,' she said to herself.

'Yes, you are,' said Bolshy Jane, with enthusiasm.

'Daughter of Helen Portman.'

'Yes, you are,' said Bolshy Jane.

'I am Time Police. Hear me roar.'

'Don't get carried away,' said Bolshy Jane.

It seemed to have dawned on their captors that their prisoner wasn't going to talk. Grint, peering up from the floor, saw the same thought occur to them both simultaneously. Slowly, they turned to look at Jane.

'Well,' said Raffy, an unprepossessing specimen of villainhood – short and skinny with greasy skin and spectacularly underdeveloped musculature. 'This could be fun.'

'And pointless,' said Jane. Lifting her chin and channelling Officer North – her role model – she made her voice clipped and authoritative. Someone not to be messed with. 'He's just a grunt. He's not going to tell you anything because he doesn't know anything. Look at him. The only use they would have for him is hitting people.'

The men approached. One of them looked her up and down. 'And what do they use you for?'

'They don't use me at all,' said Jane. 'I'm not Time Police.'

They stared at her. 'Yeah, you are.'

'No, I'm not.'

He picked up her ID. 'This says otherwise.'

Jane nodded. 'So I should hope, for the amount of money it cost me. I also have the appropriate ID for MI5, MI6, and CP24.'

'Never heard of that one.'

'No one has,' said Jane, amazed at her own fertility. 'That's rather the point.'

'If you're not Time Police – and you certainly ain't MI5 or MI6 – then what are you doing with him?'

Jane made her first public attempt at a smirk. 'Pumping him for information on the whereabouts of Ruth Wedderburn.'

He looked Jane up and down again, plainly disbelieving. 'You? And that works, does it?'

Jane half closed her eyes and slowly smiled. 'It does the way I do it.'

Grint looked across at her and held her gaze for a long moment. Battered, bruised and in some considerable pain, he raised one amused eyebrow. Jane fell in love with him on the spot.

'You said he didn't know anything,' said one man, recalling her to the moment.

'He doesn't. I've wasted over a month on this idiot and trust me, he doesn't know jack shit.'

'Even after all that pumping?'

Jane smirked again. Slightly more convincingly this time. 'Even after what could only be described as *extensive* pumping.'

'Sweetie,' said Bolshy Jane. 'If I thought you had the slightest clue what you were talking about, I'd be impressed.'

'So what *does* he know?'

'Well . . .' Jane attempted to cross her legs nonchalantly, failed, and abandoned the attempt. 'The Time Police know about Ruth Wedderburn. You slipped up badly there. Worst of all, from your point of view, they know about the candyfloss stall.'

Sitting in the chair, Jane's view of the shed was better than Grint's – which consisted mostly of dead spiders and mouse droppings. The two men looked baffled. 'What about the candyfloss stall?'

Good question, thought Jane. Don't lose control of this conversation. She shrugged. 'You tell me.'

'Don't know what you're talking about,' said Whiney-voice.

'If you say so,' said Jane, politely disbelieving. 'Tell me about all this, instead.'

She nodded her head towards the non-horticultural end of the shed – a wobbly trestle table covered with various bits of Heath Robinson electronics, one unit stacked haphazardly upon another, and with three heavily earthed cables running therefrom.

Each of the three cables ran to an equally heavily earthed metal upright pole, around three feet high, which, in turn, was firmly secured to a rubber-legged tripod. The three were arranged as an equilateral triangle. A rubber mat painted with a large X had been carefully positioned at the exact centre. X marked the spot, presumably. What the function of the spot was, Jane had no idea, although she could hazard a horrible guess. X was obviously a carefully designated place in which to stand in order that something should occur. With the memory of Henry Plimpton's disastrous Time-travelling bracelets and the problems they'd caused still fresh in her mind, Jane was convinced she was looking at something amateurish but similar.

Except . . . something wasn't right. What was it he had said? *She never said anything about fog.*

And there had been that sea fog on the horizon. Slowly rolling towards them.

Her mind flew back to her training days and the series of lectures on the many and varied ways of screwing with the Timeline. There had been Time-slips – still occasionally encountered, although not so frequently these days; anomalies – so many different types of anomalies, and new ones were being created all the time; time-stops – only one had come her way so far but one was one too many; Bluebell Time – which required prompt and direct intervention by the Time Police; alternate universes – one wrong word or deed at a critical moment could send the universe spinning down an entirely different Timeline; and last, and certainly not least, the result of bungled Timeline manipulation – the dreaded bubble universes.

These idiots must have attempted Time travel, botched it – hence the candyfloss hiccup – and the universe had created a bubble into which she, Grint and Simon had unknowingly stumbled.

A bubble universe is a physical thing. It exists – right up until the moment it doesn't. Bubbles are created by the universe to protect itself from the damage caused by idiots who think physics is something that can be messed with. It's a temporary protection while the Timeline does whatever is necessary to resolve itself. Think of it as a giant scab.

The downside is that, sooner or later, the giant scab is no longer required. The damage has been repaired. Rather like a ten-year-old child, the universe gleefully picks off the scab. It has fulfilled its function and is now surplus to requirements, along with everyone and everything else inside the bubble. The original universe, now healed over, continues on its merry way. But nothing inside a bubble universe survives. Ever.

Sometimes it just disappears. Suddenly. Like popping one of Luke Parrish's festive balloons. One minute there – the next minute gone. Along with everything inside it. Sometimes – usually – the bubble slowly shrinks – smaller and smaller – until, finally . . . nothing left.

This is not normally a problem. In fact, it's the universe protecting itself by destroying the unwanted duplicate. But – and it's an enormous but – bubbles are one-way. You can get in – usually by accident – but you can't get out. Not unless you have a pod. And Jane and Grint didn't have a pod. They were trapped here and would share the same fate as all the other inhabitants.

Not that she was likely to live that long. A rich array of possible fates lay before her. Either or both of these half-wits could kill her – by accident, probably. Or the Time Police would track them down and shoot them on the spot. Or – and this seemed most likely – this very dodgy-looking equipment could explode, blowing the shed and its occupants sky high. Because whatever was going on here – whatever the purpose of this equipment was – something had gone horribly wrong, temporally speaking, and a bubble universe had been created. Either by Ruth Wedderburn before she disappeared, or by these idiots attempting to operate the equipment without having a clue what they were doing.

In which case, the question now was – how big was the bubble? Was it still growing? Which it might be if the damage to the Timeline was very great. Or – worst-case scenario – had the Timeline righted itself and the bubble was already shrinking? Meaning this world would become smaller and smaller and smaller until they were all standing on each other in an attempt to escape being sucked into the all-consuming void? Never mind that. The really important thing was to get out. As quickly as possible. Which could prove problematic, since not only were she and Grint under restraint, but they had no pod in which to escape.

And where was Simon? Finding him must be her absolute priority. And his mother, of course. Wherever she was.

Her second priority must be to ensure no one did any more damage to Grint, because carrying him was out of the question unless someone had a fork-lift truck tucked away somewhere.

And even if they did manage to escape, their problems wouldn't be over, because then would come the challenge of keeping Grint out of prison. And herself. Good grief, when you looked at it, the list was endless. Jane sighed to herself. A woman's work is never done.

'Better get cracking, then,' said Bolshy Jane very unsympathetically. Wimpy Jane, overcome by events, appeared to have gone for a rest in a darkened room.

'Please listen to me,' said Jane, still striving to emulate Lt North without actually sounding like a Time Police officer. 'I can see that things haven't gone quite according to plan for you, and I definitely think your easiest course of action is to let us go. But . . .' she said loudly, talking over their protests, 'I'm prepared to do a trade. You let us go and we lead you to Ruth's son, Simon. Once you have him, I'm certain she'll do whatever you want. I rather suspect Joe will be so pleased at your initiative he'll increase your share. Think about that.'

She watched their faces as they looked at each other. Would this work? Greed often overcame sensible thinking.

Still they said nothing. Jane looked down at Grint.

Grint put things more bluntly. 'Listen to her. You two are in deep shit. I'm Time Police. Kill me and they'll hunt you down. You know they will. And there won't be a trial. Only an execution. She's offering you a way out.'

Jane drew a deep breath. 'Perhaps,' she said, 'if you could tell me what you've done, I could help.'

Whiney-voice said nothing. Raffy was truculent. 'Why should we . . . ?'

Jane kept her voice calm. 'Do you know who I am?'

'No.'

'Good – that means I can let you live.'

He scoffed. 'You're tied to a chair and *you'll* let *me* live.'

'If you cooperate, yes, I think I can save us all. For instance, are you aware that while we've been talking, another three red lights have appeared on the equipment behind you? Gentlemen,

I appreciate your reluctance to cooperate, but can I remind you that being dead never solves anyone's problems? I suggest we pool our resources and prioritise our survival.'

Which, since they didn't have a pod, did rather beg the question of how they were to survive, but she'd get to that later. Her first priority was to secure their freedom.

Silence filled the shed while everyone thought about this, broken only by the sound of blood bubbling from Grint's nose as he struggled to breathe. Jane stretched her legs in front of her, striving for that casual captive look. How long did they have? Days? Hours? Minutes? She had no idea.

At about the time Grint and Jane had encountered their unexpected surplus candyfloss anomaly, and – as it turned out – in an entirely different universe, Captain Farenden was working on his spreadsheet for the finance meeting happening the day after tomorrow. Not something that ever put him in a good mood even when there *was* money in the budget. He sighed. That was a lot of red for just one spreadsheet. To be fair to Commander Hay, she wasn't one to shoot the messenger, but she still wasn't going to be happy.

Fortunately – or so he thought at the time – his telephone rang. An outside line – voice only. Sighing, he lifted the receiver. Other than stating his name and rank, he said nothing for a long while. Actually, he wasn't granted the opportunity. The person on the other end had no intention of being interrupted and after a few feeble attempts, he didn't even try.

Eventually the flow of words ground down into silence. Deliberately keeping his voice calm, he said, 'Thank you for this information, Mrs Caldicott. If indeed an officer has removed a child from his place of residence, then he must have had a very good reason. I can also assure you that if this is the case, then the child in question would be in excellent hands. Please allow me thirty minutes to check the progress of this particular investigation, after which I shall contact you with an up-to-date report. In the meantime, please do not be alarmed – Simon will be returned to you as soon as operationally possible.'

He put the phone down, sat for a moment, glanced at Commander Hay's closed door and then opened his com.

'Major Ellis, please. Matthew? We need to speak. No – never mind that – we're in deep shit. I'm on my way. And not a word to anyone.'

'Why are we being briefed in here?' demanded Luke. Compared with Team 236's rabbit hutch, Major Ellis's office was generously proportioned, but there weren't that many people currently assembled within it; only Officers Parrish and Farrell, together with Officer Varma representing security.

'Where is Ellis?' said Luke irritably. 'If you call a briefing then good manners demand you at least turn up for it. And where's Jane?'

'Day off,' said Matthew briefly.

'It was my day off as well,' said Luke, seriously aggrieved. 'I had plans.'

'Blonde or brunette?'

'What's the date?'

'Um . . . twenty-third.'

'Odd. Brunette.'

Matthew sighed. 'One day your sins will find you out.'

Luke grinned. 'But not today.'

The door opened to reveal Major Ellis deep in conversation with Lt North. Their faces were grave. Ellis nodded, glanced at his scratchpad, and said, 'Yes, I've got the info. Thank you, Lieutenant.'

He glanced over his shoulder at the waiting officers and then said very quietly, 'No, Celia, you're not included on this one. If this goes pear-shaped then we'll need you on the outside to organise our defence.'

North nodded, paused for a moment and then departed.

'Right,' said Ellis, closing the door behind him. 'Sit down and shut up. This is serious. I don't want any wisecracks or arguments. We have a situation. I can't see any way out of it, but we have to try. Don't bother with notes – the less evidence against us the better.'

He paused and then, when he had their complete attention, said very quietly, 'According to information received – unimpeachable information – Lt Grint has kidnapped a small boy and disappeared with him.'

Someone drew a sharp breath but otherwise there was silence. Even Luke Parrish had nothing to say.

'Exactly,' said Ellis. 'I have a possible location and our job this afternoon will be to locate and return them to TPHQ. As quickly and as quietly as possible. The crime has already been committed. There is no way of covering it up – nor should there be. Our purpose is damage control.'

'What happens then?' said Luke.

Ellis hesitated. 'Out of our hands, I'm afraid, but we'll cross that bridge when we come to it. Civilian dress, everyone. Concealed weapons only. Maximum discretion means we won't be

342

taking a pod. Report to the helicopter pad in ten minutes. Move.'

There are various interpretations of the phrase 'civilian dress'.

Luke Parrish, who looked good in everything and knew it, was wearing a casual jacket and trousers. Officer Varma, with her previous experience of Team 236 and their eccentricities, had stuck to a basic black T-shirt and combats, on the grounds that someone was bound to need a good thumping sooner or later. Only Matthew had truly embraced the furtive nature of the mission and donned his traditional undercover gear. He appeared before them now in a death-metal T-shirt that had seen better decades, ripped jeans that were more rip than jean, a backpack adorned with anarchist stickers promoting the end of everything, and orange and purple light-up trainers. An astonishing amount of hair product ensured his never regulation style hair stood out around his head in a manner reminiscent of an exuberant cactus. Far from blending into the background, he could probably be seen from all five space stations. Without the benefit of telescopes.

Luke stepped away from him. 'I am not going out with you looking like that.'

'Don't be like that,' said Matthew. 'I quite like *your* outfit. Very age-appropriate.'

Luke looked down at himself. 'What?'

'Well, you know – everyone has to grow up. Once they've reached a certain age.'

'Not something you're ever likely to have to worry about.'

'Don't be unkind. As a member of the older generation, you should be showcasing tolerance and acceptance and . . .'

Major Ellis appeared, neat in smart casual. 'Everyone in the helicopter.' He became aware of Matthew. 'Oh, dear God.'

'What?'

'Nothing. It's too late for you to change now. Just get in the chopper before you blind someone.'

Not thirty minutes later, the smaller of the Time Police helicopters, Delta Zero One, set Major Ellis and his hastily assembled team down on the cliffs above the main body of the town, then obeyed instructions and returned to base until called for.

Ellis gazed around. This was a pretty place. Blue sea and sky. Gentle breeze. Charming town. Even the sea fog rolling gently towards land was picturesque. He would like to have visited here with North. They could have explored the antique shops, colourful cafés and busy harbour. He sighed. 'Farrell, sitrep.'

Matthew activated his tag reader, his eyebrows arching in surprise. 'I have two faint traces.'

They looked at each other. 'Two?' said Ellis. 'Who on earth would Grint bring with him on something like this?'

Luke and Matthew exchanged glances. Who was the only person not here? Surely not. Not Jane. Why would she . . . ?

'Can you give me a specific location?' demanded Ellis.

Matthew frowned. 'I should be able to but . . . there's . . . I can't get clear readings, sir. Perhaps if we can get closer, I could be more precise.'

'Then let's try lower down.'

They set off through the town, following, had they but known it, Grint and Jane's route almost exactly. Minus the shop-window peering.

Ellis consulted Matthew's tag reader. 'Can you identify their last known position?'

'There's something about two hundred yards south-west, sir. Down in the town. Near the little pier.'

'Good. A starting point. We'll check it out. In pairs. We're not an invasion force, remember. Quietly and quickly, people.'

They made their way separately down to the seafront. Major Ellis went first with Matthew at his shoulder, followed by Luke and Varma. It would seem Luke was unable to resist the challenge of the notoriously difficult Officer Varma, chatting charmingly as they went. Varma, on the other hand, had all the appearance of one barely resisting the temptation to hurl him off the picturesque cliffs.

They twisted their way among the narrow streets, dodging tourists and street vendors alike, eventually reaching the promenade where they paused for Matthew to reorient his reader. The day was still warm even though the sun had disappeared behind the sea fog being blown inland.

Ellis stared. A memory stirred. He looked back the way they had come. A gentle mist now obscured the top of the cliffs.

'Sir?'

He shook himself. 'Yes, Farrell?'

Matthew was frowning. 'They *were* here, sir. Two distinct readings.' He moved to his right. 'No – a definite reading. I've got them. They're up there. At the top of those steps. One of those cottages, probably.'

'Four Marine Terrace?'

Matthew nodded. 'Could be. I can give you a more definite location when we get closer. Although they were here . . . for a while . . . and . . .' He began to rummage in his backpack.

His colleagues looked about them.

'Ooh,' said Luke. 'Candyfloss.' He set off towards the stall.

'Stay where you are,' said Ellis sternly.

'Aaaw . . . Dad . . .' said Luke, causing Major Ellis to briefly contemplate drowning him. There was an entire ocean over there. Shouldn't take him too long.

'I haven't had candyfloss in years,' said Luke.

'So I should hope,' said Varma. 'How old are you?'

'Old enough,' said Luke, grinning at her.

Varma set her hands on her hips. 'You just can't help yourself, can you?'

'Can we concentrate, please,' said Ellis.

'I think shooting him would greatly aid my concentration, sir,' said Varma.

'Varma,' said Luke, smiling down at her. 'I don't think I've ever caught your first name.'

'I don't think I've ever thrown it.'

'I'm thinking it will be something sultry and sexy.'

'I'm thinking a handful of testicle and twist to the right.'

He grinned. 'How about Scheherazade?'

Varma shifted her weight. 'Naz.'

He blinked. 'Short for Nazreen? How pretty.'

'Short for Nazgûl.'

Even Major Ellis had to turn his head and pretend to cough.

'Actually,' said Matthew, pulling another piece of equipment from his backpack. Anxiously he consulted something that looked as if a coat hanger had mated with a long-armed stapler. To the detriment of both. There were, however, a dramatic number of red lights. 'We all need to stand very still, please.'

Astonishingly, everyone stood very still.

346

'What?' said Ellis.

'I'm reading an . . . anomaly.'

'Of course you are,' said Luke, rolling his eyes. 'Why wouldn't you?'

'What sort of anomaly? Grint didn't specify,' said Ellis.

'Not sure. If I stand here, I get one reading, but if I stand over here . . .' he moved over there, 'I get something completely different. This is odd. One candyfloss stall but two different . . . Look out, Major.'

A small boy had appeared on the steps, running hell for leather, his little legs pumping. His eyes were huge and terrified, his arms windmilling. It was obvious that at some point in the descent, his legs had got away from him and without outside intervention, he would probably end up in the sea.

Fortunately – not the word used by Major Ellis at the time – the little boy ran straight into him, staggered, made a grab for the safety railings, missed, overbalanced on his still not quite properly working legs, sat down with a bump and burst into tears.

Four Time Police officers stared at each other in disbelief while juggling a number of important questions.

Firstly – could they assume this was Simon Wedderburn? How likely was that? In their experience, things were never that easy.

Secondly – assuming this *was* Simon – where was Lt Grint? Was the little boy actually trying to escape from him? And for what reason?

Thirdly – were either Grint or Simon connected to the recently discovered temporal anomaly? And if so – were they victim or perpetrator?

However – first things first. Time Police procedures dictated they secure the suspect/victim/witness/sobbing child.

Ellis motioned to Varma who motioned to Luke who motioned to Matthew.

'Um . . .' said Matthew. He approached the sobbing heap. 'Are you all right?'

The little boy lifted his head. Tears streamed down his grubby cheeks. His nose was, at one and the same time, both dry and crusty and wet and bubbly. A very unattractive combination. His mouth was outlined in something pink and sticky. There was a matching patch in his hair. And his ear. And something awful was hanging from one cheek.

'I know you,' said Matthew, apparently recognising this unappealing heap of dust-covered stickiness. 'You're Simon.'

'Are you sure?' said Ellis, coming forwards but careful to remain outside touching range. This was a very sticky little boy. 'Are you actually Simon Wedderburn?'

Simon sobbed and gulped. Or possibly the other way around.

Mindful of the very short paragraph in the Time Police handbook relating to not intimidating nervous witnesses, Ellis crouched alongside. 'Do you know where . . . ?'

He got no further. Matthew uttered another cry of warning, and at the same moment a voice shouted, 'GET AWAY FROM MY SON.' A woman erupted from the shed behind the candy-floss stand and began to rain down a flurry of blows upon Ellis's head and shoulders.

He fell to one side – more a case of overbalance than as a result of his brutal beating at the hands of an outraged mother – as he would claim in his report. It is possible that his loyal team could have rushed to their leader's aid slightly more rapidly, but, as they later unsuccessfully explained, everything happened so quickly. Eventually, Varma efficiently pinned Major Ellis's assailant's hands behind her back and she and Luke pulled the woman off him.

Matthew helped Simon to stand up and then surreptitiously wiped himself down on Simon's hoodie. Luke offered a helping hand to Major Ellis and finally everyone was on their feet, no one was hitting anyone else, most people had stopped crying and more or less everyone was the right way up. Varma drew breath to arrest everyone in sight but at least two of the party had differing priorities.

Ruth Wedderburn struggled free and the next moment Simon found himself enveloped in loving arms. Two voices gabbled simultaneously.

'Simon – what are you doing here?'

'Mum? What's happening? Why are you here?'

'They told me they had you.'

'Mum, what's going on?'

'Never mind that – I'm so pleased to see you but you have to go now.'

'Where are . . . ?'

'You mustn't let them . . .'

'Time Police,' said Varma, who, having allowed them a generous seven seconds for a mother–child reunion, was keen to get down to business. 'You are both requested and required to return with us to TPHQ.'

There have been occasions when the very presence of the Time Police is sufficient to calm things down, restore order, and resolve the situation. This was not any of those occasions. Neither of the potential prisoners took a blind bit of notice, both of them too wrapped up in each other to heed the outside world.

'Where did you go? I thought you didn't want me.'

'Of course I want you, Simon, but these aren't nice people. How did you . . . ?'

'I had my operation. My legs are better. I can live with you now. We can . . .'

Major Ellis, listening with only half an ear, stared out to sea. The day was beginning to turn cold. Sea fog was now rolling across the harbour. Again, he experienced a sensation of unease. He was missing something.

On the plus side, however, it would seem they'd found the kid. Sadly, his mother had turned up as well and would be demanding explanations. Worse, there was no sign of Grint. Or Lockland. Could they both have fled the country? Given what he knew of them that seemed unlikely. Jane and Grint might be the most mismatched couple on the planet, but they were both proud possessors of a supremely overdeveloped sense of duty. On the other hand, given the seriousness of the charges against Lt Grint . . . He paused. There was no point in speculating. The situation had changed somewhat. Now that they had secured Simon, their first priority should be to investigate this anomaly.

'If you'll excuse me, sir.' Officer Varma pushed past him. 'Mrs Wedderburn, for your own safety, we need to remove you and Simon from this vicinity. Will you come with me, please?'

Ruth Wedderburn glowered suspiciously. 'Why?'

'We need to carry out our investigations and your assistance would be gratefully appreciated.'

She clutched at Simon, looking both defiant and afraid. 'No – you've got it wrong.'

'Mrs Wedderburn, you appeared from the shed over there very shortly after my colleague recorded a temporal anomaly. Please, if you would be kind enough . . .'

'How do I know you're Time Police?'

Varma pulled out her ID. 'All right? Although,' she gazed around at her colleagues, 'your confusion is understandable. Frankly, some days even I'm not too sure.' She looked around for somewhere more discreet. 'Let's go in here.'

She led Simon and his mother into one of those glass and wooden shelters from which one could admire the view. Or, in Varma's case, conduct an interrogation. The others remained a little distance away, carefully casual and, as Luke said, probably standing out like a dog's bollocks.

Ruth sat herself down with Simon, who had discovered he wasn't too old to sit on his mum's lap.

'Mrs Wedderburn, would you like to begin?'

For a moment, Ruth hesitated and then she said, 'Yes, of course. My name is Ruth Wedderburn. I've been building a . . .'

'Bubble,' said Matthew, who had remained outside the shelter and never taken his eyes off his mismatched equipment.

Ellis smacked the railing. 'I knew something was going on here. Where?'

'There,' said Matthew, rotating slowly. 'Here. Shit – all around us. That's what the fog is.'

'And we stood here like idiots and let ourselves be surrounded. Expanding or contracting?'

'Contracting. But quite slowly. No immediate danger here except . . .'

'Yes,' said Ellis, grimly. 'We can't get out, can we?'

Matthew nodded. 'We've left it too late, sir.'

'The chopper?'

'Gone, sir. On its way back to base as instructed.'

'Can you contact . . . ?'

'No. Sorry.'

'Focus?'

Matthew waved the coat hanger again. 'Over there, I think. North-easterly. Up near those cottages, perhaps.'

'Where you picked up the tag reading,' said Luke.

'Four Marine Terrace,' interrupted an exasperated Ruth Wedderburn. 'Along with a ton of illegal equipment, a couple of morons, and, according to Simon, a giant called Uncle Lieutenant and his friend Jane.' Simon whispered something and she continued, 'Who possibly are being held by the aforementioned morons who thought they could force me to work for them.'

Varma prepared to pounce. 'Which morons and what work?'

Ms Wedderburn stared at her. 'Which and what what?'

'What does your work entail?'

She sighed. 'Teleportation.'

Varma moved in. 'That's illegal.'

'No, it's not, but yes, the one I built is.'

'Is what?'

'Illegal.'

Varma regarded her closely. 'Just so everyone is absolutely clear: you are admitting you deliberately made an illegal teleportation device?'

Ruth made an impatient movement. 'No, you're getting it all wrong.'

Varma compressed her lips and strove for inner tranquillity.

Ruth continued, talking fast. 'I was forced to design and manufacture a perfectly legal teleport device . . .'

'Does it work?' asked Matthew, interested.

'No – but it wasn't supposed to. But, yes, I deliberately included an illegal temporal component.'

'Why?'

'To attract the attention of the Time Police, of course. Isn't that why you're here? To check out the temporal anomaly I've been signalling? Why aren't there more of you? Where's your pod? And why did those other two bring Simon?'

There was a bit of a silence, during which Simon scrambled off his mother's lap and wandered over to the railings to look at the sea again. 'Jane said I could paddle.'

'It's a bit nippy, mate,' said Matthew. 'You sure?'

'Yeah. Can I do it now?'

'In a minute,' said his mother absently. She turned to Ellis. 'I know you'd probably like to arrest me . . .'

'No *probably* about it,' said Varma.

Ruth Wedderburn was close to losing her temper. 'Look – I've been held in a cottage up there by . . .' She glanced at Simon. 'Someone . . . and so I incorporated something naughty to try to attract your attention. And here you are.'

'Actually . . .' said Ellis heavily.

She looked at him. 'What?'

He gestured at the fog. Now noticeably closer. 'Ever heard of a bubble universe?'

She went white and clutched at Simon. 'This is a . . . ?'

'Yes. I see you know what that means.'

She stared out at the sea for a long moment before saying, 'I can't go back, can I?'

Ellis shook his head. 'I'm sorry.'

'But Simon . . . ?'

'Is not of this universe. We can save him.'

She took a deep breath. 'All right. All right. That's the important thing. Yes.'

'Tell me about your apparatus.'

'It's harmless. It's a teleportation system carefully designed not to work.'

'With a temporal addition,' said Varma grimly.

'Also carefully designed just to attract your attention. Trust me, I know what I'm doing. It's harmless.'

'Well, someone . . .'

'Oh,' said Ruth Wedderburn, suddenly enlightened. 'Of course.'

Varma nodded. 'The two morons tampered. But why?'

'Because . . .' She looked at Simon. 'Someone might be angry that I'd escaped and the morons probably thought if they could get it to work, they wouldn't need me and J— someone wouldn't be so furious I'd got away.'

'How *did* you escape?'

'They were careless. J— They were told to stay with me at all times. Both of them. After a while they became bored. One went out to buy beer. I hit the other one with a table and ran. I hid behind the candyfloss store because . . .'

'Yes?'

'Because that's where the other half of my transporter is. Only, about an hour or so ago, everything went haywire. That must have been when the two morons tried to start it up.'

'Ah,' said Matthew, suddenly enlightened. 'Anomalous readings issue resolved. Does your transportation thing work?'

Ruth grinned. 'It's actually quite hard to deliberately design something that doesn't work, but I managed it. The whole thing was dead. Inert. Harmless. I don't know how those two morons managed it, but you have to get me up there to sort it out.'

Ellis looked up at the cottages. 'A stupid question to which I'm sure I know the answer, but I'm clutching at straws. If we switch off your device, will that affect the bubble in any way?'

Both Matthew and Ruth shook their heads. She said, 'I don't think so. I think the damage is done. The bubble's been created and must now live out its natural lifespan.'

'Fog's getting closer,' said Luke, appearing in the entrance to the shelter. 'If we're going to move, we should get a move on.'

Ruth caught at Ellis's arm. 'I'm perfectly willing to show you where the equipment is, but I don't want Simon involved in this. I won't leave him here alone.' She looked at Ellis. 'You seem to have a number of people at your disposal. Can one of them take him back to your pod? Out of the way?'

Now didn't seem quite the moment to tell Ruth Wedderburn there was no pod, so Ellis listened instead to the sound of frantically thinking Time Police officers seeking to avoid childcare duties.

'People to arrest,' said Varma, quickest off the mark.

'Hate children,' said Luke.

Everyone looked at Matthew – who sighed. 'Fine,' he said. 'With me, Mr Sticky.'

As before, they did their best to assume an informal formation. Ellis walked at the front with Luke. A few yards behind, Varma and her prisoner/witness/Simon's mother argued over her exact

355

status, Ruth Wedderburn maintaining she couldn't possibly be under arrest since not only had she done nothing wrong, but her actions had actually brought this illegal activity to their attention. Which illegal activity, she said, the Time Police would otherwise have known nothing about. And while they were discussing recent Time Police actions, what exactly was going on with Simon and why had they involved him in a possibly dangerous situation and questions were certainly going to be asked even if they had to be asked from her prison cell.

At this point she had to stop to get her breath back – they all did – but as Luke said, the steps were very steep and there was no point in arriving at their destination winded and wheezing.

Number Four Marine Terrace gleamed in the spring sunshine. Bright, welcoming, deceptive . . .

They halted at the top of the steps and found a convenient bench, placed there, presumably, to give those using the steps a chance to recover from any temporary cardiac or pulmonary difficulties. The steps weren't high but as had been mentioned, they were very steep.

Ellis turned to Luke. 'Parrish – you go on ahead. Just a casual stroll past the cottages. Check around the back if you can. I want to know what we're dealing with. Farrell, you and Simon will stay here. Don't come any closer.'

'Parrish?' said Ruth Wedderburn in surprise. 'Are you . . . ?' and then clamped her lips together.

Luke pushed past them and strolled slowly towards the row of cottages, hands in pockets, pausing occasionally to look around and admire the scenery.

Ellis continued. 'Farrell, report. Bubble status?'

'Still contracting but only very slowly.' As one, they all turned out to sea. The fog bank was very much closer. Gulls still screamed and wheeled but their cries were cries of alarm and it was noticeable that none of them would approach the fog.

'We have an hour, perhaps. Shutting down whatever's causing it might buy us a little more time.' He looked up at the cliffs. 'But no power on earth can prevent its inevitable end. We have to find Grint and Jane and get out. Somehow.'

Everyone looked at Ruth Wedderburn.

'Look,' she said, folding her arms defiantly. 'I'd like to make it very clear – I never set out to build a Time-travel device. I've spent years looking at teleportation and its commercial uses. I'm well recognised in my field. About six months ago, I was approached by a man and woman. Representing a large corporation, they said. They wouldn't give me the name because of commercial espionage, they said, although they'd tell me everything after I signed. Initially, I didn't want to. I prefer to work freelance and then to sell my work on. That way I retain control over my own projects. I don't like being told what to do.'

She paused, compressing her mouth.

'But . . . ?' said Varma.

'But they offered to pay for Simon's treatment. A private clinic, they said, and as soon as possible.'

'They kept their word,' said Varma, watching Simon running up and down the last flight of steps. 'Which makes me think . . .'

'Yes, you're right.' She motioned with her head. 'The people here are not the same as the people with the contract.'

Varma was astonished. 'These two people offered a contract?'

'They did. They had it with them and we sat down, there and then, and we went through it together. Line by line.'

At the mention of a contract, both Ellis and Varma stared at each other, puzzled.

'They forced you to sign, right?' said Varma.

Ruth Wedderburn scowled at her. 'No, of course not. For heaven's sake, how stupid do you think I am? I'd have been on to the police the very moment they were out of the door. No, they left a copy with me and advised me to have my own legal representative check it over. They gave me a month to find one and gave me their contact details should anyone have any queries and then they went away. Long story short – my legal rep came back to me saying it was a fair contract. Not brilliant but fair. She highlighted several areas I might want to try to haggle over and I did. The date for Simon's op was settled – a golden hello, they said. I signed and . . .'

'And they reneged on the deal.' Varma was still searching for signs of villainous intent.

'Nothing of the kind. As far as I know, the deal still stands. Simon's obviously had his op.'

Varma blinked and gestured towards the cottages. 'So who are *these* clowns?'

Ruth Wedderburn sighed and cut her eyes to Simon, who was some way off with Matthew, gazing at the sea.

'Joe Wedderburn. Ex-husband. Bit of a dead loss. Well, enormous dead loss, actually. And his brothers. Morons, all of them. I don't know how, but I think he must have somehow learned I was working on something profitable and thought he'd get there first. I don't know. You'll have to ask him. If you can find him.'

358

'Where is he now?'

She shrugged. 'He's too important to stick around – or so he thinks. He left his idiot brothers to supervise while he disappeared. Presumably to sell me and my work to someone.'

Varma leaned forwards. 'You're definitely *not* building a time machine.'

'Of course I'm bloody not. Why would I? I keep telling you – I'm looking at the commercial applications of teleportation. Or I was until this bunch of thugs turned up. We – Simon and I – were living in my flat in London at the time. I was out shopping. Joe stepped out of a doorway and said hello. I stopped dead, and the next thing I knew I was being bundled into a van. In broad daylight. I was frantic. Simon would come home from school and find me gone. Joe told me he already had Simon and if I didn't cooperate . . . Well, he didn't specify, but he can be nasty if he doesn't get his own way and I wasn't going to take the risk. Joe kept saying if I completed my project then he'd let me go. Which I didn't believe for a second. I don't know whether they would actually have harmed either me or Simon but I couldn't take the chance. I was frantic most of the time because Joe wouldn't tell me anything about Simon or where he was.'

Varma, who had done her research on Simon before setting out, was able to fill in the details.

'Because they didn't *know* where he was. They never had him. Simon took himself off to the police station saying he'd lost his mum, expecting them to find her, and when they couldn't, he went into care. Somehow Simon's operation went ahead – thanks to the orphanage, obviously.'

Ruth nodded. 'Then one day it dawned on me that if I could

somehow bring my work to the attention of the Time Police, they'd despatch a squad of professionals . . .'

Ellis and Varma refrained from catching each other's eye.

'. . . to investigate and clear everything up. And tell me where Simon was.'

'You deliberately made your teleporter unsafe?'

'No,' she said indignantly. 'I did not. But I suspect Raffy and Jugs thought they could operate it, and they've done something stupid, so yes, I suppose it is partly my fault.'

'Small cottage,' said Luke, suddenly back among them. 'Fourth one along. In good nick. Typical holiday let. Some signs of occupation. Empty at present.'

'That's where they've been keeping me,' said Ruth. 'Can we move this along, please.'

Luke hadn't finished. 'Large wooden workshop-cum-shed in the back garden. One door. No windows. Two tag signatures inside. A lot of power going in. None coming out. No one in the houses on either side. Probably holidaymakers out for the day. No access from the rear but that's unimportant because the front door's wide open.'

'Never mind all this,' said Ruth, impatiently. 'The important thing is that my apparatus is in the hands of a bunch of thugs who don't know what they're doing.'

'No,' said Ellis. 'The important thing is that two of my officers are probably inside and we have to get them out of there. And quickly. Before this universe collapses.'

Ruth looked around. 'Well, that's not a problem, is it? Where's your pod?'

There was one of those special sorts of silences.

'You *have* brought a pod. Haven't you?'

The special silence did not go away. Not even a little bit.

'How did you get here?'

'Helicopter,' said Luke briefly.

If possible, the silence became even more special.

She was bewildered. 'But . . . surely . . . I thought you'd come about the temporal anomaly. I've been switching things on and off and on and off trying to attract your attention and when you finally do turn up – you come in a bloody helicopter and now we're all trapped.'

There was more foot shuffling and eye avoiding.

'So why *are* you here if not for . . . ? And to return to the question you keep not answering – *why is Simon here?*'

'Oh,' said Simon, materialising at her side at the worst possible moment and pleased to be able to show off his knowledge. 'Mrs Caldicott said I couldn't go to the seaside without my mum and then Uncle Lieutenant said not to worry because he'd take me, so I escaped from that stupid Little Petals place and we came here. With that lady. Who's his girlfriend, I think. Although they don't seem very sure.' He reflected. 'There's no gooey kissing.'

'Wait,' said his mother. 'Wait, wait, wait . . . A Time Police officer took you without permission?' She eyed the Time Police. 'And if you're not here to investigate the anomalies then . . . you're here to . . . what? . . . cover things up? Oh my God – you're only here to get Simon back. You haven't got a bloody clue what's going on, do you? Oh God – come on, Simon. We have to get you out of here.'

'No one's going anywhere,' said Ellis, possibly feeling it was time to reimpose Time Police authority. None of this was panning out as he had expected. In fact, this bore all the hallmarks

361

of a typical Team 236 debacle. With added Grint. 'Farrell – you and young Simon are to stay outside until I give the word.'

'Aw,' said Simon mutinously.

'We'll be protecting our rear from possible attack,' said Matthew swiftly. 'The most dangerous job of all.'

'Cool,' said Simon, eyes sparkling. 'Can I have a blaster?'

'NO,' said his mother, Major Ellis, Officer Varma, Officer Farrell and Officer Parrish simultaneously.

Ellis continued. 'Varma, you and I in the lead. Parrish – you're responsible for Mrs Wedderburn's safety.'

It was hard to tell which of those two were least impressed with the other.

'Right – speed and secrecy, everyone. Hit them before they know what's hit them. Let's move.'

Back in the shed, things had not improved for Jane and Grint.

'Your boyfriend's trussed up like a turkey,' observed Bolshy Jane. 'I think it's going to be up to you, sweetie.'

Jane, who had come to that conclusion herself, nodded quietly.

The Time Police have a procedure for dealing with hopeless situations. If you can't change the situation, then look at reducing the odds.

Her legs were free. True, she and the chair were currently as one, but her legs were unbound. Hoping her face was professionally blank, she began to calculate her moves. Cautiously she flexed her feet and ankles. No pins and needles. Good. Right, then. On three.

'Have at them, sweetie,' cried Bolshy Jane.

Three.

Jane planted her feet flat on the floor and stood up. The

plastic chair was light enough but clumsy, and she was forced to bend at the waist, which hampered her vision. She swung around, meaning to jab at their captors with the legs, but misjudged the distance. At least one leg smashed into the bank of equipment on the trestle, knocking her off-balance. Something she'd planned to do to *them*.

She staggered sideways and another leg caught on something else. Everything was taking place behind her – she couldn't see what she was doing – but she felt the impact and heard the shout of pain.

Good. She did it again, swinging her backside from left to right. Someone was shouting at her. Actually, it was Grint.

'Jane, for God's sake, stop hitting me with your bloody chair.'

'Sorry,' she shouted, and swung herself around again, searching for a more legitimate target. She heard something clatter to the floor – flowerpots, perhaps. Something moved to her right.

'Impale the bastards,' shrieked Bolshy Jane.

With no clear idea of where she was, where she was going, or who she was aiming at, Jane ran backwards, impacted something and just kept going. There was an enormous crash and suddenly she wasn't moving at all. By the sound of things, she – or, more likely, the chair – had run backwards into the table full of sensitive and fragile equipment. There was an electrical sort of bang that was probably not good news for anyone.

One of the men grabbed hold of her, chair and all, and hurled her across the workroom, knocking over two of the three rubber-legged posts. Jane's feet became entangled in the rubber matting, causing her to stagger sideways.

The first thing she hit was Lieutenant Grint, attempting to struggle to his knees while still tied up. He fell sideways. Raffy's efforts to avoid a toppling Grint led to him colliding with Jane, who by now had lost all sense of direction, together with any clear idea of what was happening. Her chair caught him amidships, knocking the air out of him. He went down with a crash but not before making a grab for her. Still wearing this year's fashionable look in garden furniture and completely out of control, Jane was dragged in a ragged circle. Her chair collided with assailant number two – Whiney-voice, presumably – who had scrambled to his feet, only to be propelled back towards Grint, who swung his legs around, attempting to knock him off his feet.

Jane fell backwards, hitting her head on what she thought might be one of the table legs. Which might have been the reason why she wasn't immediately aware of what had happened. Blinking, she attempted to sit up and found that she could. Her cheap plastic chair had shattered on impact. She was tied to a chair that no longer existed.

'Come on, sweetie,' shouted a thoroughly excited Bolshy Jane.

Jane staggered to her feet. Even bound, Lt Grint was a formidable foe and had dealt with his adversary by simply rolling on top of him. Jane just had time to make out – somewhat blurrily – a pair of kicking legs and one arm before the second man threw his arms around her and attempted to drag her away.

Instinctively Jane drew up her legs and, bracing her feet against the wall, kicked backwards. The two of them staggered across the workroom, straight into the remaining equipment. The cheap trestle table proved unable to withstand this final assault. The left set of legs collapsed, and everything – equipment, monitors, cabling, keyboards, electronic bits and pieces, Jane and assailant number two – slid noisily to the floor.

Something went bang. Again. There were sparks. Jane was suddenly very thankful she was sprawled across the rubber mat. Which smelled pretty bad, by the way.

There was beeping. Beeping is never good.

'Stupid bitch,' shouted the man currently sprawled across her. 'Look what you did.'

Jane would have reflected on the injustice of his accusation but there wasn't time. The beeping increased in volume and frequency. Those lights still working were flashing red. Glass and broken pieces of electronic paraphernalia had been scattered everywhere. More sparks sparked and there was that smell of burning fish that never bodes well, electronically speaking. The droning noise was rising in tone and increasing in volume, working its way up to an eardrum-piercing whine.

Jane had a horrible feeling this bubble, originally manufactured to protect the universe, had suddenly been rendered so unstable as to present a direct threat. In which case, it could roll up and disappear at any moment.

She tried to shake her hair out of her eyes and look around. Everywhere was utter chaos. Four people sprawled across the floor, their limbs entangled and in various stages of dishevelment. Other than the lack of togas and the emperor Caligula, this could have been a small but enthusiastic Roman orgy.

'Sweetie, you wouldn't know an orgy if it jumped up and bit you,' said Bolshy Jane. 'Roman or otherwise.'

There was a small earthquake as Grint struggled to sit up. 'Jane?'

'In a minute,' she said. 'You.' She grabbed the nearest illegal by the front of his shirt. 'Where's the off switch? Switch it off before it blows us all up.'

He shook his head to clear it. Blood was running down from a cut on his hairline. Jane very much hoped she'd done that. She shook him. 'Where's the trip switch?'

'Nnggggg . . .'

She shook him again. 'I'll do it. Just show me where it is.'

'Nnggggg . . .'

'Yank out the cables,' shouted Grint.

Jane tried to get up, but her legs were pinned by the bleeding man, who in turn was half buried under his colleague, who was himself being used as a ground sheet by the biggest man in the Time Police, who couldn't get up because his hands and feet were bound.

'It's like Fred Karno's fire-trucking army in here,' said Bolshy Jane in exasperation. 'Somebody move or we're all going to die.'

It was at this improbable but dramatic moment that the door was ripped open to reveal Major Ellis and Officer Varma standing framed in the doorway. Jane was unsure whether this was a Good Thing or a Bad Thing. First, however . . .

'Quickly,' she shouted. 'It's all going to blow. Whatever it is. Find the trip switch. Cut the power.'

Clear and concise, she thought. Outline the problem, offer a solution, advise the time scale. My last act as a Time Police officer. I'm just getting the hang of it, and they're about to throw me into prison. Where I might possibly be better off.

'Oh sweetie,' said Bolshy Jane sorrowfully. 'You are so not going to do well in prison.'

Ellis looked down. The floor was full of people. He could see thick black cables but no beginnings or ends. He had no idea what was connected to what. Yanking at random didn't seem the best idea. On the other hand, they were trapped in a highly unstable bubble universe and there was no doubt they were all going to die. The only questions were when and of what?

He turned his head. 'Mrs Wedderburn, I think we could do with your expertise. And quite quickly, please.'

Ruth appeared in the doorway. 'Shit.'

Without hesitation and ignoring the shouts of pain and protest, she ran across the human carpet. 'I'm not sure what I can do. The regulator's smashed. The field generator's overloaded . . .'

'Cut the power,' shouted Jane.

'Not that simple.'

Jane let her head fall back. Of course it wasn't. People who built machinery capable of destroying the universe and everything in it never thought to build in an off switch.

Luke was staring at the shambles in disbelief. 'I can't believe I'm going to die like this.' He peered hopefully at Varma. 'It's not too late . . .'

'Shut up, Parrish.'

'Don't you want to die with a smile on your face?'

'I could shoot you and put a smile on everyone else's face.'

'You see,' said Bolshy Jane. 'You're the only one holding back, sweetie. Everyone else is just itching to kill him.'

Ellis was looking back out through the door. Behind them, the little cottage was slowly being enveloped in a whitish-grey mist. The droning sound was growing louder with every second. Ellis estimated less than five minutes left. And that was probably being wildly over-optimistic.

What did he regret losing most of all? Well, Celia, obviously, and their carefully conducted relationship no one knew anything about.

(In the interests of accuracy – it should be noted he was completely wrong about this. There are no secrets in the Time Police. Bets had been placed.)

Matthew arrived with Simon in tow, saying quietly, 'The front of the cottage has gone, sir. It's right behind us.'

Ruth Wedderburn put her arms around her son. There were tears in her eyes. 'I should have just given Joe what he wanted.'

'He'd probably have killed you if you had,' said Varma. 'You'd still be dead.'

'But at least Simon might not be here.'

There was no answer to that.

Ellis shook his head in despair. There was nothing anyone could do. Simon was crying with his mum. Luke was cursing everyone and everything. Varma was telling him to shut up because she couldn't think straight with him banging on all the time. The two men on the floor were just screaming in general. It would be reasonable to say there was a fair amount of noise going on.

Over all the babble – or possibly under all the babble – someone said quietly, 'Jane.'

Jane turned her head. She had no knife with which to free him; all they could do was look at each other. Jane thought suddenly, *This is it. This is how I die.*

'Jane . . . I . . . it's been fun.'

She smiled. 'It has, hasn't it.'

'Any regrets?'

Emboldened by the knowledge she was about to die, Jane looked him in the eye. 'Yes. One.'

He frowned. 'Really?'

She waited for the familiar inferno to sweep across her face. Nothing happened. Perhaps, when it has only seconds left to live, the body has other things to think about.

She opened her mouth to articulate her one regret. No one would hear her over the sounds of so many people yelling at each other and the whine of terminally overloaded equipment. She put her hand on his arm. 'I wish we had . . .'

Luke began to shout, 'The fog's coming. The fog's coming.'

Tendrils of mist crept out of the back door towards them.

An unexpected breeze blew cold in Ellis's face. The mist shifted and swirled in the draught.

'I don't believe it,' he said. 'There's something out there.'

Ellis and Varma lined up in the doorway, weapons raised. Luke gently pulled Ruth Wedderburn and Simon to stand behind him. Which would keep them safe for the length of time it would take the mist to snuff out his life. And then it would be their turn.

The sun had gone. There were no shadows. Darkness was falling. In every sense. The mist was almost upon them. Jane tried very hard to rid her mind of the word *tentacles*. It was very easy to imagine something monstrous emerging from the fog. Perhaps this was how universes ended – not quietly fading away to nothing, nor being swallowed by the void, but consumed by monstrous universe-eating entities. Her limbs would be torn asunder. Her still-beating heart would be tossed aside as something hideously grotesque gnawed on . . .

'Well, hello there,' cried a voice. 'Can we be of any assistance?'

It took a moment. When you're braced for tentacle-waving monstrosities and the End of All Things, a cheerful voice redolent of Cheltenham Ladies' College and Mademoiselle Leonie's Finishing School for Wayward Daughters of the Aristocracy can come as rather a shock.

'May we come in?' enquired the voice at the door. 'Goodness, what a mess. Lots of broken glass, Pennyroyal. Do be careful where you put your feet. We don't want any nasty accidents, do we? Speaking of which, we are all aware we're standing in a bubble universe, aren't we?'

'We are,' said Varma, pulling herself together at the prospect of fresh arrestees.

'Oh, jolly good. Just checking. Now obviously I don't want to ruin your day, but we really need to be going quite quickly. Are we able to offer anyone a lift?'

Pennyroyal was already making his way among the fallen, pulling those who could stand to their feet and efficiently severing the bonds of the one who couldn't.

It is worth noting that he and Grint eyed each other professionally, apparently came to the same conclusion, and thereafter steadfastly ignored each other.

Ellis sighed, muttering, 'This should not be how Time Police ops go down.'

'You'll get used to it,' said Luke comfortingly.

Smallhope mustered them all in the doorway. 'Follow me, everyone who can.'

Ruth pushed Simon at Major Ellis. 'Look after him.'

'Mum?'

'It's OK, Simon. I'll be fine.'

Simon gazed up at her, his mouth slack with shock. 'Aren't you – aren't you coming?'

She smiled sadly. 'I can't. None of us who were here at the bubble's inception can leave. We're of this universe. If I go with you, then there will be two of me and that's very bad.'

Two huge tears spilled over. 'Mummy . . . ?'

'No, no. It's fine. I'll be fine. Your friends will find me in the real world.' She looked at Ellis. 'Won't you?'

He nodded. 'Yes, Mrs Wedderburn. I promise we will.'

'There, Simon. You'll see me soon. Now go.'

Grint picked up Simon, who struggled and kicked out at him. 'Put me down. I want my mummy.'

Ellis was the last one out. He turned back. Raffy and Jugs stared at him. Ruth Wedderburn nodded and then slammed the shed door shut in his face. There was shouting. Ellis turned away.

The pod had made a terrible mess of the garden. The fence had been crushed, along with a garden swing, a barbecue, the fellow of Jane's shattered plastic chair, and a sad clump of fritillaria meleagris.

'Doesn't matter,' said Smallhope, waving an airy hand. 'None of this will exist in' – she consulted her watch – 'one minute twenty-nine seconds. Come along, everyone. Chop-chop.'

Major Ellis led his team into the pod, including the struggling Simon. Grint held him tightly as the first faint tendrils of fog swirled in through the door.

Pennyroyal was last in, taking a final look around outside and then closing the door.

'All present and correct, my lady.'

'In which case . . .'

The world faded . . .

They landed in Battersea Park. At about half past three in the afternoon, as far as Jane could make out. No one screamed and ran away so Jane assumed Lady Amelia had a camo device similar to the one employed by the Time Police.

'Well,' said Lady Amelia, turning from the console. 'Wasn't that exciting? Sorry to have cut things so close. We've had the devil's own job tracking you down. If the other Mrs Wedderburn hadn't had the brains to cause a series of temporal anomalies, we might never have found you, I'm afraid.'

Every Time Police officer present silently noted that just about everyone had been aware of the temporal anomalies before they had.

'Where's my mum?' sobbed Simon. 'Where did she go?'

'Your mum's in Rushby – in the cottage, waiting for us to come and rescue her,' said Grint.

'But you left her behind.' He beat his fists against Grint's shoulder. Tears ran down his cheeks, cutting channels in the dust, dirt and candyfloss.

'Give him to me,' said Pennyroyal. He set Simon down on the floor. 'Now then, young soldier. That wasn't your real mum back there. That was a ghost mum. You and me, we're gonna go and rescue your real mum right now. You're coming too.'

'Just a minute,' said Ellis, his Time Police instincts rising to the surface. 'Mrs Wedderburn will be arrested for . . . something . . . and Simon must be returned to the . . .' He paused.

'Little Petals Exceptions for Residential Children,' supplied Luke helpfully.

Ellis ignored this. 'And Grint and Lockland have questions to answer. So, with many thanks to you and Smallhope for your timely intervention, we'll take Simon and complete our mission.'

Heads turned from Ellis to Smallhope. Who smiled. With just a hint of steel. 'Oh dear – and we were all getting on so famously. As I am sure you're all aware by now, Ms Wedderburn is an employee of Parrish Industries and, as such, is entitled to their legal protection. As the victim of a dastardly attempt to force her to work for . . .' she flicked Simon a glance, '. . . nameless miscreants, she and her delightful son have been subjected to a great ordeal. Obviously, Mr Parrish was anxious we locate their whereabouts so they can receive the very best care as soon as possible.'

Ellis, who had a very good idea that once Ruth Wedderburn and her son disappeared into the maw of Parrish Industries, it would prove almost impossible to dislodge them, battled on. 'I regret, Lady Amelia . . .'

'Oh, so do I,' she assured him.

'But the Time Police . . .'

'You can have the miscreants,' she said. 'A gesture of good-will on our part.'

Major Ellis was prepared to go down fighting. 'Nevertheless, the Time Police . . .'

'Will emerge from this incident with nothing but credit and the highest esteem.'

Ellis was very far from convinced of this. There was still the tiny matter of Grint and Lockland.

'Quit while you're ahead, major,' growled a low voice behind him and Pennyroyal opened the door. 'Toot sweet, now.'

373

Ellis made one final attempt. 'Can you prove that Mrs Wedderburn is actually . . . ?'

'Pennyroyal, the contract, please.'

Pennyroyal produced a document. No one saw whence it came. Another dimension, possibly. Ellis wouldn't be at all surprised. He flicked through the document and there was Ruth Wedderburn's signature. Dated six months ago. Ellis sighed. Smallhope was still smiling. Pennyroyal was still politely at the door. All that could change in an instant, of course. And how much fuss should he make over this? There was still the matter of Grint and Lockland to resolve with the Residential Community for Exceptional Petals. Or whatever. He was conscious this really hadn't been the best day for the Time Police. And it wasn't over yet.

With a sigh, he handed back the contract and marshalled his troops out of the pod.

Once they'd checked in at TPHQ, Varma disappeared back to security. Matthew wandered off to find Mikey. In a spirit of pure mischief, Luke followed Ellis, Grint and Jane to Ellis's office. Where Captain Farenden was waiting for them and looking unfamiliarly harassed. No Hay, thank God. This was all still under the radar, presumably.

Captain Farenden wasted no time. 'Where the hell have you been? And what have you done with Simon Wedderburn? I've had the bloody Little Childcare in the Community for Petals people on at me all afternoon. Hay doesn't know anything about this yet, but I can't sit on things for much longer without incurring her wrath, which will increase exponentially for every minute I keep it from her. I'm really hoping you managed to resolve this.'

'Well,' said Ellis, who had been thinking. 'Simon's on his way to join his mother, who is living in Rushby. The official line will be that Lt Grint, with Officer Lockland to act as the appropriate chaperone, escorted him there for a family re-union. His mother, apparently, has a position of some importance in Parrish Industries R&D department.'

Luke nodded vigorously even though no one had asked him.

Ellis continued. '*We* only became involved because she had been snatched by people who wanted her to work for them instead. When we arrived, Grint and Lockland were already dealing with the miscre— illegals. The equipment has been destroyed along with any evidence. Ruth Wedderburn is about to be returned to Parrish Industries . . .' he crossed his fingers, 'and will – no doubt with the assistance of Parrish Industries' frighteningly efficient legal department – issue a statement confirming all this when she has recovered from her ordeal.'

'That's all very well, Matthew, but what about the . . . Thing for Exceptional . . . Things people? They're out for blood.' Captain Farenden turned to face Lt Grint. 'Worst of all, they tell me you already made one attempt to take Simon out of the home a couple of months ago. You idiot – what the fire-trucking fire truck did you think you were doing?'

Jane wished the ground would open up and swallow her. And Grint. And the bloody Little Petals Thing for Something.

'It was all my fault,' said Grint doggedly. 'Officer Lock-land's only reason for accompanying me was to persuade me to return Simon. I wouldn't listen. She did her best. All blame should rest with me.'

'It does bloody well rest with you,' shouted Captain Faren-den, reaching for his com.

'Sweetie, you need to think of something,' said Bolshy Jane. 'And pretty damn quick or his life is over. And yours, too.'

'I don't know what . . .'

'For fire-truck's sake – do something. Anything.'

'Um,' said Jane, reverting to type with her usual sunset flush. 'Sirs, I wonder if I could . . . ?'

'You?' said Farenden, apparently just realising she was there. 'What can you do?'

'Well, I'm not really sure I can do anything,' said Jane. 'But . . . um . . . I think I know a man who can.'

'And finally . . .' said Bolshy Jane.

Jane turned to Officer Parrish. 'Luke – I want you—' She got no further.

'Jane – I knew you'd eventually come to your senses. Find somewhere comfortable, take off your clothes and I'll be with you as soon as I've finished making out my report.'

Other than not being green, it might have been difficult to distinguish Grint from the Incredible Hulk.

Jane closed her eyes and persevered. '. . . to do me a favour.'

Luke was disappointed. 'Oh. Well, that doesn't sound like half as much fun.'

'That could depend on how you do it.'

He grinned. 'Intriguing.'

Reluctantly, Grint began to assume a more human appearance.

Jane talked for a few minutes, and when she'd finished speaking, it would be fair to say that this was one of the few occasions in his life when Officer Parrish was absolutely gobsmacked.

'You're kidding.'

'No.'

'But . . .'

'Just do it, Luke.'

'Jane, your faith in my powers of persuasion is . . .'

'Fully justified, Parrish. If anyone can do it, you can.'

'That's very true, but . . .'

'Please, Luke.'

Conscious of all eyes on him, Luke stared blankly at the wall for a minute or two, engaged in unfamiliarly deep thought. Then he blinked, grinned, blinked again, grinned again, sat down at Major Ellis's desk and opened up his screen.

'Please could everyone oblige me by not saying a word for the next few moments.' He paused. 'No matter what you hear.'

'Parrish,' said Ellis, 'if you think this is an excuse for some silly . . .'

'Hush, please,' said Luke. 'I'm about to push my luck to the limit and enjoyable though that is, I need to concentrate.' He looked at Grint. 'If this goes wrong, I'm likely to be in even deeper shit than you.'

'Unlikely,' said Grint.

Jane was beaming at him. 'Thank you, Luke.'

'I haven't done it yet.'

'But you're trying. Thank you.'

Luke took a deep, steadying breath, and called up his father.

'Luke, my boy – how are you?'

Luke wasted no time with pleasantries. 'Dad, I want you to fund the complete refurbishment of a local children's home.'

There was a short silence, presumably while Parrish père replayed that sentence again. And then, possibly, again after that. 'What?'

'Fully equipped, up-to-date, all-singing, all-dancing, top-of-the-range facilities for staff and inmates, climbing frames, cattle prods – you know the sort of thing.'

Raymond Parrish blinked. 'Now?'

'Well, no need to start carving out the foundations right this very moment, but putting up the cash – yes.'

'Do we know how much . . . ?'

'Well, I don't have a clear idea, obviously, but you did that thing for the Westgate Foundation, so say around the same amount, give or take a bit. Six point five million pounds. Sterling.'

There was another short silence before Raymond Parrish cautiously enquired, 'Are these facilities to be made of solid gold?'

'Up to you, Dad. You're the one putting up the money. Can I say yes?'

'To whom?'

Luke took a deep breath and went for it. 'The Little Petals Residential Childcare Community for Exceptional Children.'

'The what?'

'To be honest, Dad, I'm not sure I can say that again.'

'Why?'

'Because they're the ones that need the endowment.'

'I meant, why am I doing this at all? If you cast your mind back two years or so, you will remember I trafficked you to the Time Police precisely to put a stop to your expensive and profligate ways.'

'I do remember, Dad. How's that working out for you?'

'Unexpectedly.'

'But will you do it?'

'To what end?'

'So many reasons. I'm sure you know by now that Mrs Wedderburn and her son are being returned to you and your investment is safe. Courtesy of Lt Grint and the Time Police, Dad.' He paused. 'And after Lacey Gardens, we owe Jane.'

The silence went on.

And on.

And on.

And on.

Everyone stood stock-still. Jane hardly dared breathe.

Luke said quietly, 'Are you still there, Dad?'

'I am not entirely sure. Ms Steel, could you confirm that I am in fact sitting at my desk, appropriately clothed, sober, and in full possession of my faculties, please?'

There was a short pause and then the screen split to reveal Ms Steel. 'To the best of my knowledge, Mr Parrish – yes.'

'Ms Steel seems to feel that all is well with me, although I confess, I do still harbour doubts.'

'Dad – I need to know now.'

'This very moment?'

'Yes. Salient points for the publicity people: Simon Wedderburn. Promised a holiday at the seaside. Mother disappeared. Heartbroken. Grint – you remember him? Built like a high-sided artic? Offered to take him. Home wouldn't release him. Grint took matters into his own hands. With Jane. All sorts of shit hitting all sorts of fans. Need to bribe the home. No need to mention that last bit. Hence requirement for masses of cash, Dad. Masses of immediate cash.'

'This does not sound even remotely legal.'

'Doesn't normally stop you: Yes or no, Dad?'

Raymond Parrish appeared lost for words. Luke chewed his bottom lip. The longer this went on, the less chance there was of his father cooperating. And no help from either Ellis or Farenden, both of whom appeared too stunned to speak. He had a horrible feeling this wasn't going to work.

Ms Steel leaned forwards. 'Mr Parrish has signified his agreement, Luke. Flash me the details and I will start the ball rolling. The new building is to be redesignated the Raymond Parrish Facility and there will be an opening ceremony which Mr Parrish will attend. Together with as many carefully selected minor royals and major dignitaries as Parrish Industries and the Time Police can muster between them. If Lt Grint is mentioned at all, it will only be in a very favourable light.'

'Um . . .' said Grint, and was ignored.

'I shall notify the . . .' she continued without even the slightest hesitation, 'supervisor of the Little Petals Residential Childcare Community for Exceptional Children of their unexpected good fortune on completion of this call. Mr Parrish sends his very best wishes for the success of this project.'

Raymond Parrish assumed his *et tu, Brute* expression. 'Do I?'

'I'm sure you were about to, sir.'

'You don't know that.'

'It is the duty of every competent PA to anticipate and implement the needs of their employer.'

'You sound just like Captain Farenden,' said Luke.

'All PAs are connected by a psychic link. Hurt one and you hurt all. To your detriment.'

'I think that's the most frightening thing I've ever heard.'

Captain Farenden, who had been staring, stunned, at the screen, cleared his throat. 'This is Charles Farenden. I am adjutant to Commander Hay.' He smiled. 'Ms Steel is not wrong. There is a Code.'

'Never heard of it,' said Luke.

'It is unspoken.'

'Or seen it.'

'It is unwritten.'

Ms Steel smiled at Captain Farenden. 'Every newly qualified PA signs up to the charter upon admittance to the Secret Guild.'

'In their own blood, I assume,' said Raymond Parrish drily.

'Not if we can use someone else's, sir.'

Major Ellis, who had been watching carefully, leaned forwards. 'Ms Steel, this is Major Ellis speaking. The Time Police will be delighted to assist in any way necessary, and I feel this enterprise would greatly benefit from you and Captain Farenden getting together – as soon as possible, in fact – to ensure everything is steered to a successful conclusion that will benefit all parties. Captain Farenden is an officer of considerable resource. Allow me to make him available to you.' He paused and then added blandly, 'For whatever purpose you may think fit.'

'Thank you, Major. Your offer is greatly appreciated. Please inform Captain Farenden that I can be with him in an hour and we can work on the wording of the statements. We will need to put together something that reveals Lt Grint's recent actions to be motivated solely by a selfless desire to do good and benefit his fellow man.'

'What?' said Grint, who had never, in all his life, felt the slightest desire to benefit his fellow man and was buggered if he was going to start now.

Ms Steel ignored him. 'We will need a soundbite, I think.'

She closed her eyes. 'How about – *The Time Police Officer with a Heart*.'

'Perfect,' said Luke, before any of his fellow officers could pull themselves together and object. 'I'd definitely run with that if I were you.'

'In one hour then, Captain Farenden.'

'Well, there we go,' said Luke. 'Wasn't that easy? Keep me posted, Dad.' He shut down the screen.

There was a short silence. 'What just happened?' said Captain Farenden, slightly bewildered.

'I think you've been trafficked,' said Major Ellis.

Some forty-five minutes later, a stealthy figure crept soundlessly along the corridor – soundlessly, that is, apart from the occasional 'chink'. Just to make things clear, there was no reason on earth why the figure could not have proceeded in a perfectly normal fashion. The figure had every right to be there and its purpose – if a little unusual – was certainly not illegal. However, this was Luke Parrish, whose main talent, according to most Time Police officers, was making life difficult for himself.

He paused outside Captain Farenden's office, glanced swiftly up and down the corridor and listened carefully at the door. After a few seconds, he tapped gently.

There was no response.

He opened the door and slipped inside, where he remained for some seven or eight seconds. Emerging empty-handed, he cast another careful glance up and down the corridor. A door opened and Captain Farenden's voice was heard informing someone his meeting would commence in fifteen minutes and could he have that information by then, please.

Luke whisked himself off down the corridor.

By the time Captain Farenden returned to his office, it was empty again and almost exactly as he had left it.

With the exception of two glasses and a bottle of very excellent wine sitting sedately on his blotter.

Having caused as much trouble as possible for as many people as possible, Officer Parrish was sitting contentedly in Team 236's office. An illegal coffee, liberally laced with illegal vodka, sat at his elbow as he considered what to put in his report. And more importantly – what *not* to put in his report.

One very unproductive quarter of an hour later, he sighed and stood up, intending to go in search of more vodka, Matthew and inspiration. In that order.

The door opened and Luke found himself eyeball to nose with the mountain commonly known as Lt Grint.

Neither man moved.

Neither man spoke.

Almost certain he was about to find himself drop-kicked through the nearest window, Luke braced himself.

Finally, the mountain spoke. 'Thank you.'

'You're welcome,' said Luke, too surprised to say anything else.

Grint nodded and walked away.

Cue flash-forward music and wavy images, signifying a return to the present.

Having opened her eyes and not found Lt Grint standing in front of her, Commander Hay was questioning her adjutant as to his – Lt Grint's – precise whereabouts.

383

Captain Farenden had prepared for this. 'Alas, ma'am. Lt Grint's mission was bumped up the list and he was forced to depart for Paris, 1811, directly after his briefing.'

'Forced?'

'Yes, ma'am.'

'By whom?'

'Operational requirements, ma'am.'

'Really?'

'Yes, ma'am.'

'That is unfortunate.'

'Deeply, ma'am.'

'For you, I mean. Baulked of my prey, I must now rely on you to satisfy my curiosity.'

'Obviously, I shall do my best, ma'am.'

'A statement that fills me with the gravest misgivings. Not least because I could be here until midnight while you meander your way through yet another rambling attempt to distract me from something from which you consider I should be distracted.'

There was a pause while they both disentangled that sentence.

Captain Farenden looked her in the eye, saying, 'I shall be very happy to supply full details, ma'am, should you directly order me to do so.'

Commander Hay held his gaze. 'Perhaps, in that case, you should confine yourself only to the facts you consider relevant.'

'Well, ma'am. Christmas party. Shabby orphanage. Officer Parrish mentioned to his father. Raymond Parrish stepped up with appropriate funds. Lots of excellent publicity for him and

384

the Time Police. As, I believe, you requested back in November, ma'am.'

'And yet, still no mention of Lt Grint.'

'I believe, given our involvement with the scheme, Parrish Industries were searching for a suitable officer to be the public face of the Time Police for this enterprise.'

'And they selected Grint?'

'So it would appear, ma'am.'

'Who were the other candidates? Herod? Hitler? Vlad the Impaler?'

'Regrettably, ma'am, I am not privy to that information.'

Having lulled her prey, Commander Hay pounced. 'Really? Even after all those late-night sessions with Ms Steel?'

Captain Farenden blushed.

Unkind people might have said Commander Hay savoured the moment.

'Can I take it that Lt Grint has never figured in any of your frequent . . . discussions?'

'I can honestly say that no one has been further from our thoughts, ma'am.'

'Understandable, I suppose.' She looked up. 'And Lt Grint is to be the public face of the Time Police?'

'Yes, ma'am.'

'Our – for want of a better phrase – poster boy?'

'Yes, ma'am.'

'The best option?'

'So I firmly believe, ma'am.'

'Well, yes, it is marginally better, I suppose, than Lt Grint being arrested for kidnapping. Followed by a sordid trial. Followed by prison time for him. And probably Lockland, too. To say nothing of the end of your career for attempting a cover-up. And Major Ellis. Dishonourable discharges for both of you. And a massive scandal that would probably have finished me as well.'

Captain Farenden regarded his commanding officer with resignation. 'I should have guessed you already knew, ma'am, shouldn't I?'

'Yes, you should, but I do agree – yours was an infinitely better option. Good call, Captain.'

'Thank you, ma'am.'

'Goodnight, Charlie.'

THE END

JOY
TO THE
WORLD

This story is for Jay.

JOY TO THE WORLD

My name is Joy Rebecca Checkland and I am nearly fourteen years old. Which was what I tried to tell my dad when he grounded me and it so totally wasn't my fault but he wouldn't listen. He never listens to me. Mum says he never listens to anyone. Uncle Andrew says it's because he's a famous artist and lives in a different world to other people. Auntie Tanya says it's because he's an idiot. Auntie Franny says don't bother me now and what do I think of these shoes?

Nobody ever listens to me.

Except for my friend Tommy. The bright light in the dark hell of my life. Tommy always listens because she totally understands weird parents and how to deal with them although no one's got worse parents than me. My dad drives me spare and Mum's so weak. She never stands up to him and he's always shouting and we live in this stupid big house right in the middle of nowhere so there's never anyone to talk to and it's the last stop on the school bus route so I'm all alone at the end of the day and it's too far for my friends to come and visit. It's all so unfair.

And Rushford is such a dump. And it's miles away. And there's nothing to do when you get there anyway. Dad said that was good because it wouldn't matter that I was grounded until the end of time then, would it, and I said he couldn't do that because it wasn't my fault and Dad said anyone stupid enough to be caught holding the cigarette after everyone else had the sense to run away deserved to be grounded and Mum said no, that wasn't what your father meant at all and what he meant to say was that smoking was wrong and bad for your health and against school rules and I said it was a stupid school anyway and I wasn't going back there after Christmas and Dad said I'd do as I was told and Mum said we'd all talk about this when we were calmer and Dad said what was the point, Jenny, we've raised an idiot and Mum said he didn't mean that and he said yes, he did and I said it took one to know one which I thought was pretty clever actually but he just slammed into his studio and I slammed the door into my bedroom and he opened his door and shouted to stop slamming the door because I'd have the roof down if I wasn't careful and he hadn't paid for it yet. Then he slammed his own door again – much harder than me – and everything went very quiet after that.

I thought Mum might bring me up a biscuit and a glass of milk before bed because she usually does and she didn't so then I knew I was in trouble and it was so totally callus of her to abandon me. And anyway, as I had told her, it wasn't a real suspension because it was only two days to the Christmas holidays anyway and Mum had said a suspension was a suspension no matter how long – or short – and it was probably a subject I should avoid when Dad was around.

So everyone was being so totally unsympathetic and not thinking about how I felt at all. And it wasn't even as if I'd actually smoked the thing because cigarettes smell and taste horrible and you'd have to be mad to want to smell like a wet ashtray but when Celia Bradshaw – also known as Chief Bitch because she's pretty and she knows it – had asked if I wanted to come along with them to their hangout behind the bike shed I was pleased because they don't ask just anyone so I did.

Anyway they were all puffing away and then Miss Woodbridge turned up with her mardy face on and someone said, 'Hold this,' and then they all ran away and by the time I realised what was happening it was too late. So totally not my fault but no one listened and I'd miss the school Christmas Party and the presents and the carols and no one cared.

Dad had taken my phone off me so I couldn't call Childline and report him but he'd forgotten my iPad so I messaged Tommy to tell her all about it and she wasn't even interested, saying, 'Never mind all that – you'll never guess. Billy George is coming to Rushford.'

OMG!! I stared at the screen. I couldn't believe what I was seeing. Billy George was born here and the only decent thing ever to come out of Rushford. He's the lead singer for Noyze. He's got this huge grin and when he looks at you with his eyes and sings, 'I will *always* be yours' – it's just . . . WOW!! And he was coming to Rushford. No one ever comes to Rushford. Not once they've got out, anyway. This was just AMAZING!!

My iPad pinged again. There was more. 'There's a concert in Archdeacon's Park. Not a big thing. Just an hour or so. Half a dozen songs. But it's HERE. IN RUSHFORD. We've GOT to go.'

I was so excited. Billy George was coming back to Rushford! Then I remembered I was grounded. Isn't it absolutely typical? One thing – just one thing happens in my life. ONE THING! And I can't go because I'm sodding grounded.

I stared at the screen and then began to type.

'Sorry – can't go.'

The response came back almost before I'd hit send.

'WHAT? What do you mean you can't go? You have to go. WE have to go. It's literally the only thing that will ever happen in Rushford in our lifetime. And it's Billy George. He's GORGEOUS. We can get his autograph. I'm going to get him to write on my arm and I'll never wash again as long as I live. He might even ask us up on stage to sing with him. He does that. That's how that woman on TV got her break. WE HAVE TO GO.'

She followed this up with a string of emojis conveying every emotion under the sun and a few I think she'd invented on the spot.

I had two choices. One – I could ask permission to go and Dad would say no. I knew he would. He wouldn't care how important it was to me. Perhaps I could offer to serve double time after Christmas as penanse. But I couldn't see that working either while my parents were being so unreasonable. And once I'd asked and they'd said no – that would be it. I wouldn't get another chance.

Or I could sneak out. I mean – they're so old they've probably never even heard of Billy George anyway. I could tell them I was going for a walk or something and then come back and they'd never know and if they never knew then they couldn't get upset about it so really I was doing them a favour.

I clicked on the link Tommy had sent me. The concert was happening on a Saturday afternoon in Archdeacon's Park. From 3:00 – 4:00 p.m. No tickets required – a goodwill gesture for Christmas although collections would be taken for charity. Christmas spirit and so on. Which meant . . .

I sat back, thinking. There would be no cost involved which was good because I'd spent all my allowance on Christmas presents. Although with parents like mine I'd be so justified in getting my money back. That would serve them right, wouldn't it?

No, I wouldn't need much money. Just enough for the bus fare and something for a burger and a drink.

The buses to Rushford run every twenty minutes. Mum and Dad would probably be in Rushford on Saturday afternoon, enjoying themselves while I was all alone at home. Typical parental double standards. I'll never do that to my kids.

The park isn't far from the bus station. Town would be packed. It's the last Saturday before Christmas so people would be carrying on as if the shops will never open again. I know Mum has been stocking up for our Christmas lunch because I've had to carry most of it. Lots of people are coming. Lovely Mrs Crisp – or Mrs Bill the Insurance Man, as Dad calls her – and her husband, Uncle Bill.

Auntie Franny was coming – she wasn't living with Uncle Daniel any longer although I don't know why because it was making her very bad-tempered – even more than when she did live with him – and Dad had told her she might as well go back to him again because she was just as irrational and bad-tempered as ever and it was getting on his nerves and there had been more slammed doors. She stormed off to her car and he opened a window and shouted to her that it was time she and Daniel were reconciled and put each other out of other people's misery and Mum had said stop shouting out of the windows, Russell, we'll have Mrs Balasana round here again. Mrs Balasana is our neighbour. She has a really pretty little house and her donkey is called Jack and she NEVER SHOUTS OUT OF WINDOWS.

And Uncle Andrew was coming as well. To Christmas lunch, I mean. With Auntie Tanya, of course. They're really nice and I often think they might be my real parents who had to give me up when I was born for reasons they can't tell me about. They live in a lovely modern flat in town. The roof doesn't leak and they never shout at each other.

And Uncle Kevin who runs the landscaping place outside Rushford – he was coming with Auntie Sharon who has the cupcake shop and café down by the bridge. I always get free cupcakes on my way home and I'm not to tell Mum and Dad.

I wondered whether actually I'd be allowed to be at our Christmas lunch. My dad might make me stay upstairs locked in my room with just a cheese sandwich. Or just the bread. Without the cheese. Or even nothing at all. That would be so typical. They'd all be downstairs having a great time – even Jamie, my brother, and holder of the World's Most Disgusting Brother title – and I'd be up here in the cold and the dark all on my own.

Right, that settled it. I typed back:

'Of course I'm going. SEE YOU THERE.'

I left it at that because I thought I could hear Mum coming upstairs with the revolting Jamie. I switched off my iPad and shoved it under my pillow.

Things were no better the next day. Dad gave me a massive long list of jobs I had to do and I said I couldn't do any of them because I'd planned to spend my time reading and studying and he laughed all over the house.

The list just went on and on. First I had to clear away all the breakfast things. By myself. Then I had to tidy the mudroom and it was so totally gross in there. Then I had to take Marilyn, Boxer and Thomas out of their nice warm stable and into the cold damp field and none of them were very keen on that. The secret is to lead Marilyn to wherever you want them to go and Boxer will follow her. It's quite funny to see this enormous horse following on behind this tiny, tiny donkey.

You have to watch out for him though because he's frightened of everything, including the chickens and they know it. I don't know what he thinks they can possibly do to him – he's about nine feet high. So we formed the usual parade – Marilyn first, followed by an agitated Boxer, jumping about all over the place, followed by sensible Thomas. A sensible horse for my sensible mother. 'Nuff said, I think.

I shut the gate behind them, went back into the yard, let the chickens out and collected the eggs. People who buy their eggs from the supermarket don't know how lucky they are. I don't know why we can't live in a town like normal people. With shops and cafés and cinemas and no mud. There were four eggs. We have a lot of chickens and not that many eggs. Uncle Andrew says a lot of them are really old and long past laying but Dad can't bring himself to get rid of them because he's so soft-hearted, although I notice he doesn't have any difficulty unjustly grounding his only daughter which is so typical. I put the eggs on the kitchen table and took a moment to play with the kitten.

We used to have a cat. He was old and smelled like a wet

carpet but I loved him. He and Dad hated each other. He'd bring in smelly old corpses and leave them on – and sometimes in – Dad's trainers. He never did it to anyone else – just Dad.

And then, one day, he brought in a tiny kitten. We never found out where he'd got it from. I think it might have been abandoned because it was nearly dead – cold, wet and very muddy. Dad sat up all night with her until finally we knew she was going to live.

The cat died the very next day, quietly, in front of the cooker which was where he spent most of his time. He just fell asleep and never woke up.

Mum cried her eyes out – she'd once saved him from a watery grave and she loved him. Dad patted her for a bit and then disappeared. He came back about ten minutes later, blowing his nose. He'd been looking for something in the barn, he said, and the dust had got up his nose.

We buried the cat under a bush with pretty blue flowers. Dad said he'd probably come back and haunt us but if he has, then I haven't seen him which I wouldn't mind at all. My life is SO boring and I think it would be quite exciting to have a ghost.

I fed the kitten – who still doesn't have a name. Mum says our old cat must have trained her up because she craps in Dad's slippers and Dad goes mad and there's a lot of shouting. Mum tells him to buy another pair of slippers and keep them in his bedroom this time because then they won't get crapped in, will they, Russell?

My friend Tommy doesn't have this problem. Her parents are super rich. She says they don't speak to each other much and to her hardly at all. I tell her she's lucky. She goes to the posh boarding school on the other side of Rushford. And she has ballet lessons, plays the piano and violin and rides a pony named Candy who isn't frightened of butterflies like Boxer. And they have a villa on Crete. They go there a lot. I'm lucky if I'm able to get into Rushford once a month.

Like me, her parents don't let her out on her own very often and I think this is why we were both so keen to go to this concert. In fact, I think the sneaking out just added to the fun.

Tommy and I had met online last summer when I was telling everyone how awful Rushford was and she said you think you've got problems – you want to live in . . . actually I probably shouldn't say the name because I'll get sued or something but it's covered in seagull shit and you can't get up the high street for people lying on the pavement and there aren't any shops. Or only shops for old people, anyway, and nothing ever happens unless someone gets murdered or the river floods.

She has a banging Facebook page – my dad won't let me have one, of course – and we had a great time with our competition to see whose parents were the worst. The noisy overprotective nuisances or the remote really-couldn't-care-less icebergs. Her dad's in what he calls financial services – we discussed him being an accountant for the mob, maybe – and she said no, he was too short and too . . . nothing. And, she said, as if that wasn't bad enough, her mum works for the local council and could I imagine anything more dreary and how cool was it to have a dad who was an artist and I had to put her right on that one.

Her family's from Sri Lanka which must be so exciting. Her grandparents came over hundreds of years ago and her granny HATED it. Absolutely hated it. She refused to speak English at all and CURSED her husband for bringing her to this cold wet country and HE DIED. That is so awesome. Tommy says after that her granny got her own way on everything right up until the day she died and she was going to be just like her gran. She couldn't wait to get a husband so she could curse him.

Tommy says her parents have Great Expectations of her because Asian parents do. She's going to be a doctor or a lawyer according to them although she actually wants to be a singer. She's posted a couple of clips on YouTube and she's really good but they just won't listen. Parents should be banned by law.

Anyway, back to my dreary life. Dad wanted me to take something up to the Braithwaites' farm further up the road even though it was freezing cold out and I'd probably die of newmonia, but then I remembered I could use their Wi-Fi so I smuggled my iPad under my coat and asked to use their toilet when I got there. Reception wasn't very good – this is what happens if you live miles from anywhere. Even the stupid government doesn't think you're important enough to be able to log on properly – but there was a message waiting for me. Tommy had NEWS. Employing Granny's tactics – I must remember to ask her if she'd actually cursed him – she'd persuaded her dad to let her go.

'I'll come by train,' she had typed, 'and we should meet somewhere beforehand because we'll never find each other once we're in the park. Outside the post office or something and then go on together – it's going to be GREAT.'

I sighed and pointed out I was still unfairly grounded.

'You have to get to Rushford somehow. The concert's in the afternoon, so it's not as if you'll have to climb out of your bedroom window at midnight – although wouldn't that be FUN? All you have to do is get to Rushford and you do that every day, anyway.'

'No problemo,' I said because I was sure I'd think of something.

And I did. It was way easier than I thought it would be. And also more difficult because my parents were going into Rushford for a bit of last-minute shopping and for a nasty moment I thought they would leave Jamie with me but, in the end, Mum took him to Auntie Monica's up the lane. Auntie Monica thinks he's wonderful although I suppose after a couple of hundred sheep even Jamie would look good. So that was them out of the way. The difficulty would be avoiding them once I was in Rushford. The town's not that big. I'd have to be careful.

I had been instructed to tidy the yard, feed the chickens and behave myself.

I nodded and didn't argue although it made no difference because, as usual, no one paid me any attention at all. Dad was thinking about his painting and Mum was fussing about her list. They got into Dad's old Land Rover – that car is so totally embarrassing – and drove away.

I scattered a bit of grain around the yard, dodged the chickens who were trying to kill me as usual and climbed over the gate into Boxer's field. From there I crossed two more fields, jumped over the stream and into the village to pick up the bus to Rushford. Simples.

I was there on time. It was still early afternoon but getting dark already. I think it might have been the shortest day or something.

Rushford was full of Christmas lights and Christmas crowds. They'd floodlit the castle and the reflections in the river were really pretty. And it was very cold. Probably a good idea to make the concert so short. I spared a thought for Chief Bitch who would almost certainly be there in her new strappy top and covered in icicles. As Tommy had said, there's looking cool and then there's looking frostbitten.

I shot into the public toilets in the market square and tried to put on my make-up in the spotty mirror. I couldn't see very well and my hand was shaking with cold and excitement but I didn't think it looked too bad when I'd finished.

I turned back along the high street, careful to keep my head down just in case anyone recognised me. I didn't think they would but everyone knows Dad so I couldn't afford to take any chances.

We were meeting outside the post office. It would actually be the first time we'd met face to face. 'You can't miss me,' she'd said. 'I'll be wearing my red bomber jacket – you know, the one they don't know about yet – and black jeans.'

I waited. And waited. There was no one anywhere wearing a red jacket. I looked at my watch. She was five minutes late. Then nearly ten minutes. I began to worry.

My phone bleeped – typically, Dad had torn it from me and then left it on the bookcase and forgotten it. Classic Dad. I would have to remember to put it back before he missed it. There was a text from Tommy.

Train late. I'm behind post office. Changing in alley. Come and give me a hand.

There's a wide alleyway behind the post office, mostly full of wheelie bins. What with the rubbish and the cold, I wouldn't have fancied taking my clothes off there. Obviously her red

402

jacket was too much for her parents and she'd had to leave the house wearing her normal clothes.

It's well lit – there's a lamp post at both ends – but . . . well . . . it's an alleyway and it's full of rubbish. It wasn't very nice and I really wasn't keen. All the noise and the bustle and the lights were behind me. Ahead lay silence. Then I thought, she might not know Rushford very well. I'll take her to the public loos in the square instead. She can change there.

I called, 'Tommy?'

She didn't reply. Just the dark shapes of the wheelie bins and their shadows.

'Tommy!' I called again. I thought I saw something move. She might not have heard me. For some reason I wasn't shouting very loudly.

I took a couple of reluctant steps. 'Tommy?'

Where was she? I was getting anxious because time was getting on and we didn't want to be late. Imagine Billy George actually here in Rushford and not being able to see or hear him because we arrived too late for a good place. No one would be talking about anything else when we went back to school after Christmas and if I had to tell people I missed it . . . As I keep explaining to Dad – it's bad enough being physically separated without being culturally separated as well, but I don't think he understands.

Just as I had set off down the alley, past the overflowing wheelie bins, a van pulled up at the far end, blocking the street lights, which meant I couldn't see at all. I called again, 'Tommy – are you there? I can't find you. Let's go to the public loos over the road.'

No one replied. This alleyway really wasn't a very nice

place and suddenly I didn't want to be here. Not at all. Not even a little bit. But I couldn't go off and leave her here.

'Come on. We have to go. We'll sort you out on the way.'

Nothing.

'Tommy, come on.'

Nothing.

Except for footsteps behind me.

They were just ordinary footsteps. People used this alleyway all the time. But something wasn't right. I turned. A man was walking towards me and he was smiling at me . . .

I turned quickly and began to walk towards the other end. Away from the footsteps. To find other people. Dad always says if I have a problem the first thing I should do is get away and then get myself to where people are. Go into a shop or something. Ask for help. Then ring him.

I pulled my bag down off my shoulder and rummaged for my phone. In my haste I hadn't put it back in its special pocket. I'd just shoved it in my bag and now it had dropped to the bottom and I couldn't find it. Stupid bag.

Ahead of me, the van's sliding door opened and a man climbed out. The inside of the van was very dark.

Now there were two of them. And where was Tommy? I had a sudden horrible thought. Where *was* Tommy? Had she been pushed into the van? Was that where she was?

I went suddenly very cold. I started to shiver. Dad bangs on about this sort of thing all the time and I'd only ever listened with one ear because, of course, he was being ridiculous and it would never happen to me. And now it was. I was frightened. And I was all on my own. I was in this horrible dark place and I was trapped and it was scary and I couldn't see and everything smelled of wet rubbish and . . . something like ginger biscuits.

I stopped. Whichever way I ran would take me closer to them. So I put my back against the cold brick wall. 'Tommy – where are you? Are you all right?'

The nearest man looked at his mate and then grinned at me. 'Tommy's not coming.'

Now – now I suddenly saw what Dad had been on about all these years. Now that it was too late. He'd been right. I really, really wished he was here. Suddenly I wanted my shouty dad more than anything else in the world.

I didn't know which way to run and the wall was too high to climb. And then a voice, which may or may not have been inside my head, breathed, *'Hide.'*

There was only one way to go. There were bins all around me. I dropped to the ground – which was sticky and smelly and revolting – and crawled away. I scuttled around and between the bins, trying to be hidden.

Finally, I stopped, panting, to listen. I could hear them heaving the bins around trying to find me. They were getting closer all the time.

I was terrified. My heart was thumping so loudly. I was too frightened even to cry. I just didn't know what to do.

They started calling to each other. 'Where the duck is she?'

Mum says if someone says that word, I have to hear it as *duck*. Which is so typical of her – I don't think she knows bad words even exist. So he was shouting, 'Where the duck is she?'

'She can't have got away. We've got the ends blocked. Keep looking for her.'

'You said this would be easy.'

'It will be. She's not going anywhere. She can't.'

'She'd better not – I've already spent the money.'

What money? What was happening? If anything, it was even more freezing down here on the sticky concrete in among the tiny wheels and I was kneeling in something horrible and I couldn't see anything. I was ice-cold and shivering and I wanted to go home. All Dad's warnings. Everything he'd ever said. And Mum. And Uncle Andrew. Why hadn't I listened? Even at school they'd banged on about this sort of thing. A giant policewoman – Seargant Bates – had talked to us about it and I'd sat at the back and thought about something else. The one useful thing I might have taken from school and I hadn't bothered to listen.

They were still pulling the bins about. There weren't that many left. I had a minute. Possibly not even that.

Then I had a bit of luck. I found my phone.

I scooted back as far as I could go. I wanted my dad. I wanted to see him more than anyone but I had to be sensible. He wasn't here. They were.

I dialled 999.

To my surprise, they answered immediately. Before anyone could say anything, I whispered, 'Help. Two men are chasing me. Behind the post office. Help. Help.'

Someone would come. There must be loads of police around today. Someone would come.

The last of the bins were being pushed aside. I hung up and hit speed dial.

'Joy, where . . . ?'

'Dad. Help. Two men. Behind the post office.'

I stood up and tried to slip between the bins and the wall.

They shouted because they'd seen me. I dropped the phone in shock and tried to run. I was sobbing with fright. I tried to shout for help. One grabbed me so tightly I couldn't breathe. I tried to kick them but they simply picked up my legs and carted me off towards the van.

I hurt my throat trying to scream. I was twisting and bucking but I couldn't get away. One man fell against the wall and it hurt him. I heard him swear. He went to hit me but his friend stopped him saying, 'No damage. They'll take it out of the price.'

The van wasn't far away. The open door looked like a giant black cave.

And then, over the smell of rubbish and wet concrete and dirty old men I could smell warm ginger biscuits again. I wondered if I was going mad.

A voice over my head said, 'Wossat?'

'Woss what?'

'That. Over there. There's someone there.'

I felt one of them turn.

'Nuthin'. I don't think . . .' He sounded uncertain. 'Nah . . . it's nuthin'.'

But it was.

I could hear hoof beats. Right in the middle of Rushford I could hear hoof beats. Coming from a great distance. Then I thought, it's the mounted police. From the park. The police are here.

The hoof beats drew closer and louder and suddenly a huge glowing golden horse exploded into the alleyway, galloping full tilt towards us. I could see every detail. I could see its mane and tail flying. I could even see sparks where its enormous hooves struck the ground. It was huge and fierce and coming straight at us.

I screamed. Or tried to.

They dropped me. The ground was very hard. I hurt my elbow quite a lot. I lay, rubbing my elbow while they shouted over my head.

'Whatya do that for?'

'Quick. Grab her legs.'

I was already rolling away. To be fair, mostly because I was trying not to be trampled by this giant horse that was nearly on top of us. It wasn't wearing a bridle or head collar and I had no idea where it had come from.

Joy, get back under the bins.'

Obviously the owner was around here somewhere which was a huge relief. I crawled away between the bins.

There was a light over there. On the ground. It was my phone. I hadn't ended the call. I could hear Dad shouting. He must have been going spare. I grabbed it. 'Dad . . . help me.'

'Hold on, sweetheart. I'm coming.'

I crouched on my hands and knees and peered round a bin. The horse was between me and them. It was a vicious-looking thing, baring its teeth and half rearing. All I could see was horse. It was huge.

The men were funny though. It was as if they knew something was there but they couldn't see it. They kept looking from side to side and spinning around. As if they thought something was creeping up on them. One of them even had his back to it, which wasn't very clever. I thought, how could they not see it? It was enormous. And scary. And wonderful. But scary. I stared some more trying to work out what was happening.

This wasn't a real horse. It couldn't be. Was it a projection? Or a ghost? Or perhaps I'd banged my head and was seeing things. But it seemed very real and solid.

I stuck my head out, wondering if I would be able to run away.

'Joy – stay back. Help is here.'

And it was. Two figures appeared at the entrance. Oh no – this wasn't good at all. It was my mum. What was she doing here? And why wasn't Dad with her? He must have rung her to come and get me. There were two nasty men here. What could she do? And oh God, no, Auntie Franny was with her. They must have met for coffee. This was no good at all. I needed a rugby team at least. With tanks. Not my mother and a fashion model.

'You're quite wrong there, Joy. Very good in a crisis, your mother. Stay back, now.'

Mum shouted something and began to run, followed by Auntie Franny. I didn't know my mum could run. I definitely didn't know Auntie Franny could run.

The two men stood their ground. 'We 'ave to take her,' said one to the other, 'she's seen our faces.'

'You tek her. I'm not hanging around.'

'For duck's sake – they're just a couple of old women,' and the next moment one of Auntie Franny's spiked purple Jimmy Choos slapped him between his eyes.

I was so surprised I forgot to be afraid.

He realed backwards, hit a bin with a bang and slithered down on to the ground. I only just got out of the way in time.

Mum was on the other one, clawing at him in her fury. 'Where's my daughter? Where's my daughter? Where's my daughter?'

I might have forgotten to mention she's got a bit of a stutter sometimes, especially if she's upset, but not today. She was really pitching into this bloke and he was much bigger than her. I should help.

I crawled out and hung on to the back of his coat to try to slow him down.

Auntie Franny was hammering away at the man on the ground but she couldn't keep him down there for ever. They'd been taken by surprise but when that wore off . . .

There was a shout from behind us.

'Jenny.'

My dad was here.

Mum shouted, 'Russell – help.'

And so was Uncle Andrew.

'Quick – back under the bins, Joy. This is going to be good. I mean – this is no place for a young lady.'

I heard Dad roar, 'Get out of the way, Jenny.'

Mum let go and Dad waded in.

'Excellent bloke to have around in a fight,' said the voice again. I looked around. Other than the giant golden horse standing between me and the fighting men, I couldn't see anyone. I felt suddenly safe and comforted. *'Are you all right, Jenny?'*

Who was talking to my mum?

'Yes, yes,' she said impatiently. 'I'm fine.' Still no hint of a stutter. Her hair was tousled and she had blood on her hands. She didn't look anything like my mum. 'Joy, come here.'

I scrambled out from behind the bins. Across the alleyway, Uncle Andrew had wrested Auntie Franny's shoe from her so she was using the other to put the boot in. I had no idea old people were so violent. If I'd carried on like that I'd have been grounded until I was a hundred and eight. And they'd have taken my phone away for ever. Parents are such hippocrits.

They're always going on about violence not solving the world's problems, but clearly it does.

'Should I break it up, do you think?' asked Uncle Andrew, still clutching Auntie Franny's purple stiletto.

'In a minute,' said Mum. 'Poor old Russell's . . . been a bit stressed recently. This is probably . . . doing him so much good.'

Obviously feeling he had to save someone, Uncle Andrew pulled Auntie Franny off the other one. 'Now then, Franny. Let him live.'

She said, 'Don't call me Franny,' and snatched back her shoe just as Dad, with one final punch, knocked the other man to the ground.

He and Uncle Andrew high-fived.

I think the man was glad to stay put. He certainly didn't try to get up. More help was on its way. I could hear sirens.

Dad envelopped us both in a big hug. 'Joy, Jenny. Are you all right?' He dropped a kiss on top of Mum's head and smiled down at her and I thought, no matter how much they say they love me and Jamie, in the beginning it was just the two of them. Before we came along. I opened my mouth to tell him I was all right but he'd turned away. He didn't even look at me. Not once. Didn't even notice I hadn't replied. I went cold all over.

'It's all right,' said the horse quietly and I was actually turning to Mum when I realised. It was the horse that was talking to me. An actual horse. A talking horse. A giant talking horse. Was talking. To me. A horse was talking to me. His voice was very gentle.

'He's just realising what nearly happened and he's too upset to speak. Give him time. Oh look – here's Sgt Bates. I haven't seen her for ages. She hasn't changed a bit.'

411

I stared at him. 'You're a talking horse.'

'Yes, I know.'

'A horse who talks.'

'Yes, but let's not go into that now. This is much more exciting.'

There were three policemen altogether and they were trying to take us all off to the police station. I pulled Mum's arm and shook my head. 'I have to find my friend.'

'Which friend?' asked Sgt Bates sharply. 'There's someone else here?'

'My friend Tommy,' I said, pulling her arm again. 'I think she's in their van. We were meeting for the concert. She texted me to meet her here. Look.' I showed them the text.

Sgt Bates took my phone and looked at it, looked at Mum and Dad and then pressed a few buttons. Somewhere close by, a phone began to ring. She reached down and pulled it out of the first man's pocket. It was his phone. Everyone looked at everyone else.

I said, 'Oh my God, he has Tommy's phone. She must be here somewhere.' Nobody moved. I couldn't believe it. No one was trying to save Tommy.

Mum said, 'It's all right, Joy. Tommy's not here,' and her voice was shaking and so was I. I buried my head in her warm coat.

Once inside the station, in the warmth and the light, Mum said, 'Let's have a quick wash and brush up, shall we?' and it was only when I looked at myself in the mirror that I realised I hadn't really made a good job of my make-up. Half of it was smudged across my face and I looked like a clown.

I had a good wash in warm, soapy water and buried my

face in the paper towel. For a long time. Because whatever happened next wouldn't be good and I would be in so much trouble. And what about Tommy?

When I could see again, the giant golden horse was standing in the toilets with us. It had followed us from the alleyway. I hadn't imagined it after all. I whispered, 'Mum,' and started to edge away. 'I can see a giant horse.'

She smiled. 'So can I.'

'What does it want?'

'This is Thomas. He . . . brought me up.'

'I thought that was your aunt and uncle.'

'No, it was Thomas.'

I looked at the giant horse who was carefully inspecting the hot air dryer.

'Jenny, what does this do?' He turned to the machine on the wall. *'Good heavens! What are these for?'* and he sounded so surprised I nearly laughed.

'That's better,' he said.

'Those men – they couldn't see you, could they?'

'No.'

'But I can.'

'That's because you're special, Joy. Would you excuse me for just one moment, please?'

He turned to my mum, lowered his enormous head and said simply, *'Jenny.'*

His voice was warm and deep and full of love and somehow, I just knew everything was going to be all right.

I looked at Mum and her face was glowing. I'd never seen her look like that before. She said, 'Thomas,' put her arms around him and rested her forehead on his. The smell of warm ginger biscuits was overwhelming. 'Are you staying? Please stay. Even if only for a little while?'

'Oh yes. For a little while. Watching the Checklands' attempts to mislead the majesty of the law and explain their actions is usually the best bit.'

I thought it would be all bare and horrible but the little room was bright and comfortable. Not at all like the interview rooms you see on TV.

'They wouldn't have been able to get us all in,' said the horse, who appeared to know what I was thinking before I thought it. And how come Mum could see him? And me? But no one else? It was weird. I wondered if my mum was mad and I'd got it off her, which was surprising because I'd have thought if I'd inherited madness from one of my parents it would definitely have been my dad.

They tried to make Uncle Andrew and Auntie Franny wait outside and I insisted on them coming in.

'It's usually family only,' said Sgt Bates.

'They are family,' I said and so we all squeezed in. Even the horse, who winked at me.

Sgt Bates cleared her throat. 'Do I gather Miss Bauer will be joining us? She usually does.'

'She's Mrs Checkland now,' said Uncle Andrew.

The horse started dramatically. *'I always knew Russell was unconventional, Jenny, but I never thought he was a bigamist. When did that happen?'*

'She's Andrew's wife,' said mum.

'Ah. Good job you mentioned that, Jenny. I'd got hold of completely the wrong end of the stick, there. In my defence, of course, it is Russell.'

414

Mum said, 'Idiot,' and then Sgt Bates pulled open her note-book and sighed. 'You've all been here before so it isn't as if you don't know how these things go.'

I blinked. Had they? All of them? Well, that was news to me. My parents had never said anything about this. Had they been lying to me all these years?

The horse said, *'Oh, Joy – you don't know the half of it,'* and snorted.

'Language,' said my mother. 'Young foals present, remember.'

Sgt Bates continued. 'I suspect the new Mrs Checkland's advice to you would be to say nothing until she turns up.'

How long would that be? I was still cold and every now and then I had a little shiver. Sgt Bates looked at Mum. 'Do I need to call a doctor?'

I shook my head. I just wanted to go home.

Mum put her arm round me. 'She's too upset to answer any questions at the moment.'

'I agree.' Sgt Bates smiled at me. She seemed very nice. 'I'll just take a very short statement tonight. We have the two men. They'll be questioned over the next couple of days. Depending on what they say I might come back after Christmas with a few questions. And I'd like to keep your phone for a while. Is that all right, Miss Checkland?'

'Tommy,' I said, because no one was talking about her.

'Yes, who is Tommy?'

'My friend. I was meeting her by the post office. We were going to the concert.'

She looked at Mum and Dad and then at me. 'Joy, there is no Tommy. There has never been a Tommy. Tommy does not exist.'

'Yes, she does. I've been talking to her for months.'

'No, I'm afraid you haven't. We think you were talking to whoever those men worked for.'

Mum had turned as white as a sheet and I thought Dad was going to get up and hit someone all over again. Uncle Andrew put his hand on his shoulder. I couldn't take it in. 'But Tommy lives with her mum and dad. They want her to be a doctor or something but she wants to be a singer. Her parents are always arguing. She goes to school in Rushford.'

'Have you ever met her?'

'Yes, of course I have. We talk nearly every day.'

'Online. Have you ever met her face to face?'

'Well, no . . . the buses aren't very good and her dad's too busy to drive her and her mum can't drive . . . She's sent me photos of her family. And her house. And her pony, Candy . . .' I trailed off.

'You've never actually met her, have you?'

'We keep meaning to, but . . .' But there had always been an excuse. There had always been some reason why it couldn't happen. Why hadn't I noticed that before? Things began to fall into place. Mum took my hand. Hers was nearly as cold as mine.

'Shall we begin,' said Sgt Bates, quietly. 'I promise you this won't take a minute. Present at the interview are Mr Russell Checkland, Mrs Jennifer Checkland, Miss Joy Checkland . . .'

'Just like Happy Families,' said Uncle Andrew, cheerfully.

She just looked at him. 'Also present – for some reason – Mr Andrew Checkland and Ms Francesca Kingdom.'

I wanted to say, 'And an invisible horse named Thomas,' just to see what people would do, but Mum shook her head.

I told them what had happened. They didn't ask any questions. No one told me off. Once again, no one said anything at all.

Back home, I had a hot bath and a drink of cocoa, and Mum put me to bed. As she was tucking me in, I said, 'Where's Dad?' He'd been very quiet while we were at the station. I thought he'd be shouting at everyone and he hadn't. And then when we'd arrived home, he'd muttered something and gone out into the yard.

Mum smiled. 'He's making sure everything's locked up and we're all safe.'

'Is he . . . is he very angry?'

'Furious,' she said, patting the sheet, 'but not with you.'

'But he won't speak to me . . .'

'He's upset. Go to sleep, now. I promise you everything will look . . . better in the morning.'

I looked around my room. Suddenly, it wasn't my lovely bedroom any longer. The little flight of stairs leading down to my bathroom was in shadow. Anyone could be hiding there. Or in the wardrobe. Or under the bed. Should I ask Mum to pull back the curtains so I could see if anyone tried to climb through the window? There were too many shadows. Too many windows. Too many doors.

Suddenly, I could smell ginger biscuits again. Warm ginger biscuits. It was a lovely smell. I closed my eyes and breathed in and when I opened them again a giant golden horse stood at the foot of the bed. Mum never turned a hair.

He smiled at me. *'How are you feeling, Joy?'*

'How do you know me?'

'I was here when you were born. You've grown a bit since

then. Too much protein, Jenny. Stop feeding her so much or you'll need a bigger house.'

They smiled at each other again and then Mum stood up. 'Try to sleep.'

I wasn't ashamed to admit it. 'Mum . . . I don't think I can.'

'If you would like me to,' said Thomas, *'I can stay. I often used to guard your mum when she was small. And when she first came to live here at Frogmorton, as well. This was her bedroom. I used to stand over there.'* He walked over to the corner, where he stood, gently glowing in the dark. *'Just think of me as a very upmarket night light.'*

I didn't think I'd sleep, but I did. My bed was warm and comfortable and I dropped off almost immediately. I woke once – the bedroom door was just closing. I sat up with a jerk, full of fear.

'Just your dad, checking you're all right,' said Thomas quietly, from the corner. *'Don't worry – I'm here.'* The room was full of the smell of warm ginger biscuits, comforting and safe. I lay down and went back to sleep.

I didn't want to get up the next morning and I definitely didn't want to face the day. No – that wasn't quite true. It was Dad I didn't want to face. I didn't know which was worse – Dad shouting at me or Dad not shouting at me.

Mum brought me breakfast in bed which wasn't something she'd done since I had mumps. I wasn't particularly hungry, but it was scrambled eggs on toast which is my favourite.

'Looks delicious,' said Thomas, as Mum went off to run my bath. *'I'd get stuck in if I were you. And don't forget your orange juice. It counts towards your five a day. Helps you grow*

up to be a big strong filly – good bones, sloping shoulders, glossy coat, that sort of thing.'

I sighed and shook my head. My lip wobbled like a little kid's. 'He hasn't been in to see me. He must be so angry with me.'

'Joy, I was here when you were born. I saw his face the first time he saw you. You should never doubt that your dad loves you very much.'

'But he's still cross with me.'

'Well, yes, probably, a little bit. Would you rather he didn't care?'

'Thomas, he can't even look at me.'

'Why don't you go and find him.'

I shook my head.

He sighed. *'You know, the two of you are really very much alike.'*

'No, we're not.'

'Oh yes, you are,' said Mum, coming back into the room. 'Eat your breakfast. I'll be back in a little while.'

She went out.

'Thomas, my dad doesn't love me any more.'

'Of course he does. More than ever now but you frightened him. Yesterday was his worst nightmare and he's not dealing well with it. I think it's going to have to be up to you.'

No, that couldn't be right. Not my big, shouty dad.

'He shouts at me all the time.'

'Of course he does. He's Russell Checkland. He's terrified something will happen to you and it's his way of trying to keep you safe. And now, after yesterday, he thinks he's failed. He was the same with your mother until she sorted him out.'

'No,' I said, impatient because he didn't seem to understand.

'Mum never says anything. She never stands up to him. He just walks all over her.'

If a horse can twinkle, then he twinkled.

'Joy, your mother can control your father by lifting an eyebrow. You must have noticed – he never does anything she doesn't like. And your mum's clever enough to let him do as he pleases – right up until the moment she decides otherwise.'

I sat back to think about this. Now that he came to mention it . . . I sipped my orange juice thoughtfully. This was a lot to think about. I thought about it while eating my scrambled eggs.

I was allowed to stay in bed. Mum was in and out all morning, checking to see I was all right. I felt so lost. Normally, I'd have been messaging Tommy every few minutes but she was gone. Worse than that, she'd never actually been here. I tried to imagine who Tommy had been.

'Don't,' said Thomas. *'They're not important. And certainly not as important as you.'*

Still no one told me off about yesterday. Especially not Dad. In fact, he didn't come in at all. I hadn't seen him since the police station. I was half relieved and half . . . hurt.

I said to Thomas, 'It's nearly lunchtime and Dad still hasn't been to see me.'

Thomas was peering out of the window. *'Your father's just driven off in . . . I can't believe it. He still has that old Land Rover. Oh Joy, he brought Marilyn home in that. And then she wee'd on him. And then her owner turned up and your mother and Sharon attacked him with household ornaments. What an exciting day that was.'*

'What?' I was beginning to wonder if he'd confused my mother with someone else's.

He was still looking out of the window. *'Where's he going?'*

'It's the carol service this afternoon. A bit of the church dropped off because it's falling to pieces and so the vicar's holding it in the open air this year. On the village green. I'd forgotten all about it. It'll be cold. I don't want to go.'

Thomas said nothing. I hadn't known him very long but he had a very particular way of saying nothing.

I felt *I* should say something. 'Dad's been helping to build the stable.'

'Are you taking part?'

'No. It's the adults' turn this year. They said it would be too cold for the kids. And for me too.'

He said, *'You should go.'*

I pulled at my sheets. 'I don't want to.'

'You should go.'

There was something in his voice. I sighed. 'We'll see.' That's what adults say to me all the time. It's grown-up speak for 'no'. I don't see why I shouldn't get to use it occasionally.

I could hear Mum and Dad arguing in their bedroom. I worried it was about me but it was Dad's old coat again. He likes his old coat. It's a giant thing with a hood and cuffs. It was dark blue and woolly once, but it's so old now that it's grey and gone all bobbly. She keeps throwing it out and it keeps finding its way back home again. Dad says it's got a better homing instinct than Boxer.

'Russell,' said Mum.

'What?' he said, although he knew perfectly well what.

'You're surely not wearing that old thing.'

'What's wrong with it?'

'You don't have . . . time for me to . . . tell you.'

'I'll have Marilyn and Jack with me, Jenny. It would be silly to wear anything decent. Anything could happen. You wouldn't want my good overcoat getting dirty, surely.'

'It's covered in paint.'

'I'm an artist.'

'And slobber.'

'Well, don't blame me – it's not my slobber. It's not yours, is it?'

'Russell, it . . . smells.'

'All the best clothes do.'

They closed the door then but Dad must have won that one because he wore his old coat.

Thomas winked at me.

I went to the service after all. It seemed easier and they said it would be good for me to get out.

'Everyone will stare at me,' I said to Thomas.

'No one else knows anything about it,' said Thomas. *'Or ever will. Just go and enjoy yourself.'*

I hunched a shoulder. 'It'll be cold.' Even I could hear how petty I sounded.

'Dress warmly.'

'But . . .'

'If you don't go, then your mum won't go and she's been telling me how much she's been looking forward to it.'

I sighed again. 'We'll see.'

Mum put Jamie in his pushchair. We could hardly see him for his furry teddy bear onesie and half a dozen blankets on top of him. Only his eyes were visible. If only he could stay like that.

I followed them down the lane and joined the crowd on the village green. Dad was already there putting the finishing touches to the stable.

It was really quite nifty: an open wooden shed, with a roughly thatched roof. They'd filled it with straw bales for Joseph and Mary and the shepherds and the wise men to sit on and the empty manger waited for Baby Jesus. The inside was softly lit by a giant star suspended from the roof.

Dad had brought the animals. Marilyn looked very smart in her blue coat with the red piping. She was an old hand at this. She stood near the manger making sure she looked cute and appealing. Lots of kids were stroking her and she was lapping it up.

Jack, our neighbour's donkey, looked very handsome in his red coat with the blue piping. I think he'd gone to sleep. Two of Martin Braithwaite's sheep, selected for their plassid natures, were half asleep at the back and a cow – a real, glossy, black and white cow – was standing at the back, chewing the cud, sleepy and uncaring. Dissapointingley, there was no camel. Dad had offered, but Mr Wivenhoe had said no. Very quickly and unusually firmly.

The cast were assembling. As usual, Fiona Braithwaite was the Angel Gabriel. She and the Virgin Mary were looking daggers at each other. Joseph cowered behind them.

'They have form,' whispered Mum. 'Anything could happen.'

Silence fell. The Reverend Wivenhoe stepped forward and welcomed everyone, his voice carrying easily in the still night air.

Someone rang a bell and the crowd parted as Joseph and Mary followed the Angel Gabriel to the stable. Marilyn carefully positioned herself so that everyone would know she was the star of the show and we all sang 'O Little Town of Bethlehem'. Except me. There was a big lump in my throat and the words couldn't get past it. I shoved my hands into my pockets and stared at the frosty grass.

Martin Braithwaite was Head Shepherd. He wore his thick farm jacket with his dressing gown over the top, with a black and white checked tea towel over his head, tied in place with his dressing-gown cord. His two enormous sons followed on with the sheep. I could see Marilyn batting her eyelashes at them because she knew there were carrots in there somewhere.

The three wise men – townies who hadn't done this before and hadn't thought to bring the wherewithal to bribe a tiny donkey – wisely stayed well back.

The night was bitterly cold. I could see people's breath puffing as they sang. The grass was white with frost and the sky was white with stars.

The procession approached the stable and, as Mary settled the Baby Jesus in the manger, a solo choirboy sang 'In the Bleak Midwinter'. His voice rose up towards the stars and it was so beautiful that I knew I'd remember this moment for ever and suddenly I found myself crying. It was so embarrassing. I didn't know what to do so I did nothing. I couldn't. I just stood and sobbed and wondered if I'd ever stop. It was my dad who came to my rescue.

He walked across the frozen grass. Unfastening his coat, he pulled me inside and wrapped it around both of us. It was warm inside and he smelled of horse, paint, hay and creosote. It was his 'dad' smell.

He didn't say anything. Not a word. I cried and cried. All down his front. I don't know where the tears came from. I just stood with the weight of his smelly coat wrapped around me and thought how amazing my dad was. Eventually, when it was over, he even found me a handkerchief. Well, I say 'handkerchief', but I think I mean painty rag.

I blew my nose and felt better.

Still envelopped in his coat, I wriggled around to look at our village. This place where I lived. My home. The street lights had golden halose around them in the frosty air. People's lighted windows looked pretty and warm. Everyone was singing away. We'd moved on to 'Away in a Manger'. Nearly everyone in the village was here. The big bright moon shone down. I leaned back against my dad. It was freezing out there but I was warm and safe in here. Everything might be all right after all.

I turned my head. At the far edge of the green a giant golden horse was standing, swishing his tail and watching us.

Little knots of people were dotted all over the green, all singing their heads off. Thomas began to pick his way carefully through the crowd. Not one person seemed to notice this giant golden horse in their midst until he stopped in front of Charlie Kessler and his mum.

Charlie's special. Sometimes he does some work for Uncle Kevin at his landscaping place. He's really strong and can lift sacks and rocks and everything but mostly they like him to plant things because his giant hands are really delicate and everything he plants grows brilliantly and has millions of flowers. Thomas stopped and bent his head down to Charlie who broke into his usual enormous smile. Charlie could see him as well.

I was so surprised and then I remembered Thomas saying that only special people could see him.

He stopped in front of Mum. They looked at each other for a long time and I knew they were saying things no one else could hear. Again, they rested their heads together. Like old friends. I looked away because it was private. They were saying goodbye.

He was leaving us. I knew he was leaving us. I wanted to run to him. To throw my arms around him and make him stay. Why couldn't he see I needed him? He couldn't leave me all alone again. Not now.

'My darling girl – I am always with you. You won't be able to see me but never doubt that I am there.'

'I haven't said thank you.'

'Yes, you have.'

I was going to cry all over again.

'You have to release me, Joy.'

'I don't understand.'

'You have to let me go. Then we can both move on.'

'Will I ever see you again?'

He laughed. *'We'll see.'* And I laughed too although I think my heart was breaking.

'Farewell, Joy, my golden girl.'

I nodded. 'Goodbye, Thomas.'

I caught just the very faintest scent of ginger biscuits as he wound his way carefully through the singing people.

Emerging at last, he broke into a trot. And from there into a gallop. He dropped his head and thundered across the village green. His mane and tail streamed behind him – a great golden horse, exactly the same colour as the huge moon above him. No one looked. No one pointed. No one else could see him. No one except me and Mum and Charlie. The special people.

Everyone was singing 'O Come All Ye Faithful' and even

426

now, whenever I hear that carol, if I close my eyes, I can still see him. And sometimes, if I concentrate really hard, there's just the very faintest whiff of ginger biscuits.

Now he was going really fast – galloping full tilt – his neck outstretched, his powerful muscles bunching under his golden coat. He was beautiful and strong and graceful. Tossing his head, he kicked up his heels for the sheer joy of living and I couldn't help myself – I laughed. I heard Mum laugh, too. Gathering himself, he leaped the hedge, the one that divides the green from the pub car park.

The world slowed. For a moment, he hung in the air, motionless beneath the stars. As if he'd never touch the earth again. And then, right in front of my eyes, he faded quietly away and all that was left was the brilliant moon.

THE END

To discover more about

JODI TAYLOR

visit

www.joditaylor.online

You can also find her on

Facebook
www.facebook.com/JodiTaylorBooks

X
@joditaylorbooks

Instagram
@joditaylorbooks